The author lives in The United Kingdom with a wife and grown-up family.
He had a traditional British public school education followed by a short army career before going into the chemical industry.
Now he is a semi-retired international businessman, having managed many technology based businesses in ASEAN, Japan, China, Australasia, USA and Northern Europe, and gaining exposure to many cultures and traditions.
It is the author's love of travel that has given birth to the story line of *Bad Chemistry*.

To my friend
Tim Thompson with
best regards.

Bertie Fairbank

Stephen Firbank

BAD CHEMISTRY
– VOLUME ONE

AUSTIN MACAULEY PUBLISHERS™

LONDON • CAMBRIDGE • NEW YORK • SHARJAH

A CIP catalogue record for this title is available from the British Library.

ISBN 9781398472174 (Paperback)
ISBN 9781398472181 (Hardback)
ISBN 9781398473560 (ePub e-book)

www.austinmacauley.com

First Published 2022
Austin Macauley Publishers Ltd®
1 Canada Square
Canary Wharf
London
E14 5AA

Chapter 1

Sunday morning was never his favourite time. After a night of Japanese entertainment, he wasn't sure anyway whether his head was on the pillow or beneath it. He turned over, and with dim light filtering from the top and bottom of the heavily insulated curtains, he could tell it was light outside. Beyond that, he had no way of estimating the time unless he lifted his head and looked at the digital display inconveniently placed to his right in the bedside console. He resisted the effort to view it and lay back. After a while, the numbed brain engaged itself, and he wondered what had actually been said last night. Were they seriously interested, and if so, was the technology advanced enough to make them move or not? These questions fought for space alongside the pulsating headache. He lifted his head again and made the essential effort to look at the digital display.

'Oh my god,' he groaned, '10:21.'

No longer do we tell the time by saying, 'It's about 10:15.'. Life has moved on. Digital displays leave no room for maybes; they tell us in stark clarity what we sometimes want to know approximately—10:21, the hour and the minute, sometimes the second, clocks that speak to you. Does it make life any more precious, or does it just tell us that our mortality is running out inexorably? Did he even want to know? Philosophy before breakfast was best left to the Japanese.

He raised himself and sat on the side of the bed. It really didn't feel too bad. Gingerly, he straightened his legs; the pain was still there in his left heel. He had bruised it earlier in the week in Tokyo, and it just would not go away and made walking difficult, so he hobbled across the room to the window. During the day, the pain seemed to wear off somewhat, but it was only because he had come to accept it as one might a nasty cold; it didn't make it any less of a pain. He pulled back the curtain decorated on one side with stylised trees and birds that appeared to be flying in a manner unknown to man and insulating silver plastic on the other. The sunshine hit him and, magnified by the glass, was so strong, he felt as though it was pushing him back into the room, but he stood his ground and, using a rapid blinking movement to accustom his eyes to the light level, eventually focused on the traffic below already piling up on the expressway.

He breathed the air-conditioned air deeply and, satisfied with this minor form of exercise, returned to his bed. He sat down on the edge again and waited for his mind to relate to his body. Slowly, a thought formed and grew rapidly in urgency and intensity.

'Coffee.'

Standing on what the Japanese use in a hotel bedroom as a combination dressing table and writing desk was a pregnant white plastic object whose use could only be guessed at by the first time traveller, but to Victor Stanley, a seasoned veteran, it was a constant source of water hot enough to make coffee and Japanese tea but not hot enough to brew English breakfast tea to its full rich flavour. It seemed to have a perpetual method of replenishing itself no doubt assisted by the ever-silent and efficient maid service.

He took out from the bottom drawer a jar of Nescafe, the virtues being extolled in both Japanese and English on a crowded label. The same applied to the creamer from Nestle. He had purchased both the day before in a small twenty-four-hour shop nearby and would have normally had them to hand except that he had, in a moment of boredom, leafed through the rules on using 'accommodations' at the hotel. The rules told him that the bringing of beverages and food into the hotel without the management's permission was frowned upon, and he was old enough to remember the times when hotels used to charge if they found such things in guest rooms.

He had read on to discover that they didn't like pets or malodorous articles or even too large a number of personal effects. They also failed to permit gambling or the engaging in indecent or immoral behaviour in the hotel. He wondered for a moment whether this was really Japan.

He went into the bathroom and stood in front of the mirror. A man of late middle age peered out at him; it was not an unpleasing sight if one discounted the temporary effect of alcohol. He was reasonably fit if a bit too heavy, but that was the life he led. Twenty-three meetings in five days in Tokyo, young men of today could not keep up that pace; he still had the stamina. The headache pulsed dully, and behind his strong white teeth, there dwelled a tongue like the bottom of a parrot's cage. He picked out from a small bag of miscellaneous drugs a packet of Nurofen telling him that it was still a breakthrough in pain relief; that's exactly what he needed—a breakthrough.

One of the nice things about ablutions in Japan is the design of the small but functional bathroom that usually has a bath deep enough to fill and wallow in, sometimes with an immersed seat, which makes reading a book a less hazardous exercise. He started to run the water as he carefully shaved using the razor provided. He drew it down one side of his face and discovered it was not designed to deal with the tough growth of a Western beard but with the softer fur of the East; nothing changed. He took his Wilkinson out of the toilet bag and completed the job. At least the toothbrush worked and was supplied with its own tiny tube of toothpaste that had a taste and quality all of its own, not dissimilar to parrot. Victor turned off the bath and lowered himself slowly into the steaming water. It was marvellous, and if endured long enough, it would restore him to near normality. The all-enveloping heat soothed away minor aches, and even the head started to feel better. He leaned back and closed his eyes. The phone rang.

'Shit!' If left alone, it will go away, so he plunged his head below the surface. It was still ringing when he ran out of breath. He started to raise himself out of the water, and as he put a foot on the floor, it stopped. He waited several moments and gratefully lowered himself back into the water. It started to ring again. It was too far away to reach. With more cursing, Victor scrambled dripping out of the bath and, sitting inelegantly on the toilet seat, lifted the receiver. It was Takeo Koizumi.

'Good morning, Stanley San. I hope you slept well?'

Whenever his name was said this way, Victor always had the feeling that he was being referred to as an item of bathroom sanitary ware, and currently seated on a piece with the phone to his ear, looking into the mirror, he felt like one. The mirror image did not improve his mood. But Koizumi was important, and he couldn't take lightly the fact that he had telephoned on a Sunday morning.

'Koizumi San, I am in excellent health apart from too long a memory of your excellent hospitality last night, but I think with some coffee and breakfast, I will recover.'

He gave a short bark of a laugh, and Victor could hear the involuntary sucking of teeth.

'Stanley San, it is important that we meet as soon as possible to discuss the NTI invention further as news is already reaching us about your earlier talks in Tokyo.'

Victor could understand this as the grapevine in Japan had always surprised him with its speed and accuracy. You talk to someone about something new, and within a matter of hours, the whole of their company knows about it, and probably three or four others as well.

'Koizumi San, I am perfectly happy to meet you again, but I have to repeat there is no point in doing this unless you are prepared to discuss substantial investment in the project, and when I talk substantial, the price for entry will be what we have already discussed.'

'We understand,' said Koizumi. 'We have no problem with regard to the investment, but we are having some difficulties understanding the chemistry, and it is difficult for us to make an investment without this information.'

Victor knew what he meant. He could be the greatest confidence trickster in the world; he could be using all his knowledge of Japan and the contacts that he had to extract money for what appeared to be a magic trick. Indeed, it had occurred to him that the project he was working on would be of significant benefit to any stage magician, and he filed that thought away under trivia.

'Koizumi San, I am just a simple marketing man.'

'If you are simple, Stanley San, then may the gods protect us against those who are clever.'

'You know what I mean, Koizumi San. My role is to bring people together. It is to put into your hands our products and ideas in order that we can both grow richer, and this time, you are looking at a product that is so revolutionary that I dare not even ask about the chemistry because a little knowledge in that area would be of great danger to us if I was to impart it to you accidentally. I have told you that you are welcome to come and see our facilities, you are welcome to talk to our scientists and to determine that the project is real but I also, have to tell you that already I have one very good offer on the table.'

'Stanley San, we are trying to understand what you are telling us, but it is difficult as you know to move very quickly in Japan. The system of consensus does not always allow it, and although we are working rapidly to bring all interested people together, we cannot do this until Monday afternoon.'

Victor was beginning to get cold seated on the vitreous enamelware looking at his reflection, and speaking into the phone, he realised he was no longer built for speed, but at least he did not have to consult a committee every time he wished to take a bath. Progress was going to be slow as usual. He tired of his reflection and turned away from the mirror to concentrate on the conversation.

'Koizumi San, I am at your disposal anytime for another meeting, but if this is not a meaningful discussion resulting in some sort of offer, it is unlikely that you will end up being anyone very special. I need to take offers home with me based on what you know now. Offers later are of no interest. If your company waits too long, you will lose the opportunity.'

'Stanley San, I know that. I am just asking that we get together in the morning at nine o'clock and that you allow the day for our further discussions.'

'OK, I'll agree to that, but if no conclusion is reached, then I will not hold open any options. I'll be in the lobby waiting for you.' There was a gap in the programme anyway because of a cancellation.

'One final thing, Stanley San—not all the people who have heard about this new and revolutionary invention are to be trusted.'

'What do you mean?' asked Victor. 'I haven't spoken to anyone who wasn't a member of a completely reliable and honourable organisation.'

'Stanley San, it is not whom you have spoken to but those with whom you have spoken have spoken to others not so reliable, and, regrettably, and the news is out.'

Victor knew what he meant.

'So please be careful with the sample kit. We will see you tomorrow.'

'OK, Koizumi San, and thank you for the warning, but I think perhaps you are being over cautious. Until tomorrow, then.'

Victor put the phone down. He climbed back into the bath. The water felt colder; it was, but it wasn't just colder physically. There was something else now, something he could not quite explain. Surely there couldn't be a danger in going round the market trying to sell a new invention like this? Admittedly, it was novel, it was fundamentally new, it was exciting, and, of course, it was British; but above all, it would stop a lot of criminals making a lot of money—that's why the warning chilled him. He turned on the hot tap and restored his well-being. He started to soap his extremities; it was not easy.

At least it was Sunday and the sun was shining. At last, his headache was going. He was clean and refreshed, and after rubbing himself briskly dry, he put on some lightweight trousers and a baggy shirt that hid his bulging waistline.

He left his room and limped along the corridor and pressed the descend button for the lift. It was ingenious system in this hotel; when you pressed the descend button, the display indicator outside the appropriate lift told you it had arrived. It did this within a few seconds, but this was designed only to delay the traveller's degree of impatience, which rapidly built up when it was realised that it was a lie and that it would in fact take several minutes to be transported. When eventually it arrived, it did so at the designated spot and, as if to make up for tardiness, descended in almost free fall from the twenty-fourth floor.

By now, it was late for breakfast, but the hotel was packed with people mid-morning entertaining friends and family and spending huge amounts of money on very small amounts of food. Victor walked into the coffee shop, which was situated on the second floor, and was greeted immediately by an exquisitely polite waiter in formal attire and shown to a non-smoking table.

Looking around the room, it struck him how many weekend brides there appeared to be. He didn't mean by this that Sunday is the traditional day for weddings in Japan, which it is, but that there were a large number of young attractive girls with rather older men.

At the next table was an excellent example. The girl, who was exquisite in a white silk suit and whose waist could have been no more than twenty-two inches, was seated opposite a slab of a man whose eating habits would have made a chimpanzees' tea party seem like tea at Buckingham Palace. She sat erect with her

9

handbag tucked in between her and the back of the chair for safety; her diminutive bottom occupied just a quarter of the seat area. By comparison, her companion spilled at least a quarter of his lower anatomy all around his. The money must have been good.

It made Victor think fondly of home. He wondered where his woman was and determined to phone home this evening, by which time England should have struggled into its early morning weak summer sunshine.

He ate a good breakfast. The headache having virtually gone; he was hungry again, and after an endless week of Oriental food, he enjoyed a corned beef hash. The little basket that contained the toast also had within it a message for the diner neatly printed on a small card informing him discreetly that should he wish to eat more toast or croissant, he could go on doing so for as long as he wished at no extra charge, so a late breakfast could run through until dinner time.

Victor read the English language paper *Mainichi Daily News,* which, although it gave a heavy American slant, nevertheless kept one reasonably well informed about world news. It even extolled the virtues of the latest Hungarian underwear showing a picture of models with farmworker's legs wearing garments that would almost entirely have enveloped the girl in the white silk suit.

The business news was its usual mixture of 'no news' or 'bad news' arising out of manipulation of currency rates and computer-controlled stock markets. The dollar was going down having been going up the first part of the week, and the markets were generally flat, again worrying about interest rates and waiting for the next event. Since young men and computers took over the City of London, Victor had lost interest in the market, and, anyway, he didn't really have the luxury of surplus money that he could afford to lose. He looked casually down the headings, Tokyo, New York, London. Surprisingly, and against the trend of improving company results, there appeared to be fears of another economic recession. He blinked; there in front of him was the company name in capitals.

'NTI (New Technology Industries) plc saw its share price rise 30p on rumours of a new wonder product produced by their Fine Chemicals Division that would combat anti-counterfeiting and terrorism.'

There were no other comments. Victor quickly finished breakfast and went over to the message desk.

'Any messages for Stanley?' he asked the diminutive person whose job it was to communicate to guests those pieces of information usually lost by hotel staff after assuring the message sender that their job depended on delivering it into the right hands. Lost or not, there was no message.

Victor was surprised that with all the communication aids at their disposal nowadays, someone within the company had not contacted him to let him know what this was all about, but then he was out of sight and mind doing what he always did—bringing home the bacon, despite the shortage of pigs.

He knew rumours were flying around in Tokyo and that they had spread to Osaka. The market was talking about it in London; at least his share options had gone up this week.

It was noon, and although Victor had some bits and pieces of paperwork to do, there was nothing that couldn't wait. He had no business or social engagements planned, and that meant he would soon be bored. Fortunately on Sundays in Japan, the department stores are open, and he decided to go and join the fight.

The Nikko Hotel, where he was staying, is opposite the stores Sogo and Daimaru, and he descended the escalator from the second-floor reception to the lobby to be greeted courteously by porters in white tailcoats and tall white hats more reminiscent of an army in Africa than a hotel porter in Osaka. The girl in the white silk suit, whom he had seen earlier at breakfast, had changed into jeans and a white shirt and was just ahead of him as he walked out of the hotel and turned right towards the crossing. A white-helmeted policeman was discussing energetically with an offender the merits and demerits of parking in a restricted area. Victor waited for the little green man to appear, as that same white-helmeted policeman would have probably wanted to talk to him if he took the stupid risk of jaywalking, and with eight lanes of traffic, it was not to be recommended.

There was still an abundance of high-priced left-hand-drive European cars, mainly Mercedes and BMW. They are status symbols. Perhaps the girl in the white silk suit was fortunate enough to ride in one, but he had lost view of her.

Victor walked by the side of Daimaru being carried along by the crowd and passed the Shinsaibashi subway station entrance. The windows told him to buy the products of Givenchy, Chanel, and Shiseido. On the other side of the street, a jewellery store proudly announced that it was Tiffany and also stocked the products of Yves St. Laurent.

Street stalls sold everything from tea in teapots to health drinks, one of the most popular of which was called Pocari Sweat. Victor recalled having seen reference to this stunningly dreadful name back home and wondered at its uptake in the British market. This, along with the restaurant in the basement area of the hotel called the Pooh Curry Centre, did not encourage him to try either.

The crowd carried him towards what appeared to be a covered shopping arcade, and he wished for the hundredth time this trip that he had brought his Nikkon camera with him, but it was just another unnecessary piece of extra weight at the time of packing. The sights he wished to record would have to remain in his memory.

It was hot for May; everyone in summer clothing, and the temperature in the mid-eighties. Sweatshirts held various Western messages; they told him people were 'neat', but they wanted a 'peaceful future'. One was a 'Mr Junko', although he doubted it. One unintelligible message told him that the girl sporting it was a 'Big Swishi'.

He stopped to look into a pachinko parlour, where mindless thousands of people throughout the country flick little silver balls around what appear to be old-fashioned slot machines to win prizes. They are controlled by the police, but the Yakuza removes large sums of money, some of which finds its way to North Korea. The police were currently embarked upon a major programme to stop money being siphoned off and to prevent the system from being used as a laundering exercise; there was a major potential use for the new products NTI had developed.

He took a look inside and turned back to look down the covered street. To his surprise, the girl of the white silk suit was close by. Victor remembered looking up from the breakfast table and meeting the eyes of the man who was her weekend husband, or was he? Maybe the quizzical look he received in return was something different, and the cold shiver that he had felt in the bath travelled down his spine again. Here he was on a Sunday afternoon surrounded by thousands of people, the sun was shining, the crowd was happy, yet he felt cold and alone. Perhaps it was just coincidence that she was there, and he walked on past other Western names. Printemps was selling French patisseries like hot cakes; Ethnic Summer was discounting inferior clothes, and you couldn't have stuck a pin between the people wanting them. He passed another game parlour; this time, Hicari, where an attendant was meticulously taking marks off the floor with a paint scraper and a cloth with solvent, and it made him think of what it would be like in Soho, only the games were similar and maybe the route the money eventually took. He walked past Daimaru and found Mickey Mouse skipping in a box.

Ahead was a small cross street and on the corner a pharmacy called Sasanami. The populace thinned out there with most of the shopping crowds going up and down the covered way, so Victor turned left. He had walked some fifty metres and was outside a building that obviously offered the pleasures of the night to anyone who wished to pay £50 a head or so to go in. Two young men stepped out of a door immediately in front of him. They both wore black T-shirts with the emblem 'Voire Africa' on them and white trousers. Victor stepped aside to avoid them, and they stepped aside too, blocking him. Victor looked back. There was another person behind him, the girl of the white silk suit. In impeccable English, the one on the right spoke.

'Mr Stanley, we would be very pleased if you would accompany us and talk to a gentleman who wishes to meet you.'

Victor was alarmed; his intuition ran true. 'Do I have any alternative?'

'Not if you are sensible, sir.'

Victor was no James Bond, and although he used to be built for speed when he was younger, he could not move at speed now, at least not over a long distance, and in these crowds, it would be impossible anyway.

He considered the alternatives, and none of them looked very good. He had read that in situations such as this, the victim usually got hurt if he resisted and they had been polite about the request. Koizumi was right; the news was out, and the recent press cover would not have helped. How was the girl involved? At least if she was around, it was unlikely any serious damage would be done, but he did not know why he thought that.

'I don't like being asked to meetings in this way', said Victor, 'but you seem to be in command, so lead on.'

His voice seemed to be that of another less fearful man; it surprised him.

He was led into a building that advertised many entertainment bars so favoured by tired businessmen at the end of the day when apparently coy hostesses would bring them drinks and giggle. They all squeezed into the little lift with the two young men facing him and the girl by his side; she smelled wonderful but said nothing. The lift stopped at the fifth floor, and having extricated themselves from it, the little group stood in front of an intricately carved door that should have been opened by a kimono-clad hostess; today, it remained closed.

The Voire Africa number one—he was the shorter of the two and the one who appeared to be in charge—knocked on the door. It was opened by a girl in one of the ubiquitous T-shirts that informed the world that she had 'British Taste'. She led the way down a short corridor, opened another door, and they were in what would have been, had it been night, the elegant surroundings of an expensive bar. Standing behind it was one of the biggest men Victor had ever seen. It wasn't that his height was anything particularly special; it was just that everything about him was simply enormous and very much in the fashion of the weekend husband Victor had first noticed with the delectable girl now so surprisingly by his side.

'You may go.' He made this pronouncement in a stentorian voice and waved his ham-like hand around in the air; some instinct told Victor he was not included in the command. The acolytes withdrew as if from royalty backing out of the room swiftly and no doubt with some relief.

The door closed behind them, and they were left alone. The slab of a man came round from behind the bar at speed; for his size, he was surprisingly light on his feet.

'Mr Stanley, it is a great pleasure to meet you. So much has been spoken about you this week in Tokyo,' he bellowed.

Victor was visibly shaken. If such a man as this knew all about his movements, he should be seriously frightened; it came as no surprise to him therefore to find that he was. Businessmen are not meant to get themselves into situations like this. Normally, it is only the sort of thing you read about in books, but here he was in the middle of Osaka standing in a bar facing a man who could probably tear his arms off, whose English was as good as his young bodyguard, for that's what he presumed he was, and who, despite his size, obviously had his suits made at a high and mighty version of a Saville Row tailor.

Victor distinctly felt the urge to go to the toilet, but he was damned if he was going to ask, not yet. Until now, the heat of the day had not seemed to matter, and he really hadn't perspired at all; but now, despite the air conditioning, he felt as though his armpits had taps fitted to them.

The slab spoke. 'Allow me to introduce myself, Victor—you don't mind if I call you Victor, do you?' He did not need a reply.

How the hell did he know my first name? speculated Victor. He didn't like it being used at this exact moment. They hadn't been formally introduced, and he felt far from being a Victor.

'My name is Lee Doo-hwan.'

At least Victor could identify the country he came from as he had remembered that name from his reading of events in the politics of South Korea.

'Please understand, Mr Stanley, that although I have had you brought here today, you are under no threat. I am merely detaining you for a short conversation. My young men are not armed, and you have no need to fear anything other than physical restraint.'

'I'm pleased to hear it,' Victor said with no feeling of relief whatsoever. 'Was any intended?'

'I still want to know why I have been dragged in off the street. I suspect there is some rather sinister aspect to all this, Mr Doo-hwan. After all, I leave the hotel quite innocently, and just twenty minutes later, I am miraculously picked out of the crowd and deposited in front of you. Furthermore, you seem to know a great deal more about me than I do about you.'

'Mr Stanley, we have been following you since you left Tokyo. The young lady whom you saw with my men accompanied you on Shinkansen—the bullet train, as you call it—yesterday afternoon and then followed you to the Hotel Niko. We have

14

sophisticated communications, Victor, and she followed you when you left the hotel. We were quite easily able to pick you up. It was our good fortune that you turned in this direction.' The man sighed and smoothed out a wrinkle on his huge belly.

Victor then realised the purpose of the girl of the white silk suit. He had seen her in the crowd, twice she had been in his direct view, and he had shrugged it off as though it was a coincidence. So he hadn't been wrong at breakfast; the weekend bridegroom had looked at him with more than just casual interest.

Again, the conversation Victor had had with Koizumi San this morning came back to him when he told him that the information about the invention was passing around very fast indeed; quite clearly, it had already gotten into the wrong hands. At this stage of the development, it was still very much a research project, and Victor only had a few grammes of the material to demonstrate. The problem with selling products in their early stage of development is that the salesman is out there ahead of the commercial product telling the story in all its wonderful detail and showing small examples as a come-on; if you don't, then no one gives you the encouragement to go on. Apart from anything else, it is all part of the market research. This time, the product had crossed over from being just another brilliant invention for the good of mankind and was quite clearly being regarded as an extremely dangerous substance to be packed in cans with the instruction on them, 'Do not spray on counterfeiters. They are likely to disappear.'

'I am forgetting my manners,' Doo-hwan said. 'Please be seated, and allow me to send for a drink.'

Involuntarily, Victor looked at his watch; it was well into the permitted hours for consuming alcohol in the middle of the day, and although he didn't normally do so, apart from the necessary courtesies during entertainment, he requested a Jack Daniels on the rocks and a glass of water. Doo-hwan made a sign with his hand, and one of the young men appeared silently at his side. He spoke rapidly to him in a language that Victor took to be Korean, and he disappeared behind the bar. There was the sound of bottles and glasses and ice, and then a nasty thought struck Victor. *Oh my god, what if they drug me?* But then, why should they, as he wasn't any good asleep and the man had promised no harm would come to him?

The Voire Africa brought the tray over, and Victor looked suspiciously at the water and even more closely at the Jack Daniels, which he desperately wanted a swig of.

Doo-hwan read his thoughts.

'I assure you, Victor, there is nothing wrong with the drinks. Look,' and he took the glass and sipped it and followed it with a mouthful of water. Comforted, Victor did the same, and the second horrific thought struck him. Perhaps the slab had AIDS, but surely not even that would live in Jack Daniels. Today was full of surprises, and the next one was just one of many. The giant fat hand was again waved in the air, and another of the young men reappeared, or was it the same one?

This time, he had a small black case, and to Victor's horror, he realised that it was his sample kit. They must have been into his hotel room and removed it from his voluminous briefcase, which he normally kept locked. No lock would deter these men, though, not even his trusty and battered Samsonite.

'These are my samples. You have been into my hotel room and removed them. For heaven's sake, tell me what on earth I am getting myself into.'

The slab settled himself in the ample leather chair. His hands rested lightly on the arms, and Victor noticed that on the index finger of his left hand was an enormous gold ring whose flat face was inlaid with a serpent in red stones that he took to be rubies with a diamond for its head. His immaculate jacket, which disguised his enormous size, fell open to show the same design emblem on the pocket of his shirt.

'Victor, this is going to take a little time, but perhaps we do owe it to you to explain why you are here and how we know so much about you.'

He leaned forward and took a drink. He then moved a large carved teak box towards Victor, sliding it across the surface of the table.

'Please help yourself,' he said and opened the lid. Inside, there was a selection of Bolivar and Montecristo cigars. They even understood his tastes, and seeing he was about to be told a good tale, Victor took a short, fat Robusto Bolivar, which he enjoyed so much, and sat back. With a good drink and a good smoke, he could die happy.

'You have within your company', said Doo-hwan, 'a scientist who has made an incredible discovery. His name is Dr George Yoreen.' He pronounced it 'urine', but Victor didn't dare correct such a dangerous specimen.

'Your Dr Yoreen is not altogether honest, and some long time ago, I had reason to be in contact with him.'

Victor recalled that George Yoreen had joined NTI some three years ago and had been put in charge of one of the research groups dealing with conductive polymers. No one seemed to know exactly where he had come from; although his chemical background was academically sound. It was said that NTI had picked him up after he had made a series of catastrophic investments that had bankrupted his small research company.

The slab went on. 'Dr Yoreen sold my organisation some material some years ago that failed to work. He had demonstrated it to us, and it had been extremely efficacious at the time, but when we purchased a substantial quantity, we were unable to make the material function. Your doctor had, as the Americans say, then taken a powder and disappeared. The purchaser of this technological miracle that was meant to revolutionise a certain aspect of electronic manufacture was a company in which my organisation had a legitimate interest, and we therefore diligently searched for the bad doctor in order that we could bring him to justice in our own way.'

Victor did not care to speculate as to what form this justice might take.

'The doctor covered his tracks extremely well, and we began to believe that perhaps he was a professional, someone well versed in the arts of the confidence trick, and it wasn't until a few months ago that, quite by chance, we read an article in an English technical publication referring to your company's work with conductive polymers, and my colleague, remembering the history of our association with Dr Yoreen, felt that it was too much of a coincidence that your company would be separately pursuing a similar line of research. From there, it was not difficult for us to determine that the infamous doctor was now an employee of yours, but where he was between the time his research company went bankrupt and his partner became deceased, we do not know.'

The way he said 'became deceased' did not have a nice sound to it, and Victor wondered how the doctor's partner had become deceased.

'Having relocated Dr Yoreen, we felt it wise to watch what he was now doing as the learned article had informed us that the activity had far-reaching implications with regard to the control of certain types of criminal activity, and my organisation is most interested to support the endeavours of the good doctor in order that when the time comes, we may also benefit from his invention. He will then have repaid the debt that he owes us, with interest, for we are not totally unforgiving or ungenerous.' He refreshed himself with another delicate sip, which emptied half the glass.

'Your arrival in Japan has unfortunately forced us to act quickly with regard to re-establishing contact with the doctor, and last week, an ambassador was sent to England to have a conversation with him. Your demonstrations of your company's admirable product have convinced us that you are at a much more advanced state of development than we had thought possible, and if your product were to be introduced here in Japan, in due course, it just might present certain of our group members from going about their profitable business.'

Various thoughts raced through Victor's mind. If the doctor was truly crooked, then NTI was in trouble. To have sold a product that didn't work to an organisation of which this man was quite obviously the head was not good for the health, and NTI very much needed the health of Dr Yoreen for the time being. Victor wondered what was happening to the said doctor, for if this man had dispatched an ambassador to the UK last week, then by now, Dr Yoreen must have had a meeting, and there must have been a conclusion. There were no messages for Victor from the UK, and therefore George Yoreen couldn't have collapsed and died or anything horrific like that, and this meant that if there had been any negotiations, then the doctor was unsound, to put it politely. Worse still, he could have sold NTI down the river. If the doctor's partner had become deceased through the agency of this Doo-hwan, then he could frighten George Yoreen seriously. Quite literally, he could put the fear of death into him. George was going to either tell the authorities or accept the forgiving and not-ungenerous escape route hinted at by Doo-hwan; Victor suspected the latter would be the more comfortable way out.

Victor was having to absorb these facts too rapidly; it was surreal sitting opposite this very dangerous and yet very credible character sipping whisky and smoking an expensive cigar to all intents as though nothing was wrong in the world. Even the desire to visit the toilet had disappeared from one zone but was re-entering another.

Who in hell was going to believe me? thought Victor. *If I ring up our egregious chief executive and tell him that the doctor is a criminal, then he's just going to think I am shit stirring, and it might even be the ideal excuse to let poor old Stanley go.* Victor started to think about going to the Japanese police, but then thought of the fact that the lady of the white silk suit had followed him all the way from Tokyo and this Doo-hwan probably knew exactly where he was going and what he was doing and whom he was seeing suggested that becoming deceased became rather a real issue for him.

Perhaps when he returned to England, he could go to the police, but what was he going to tell them? They had already warned the company that being active in this sort of area would require extreme care and that NTI might be open to some sort of danger from the criminal fraternity and they had only taken this half seriously; now it was happening. The police would record events and declare an interest, but events in Japan were outside their jurisdiction. They would be unable to act on the unsubstantiated facts Victor could place in front of them. Any action on his part would be noted by Doo-hwan, and he could seriously damage his health.

Superconductive polymers are interesting little beasts, and what NTI had done was to make them intelligent. Plastics that will conduct electricity have been around for some time, and NTI was at the forefront of that technology. They realised that if a polymer could be produced that could hold an identifiable message that could be easily read, then counterfeiting would be a thing of the past.

Working with nanochips, microchips so small the human eye could not easily see them, they had devised a means of suspending these intelligent particles in a liquid that could be laid down like an ink or incorporated within a plastic such as a credit card. Using a very simple piece of electronics, the article or articles could have a code inserted that could be read by a number of different types of machine. At its most simple, the SCP, superconducting polymer, could be printed without a message, and a small handheld device placed on its surface would pass an electric current between two contacts and identify the SCP itself.

At its most complex, the SCP would carry an individual code for such things as American Express credit cards or banknotes, and a swipe device or other more sophisticated readers would show the code to the inspector. It was simple and foolproof provided the technology was secure.

The good doctor had most of this technology at his fingertips, and Doo-hwan knew that very well, but he clearly didn't know the electronics and chemistry; probably only three or four people in the world did—Victor was not one of them. All he had to do was expose himself with half of the story in this trip to the major market and pick up a 100 per cent of the danger.

The slab leaned forward and slid the black sample box towards Victor; it ended up alongside the cigar box.

'Please show me, Victor, how this wonderful product works.'

This was more than a request; it was an instruction. Victor had been showing potential clients how the product worked all week; it would reveal nothing Doo-hwan had not already heard about, so why not?

For some reason that Victor could not explain, he had removed from the kit the small bottle of the polymer mixture that was the conductive fluid. He had shown this during the week to two or three highly specialized electronic companies who were also active in the chemical sector. Each of them had nearly wet themselves in their desire to obtain just a few grammes, and he was quite sure he could have made himself a rich man if he had not been the disappointingly honest citizen he was. Some sixth sense had warned him therefore that to carry the demonstration equipment, and the SCP in the same case was not a good idea.

When he had arrived in Osaka, he had removed the SCP from the demonstration kit, and he had looked for a safe place to store it over the weekend. There was a small standard lamp in the room with the light projecting from it on a steel bracket. The arm carrying the wire ended in what appeared to be a polished copper cylinder, and the bottom was ornamented. Victor had twisted it to see whether it unscrewed—it did—and, having unscrewed it, made a perfect hiding place for the small bottle, which he placed in the opening and screwed it up again.

Victor just had to pray that whoever had told Doo-hwan about the demonstration was not one of the people he had shown the sample to. Fortunately, Victor had told most of those who viewed the demonstrations that he did not carry active material with him. Now he wished this was true.

He opened the case and took out a piece of white paper with a red cross printed in the centre, a piece of plastic marked in the same way, a piece of glass, and a small piece of stainless steel. He laid them in a row on the table surface. He then took out what appeared to be some sort of gun with a short fat barrel extending at right angles to a piece of moulded plastic designed to comfortably fit into the hand. The barrel was about four inches long and was of a rigid plastic material with a white translucent disc at the end, which protected the sensor. At equidistant points on the edge of the sensor area were two small copper contact points.

Victor had been educated in the use of the device but did not understand the complex electronics. The wizards who had put it together had told him only what he needed to know and then had assured him that nothing could go wrong. They had not envisaged these particular circumstances.

There was a trigger where barrel and handle joined and a small screen at the rear of the device easily viewed by the user. Like a high-technology camera, it had a liquid crystal display. In the simple form, the gun barrel was placed on the marked surface of a product, and when the trigger was squeezed, it would emit a series of sound pulses, while at the same time, the display would show a preprogrammed selection of symbols, letters, and numbers. For particular clients such as credit card companies or central banks, special batches of SCP were produced with codes built into them by an electrochemical process. The identification worked in the same way, but the code was specific to the client, enabling him to clearly identify his own product. If the test device did not detect SCP, the sound emitted would be continuous, and the liquid crystal display would show a line of zeros.

Victor was no scientist, and he did not fully understand the system, but he presented it in a highly professional manner and used all the buzzwords collected during his numerous discussions with the boffins at NTI. Clients came to believe that he was the font of all knowledge; some sat open-mouthed believing him to be some sort of magician.

He switched on the device and waited for the display to produce the signal that indicated it was ready for use. He then placed it on the centre of the cross on the piece of paper and pressed the trigger; the device emitted a series of low fart-like sounds. The slab looked towards Voire Africa, who shifted uncomfortably. Victor turned the small knob that controlled sound volume and pressed it again. This time, it was a more effective high-pitched pulsing squeal. On both occasions, the display had clearly lit up with the figures 1-2-3-4-5. Victor moved it to the plastic and did the same thing again; the number appeared accompanied by the noise. He then moved it to the glass, and this time, the sound became continuous, 0-0-0-0-0 appearing in the display. The steel had a transparent coating on it, and this time, the device produced the noise but a new code 2-4-6-8. Victor switched off and sat back in his chair.

Doo-hwan looked at him for a full minute before speaking. 'Victor, I am a man who understands threats when I see them, and I have just seen a threat.'

Victor remained silent. Doo-hwan reached over and picked up the sensing device and switched it on, not a difficult thing to do if one had observed what Victor had been doing. There was a little switch in the side that had to be depressed; once again, the device came to life. Doo-hwan then repeated exactly what Victor had done and satisfied himself that he could get the same response. He switched it off and laid it gently, almost reverently, in the box.

Chapter 2

Dr George Yoreen was fifty-eight years old; his long suffering wife, Sybil, was fifty-four. She had experienced the ups and downs of George's life stoically and was now, much to her surprise, in the middle of a series of ups and downs that were quite unexpected, for George was making violent and passionate love to her; she could not remember the last time that such a session had occurred. Oh, yes, she could remember the half-hearted efforts that he usually called lovemaking, for she had been a very sensual woman all of her life, and it had been her undying regret that although she loved George dearly, he had never been an absolute wizard in bed, but because they had moved around the world so often, she had found time to have discreet affairs when George was away in the laboratory fucking up other things.

At least seven inches of him wasn't the same man she had lived with recently, and she had to admit it was a very exciting change.

'Now … now … now … now …' gasped George, and she sank her nails into his back and called out in ecstasy, or was it surprise? 'George, that's fucking beautiful!' for she had always been a woman who was boisterously noisy in her sexual enjoyment. The noise deflated George, who had crept up silently on this event, but he was still held in the vice-like grip of his wife, and on this occasion, he dare not extricate himself for fear that the claws clinging to his back would rip him to shreds. Slowly, ever so slowly, she released him.

'George, I don't know what has come over you. That was absolutely wonderful. It was just as though we were young lovers again. Has something happened you have not told me about? Not a new pill to rival Pfizer surely?'

George rolled out of the embrace and looked up at the ceiling. It was cracked and needed painting; in fact, the whole room, the whole house, indeed his whole life was cracked and in need of urgent attention, now perhaps he could afford it. He sighed and then scratched his hairy stomach and looked somewhat in surprise at his now quiet organ and then over at his wife, who he had to admit was still quite a striking woman despite her fifty-four years; he wondered how many times she had been unfaithful to him.

'Something extraordinary happened last week, my darling, which I dared not tell you about at the time. It is likely that we will soon have money again and will be able to enjoy all those luxuries we have promised ourselves for so many years but have been unable to afford because of my past failures. Events have removed financial worries from my mind, the age from my body, and probably the sense from my brain.'

Sybil snuggled up to him. 'George, it must have been an incredible event to have had all these effects on you at the same time, and long may it continue, but as you are an employee of a company, I don't see how we can possibly have come into a quick fortune, and you certainly don't have any rich relatives and you haven't won the lottery, so tell me more.'

She ran her fingers through the thick mat of hair that covered his chest, but despite this, George was not inclined to tell her more at the moment, and he didn't particularly like entering into long conversations when they had just finished lovemaking. It had been some effort for him despite his excitement, and he was now quite exhausted.

'Sybil, let's leave it till the morning and then I'll tell you about it. Just go to sleep in the knowledge that our fortunes have changed.'

Sybil could remember the times in their past when George had not been altogether honest either with himself or with some of his partners in the many businesses he had been associated with. She had stuck with him despite his dubious ways and lack of business sense, but she was no fool, except in her all-consuming love for this strange man. It wasn't that he was handsome or good in bed, but he had a certain pathetic magnetism about him that appealed to her. She knew that any good fortune that must have come along was bad fortune for someone else, but what the hell, he was going to be retiring in a couple of years, for the one thing they had done when money was available was to stuff it away in a suitable fund to protect them in their old age, and because these various pieces of money had been invested in the various different countries in which they had lived, they had resulted in a not-inconsiderable accumulation for the simple reason that they had avoided paying tax.

Sybil had been entrusted with the guardianship of these retirement funds, and she had locked them away so that neither of them could legitimately put their hands on any money until George's sixtieth birthday or in the event of his or her prior death. They were not huge, but they would not starve in old age, but if a bonus could be added, then retirement would look altogether rosier.

She awoke, as was her custom, at half past six, got up, and went into the bathroom before going downstairs to be greeted by her dog, Sesame, who had gained this name because of her unique ability to open almost any door. The dog hurled itself across the kitchen and nuzzled her with delight. She opened the door into the garden, and it hurtled out with equal enthusiasm seeing in its imagination first a rabbit and then a cat before realising what the garden was really for and finding a stunted bush and adding to its retardation.

Sybil switched on the kettle and got two mugs out of the cupboard and placed tea bags in them. Into George's, she reluctantly put two spoons of sugar and into her own a piece of lemon; she poured the boiling water in. Sesame re-entered and shot through the inner kitchen door and upstairs. George was slowly awakening, aware that a new day was about to dawn and that something wet was happening to his face.

'Bugger off, Sesame,' he growled, pushing the wet face away from his. Sybil came in.

'Good morning, darling. It's quarter to seven,' and she turned on the morning television. Some female was encouraging the world to start the day by hurling themselves around the bedroom in a manner that would either destroy it or the body.

'God, she's boring,' said George as he usually did and took a noisy gulp of his tea. Sybil sat there unusually silent, for, normally, she started talking at the beginning of the day and didn't stop until the end. They watched the weather forecast, which wasn't all that good, but then it never was. She broke the silence.

'George, for heaven's sake, stop keeping me in suspense and tell me how on earth we have come into this good fortune you keep hinting at.'

He looked sideways at his wife and realised that the moment of truth had come. He was now going to have to tell her what he already suspected she knew—he was a dishonest but potentially quite wealthy man. He also knew in his bones that this time, if he failed to deliver on the deal, he was probably going to become a deceased man.

'Sybil, you know that most of my life, I have drifted from one thing to another. Admittedly, I have a brilliant chemical mind but absolutely no business sense, and yet I have always wanted to make money, not products. We have on several occasions had to run away from situations that were getting to the point where either we were going to lose what little money I had accumulated or somebody was going to take it away from us.'

'George, I—'

'No, Sybil, let me finish. I am not a good man, and if I had my life to live over again, I would probably try and do different things with it. I admit to being weak and greedy. I am also fifty-eight years old, and this is the last chance that I will get to make a fortune. I have invented a very novel product using some of my accumulated knowledge added to a research project under way at NTI, and as a result, I have created a fascinating hybrid polymer. Without the two pieces of technology, NTI would never have had this breakthrough, and yet I will see nothing much from it apart from a reasonable salary and some acclaim and, if I am very lucky, a bit of bonus as well, but most of it will go into the pockets of the shareholders and a lot to that lousy chief of mine.'

George shifted his bulk in the bed and pushed his fingers through his hair to break up the unruly mess it had become during the night.

'You will remember four and a half years ago, Fred Latham and I fell out and our company went bust and we had to rush off and hide away in France for a while. Well, shortly before the company went bust, we sold a relatively large quantity of the product I was working on to an organisation in the Far East, but our research had not been completed, and I took a risk by contracting out the manufacturing hoping that the material would be satisfactory. Unfortunately, it wasn't.

'The client's approval had been gained from a large sample we had made in the laboratory and sent as a representative sample of the manufacture. The client approved it and paid in advance with an irrevocable letter of credit against a substantial discount. I received the money, and it kept us until I joined NTI. Poor Fred Latham didn't need to worry about it for too long because, as you know, he was sadly killed in that strange car accident.

'The product eventually arrived in the Far East, in fact in Korea, and didn't function properly as I suspected it might not. The man who headed up the organisation, which turned out to be much larger than the small electronics company I took it to be, has tracked me down, and last week, he sent a man to talk to me whom he called his "ambassador".'

'Oh, George, you fool—'

'Wait, Sybil, there's more. The ambassador told me that a man called Doo-hwan was determined that I should pay fully for having swindled his company but that he was a very fair man and I could satisfy the debt in one of two ways. The first is unacceptable, as it is with my death',—and he grimaced convincingly—'but the second is much more attractive. I am to supply him with some of our new superconducting polymer and help with the formulation know-how for his company to produce it, for, as you might be aware, Korea is not particularly worried about international patent law. In return for this and when his scientists have successfully reproduced it to match my initial sample, he will pay into my bank account at any nominated bank the sum of £1 million, and as a positive gesture of his goodwill, he has already deposited £250,000 in cash in a deed box in a bank in London for which I have the receipt but do not yet have the key. When he gets the sample, I will receive the key. If I fail, I shan't need the key,' he added unnecessarily.

He turned to look at Sybil; she was studying him open-mouthed.

'George, you are the biggest idiot I have ever known. Why I love you, I don't know. You are basically dishonest, and, worse, you are trusting. I have faults too, I know, but at least my faults don't lead me into danger, and I am always here at the end of the day, but you, my darling, have a death wish. Good god! George, you earn a good-enough salary now, and we have a good-enough pension in prospect, and even if you had stuck with Fred Latham and patched up the row, we'd have gotten by, but, no, you bloody well have to con someone out of enough money to satisfy your immediate greed, and this time, you picked a man whose connections were more unsavoury than your own.' She paused dramatically and drew in breath before continuing.

'You can't possibly accept the money, George. You have got to go to the police. At the very least, you must tell Hipkiss what's going on in order that he can inform the law. They'll protect you. What you have done in the past is not against the criminal law of England, and these new products you have invented are going to protect the law.'

'Sybil, it is not as easy as that. Apart from anything else, I am frightened, and I have no doubt that this ambassador from Mr Doo-hwan meant everything he said. One way or another, if I don't deliver, I am dead.'

Sybil's lower lip started to tremble violently, a sure sign she was about to burst into tears; with supreme effort, she controlled herself.

'You don't believe, do you, that all that money is ever going to find its way to our bank account George? If you do, then you are an even bigger fool than I thought.' The effort made, she now subsided into tears, not just little ones that flowed gently down the cheek but huge storm drops of tears that burst forth in uncontrolled fury. She was crying both for herself and for the fool of a man she was married to.

'Please don't cry, Sybil,' said George, tentatively moving closer in what he thought to be a comforting crablike movement. Sybil backed away. 'You know how it upsets me.'

'Upsets you, George?' She sobbed. 'You sit there and tell me that you're in imminent danger of being murdered and you won't do anything about it, and you expect me to be the good little wife, keep a stiff upper lip, and support you through thick and thin.' She looked for and found a crumpled handkerchief and blew her nose noisily and wetly.

'I am not going to be murdered, Sybil. I am going to produce the goods—it's the only way.'

She looked at him again through her tears. They had run down her face, and despite work with the now sodden rag, one or two hung precariously from her chin and were in imminent danger of disappearing down her cleavage. She sniffed; they dropped. *A million pounds,* she thought, *would they give it to him?*

'Oh, George, what would I do without you?' she sobbed, drier now. In her mind, she was already thinking that this was just another of George's adventures. If he could deliver, if they could get a million pounds. It would make up for all the problems of the past; they would have to go away, of course, but she really didn't mind that. Provided she had George, she could put up with a lot, and a George with substantial money was very put-up-withable indeed. Despite her mood, she smiled.

On the television, which had been muttering away in the background, the start of the week's business news flashed up on the screen, and, suddenly, the voice of the newscaster was demanding attention; they both took notice.

'Late in Friday trading, the shares of NTI advanced 30p on rumours of a significant breakthrough in the conductive polymer area. It is thought that the share price increased as a result of strong Far Eastern buying, but no one at NTI could confirm this.'

Chapter 3

Victor held his breath. Doo-hwan withdrew his hands from the box and looked at him steadily for what seemed like an eternity, and then he smiled. His teeth positively glistened and owed more to the work of an orthodontist than they did to nature. They matched the whiteness of his shirt, and the black moustache on his upper lip acted like a theatre curtain lifting now and again to show the star performers.

'Mr Stanley, it does not take a very clever man to understand what has been demonstrated. The uses for this product are far-reaching and must be studied seriously by both the legitimate and, aah … other areas of my business interests.'

In hearing what he was saying, Victor realised that he was not aware that there was a sample of the product in Japan, and that enabled him to eliminate from the list of companies he had spoken to last week those that had been shown the sample itself. It would still be a difficult task to put a finger on where the leak was, but at least it was known that the enemy was in a group of businesses that need not be seen again.

Even so, this Doo-hwan knew too much, and with his links to George Yoreen, he already had the track to the source and was running his little engine along it.

The hand with the ring waved in the air, and a Voire Africa silently appeared by his side. For the first time, Victor noticed that there was an additional adornment on his T-shirt—a small pin stuck in the collar with the same red tail and silver dot for the head, though he doubted that his was picked out in rubies and diamonds. A brief conversation ensued during which the slab gesticulated and emphasised, and Voire Africa stood to attention and listened.

'I have just told him', said Doo-hwan, 'that he is to escort you back to the hotel, so let us consider for a moment what is now going to happen.'

Victor's stomach gave another violent lurch, and the shift of emphasis changed again with regard to his sanitary requirements.

'I wonder', said Victor, 'if I might be permitted to use the toilet?'

The pudgy hand again rose into the air, and Voire Africa appeared again.

'I should remind you, Mr Stanley, that we are some floors above the ground here. The toilet window is extremely small, and there is no purpose anyway in you trying to climb out of it. When I say you will be returned to your hotel, I mean it. I wish you no harm.'

Victor had no intention of escaping; his needs were entirely genuine, and he accompanied the young man to a passage at the side of the bar where a small emblem on the door seemed to inform him that he was probably entering an area reserved for transvestites, or men who wear very short trousers. Thankfully, Voire Africa left him at the door, and he moved rapidly into the cubicle and joyfully relieved himself of his gathered fear; at least now he could relax his stomach muscles somewhat and reduce sphincter control to 50 per cent. It seemed to be a habit today—sitting on toilets. The casual warning had been delivered while he was on one, and now he was undoubtedly being released with another warning, and again, he was seated on one. *Where would it all end?* he asked himself.

He washed his hands, put cold water on his face, and felt a little bit better, but the uneasiness in the stomach still hadn't gone completely, and the day was wearing on. He looked at his watch and could not believe that it was quarter to four. He looked at the window. It was too small to get through for someone of his age and bulk; besides which he wasn't too good at jumping up and getting hold of things by his fingertips and then hauling the rest of his body after them. He looked around to see if there might be some sort of weapon; there wasn't. He felt foolish; he hadn't actually been threatened with physical violence, and what could he do anyway? It appeared that time was on his side; somehow, he was going to have to use this to his advantage, but at the moment, he had no idea how.

He opened the door, and Voire Africa was standing there waiting just like a good servant should. He bowed courteously, and Victor followed him back into the bar. Doo-hwan still occupied the seat on the other side of the table, but the drinks had been cleared away, the ashtray had been emptied, and Victor's partly consumed Dunhill cigar had disappeared with it, cleanliness being more important than thriftiness. The box containing the rest had also been removed, and the sample case had been closed and placed in front of Victor's seat. Victor sat down; the leather made a sighing noise, rather too timid, he thought, for the situation in which he found himself.

The slab spoke. 'Victor, it is perhaps now time to explain some of the events of the immediate future, for you need to have an understanding of what will now happen.'

Victor wished he hadn't left the toilet.

'I have had a most informative afternoon,' said Doo-hwan, smiling hugely and bringing the curtain up on his mouth of teeth. 'You have confirmed for me both in Tokyo last week and with your excellent demonstration today that my investment in your Dr Yoreen'—Victor had stopped even smiling inwardly at the mispronunciation as it now seemed appropriate—'is going to pay off handsomely. I don't trust him, of course, as he has a most unreliable background, but he understands the situation, and as he is a greedy man, I believe that he will do his best to follow the simple rules that I have given him and stick to the timetable, which has been indicated. As I explained, my ambassador spoke to him very recently, and I have had the message passed to him that time is of the essence in this matter, and he understands that this means he must deliver in weeks, not months. I will get very impatient if he drags his feet—too much dragging could be terminal. Your good doctor is aware that threats made by me must be listened to carefully—I do not accept failure. He also knows that revealing my interests to the authorities would not be good for his health. I do not believe that I am in any particular danger from your Yoreen. I do not want to be in danger from you either, but then we have never met Mr Stanley.'

He repositioned himself in the large chair, distributing his weight more evenly across the seat, which sighed softly. His fat arms once again rested heavily on the arms of the chair. The curtain of his moustache rose again.

'You will be taken from here—'

'Now, wait a minute ...' The words, half recollected from some time long past, 'to a place of execution' rushed into his mind.

'Taken from here to your hotel,' continued Doo-hwan. 'I believe you are leaving our city on Tuesday afternoon, and I must therefore ask you to stick meticulously to your plans. A member of my organisation will maintain contact with you until Dr Yoreen has satisfied my aspirations. Enjoy yourself, Mr Stanley.'

The great man placed both of his palms flatly now on the front of the arms of his chair and pushed. The bulk seemed to come up out of the chair with jet propulsion, and Victor realised again that this was not just bulk; it was muscle too, and he remembered that Korea was famous for martial arts. He had no doubt that one chop from either hand would break in two the table in front of him and therefore, if in contact with human flesh, was likely to cause a moment of exquisite agony followed immediately by becoming deceased.

Victor also stood but somewhat unsteadily; for some reason, his legs did not really want to support the weight of his body anymore, but he forced himself into movement and picked up the demonstration kit.

Voire Africa and his twin T-shirt stood expectantly at the end of the short passage leading to the door. The girl of the white silk suit, still in her jeans, appeared out of a small door in the wall opposite the bar that he had not noticed before. She was carrying a carrier bag with 'Daimaru' emblazoned across the side advertising the name of the nearby department store. It was all Mickey Mouse to Victor.

'When you leave here, Victor', said Doo-hwan, 'it will be as though no one had ever visited. No one will remember ever having seen me or indeed my assistants. This bar is closed during the day and does not open until six o'clock. You will be escorted back to the hotel, and if you were then so foolish as to ring the police and they were to believe your incredible tale, they would find nothing.'

He stood, hands outstretched inviting Victor to reply, but he could not find the words.

'I have a simple request of you this evening, and that is that you do not leave your hotel or make any telephone calls. Tomorrow, go about your business as though nothing had happened—after all, Victor nothing really has.'

He held out his hand, and, despite himself, Victor shook it. It was warm and dry and enveloped Victor's entirely. Again, he noticed the ring and observed it more carefully; perhaps this was the only real evidence that he was going to have after this meeting, for there must be somebody who knew what that symbol meant. He kept referring to his organisation, so perhaps this was its logo, but what organisation?

'Au revoir, Victor,' said his host.

He was a precise man, this much Victor had learned. He suspected he would know of the meaning behind the French way of parting temporarily; 'au revoir' was not a final goodbye, and he believed he had chosen his words carefully. Victor hoped fervently he was wrong.

The girl of the white silk suit came over to the table and reached out for the demonstration kit. Victor handed it to her, and she put it carefully in the Daimaru carrier. Her hands were elegant, the fingers long and slim, the nails beautifully painted. For the first time, Victor noticed the ring on the middle finger of the left hand. The symbol again stamped without stones into the flat surface of a gold signet ring.

'My colleague and I', said Voire Africa number one, 'will accompany you back to the hotel. Ms Tan will lead the way. You will please follow behind her.'

It all seemed surreal. Victor was leaving as though nothing had happened. He was being returned to the hotel. He had thought that his release was unlikely at times during the meeting, at least until Doo-hwan had what he wanted from George Yoreen. Doo-hwan was obviously supremely confident of the fact that Victor was not a real threat.

They went down the short passage, and Victor looked back over his shoulder to see if Doo-hwan was following; he was not in sight. Once again, they squeezed into the small lift and descended the four floors to the entrance. The sun was still shining, people were still hurrying about their Sunday tasks, shopping bags were crammed to overflowing, and little restaurants were packed with people. There was a good-natured feeling about the crowd Victor was about to re-enter.

Ms Tan, as Victor now knew her name to be, stepped out of the entrance, and he followed. Victor kept his eyes glued to her bottom as he strode joyfully after her; it was a good day for bottoms. He realised now what a very excellent figure she presented from the back. There was a message sewn into the left-hand pocket of her jeans that he couldn't quite read, so he accelerated his pace a little to catch up. 'Elle', another French message!

A lot of men go for tits and faces; Victor had always been a bums and legs man. His life had been filled with women walking away from him, but they had left behind some wonderful memories.

It occurred to Victor that Tan was a common Chinese name, particularly in Singapore where he had spent many happy weeks, so why was a Korean involved in Japan with a girl from China or Singapore? As these thoughts came into his mind, they passed the pachinko parlour that he had walked by on the way to his unwitting rendezvous; the mindless people were still seated at the machines flicking them endlessly to win their little bag of presents, which they would go round the corner to exchange for cash, a strictly illegal act.

Somebody in the gambling parlour seemed to shout a greeting, and Ms Tan reacted. It was only a half-gesture checked in mid-flight, Victor could not be sure; maybe he had been mistaken and the man hadn't been calling out to Ms Tan at all, but then those idle rumours came back to him again. Pachinko parlours, money going to Korea, profits being syphoned off, police having to keep an eye on them, special new systems being introduced that would stop them avoiding the Japanese taxman's grasp. The product the good doctor had produced might even have an application somewhere in that, and although Victor didn't think for one minute that this was the major incentive of our friend Doo-hwan, it was possibly part of it. He looked more sharply at the man who had made the gesture of greeting, who was now standing on the top step of the pachinko parlour as though nothing had happened. There was a flash of light from something on his lapel, and Victor wondered whether it was the red snake emblem again.

It was not a long journey to the hotel, and he was almost sorry when the magnificent bottom of Ms Tan arrived at the door. Voire Africa came up beside him.

'Mr Stanley, we leave you now, but please remember the messages of Doo-hwan. He also asks me to mention that he feels sure you will have an enjoyable evening.'

Victor didn't think for one moment that these two men would be far away, and he had no intention of leaving the hotel. The way up to the lobby was via an escalator straight ahead of him. Ms Tan walked on as though to descend the other escalator that led down to the subway.

To his surprise, at the top of the stairs, Victor was greeted by one of the obsequious well-meaning guest relations people. Although he dearly enjoyed his experiences in Japan, there were habits that tended to get up his nose. The way that everyone greets you like a long-lost friend in hotels so that everywhere you go they are continuously greeting and bowing, it is the same for that matter in department stores and restaurants where, in places like the coffee shop, you never wait more than one minute between courses; they actually apologise 'for keeping you waiting'.

'Mr Stanley', said the immaculately attired customer relations person, 'would you be so kind as to follow me to the guest relations desk?'

Victor wondered, first, how on earth he knew his name, and, second, what was going to happen now. He followed him to the desk and was offered the chair opposite the hotel servant. Victor sat down. He noticed that there were invitations to a number of tours assuring the viewers that they would have the most marvellous time and with continuous commentary in 'Englis' followed, no doubt, by an unbeatable opportunity to purchase local goods at inflated prices. The thought of yet again seeing the Golden Pavilion at Kyoto did not appeal to Victor. Going on that trip or any other was thankfully not on his modified and restricted schedule.

'Mr Stanley', said the servant, 'there has been a slight change with regard to the accommodation arrangements.'

'Not as far as I am concerned,' Victor retorted. 'There is nothing wrong with my guest room accommodation.'

'Ah, no, you missunnerstan,' said the servant. 'Unfortunately, there has been a sudden demand for, ah … twin, ah … bedded rooms, and as you only have two more nights in Osaka …'

'Oh, here it comes,' said Victor. 'You want to move me to a single next to the lift.'

The servant either did not understand the heavy sarcasm or chose to ignore it.

'The management has therefore decided, at no extra cost whatsoever to yourself, to allocate you a suite on the twenty-seventh floor.'

Victor was struck dumb, for he knew that on the twenty-seventh floor, because he had read it in the hotel's publicity information, there were only suites that had been specially designed by the Japanese designer Hanae Mori, and there was no reason for him to deserve this treatment. The hand of Doo-hwan loomed large, and Victor saw in his mind's eye the imperious gesture and imagined the telephone conversation that had taken place.

'Am I to understand that you are actually going to move me to a magnificent suite at no extra charge?'

'Ah … precisely so,' said the servant.

A feeling of great contentment came over Victor. 'My god, not even Hipkiss could get this treatment meted out to him,' he said aloud to no one in particular.

'Plees?' queried the servant.

'Oh, nothing. I was just thinking aloud. I will accept your offer.'

A person in a red jacket accompanied by a person in a black jacket was summoned to the guest relation manager's desk. One of them was carrying a key held tightly by the right-hand seam of his trousers and stood rigidly to attention, while guest relations informed him in Japanese that he and his companion were in the presence of a person who warranted a degree of bowing almost parallel to the floor. For those who are not familiar with the Japanese tradition of bowing, some explanation: when you are in an inferior position and the bowee is in a ferior position, you bow lower. If you get a nod, then you are in the presence of God. If you get nothing, then you are in the presence of the emperor. The group of three guided Victor to the lift, and he was escorted to what could only be described as a sumptuous suite—two bedrooms, two bathrooms, a sitting room, and a small hallway. Victor was conducted around it being shown all the facilities and then ushered into the bedroom, which opened off the small hall to the left.

He saw his case, which was garishly covered with hotel stickers from the East in order that it could be spotted in an airport, placed on the luggage holder at the foot of the massive bed.

The servant was speaking again.

'I do hope, Mr Stanley, that you enjoy the next two days.'

The trio withdrew, upper bodies almost parallel to the ground, and Victor was left to contemplate the luxury before him. He went over and stood at the window; if he had suffered from vertigo, he would have had a problem. The traffic on the expressway was moving quite freely for a change. He lowered his field of vision and took in the roofs of several car parks. It immediately struck him that practically every car in sight was almost a reflection of life in Japan—whiter than white; the sparkle of corruption was everywhere.

He turned back into the room and noticed that his nightshirt, a garment he much preferred to pyjamas, was laid out on the bed. Someone had nipped it in at the waist, impossibly. He went through into the sitting room, and there on the table in the middle was a bottle of Jack Daniels, a box of Bolivar Robusto cigars, and a white card edged in black with the word 'Remember' on it. His feeling of well-being vanished, and the words 'become deceased' lit up in his brain like neon lights; he decided to explore the bathroom urgently.

When he had once again fully recovered from the shock to his system, he explored the suite more fully and went through into the second bedroom. It was quite different from the first. The colours were more exotic and the bed slightly smaller with a canopy; it exuded a feeling of intimacy. To his surprise, it also contained a suitcase, and laid out on this bed was a most exquisite nightgown through which he could see the designs of the quilted cover. He had hardly had time to consider what all this meant when a series of chimes rang in the hallway of the suite. Victor went to the door and cautiously looked through the spyhole. Stood in the middle was a rather distorted face of a woman; perhaps she was the owner of the diaphanous nightgown. As he had never felt threatened by any woman yet, he opened the door. The exquisite lady in the white silk suit stood there.

Chapter 4

Kevin Malo Hipkiss was a prat, a very polished, unpleasant, and superficially able prat. Kevin did not know that people thought of him in this way; they learned of it from having to work for him. His father, now dead, had known it and mentioned it again to his wife, Marjorie, at the time of his passing.

'Marjorie, you really don't have anything to worry about for the rest of your life, for I have left a suitable income by way of a considerable annuity, which will be more than enough for your personal needs despite the awful rates that currently prevail. If you see fit to give the surplus to our son, then so be it, but there is one thing I am determined about, and that is he shall make his own way in life, and therefore, apart from the property, which is the inheritance of a roof over his head, he must fend for himself as I did. Our son has a decidedly nasty streak, and he is therefore bound to succeed in the present-day business climate, and fortunately for him, he inherited a fine brain. I hope God lets him know how to use it—perhaps I can put a word in for him. Sadly, he despises his fellow man, which is a mistake. He will never develop their respect, and until he learns to correct this weakness, he will continue to be a prat.' Having delivered this last message to his wife, he passed quietly away with a wicked little smile on his lips that even the best embalmer could not remove.

Marjorie was consoled in her grief by the financial message but nevertheless wore black for a whole week after the passing of her somewhat undevoted husband. Marjorie loved Kevin and could see only sunshine in his soul; the fact remained, however, that his father was right.

Kevin stretched himself luxuriously in the king-size bed. He stretched both his arms sideways, and his yellow silk pyjamas moved with him; he had the appearance of an unshaven sunbeam. The arms seemed to reach out for contact, but there was no one for him to touch. He had already gone through one marriage, and a proposal to the second woman of his dreams had been rather abruptly refused on the basis that, although she was very fond of the good life Kevin could give her, she was still looking for the ideal partner. She had the old-fashioned view that really good relationships lasted forever, and not for the three or four years she felt would be her tolerance level with Kevin's tantrums.

Having completed his investigation of the extremities of his domain, he withdrew his hands and pushed himself up into a sitting position. He then scrabbled crablike to the left-hand side of his bed and pressed a white button set in a red plastic box that would summon his man from the kitchen.

In the bowels of the inherited house, Clinton was enjoying his second mug of tea. The kitchen around him was immaculate, and he thought, not for the first time, that he was indeed fortunate to be in the employ of a man who earned more money than he deserved and spent a sizeable amount of it maintaining his presence. The angry hornet-like signal of the buzzer informed him that his employer was awake, and he stood up and walked over to the ceramic hob unit, which was already on standby, and placed a Le Creuset pan, which already contained a sizeable knob of Cornish butter on the halogen heater. He depressed the switch on the electric kettle and moved towards the refrigerator. He took three eggs from the egg rack and a jug of double cream from the bottom shelf and returned to the halogen lamp, which was now searing the bottom of the pan. The butter was beginning to melt and bubble slightly. He poured a liberal portion of double cream into it and cracked, one-handed, the eggs. He stirred them briskly with a wooden spoon and left them momentarily, whilst he took two pieces of wholemeal toast and placed them in the toaster and depressed the activating button. He moved back to the hob unit and briskly stirred the eggs and cream and butter until they were of a consistency that his master appreciated. He removed them from the halogen unit and stood them on the side to continue their cooking process gently by themselves. He took from the oven a warmed plate and placed it on a tray that contained silver cutlery, a cruet, and a spotless napkin, all part of the household inheritance.

The toaster, as it always did, threw the two pieces of wholemeal onto the benchtop, and he picked them up, putting one on the warm plate and another on the side plate. He gave a final stir to the eggs and eased them gently out of the pan onto the toast. He placed a premium grade of margarine in a small dish on the tray and wondered, not for the first time, why on earth his employer, who insisted that he use butter and cream in the preparation of his scrambled eggs, wanted margarine on his toast particularly when accompanied by a jar of Fortnum's Canadian clover honey.

The kettle switched itself off, and he took down from the shelf in front of him a large jar of Nescafe Gold Blend and placed two liberal spoons in a silver jug and added the water. Kevin Hipkiss was a creature of habit; Gold Blend coffee was his idea of a good waking-up drink but served black because he liked the initial kick of the caffeine. He inspected the tray, and satisfied that he had everything that his master desired foodwise, he added to it the Monday edition of the *Financial Times*.

He picked up the tray and went through the kitchen door into the hallway and ascended the one flight to his master's bedroom, which was situated immediately opposite the staircase in front of him. The wallpaper was not his taste, but then again, very little in this house was; Kevin employed every year an interior decorator of dubious quality to redo the house. The hallway, staircase, and landing were decorated in what was meant to be a fashionable combination of yellow, green, and purple. Halfway up was a painting by a modern artist whose name he had thankfully forgotten who had apparently broken eggs onto a canvas and then run over them with chickens. He used one hand precariously to open the bedroom door and entered the exalted presence.

'Good morning, sir,' said Clinton.

'Morning,' said Kevin.

'It is surprisingly a fine day outside today, sir.'

'Good.'

Clinton walked over to a small table by the window and placed the tray upon it. He opened the curtains by pulling a cord at the right-hand side. They revealed a not insubstantial garden with a tennis court at the far end and a small pavilion for players to relax around and change in. It was a matter of some concern to Kevin that his tennis was not very good.

Clinton pulled back the chair to a suitable position, adjusted the *Financial Times,* and moved the one slice of toast a little to the left and departed the way he had come.

Kevin eased himself gently out of bed; his silk pyjamas draped themselves around his not-inelegant frame in the manner they had been taught. He went into the bathroom and, having satisfied himself that his organ was functioning, seated himself in the chair by the window. He took a fork in his left hand and a knife in his right and in a fairly straightforward manner attacked the scrambled eggs. He took a mouthful of coffee and opened the pages of the *Financial Times*.

The information that it contained on a Monday morning concerning company matters was relatively spars, for those messages that did not hit Friday or Saturday were dead by Monday; but there was one article that he was gratified to see, for it concerned the share price increase of New Technology Industries plc (NTI), and it speculated upon the breakthrough that they might have made with their new superconducting polymer. He searched in vain for his name and frowned at its omission. He made a mental note to have their PR man in his office this morning to explain why. He again picked up the knife and fork and cut himself another small piece of the scrambled eggs on toast and placed it in his medium-sized mouth and started to chew. He stopped chewing; there was a piece of eggshell in it. He removed the offending fragment and tried again—better. Not a good start to the day—an article in the *FT* without his name in it, and Clinton not taking due care of his food preparation. What else was going to go wrong? Kevin believed in threes.

He finished his breakfast and moved into the bathroom, which opened off a short corridor whose other side was occupied by a dressing room. He stood in front of the right-hand washbasin, for this room had originally been designed for two people to brush their teeth simultaneously. The mirror occupied the whole of the wall. It reflected a medium-sized man, aged forty-two, with rather attractive wavy hair often adored by women; he had a clean complexion and appeared in good health. He undid the pyjama jacket and let it drop to the floor; it revealed a relatively hairless upper body. Kevin had always wished that he had been born with more active hair follicles on his chest, as he felt it would make him feel more masculine to accompany the macho image he liked to adopt. His eyes were brown and matched his hair. Around his neck, he wore a gold chain with a small medallion; some said that it was engraved 'I love Kevin'; some said that he had had it engraved himself, for there was no doubt that the first love in Kevin's life was Kevin, and as if to prove it, he smiled happily at himself.

Chapter 5

The chimes confused Victor until he realised it was someone at the door. He went to the small hall and opened it.

'Aren't you going to let me in?' asked the lovely Ms Tan.

Victor stood transfixed at least momentarily. He had suspected something was going to happen because of what was laid out in the second bedroom, and various pictures now started to rush through his mind, none of them unpleasant. His manners took over.

'Yes, of course, do come in.'

She walked confidently into the hallway, her small feet hardly moving the thick pile of the carpet. She walked past Victor into the sitting room and turned round and looked towards him. The window behind her seemed to create a halo around her head, and Victor began to wonder whether she was all bad.

'Mr Stanley, I have to explain to you why I am here.'

This was an understatement as far as Victor was concerned; he needed so many explanations that he had almost given up trying to obtain them.

'Let me guess,' he said. 'Our big Korean friend has dispatched you to be my entertainment for the evening and to give me no reason to leave the hotel.' He hoped it was true.

'Doo-hwan wants to see me safely on a plane from Narita to London Heathrow. That is a common objective he and I both share. You are here presumably to look after me when I am not being followed by one of his men, who will no doubt take care of door duties and make sure that I go only to the various meetings planned for the remainder of the visit. I am assuming, of course, that they know of the meetings because they were able to remove the demonstration kit and sample box from my briefcase. They must have studied everything about me that was available from the awfulness of my passport photograph to the contents of my toilet bag.' He stopped.

'Oh, shit, the demonstration kit.'

Ms Tan had it in the bag. Victor took three strides across the room in a sudden panic, but she was faster and held out the Daimaru bag to him.

'It's here,' she said. 'You must trust me. I am, after all, looking after two sets of interests—yours and ours.'

Two sets of interests be damned, the only interest she was looking after was Doo-hwan's. At the moment, it suited them to have Victor as the demonstrator of a new and fantastic technology, but they had their knives into the bad doctor. Victor knew he would be watched until his flight home; he would have no chance of informing anyone about Doo-hwan and his ambitions. Who would believe him anyway?

He needed to know more, and she would tell him more, no doubt. At least he had the essential demonstration kit back in his own hands. There weren't exactly many of them, and if he had to account for its loss, he might as well write off the rest of his career with NTI.

He took the bag and put it on the table and withdrew the black box. He opened the lid and checked the contents and assured himself that the activator was in working order. Nothing seemed to have been touched, and for the second time, he thought how fortunate it was that some sixth sense had made him hide the working sample.

Appalled, he realised that the working sample was not with him for he had changed rooms; he hadn't needed to go back to his previous room, as all his belongings had been moved for him.

'Is everything all right?'

'Yes, yes', said Victor uneasily, thinking, 'everything appears to be in order.' He had to do something.

He looked at his watch; it was now early evening, and in a few minutes, the big hand would have passed the hour mark and the little hand would tell him it was six o'clock and the time he usually reserved for the first hard liquor of the day. Perhaps a short sharp one would make his mind work better on the immediate problem of sample restoration. First, there was the situation with Ms Tan to be sorted out.

'I think it's time you and I put our cards on the table. I need to know what your role is.'

Ms Tan sat down. She sat quite upright, and the deep upholstery of the sofa hardly seemed to notice she was there. Both feet were firmly on the floor, knees slightly apart and tantalisingly far enough to make Victor think that with a little bit of luck, he might be able to see all the way up. The Western woman prefers the cross-legged style giving you a view of the bottom of her thigh, but the East is the land of eternal promise.

'I am yours to do with what you like, Mr Stanley. My only instruction is to remain close to you, and you will find that I shall do just that until we reach London, for I am to accompany you there. Doo-hwan's men will observe me as well as you and report back, but for the time being, I am yours to command.'

'What happens if I leave the suite?'

'Nothing, Mr Stanley, but please do not leave the hotel.'

At least that solved one problem, and then he realised that in his pocket, he still had the key card to his original room, but what would happen if he presented it? No doubt someone in that grand reception area was keeping a friendly eye open for what he might be doing, and if a receptionist was to hand a key over to him, they would want to know why. It was a forlorn hope anyway; the room would have been relet, and Doo-hwan would not be so slipshod as to leave that possibility open.

He needed that drink and went to the table. The ice bucket was full, and Victor put some in a glass and poured a liberal shot of Jack Daniels into it and a less liberal shot of still mineral water.

'Can I get you a drink, Ms Tan?' He paused. 'Look, I can't keep on calling you Ms Tan. If we're going to stay together for some time, at least we can get on a level of communication that is a little bit more intimate.'

Victor seemed to stretch that word as though there were hyphens in it. *In-ti-mate, yes, please,* he thought.

'My friends call me Veronica,' she said.

'Well, that's fine because I hope we will become friends even under these strange circumstances. You already know my name, so please let's be on a Victor-Veronica status.'

'OK!' in that delightful singsong Singapore accent. 'And I'll have a Coca-Cola, please.'

They sat there sipping drinks for all the world as though nothing was wrong. Here was the horny Englishman with his beautiful Oriental girlfriend in one of the best suites in one of the best hotels in Osaka, and all around him a huge criminal activity was building up, one that he couldn't even put his finger on. Back home, the bad doctor was finding ways to sell NTI technology down the river, Hipkiss no doubt was so buried in his own importance that he wasn't really aware of the plotting, and apart from Victor, the only man who appeared to think that there was anything suspicious going on was his business contact in Tokyo, Koizumi San. Victor speculated, however, that if the rumours had reached him, then his main contact in Osaka and NTI's close business associates, Nonaka Industries, would also be aware of the intense interest in the superconducting polymer.

The following morning, he had a meeting planned with his closest Japanese friend and business associate Kenezo Nonaka, heir to Nonaka Corporation. Maybe he could take Kenezo into his confidence; somehow, he had got to recover the sample.

'Veronica, I'm going to have a shower and try and get some of the dirt of today washed away. Then I have some preparation work to do for tomorrow's meetings, and under the present circumstances, I would prefer to eat here in the suite than to go down to one of the restaurants, do you mind?'

'Mr Victor—sorry, Victor, I am happy to go to my room and take a meal there. I don't want you to feel that I am an imposition.'

That she certainly wasn't.

'If there is anything you want, please come to my room,' and she looked at Victor directly; he could have sworn that the knees just consciously opened a bit. He smiled, got up, picked up the glass, refilled it with ice, and added to it another tot of liquor. He put the black demonstration case under his arm, went into his room, and shut the door behind him, but although there was a lock to turn, he did not use it.

Victor took a contemplative swig of his drink and tried to think just about the liquor and the years of work that had gone into the production of this particularly joyous invention and thought that all those years ago, there must have been some guy called Jack Daniels who thought that he had developed something pretty good and who had provided for the quality to be available to future generations. Victor wondered if NTI and its inventions would survive that long; he would try his best to ensure they did.

He took great care with his ablutions, even shaving for a second time that day and applying his favourite cologne generously to his body. He put on a clean open-necked shirt and a pair of lightweight trousers. Walking through into the sitting room, he added more ice to his drink and sat in one of the very comfortable chairs and thought about the sample and how he was going to get it back. He had difficulty keeping his mind on this subject for long. Next door was Veronica Tan. He was sure there had been a message in the intimate knee movement; she had said that if he wanted anything, he only had to ask. She was decidedly delicious.

Victor looked at the room service menu; it was quite passable, and he was getting hungry. The thought of feeding both the inner and outer man was appealing. He sat there a bit longer just enjoying the relaxation and trying to put out of his mind the other threats that wanted to crowd in. He must have dozed off as he awoke with a start. Apart from a small lamp in the corner of the sitting room, which he had turned on when he came in, the only other light came from the big windows and the night lights of Osaka. Victor leaned to the side of the armchair and turned the switch on the lamp by his side. He looked at his watch; it was quarter to ten. Hastily he got up from the chair and walked into the bathroom and splashed cold water on his face to take away that fuzzy feeling that often follows a catnap.

He walked back into the sitting room; it was still empty. He went and stood by the door of Veronica's room and placed his ear against the wood and listened. There was no sound, but there was light under the door. He knocked.

There being no reply, Victor gently opened the door and poked his head around it. The bedroom was empty, but the table by the window contained a tray and the remnants of a meal. The door to the bathroom was shut, and as he walked towards it, he could hear water running. The diaphanous nightdress had disappeared from the bed and was probably with the delectable Ms Tan in the bathroom. He walked over towards the window and picked up what was left of a small bunch of grapes and plucked one off and popped it into his mouth. He squashed it with his teeth, and the juice spurted into the dark extremities sweet with the summer's sun, soft like the body in the shower. He ate another, this time cutting it in half with his front teeth, and pushed his tongue into the soft flesh.

Veronica Tan passed the towel intimately between her thighs and thought not for the first time about how different it would be to have a Western lover instead of the hairless little bodies of the East. She looked at herself in the mirror and touched first one nipple and then the other. She rubbed them with the warm palms of her hands still damp from the water. They arose expectantly, and she shivered involuntarily with the exquisite pleasure of self-gratification. Her jet-black hair was a contrast to her pale complexion. Her skin had that wonderful marble-like appearance, not of pure white but white that pink has entered and touched it with a healthy luminescence. She was five feet six inches tall, and her hair was cut with a straight fringe at the front and dropped down to her shoulders. She shaved under her arms, and the only other hair on her body was set at the junction of legs and abdomen. She had a small waist, graceful hips, and long and extremely well-shaped legs. Her feet were well designed and without the usual lumps and scars so often the hallmark of being crammed into shoes too small and too high. She dropped her left hand, and watching herself in the mirror, she placed it over the mound of Venus and pressed with her middle finger on the most sensitive part she could find, an image of Victor Stanley placed itself in her mind, and, suddenly, she wanted to be held. She wanted something nice to happen to her. She wanted him to make love to her.

Victor picked up a third grape and licked the skin until it shone. He was still doing this when the bathroom door opened, and Ms Tan stepped through her nightdress, hiding little.

It was as though the image she had had of him had been replaced as if by magic by his presence. It was almost a physical shock to see him standing there, and, instinctively, she moved her hands to cover herself; but when their journey was halfway completed, she stopped them.

'Mr Stanley,' she cried, surprised in the way she said it, off guard.

'Victor,' he said.

'Victor,' she echoed and walked towards him. He could see every inch of her body through the fine material of her nightdress; it was as though he was looking at it through smoke, but it was Victor that was on fire.

The arousal she had experienced in the bathroom was now heightened. He was here in the room. She didn't know why he was here or even cared to ask.

The third grape remained glistening held between the thumb and forefinger of his right hand. She really was beautiful. Her progress across the carpet towards Victor was swift and silent, and with a matching swiftness, an erection grew within his trousers, which unashamedly made a statement but was uncomfortably contained. He could smell the perfume of her body as she stood directly in front of him; he dare not move. Her left hand went up to meet Victor's right still suspended in mid-flight between viewing the grape and actually consuming it. With her thumb and forefinger, she plucked it from his hand and popped it into her mouth. She looked upwards into his eyes, and he remained transfixed. What on earth was this beautiful creature, who at first seemed sinister and now was intolerably desirable, wanting with a middle-aged businessman like Victor Stanley? Maybe it was his lucky day; he was sure he was going to find out.

She chewed on the grape and put her right hand down and touched the by now very obvious protrusion; it was like an electric shock.

'Victor, make love to me.'

It was not a command Victor could ignore, and he drew her to him and kissed her more passionately and with more desperation than he had kissed any woman for many years. Euphoric, he clasped her around the waist with his left arm and placed his right behind her knees and lifted, for if this thing was going to be done, it was going to be done well. He walked the few steps to the bed and placed her gently and as nearly as he could at the centre and, straightening up, urgently and inelegantly removed the containment and with something approaching surprise looked at the strength and rigidity of his organ. Veronica looked too and, drawing herself sinuously across the bed, placed her two hands at the base and devoured the rest.

If paradise could be expressed, then that night, Victor Stanley entered it.

Victor felt excellent. It had been a wonderful night; he hadn't had much sleep, but still he felt rejuvenated. Having made love to Veronica, or more accurately Veronica having made love to him, he knew that she was acting entirely under the instruction of Doo-hwan for some unaccountable reason that gave him additional hope and confidence that the future to this apparently insurmountable problem was not all black. They had agreed that Victor would go about his business this Monday as normal, and as he knew this would include some entertainment in the evening, he told her not to wait up.

Victor showered and put on suitable attire for business meetings and, knowing that Kenezo Nonaka would telephone the room at about 9:00 a.m., went down to the coffee shop and had a quick breakfast to replace lost energy.

The telephone call was duly received, and they met in the lobby.

'Victor', he said, 'how very good to see you again. It is always a pleasure to welcome you to Osaka.' Kenezo Nonaka gripped his hand and shook it warmly. 'We have meetings with several of our departments today to explore some of the opportunities that NTI seems to be creating for itself with these new developments.'

'Kenezo, it is good to see you too, but before we rush off, I have to tell you about a major problem that I am going to need your help with.'

Victor had thought about how he was going to put this to Kenezo, and now that Veronica and he had, so to speak, become intimate, he could use her as the excuse.

'If there is anything I can help with, you only have to ask,' said Kenezo. So he did.

'An extraordinary thing happened to me over the weekend. I met a very attractive young lady from Singapore, and we have rapidly become very good friends.'

'Ah! Good friends can be very comforting.'

'Not exactly the expression I was thinking of', said Victor, 'but, yes, you are right, and because of that, I changed my room.'

'Victor, you have not just changed your room—I think you have bought the hotel!'

'It's a small luxury that I owe myself, Kenezo, but in taking on this luxury, I have unwittingly been somewhat foolish.'

Victor told him of the situation with the sample and how he had placed it in the base of the lamp to be absolutely certain that it was secure and how that in changing his room he had forgotten about it.

Kenezo looked at him quizzically.

'You remember me telling you that there was an element of risk concerning this product of yours and perhaps, Victor, you are only telling me half a story? However, you are quite right to ask for my help. We don't want others to rescue it for you—they will talk too much. What was your room number?'

Victor told him.

'Wait here,' he said and went over to the reception desk.

One of the reception staff came up and talked to Nonaka, but he was dismissed with a message to bring someone more senior. Within a few seconds, the more senior person appeared, but there was no difference in dress or facial expression to indicate to Victor from this distance what sort of seniority the man had. Anyway, Nonaka seemed to have some sort of relationship with him, as there was much bowing and polite conversation, the result of which was that Nonaka disappeared through a door by the reception area and was lost to view.

Victor moved a chair to a strategic position and sat down in order that he could watch the door and see what might happen; it also gave him a good vantage point to watch the general traffic in the area of the reception desk, which, at this time of the morning, was at its peak. As he idly scanned the multitude, he saw Veronica Tan emerge from the area of the lifts; this was something of a surprise, as he had left her in a state of undress relaxing in the suite. Victor sat further back in the chair in the hope that she wouldn't spot him and watched her walk to the escalator and descend to the street.

Veronica was wearing a very expensive-looking pink-and-white suit with pink shoes, and it didn't appear that she was going to be hanging around the hotel all day. Victor got up from his chair and looked discreetly over the rail that prevented the customer from plunging into the entrance hall. Through the glass doors, he could see Voire Africa with friend and a large black Japanese car with tinted windows. As she came through the door, Voire Africa said something to her, and she smiled in that sort of relaxed way that indicates that life isn't actually a threat.

Voire Africa's friend sprang back to the kerbside and opened the rear door; she bent down to enter. Whoever was in there was seated well back, for Victor could only see the bottom part of the legs, and there was no way of knowing if this was Doo-hwan or some other contact. The door was closed, and she was lost to view. Voire Africa's friend went round the other side of the car and climbed into the driving seat. Victor refocused his attention on the situation in hand.

He returned to the chair just in time to see Kenezo Nonaka come out of the doorway with the senior reception man and head towards the lifts; he didn't look at Victor, who, in turn, ignored him. Fifteen minutes passed, a long time to take a lift up to the floor in question, unscrew the base of the lamp, and return again. As Victor looked at his watch for the third or fourth time, Kenezo Nonaka came back into view, this time without the man from reception. He had an unhappy expression on his face, and Victor feared the worst. He came over to the chair.

'It is not appropriate that we talk here. Let's go to the office.'

Victor got up, followed him down the escalator, went through the doorway where Voire Africa paid more than casual attention to his exit, and headed towards the taxi. Kenezo Nonaka turned suddenly and walked down the short drive the cars used as the entrance to the hotel; Victor turned to follow.

'I think we will take the underground, Victor. At this time of the morning, it is faster, and I am sure it is safer.'

It was always a miracle to Victor that the underground railways in Japan were immaculately clean when so many millions of people use them. There was no crime to speak of; it was unheard of to be mugged. The trains are rather wider than the London version. Paper advertisements hang down from the ceiling in pristine condition waving invitingly in the movement of the air. There don't seem to be any yobs with a senseless desire to rip them apart. The pushing and shoving was probably just as bad, but when your body was crammed up against that of your neighbour, it was what one might describe as a clean experience. If you moved, you squeaked; dirt must be the ultimate lubricant.

It was only one stop to Yodo Yabashi station, and although Victor doubted that Voire Africa would have tried to follow them, he was sure that if he had, he would soon lose them. Common sense told him as well that if his demonstration case had been removed from his room, then Doo-hwan's people would inevitably have seen his visit schedule, and Nonaka Corporation was indicated for Monday, so, eventually, he would catch up with them.

The train sighed to a stop, the doors opened, and they were carried along in a mass of people intent on being at their desks well before the required time. They went up out of the station using a combination of steps and escalators using rather more of the former. With multitudinous exits and entrances and miles of underground walkways, it was possible to walk for miles out of the weather; in some cases, one could walk between stations, which was a relief in rush hour!

Finally, they reached pavement level and headed in the direction of Nonaka Corporation. It was two blocks from the station entrance and situated in a new state-of-the-art high-rise building serviced by a number of lifts so meticulously programmed that it was guaranteed there were never just quite enough on the ground floor to load up at any one time with the total number of people waiting. Fortunately, the executive suite of this company had an express lift reserved exclusively for the use of a senior group of managers who no doubt also had the key for the executive toilet complete with on-the-spot bottom washers. They probably had keys to other executive privileges as well including the golf club and the liquor cabinet in their favourite after-hours drinking den.

The two men were greeted outside the lift by a person bent almost parallel to the floor. An exchange of Japanese, only some of which Victor recognised, seemed to suggest that it was a wonderful experience to receive their leader here again and what could be done to make him and his guest more comfortable?

On the executive floor, there were a number of offices as well as meeting rooms, and this gave them a degree of privacy not available on the normal open-plan systems so favoured. Kenezo Nonaka opened the door to his office and waved Victor through. He waved him onward to a low table and equally low chairs that were guaranteed to make all who sat in them vaguely uncomfortable. This habit in Japan of sitting on the floor and at the end of the day lying down on it had never been popular with Victor. It put the Western businessman at an immediate disadvantage; a day with knees bent in a sort of semi-crossed-legged position was not guaranteed to make discussions run smoothly.

'Victor, just wait a minute while I do my normal sweep.'

Kenezo removed from his desk drawer a device that looked something like a microphone only with more works on it. He depressed a switch on the side, and a small red light came on. The device emitted a gentle humming noise as he walked around the room, probing it into corners and towards light fittings and finally a quick scan over Victor. The low humming noise continued unabated, and apparently satisfied, he returned to his desk, switched off the device, and put it back in the drawer.

'Now, Victor, we can talk,' he said.

'I take it', said Victor, 'that that was some sort of search device, I presume for electronic equipment?'

'Yes, it is a sad state of affairs, Victor, that we have to take precautions such as this nowadays. There are few people who will be above accepting technology from undisclosed sources. Proprietary developments are exceptionally important to businesses such as ours and yours, and we have to protect them, Victor, as no doubt you do.'

All this explanation was fine, but Victor's thoughts were more exercised by the missing sample than the possibility that they might be bugged.

'For heaven's sake, Kenezo, let's get down to the matter in hand and the sample. What happened in the hotel?'

'Well, now, the news is not all that good,' said Kenezo, spreading his hands placatingly. He removed a speck of cotton from his otherwise immaculate blue suit, momentarily looked Victor in the eyes, and then stared at him in the general direction of his navel.

'I am sorry to tell you, Victor, that when I unscrewed the lamp base, there was no sample within it.'

'Oh my god, do you realise what this means?' he said, going pale around the gills and feeling decidedly weak at the knees, not to mention starting to feel the urgencies of nervousness that had visited him earlier on this trip. This was serious; this was career blowing; this was the sort of thing that didn't happen to elderly ambassadors of the company at large in the world.

'Victor.'

He jumped.

'We need to look at this rationally, and if you will allow me, I will summarise the present situation.'

Victor nodded dumbly, thinking to himself that there really wasn't a lot of point in going back home, never mind going back to the office. He looked out of the window; it was a long way down.

'You have come to Japan primarily to demonstrate to my company the latest version of the new superconductive polymer material we have been cooperating on, which has far-reaching commercial possibilities. It is a method of positively identifying as genuine a host of materials, and beyond that, there are also various interesting possibilities that our research teams have yet to work upon. You unwisely, or perhaps wisely, placed a sample of this in hiding, maybe because you had been warned that there were certain people who would stop at nothing to obtain it, am I right?'

Victor nodded.

'You have with you the demonstration kit, and that is what we need to talk about today because I can bet, Victor, that you were not actually going to leave the sample with me, but you were going to show me that it was real and offer it as proof that you had perfected the manufacturing process.'

It was a fair summary, and Victor couldn't argue with it. The apparent loss of the sample didn't stop him demonstrating NTI's success either to Kenezo here at Nonaka Corporation or to the other two companies he was to see whilst in Osaka. He wondered if Kenezo was aware of these additional visits.

'Your summary is too close to the truth for comfort, Kenezo. It is on a personal level that I am shocked by the loss of the sample. It is unlikely that it can be successfully analysed because of the protection built into the formulation, but, nevertheless, a particularly clever team of chemists might just be able to get enough useful data from it to make a copy that would pass cursory examination. That in itself is bad enough, but what is worse is that the loss is almost certainly a passport to the cessation of my career. There were good reasons to do what I did, and subsequent events have proved that to me.'

'Victor, you are a good friend of Nonaka Corporation. Over the years, we have done good business together, and you and I have become closely associated through that business, a mutual respect has been built up, and trust and friendship have flowed from it. I trust you more than any foreigner I know.'

It was a nice compliment, and because of it, he felt obliged to tell Kenezo some of the outline details of the weekend in Osaka, so as quickly as he could, because he knew there were commercially pressing arrangements that must be fulfilled, he reluctantly explained what had happened concerning Doo-hwan.

'It would be very serious, Victor, if Doo-hwan was to get hold of the missing sample, as he would attempt to break it down.'

'So you know this man?'

'Of course, everyone in the industry here knows Doo-hwan. Out of his crime has come a certain respectability, but it is only a thin veneer that covers a still corrupt organisation, which spreads throughout South East Asia and the Pacific Rim. He is a powerful individual, and you would be well advised to avoid any future contact with him and allow events to take their course. Let us suppose, however, that something else happened within the hotel—for instance, maybe the light in your room was removed for repair and replaced with another. The electrical works are above the ornamental decoration, and if so, it is unlikely that the electrician would come across the sample. It might remain hidden for years.'

A drowning man will clutch at straws, and maybe this was what Victor was being offered, but the probability that such a set of circumstances had occurred really defied belief, and he would only know the truth about Doo-hwan if the pressure was being maintained upon the bad doctor Yoreen back in England.

'Out of adversity, Victor, comes ingenuity. I don't think you are currently in any grave danger from Doo-hwan, as he has seen what he wanted to see and has an adequate watch being kept on you.' He almost leered.

'I really don't think Veronica Tan is willingly mixed up with him,' said Victor, for he took his leer to be a direct reference to the lady in the case.

'If you believe that, Victor, you will believe anything. Just remember what I have told you—this man is dangerous and he is corrupt and he will stop at nothing to achieve his ends. You may be aware that here in Japan, he controls a very substantial amount of gambling, and when I tell you that each year millions of your pounds are illegally removed as cash from his operations, then you can understand that any new device that can be introduced that might stop such illegal activities must be of immense value in his hands. His legitimate industries could exploit it, and he could control its distribution to lessen the threat to his corrupt businesses.'

Victor had already worked out most of this for himself, although he believed that Doo-hwan would market the invention so widely that its security would be compromised, and its use against fraud and counterfeiting would then be unlikely. This would be a major blow for NTI but not one it could not recover from. The other potentials for the product ultimately outweighed the first commercial opportunity.

There was a polite knock at the door, and a diminutive girl came in carrying a tray of coffee. It was the typical very black, very strong product that was traditionally served in Japanese offices, and if having little resemblance to coffee, it at least gave Victor the boost he needed. The diminutive placed the cups on the table, placed sausage-shaped sticks of sugar beside them and small pots of coffee creamer beside those, and withdrew. Victor gratefully sipped the black liquid and felt better.

Victor still felt under threat and had a feeling of persecution. He remembered Kenezo's words 'out of adversity comes ingenuity' and thought of the Second World War and of the defeat and humiliation of Japan; they had recovered from a seemingly impossible situation. Victor's circumstances did not compare; full recovery was possible, and these thoughts together with the caffeine boost made him feel better.

The phone rang, and Kenezo Nonaka spoke for a couple of minutes in Japanese and then turned to Victor.

'It is time for us to join my colleagues and for you to make your presentation about our joint interests and how we will continue to work together, and, Victor, I know it is not easy to forget your present problems, but let me remind you that you always have a friend here at Nonaka Corporation whatever the circumstances.'

The day returned to near normality, if that is what you could call doing business in Japan. Kenezo Nonaka took Victor along to a meeting room where he sat at one side of the table and seven Japanese sat at the other; two of them he had met before. Victor exchanged cards with each of the others. Japanese tea was served, and he was then invited to describe the latest developments of NTI products and to indicate the way the two companies might be able to work together in the development of the superconducting polymer.

Victor started his presentation in the normal way and drew upon the high-technology writing board, which would automatically photocopy anything he placed there, the non-confidential part of his presentation. This covered what a marvellous company NTI was, how good their technology was, and how much they were investing in high-technology development and avoiding the dot.com sector. General statements about how inventive and entrepreneurial the chairman and board of directors were, all good standard stuff that made him sick; if only it were true.

Polite questions followed, and Victor then gave the demonstration he had given to Doo-hwan on the weekend. This time, the demonstration was studied much more scientifically, and when he started to suggest that there might be a way that NTI and Nonaka could create a joint venture company in Japan, he could almost hear the commercial minds amongst them clicking into gear.

Lunch was taken, and they then continued through the afternoon trying to work out some sort of sensible arrangement whereby NTI introduced technology and Nonaka spent a lot of money erecting plant. As always, this did not reach a conclusion during the day; it was not their style. Victor warned them that as interest was high, they should not take too long to make up their minds.

It had been a long presentation, and it left Victor mentally tired and not a little thirsty; he was dying to get back to the hotel and at least take a shower before embarking on an evening of traditional entertainment. Kenezo had already mentioned to Victor that they would be going to one of his private clubs for a drink and afterwards for a teppanyaki meal, and although Victor preferred the prospect of renewing his intimate relationship with Veronica Tan, he knew that good manners would not allow him to refuse this invitation.

The meeting concluded. Kenezo told Victor that his driver would pick him up at half past six outside the hotel entrance. Business was over for the day, and he would hear nothing more now until the Japanese system of consultation had decided whether Nonaka Corporation should do something together with NTI, and then there would be further and more protracted discussions with more people, and, inevitably, he would be engaged in those as well. The more senior members of today's party escorted Victor down to the reception area where a taxi was waiting. The rear door opened as if by magic, for no one had appeared to open it; most Japanese taxis have an arm mechanism controlled by the driver that relieves one of the necessity of opening or shutting the pavement-side door. Victor climbed into the air-conditioned comfort, which was somewhat better than the air conditioning of the offices where the temperature was controlled so as not to damage the economy too much by overcooling; fossil fuels are important to Japan, and their conservation overcomes daily comfort. Victor told the driver he wanted to return to the Hotel Niko, and they set off. He marvelled, not for the first time, at the extreme cleanliness of the interior of these vehicles. He looked round and studied the driver details. There was something shockingly familiar about the identifying photograph, and Victor looked more carefully at the driver; it was Voire Africa. He leaned forward.

'You!' he said, surprised.

'It eess with compleements of Doo-hwan,' he replied in fractured English as he pulled away from the offices at alarming speed.

'Where are we going?' Victor asked, but there was no reply. Either he didn't understand English well enough to answer or he wasn't allowed to talk or he was just being plain bloody-minded, but as the taxi seemed to be heading generally in the direction of the Hotel Niko and as Doo-hwan would want to make sure that Victor did not disappear between the end of the day and the evening's entertainment, it seemed safe enough, and so it proved to be. At least he did not have to pay.

He went up to the suite and opened up the door with a pleasurable little thrill, but this was only turned into mild disappointment when he discovered that Veronica

Tan had not yet returned. So he went into his bedroom, stripped off, and walked into the shower and let the pressurised jet of water remove the day's fatigue. He dried off and put on one of the robes supplied by the hotel and sat by the window to review the situation. There was only one major problem that he foresaw currently, and that was the fact that he was returning to England without the sample that he was entrusted with, and, somehow, this problem had to be solved. If Doo-hwan did not affect the rest of his life, then certainly the loss of this sample would, and Hipkiss would take an almost sadistic pleasure in, first of all, sacking him and then blackening his character until no sane employer would dare touch him. A glimmer of an idea came slowly into his mind. It was an idea that would need a whole lot of luck to make it work, and he had been short of luck recently; but if life teaches you one thing, it is that you can live in hope, and as that was all Victor had at the moment, that's what he had to live with.

By the time it was quarter past six, there was still no sign of Veronica, so having changed into his lightest weight suit and having put on his bravest smile, he went out for the evening.

The immaculate porter in the funny hat held open the door for Victor. Parked in the hotel yard was a large black Mercedes belonging to Nonaka Corporation; Kenezo Nonaka was seated in the back. The driver got out and opened the rear door for Victor to join his employer. He climbed in alongside him, and the car pulled smoothly away.

Kenezo Nonaka turned towards Victor.

'Victor, it was an interesting session today, and although I didn't want to say it in front of my colleagues, I can tell you now that there is more than casual interest in this product, and for that matter, there is more than casual interest in you, Victor, for I am sure you know that it is you we trust and not your company. We are going to enjoy ourselves this evening, and I do not want to pursue this matter now. However, I do want you to know that we here at Nonaka Corporation will do our best to develop a relationship that will be to our mutual benefit.'

The words were full of ambiguity, and despite the immaculate English, Victor wondered whether Kenezo could understand ambiguity and use the language accordingly. Victor could not precisely translate what he had just heard but believed a confidence was being expressed in him as the ambassador of NTI and in the produce he was meant to have with him. He knew that if he was suddenly to depart NTI, then Nonaka would be unlikely to enthusiastically follow up the business opportunity. He felt decidedly heartened.

The car pulled up in a very narrow street where many other cars were already disembarking blue- and black-suited passengers intent upon a night's fun. The street could not have been far from the club where Victor was initially interviewed by Doo-hwan, and a similar lift took them up to the fifth floor, where a sign indicated that they were entering the Lucky Club. Perhaps things were looking up after all.

A mature Japanese lady immaculately turned out in a kimono with a traditional hairstyle welcomed Kenezo by first flinging the upper part of her body horizontal with the floor and then embracing him enthusiastically. Rapid Japanese was spoken, and they were shown to a corner table where they sat with backs to the wall looking out onto this small but well-appointed club. The furniture could be described as American club room; there was a small well-stocked and beautifully constructed bar at the end of the room opposite the small reception area, and there were a number of tables and chairs discreetly placed in the rest of the area to give maximum comfort whilst occupying every possible square inch of space. Several very attractive girls were present, half of them in Western dress.

Madam withdrew from the table, and shortly afterwards, they were joined by the head of research from Nonaka Industries, who had made his way there separately. Dr Nobura greeted them and sat down. He took out a packet of cigarettes and lit one, puffing away with small nervous movements until he had apparently poured as much smoke into his lungs as they would take, which he then released with an explosive sigh and a huge cloud of smoke that would have completely obscured anyone downwind—passive smoking at its best!

Madam returned accompanied by two exquisitely turned-out girls, one quite clearly European and the other probably from the Philippines or Thailand. It was indicated that the European should sit next to Victor on his left hand side in order that he could share her with Dr Nobura. The Oriental girl was seated on his other side to share with Kenezo.

Victor had experience of these places of entertainment and knew that this was all done in the best possible taste and that really they were there to serve drinks and to enter into polite conversation; if you really fancied one of them, then a private contract might be arranged but at an exorbitant price and late at night. The girl from Europe came from closer to home than he had thought, as she was from Kent and had been selected for Victor because of her obvious charms and her ability to communicate; she also spoke good Japanese, which would work for her later in life when she had given up on being a hostess, as she explained it to Victor. He observed the niceties and commented tiredly on her good looks and desirability, but he loved the way she poured drinks; they were very large drinks and matched her breasts, which were also of significant proportion and, as she leaned forward to pour, were displayed splendidly. Inevitably, she told Victor she was lonely and would love to screw an Englishman because the Japanese were always cruel and inconsiderate to their women, and the Koreans were worse. Oh, and did he have a spare pack of Dunhill on him, and, by the way, it would only cost him something in the region of £600 to satisfy her yearnings. She would throw in for free her life story.

No, he didn't smoke Dunhill. No, he didn't feel like spending £600 at the moment but was sympathetic to her views about the treatment meted out to her by the country in which she was working, but then it was her choice. She poured him another JD and put more ice in it and talked some more until Dr Nobura decided that he wished to practice his English. Victor switched his attention to the Oriental girl, who told the same tale more prettily and smoked Marlborough. It was time to dine.

Teppanyaki is only one of many different styles of eating in Japan. Theme restaurants back home had never really interested Victor, but, unwittingly, he enjoyed them away. He knew the Japanese would have been horrified had he referred to them as such, but, nevertheless, that's what he thought them to be. Each form of serving food had a history and artistry of its own, chefs took years to train, and the event of eating out was a view of an artist at work presenting a picture on a plate and completing the event with a bill so large it took the breath away.

The restaurant was small with three cooking surfaces. Each surface looked like a polished sheet of stainless steel, but it was in fact mild steel kept in this condition by constant use and polishing. Each slab could weigh up to three tonnes and was constantly heated to maintain an even temperature. Around the edge of the cooking area, there was a polished wood surround where the food was served with the chef preparing each item and placing it from the cooking surface onto the plate. The chef performed with polished ease and exercised his skills on several groups of diners each night. When the diners had eaten, they were politely removed to the sitting area to make way for others.

Kenezo Nonaka ordered for them, and tiger prawns were cooked sizzling with oil and garlic, the flesh was delicious and tender, and the body portion, flattened and cooked until crisp, was presented as well. At this point, most Western guests refuse; Victor knew better. The Kobe beef, wonderfully marbled with fat, followed. Victor did not have words to describe it, and each piece was savoured to its full; the look of intense satisfaction on his face said what words could not.

The conversation turned to non-business topics and politics. Kenezo was worried about the reputation of Japanese politicians and the ability of Japan to recover from the recent period of financial chaos. He felt that as the new millennium developed, the power of Japan would have receded and regarded external investment in Japan as essential for the future.

'Despite the claims of our government, Victor, the trade and financial doors have never been fully opened. There has been some improvement in imports, but every small gain by the West is at enormous expense, and progress is slow. Barriers to trade continue to be imposed, and it takes something truly novel to make the major breakthrough. Fortunately, I believe we have one of those unlikely products, so let me offer a toast to our success.'

Kenezo raised his glass of whisky and water.

'To Nonaka and NTI, may we have a long life together here and overseas with not a little profit.'

Dr Nobura and Victor raised their glasses and touched them to Kenezo's before drinking.

'I sincerely hope you're right, Kenezo,' said Victor. 'And now, if you don't mind, I will return to the hotel. I have some preparation to make for the next two days and for my departure.'

A few more pleasantries were exchanged, and Kenezo once more stated the serious interest of Nonaka Corporation in the superconducting polymer.

'We want this project to work, Victor. Ideally, I would like to persuade my father to go for a joint venture for the whole of the Pacific Basin, and if I do, I hope you can pull it off for us.'

Victor knew that he could not agree; it was not up to him. He would like it to happen, though.

'Subject to what happens during the remainder of my visit, I am sure there is every prospect of a successful outcome to our negotiations. You know that I respect Nonaka and its technology, and our personal relations are excellent. You are NTI's oldest contact in Japan. I will do my very best for you.'

'I can ask nothing more, Victor.'

The car took them back to the Niko Hotel and dropped Victor. It was still relatively early, and Victor wondered what awaited him in the suite—was the lovely Veronica waiting for him?

He hurried up the escalator and across to the lifts, pressing the button to the top floor. Pictures of Veronica naked on his bed came unbidden into his mind's eye. *I'm going potty in my old age,* he thought. The lift stopped, and Victor pulled out his key. The doors slid open. Standing on the landing was Voire Africa. Victor continued towards the door.

'Have nice night, sir,' leered the minder. Victor didn't reply; instead, he inserted the key into the lock and gently turned and pushed. The door opened into the small hall, and a lamp on the table to his left illuminated the luxury of his surroundings once more.

Victor closed the door quietly behind him and stood there listening; there was no obvious sound. The door to Veronica's room was shut. The door to his own was open a few inches, and light spilled out. He went over and pushed the door fully open. Veronica was seated in the big armchair on the other side of the king-size bed. Her long robe fell away from her left leg at mid-thigh, giving Victor a clear view of the top of her black stocking held in the grip of a pink suspender with a little bow on it; she had no shoes on.

Veronica looked up at Victor and put down in her lap the copy of *Vogue* that she was leafing through.

'I thought you would be late,' she said.

Victor was very glad indeed he wasn't; he wondered if she would have still been there if he had been.

'I wanted to get back.'

'I can't imagine why,' she said, letting the robe fall open further still and increasing Victor's blood pressure as she did so.

'I think you can,' he added lamely.

Veronica stood up; the robe fell back in place. She walked over to the transfixed Victor, and standing on the tips of her toes, she kissed him on the mouth. Victor wished he had not eaten garlic; she didn't seem to notice.

'Go and put something more comfortable on, Victor,' she said. 'I cannot make love to a man in a suit.'

Victor went into the bathroom where his light but voluminous Japanese robe hung. Eagerly, he took off his clothes, and thinking he would be much nicer to handle if he was clean and sweet smelling, he stepped into the shower and turned it on. The warm water poured over his body, removing any residual trace of tiredness. He heard the shower door slide open and looked round. Veronica stepped in; she had removed her robe but still had on the black stockings, suspender belt, and small matching knickers.

'Move over, Victor. There's room for me as well.'

'You've still got some clothes on,' said Victor needlessly.

'They need washing,' she said and started to remove the little knickers, which were now thoroughly soaked. She prised the bar of soap out of Victor's hand and started to soap the little bundle of material. Water was now bouncing off more of Victor's body, and noticing the effect she was having on him, she started to use the soapy knickers as a washcloth and gently sponged his cock and balls. Victor, in utter astonishment, let her do this for a little while and then pushed her hand away and drew her to him. Her wet nipples dug into his chest, and she made room for him between her legs. They kissed as the water continued to pour over their bodies.

Victor somehow managed to open the shower doors and turn off the water without letting go of Veronica. They stepped out dripping water everywhere, placing his hands under her bottom, and with her arms tightly round his neck, Victor could raise Veronica two or three inches off the ground, and he walked with her back into the bedroom, and they fell dripping and laughing onto the big bed.

He found himself underneath her, and Veronica knelt astride him and trailed her wet hair down his body until his cock vanished behind the damp black curtain. The curtain descended, and he felt his glans encircled by a wet warm mouth. Her tongue licked him, and then she took even more of him inside her and started slowly to draw him in and out. Victor lay there, his eyes tight shut; if only he could stay like this forever.

When he was crying for mercy, she released him and crawled back up his body until she was suspended above him. Reaching down and behind, she guided Victor's rigidity into her and sank back upon him. He had opened his eyes and looked up into hers. He saw a wild abandon that did not come from a lack of interest or through a pay packet.

'Oh, Victor, Victor!' she shouted. 'I'm ready.'

There was nothing Victor could do about it; she was in charge, she was dictating the pace, but he knew what she meant and obliged her royally so that they were both shouting and moaning in joy and ecstasy. Victor seemed to go on and on, the longest ejaculation in history.

She collapsed on top of him and stayed there for some minutes panting gently. The remaining items of clothing had dried on her body. There was no sign of the little knickers; they must have been dropped in the bathroom. Eventually, she rolled off and lay by his side.

'Victor,' she whispered in his ear.

'Yes, Veronica?'

'I am coming to England with you.'

Victor sat up. 'What did you say?'

'I said I'm coming to England with you. Doo-hwan wants me to go and collect the goods, as he calls them, and what better way to know that you are safely back there than to have me travel with you. Don't worry, I won't be in the way or be an embarrassment to you.'

Victor did not doubt that she would be discretion itself; it was just a bit of a shock and brought home to him at this moment of heightened awareness that he was very much in the sights of Lee Doo-hwan and his merry band. He had his own problems to solve as well—how was he going to return a sample he no longer had, and where was it anyway?

'You don't choose the best of times to tell me things like this, Veronica. Couldn't it have waited until the morning?'

'I'm sorry, Victor. I just wanted you to know. I have enjoyed myself with you and will go on enjoying myself if allowed. I was just pleased, and I thought you would be too.'

'I am pleased, in a way. You know, Veronica, that I am married, and this little affair—wonderful, though, it is—is not going to interfere with that. Once back in England, I will have a job to do, and it looks like you will too. There may be few opportunities to have the sort of fun we are having now.'

'Of course, I know you are married, Victor. You are not for me, but I am liking what I have been asked to do, and I would like it to go on for a bit, maybe for a long time on and off if you continue to pass through Singapore. I have not often come across someone as nice and kind as you are, and for an older man, you are a very good lover.'

He was surprised; he seemed to have done little in their sexual encounters, but he had to admit it would be nice to have access to Veronica on his travels, and maybe staying in touch now would keep him informed of events with Doo-hwan and George Yoreen.

'Are you staying with me until we leave then?' he asked.

'That is the general intention. I'll have to go home and pack and do some work whilst you finish your business, but I'll be here each night if you want me.'

Victor could think of nothing he would like better. He lay down again by her side, and she snuggled close to him. Victor pulled a sheet over them. She still had on the stockings and suspender belt, and he slipped the fingers of his left hand inside her stocking top. There wasn't much else to say.

She awoke him in the most extraordinary manner the next morning, and the last two days followed in a haze of sexual fulfilment undreamed of in Victor's past. There were three unsatisfactory business meetings that left Nonaka Corporation as the favourite partner, as Victor had expected all along.

He packed his case, completed his reports, and prepared to depart.

Chapter 6

They stood in the early morning cold on the platform at Shin-Osaka, the station for Shinkansen more commonly known as the bullet train. It was an ungodly hour, and even on a clear summer morning, it was cold. Little markers on the platform indicated exactly where the carriage would stop, and armed with their Green Car tickets, they awaited one of the world's best trains.

Exactly on time, the bullet-shaped silver-and-blue-striped monster pulled into the station, and they boarded car number seven and disposed of the luggage in a small room kept for that purpose. It was one of the Hikari Expresses with twin-deck accommodation in the first-class portion, and they went up the steps and sank thankfully into their seats. Below, there was a full-scale self-service buffet with every imaginable variety of light Japanese snack and presumably available at all hours of the day and night. Two minutes later, the train pulled swiftly out of the station, and with only brief stops early in the journey at Kyoto and Nagoya, it seemed no time at all before they were skirting Mount Fuji, but the peak of that great impressive symbol of Japan was hidden in cloud.

Three hours after the start, they pulled into Tokyo's main station to fight their way across the city to the air terminal and to take the bus for Narita.

It would all have been much more simple to have flown, but Victor happened to like the bullet train and the romance of the railways; besides which one could see more and it was safer than internal air travel in Japan.

The bus from the air terminal in Tokyo completed the journey in what was good time taking only an hour and fifteen minutes to Narita airport. There was the inevitable stop at the outer perimeter security where they all had to disembark and identify bags and open them for inspection. Finally, they pulled up outside the south wing, recovered the bags, Victor's and Veronica's, and went in through entrance S42. They walked left towards British Airways, and a line of Singapore Airline girls came walking by as beautiful as ever and bearing a striking similarity to Veronica. Victor was already travelling on a club booking, and Doo-hwan had thoughtfully done the same for Veronica. The queues were relatively light, and they received their boarding cards on the upper deck seats 59A and B, BA8 non-stop over Siberia and straight into Heathrow.

They were not alone on the journey to the airport. Voire Africa and his lookalike friend, now changed into very neat blue suits, had accompanied them all the way from Osaka and were watching them now apparently as benign as ever.

The actual buildings at Narita were relatively small, and not many people frequent them mainly because it is a long way out and the authorities don't encourage guests to see off passengers. From one end of the south wing to the other, it is only a two-minute walk. Victor went over to the florists, looked at the seeds as he usually did, decided most of them were commonplace, but bought two packets of Bonsai seeds, although they were notoriously difficult to germinate. Veronica walked demurely by his side.

'Is there anything you want?' he asked her. 'Do you want some chocolates or something to read?'

'No, thank you, Victor. I have everything I need with me, and I always have you to talk to.' She gave his arm a little squeeze. 'Please don't worry about me so much.'

How did she know I was worrying? thought Victor, and he was, but not about her; he had been trying to come up with a solution to his problem of how to replace the sample. At least she cheered him up. He bought a packet of peppermints and turned back towards the customs area and the security of the British Airways Lounge. At least they would be free there from observation.

They entered the passengers-only area and went down the Hitachi escalator. Victor thought there was a time when all such moving devices were 'made in Britain'—why not now? At the bottom, they turned round the corner towards the executive lounges and entered the rather ordinary passage past Lufthansa's Senator Lounge, Korean Air, and Varig, and finally found themselves at the doorway of British Airways.

The lounge is small and pokey; there was not enough comfortable accommodation for the number of passengers flying, and despite its size, it was divided into smoking and non-smoking. Veronica and Victor hid themselves away in the farthest corner and ordered a coffee, and Victor caught up on some of the newspapers and smoked a cigar courtesy of Doo-hwan; after all, there was no point in leaving a whole box of Bolivars in the suite.

Victor flicked idly through the pages of the *Financial Times* and on page 25 found the short article about NTI. *Hipkiss'll be mad,* he thought. *They don't even mention his name.*

He turned to the *Sunday Times* and, for the first time in several days, had a good laugh; the Macallan malt whisky advertisement was hilarious. *It was a pity NTI's chairman didn't replace their fuddy-duddy advertising people with people of this calibre,* thought Victor. He had tried often enough to get their publicity head to use 'art direction'.

At just after twelve thirty and somewhat refreshed, they left the lounge. Victor couldn't help noticing the admiring glances cast at Veronica Tan. They handed in their tickets at the Customs/Immigration/Quarantine Department and joined one of the long queues waiting for exit; it seemed sensible to choose the one with most Japanese passports on view. Voire Africa came to the bottom of the escalator and stood outside immigration watching them go through.

'And that, my friend, is that,' said Victor aloud.

The queue quickly diminished, and Victor presented his passport; it was examined, and he walked through. He looked back at Veronica and, to his surprise, saw she presented a British passport; it reminded him that he knew very little about her yet, but no doubt there would be time on the long flight to find out more.

They took their bags through the security check. Victor was searched because he carried too many metallic things in his pockets; Veronica came through unscathed. Victor chose to walk the short distance rather than travel on the moving pathway, as he would be seated for the next eleven or twelve hours. Parked out to the left was a 747 of Singapore Airlines. Victor looked at Veronica.

'Do you wish you were on that?'

She nodded. 'Yes.'

BA8 had not yet started the boarding and stood there waiting; emblazoned on the side was 'City of Manchester, Breath of the North'.

Veronica sat down in one of the tired seats for holding bottoms in transit. Victor wandered aimlessly around the holding area. He gazed through the large glass windows and watched as Air France was being pushed out and Northwest Airlines was disembarking a crowd of tired-looking people from Los Angeles. Victor was wearing a favoured cotton shirt and a pair of lightweight trousers and slip-on shoes with a woollen sweater for those chilly moments. Veronica was travelling in a blue suit, a jacket that didn't meet in the front, and a plain white blouse; the suit seemed to suggest Paris, and she looked good enough to eat. He thought of nights past; she looked good in anything.

Victor walked towards the gate and turned round suddenly to check his rear. There was Voire Africa. He was standing by a blue bin that declared on one side in Japanese that drinking Pocari Sweat was good for you, and on the side next to it, it just said simply 'Trash'. He smiled.

All around people were tagged with little badges and packaged in groups, the international sign of tourism. The announcement about departure came over the public address system, and the stampede began. Victor walked over to Veronica.

'We might as well try to get on first,' he said. 'At least we can get our bags stowed.' As they waited in line, they saw SQ97 being pushed out for the haul to Singapore.

They were first into the executive cabin, seats 59A and B on the port side, and they stowed away their hand luggage, sat down, and waited for things to happen. The upper deck filled to capacity, but there was no sign of anyone Victor recognised, so perhaps Veronica was occupying the only seat to London reserved for one of Doo-hwan's team. Even he would work to some sort of expense budget; the costs of crime, after all, had to be budgeted like any legitimate business.

A feeling of relaxation started to come over him countered only by his natural tendency to prefer to be on the ground rather than in the air.

The interlude of the last few days could in no way be described as the beginning of a romance, thought Victor as he stretched himself out; it was a combination of lust, a bit of trying to get closer to the enemy, whilst taking advantage of using the enemy—or was she?—and a bit of comfort after the mental ordeal that he had just been through. For Veronica, it was a question of what she had been told to do, and there was no romance in that, or was there?

Drinks were served, and Victor chose champagne and orange juice, and Veronica stayed teetotal. He felt her hand insert itself between his arm and the side of his body, and using that grip as a lever, she pulled herself closer.

'Victor, I want to tell you something.'

He raised his eyebrows but didn't say anything.

She spoke in the characteristic English of the Singaporean and so close to his ear that Victor found it pleasantly musical if a little bit difficult to understand.

'I think you know I am a Singapore girl because you have visited Singapore many times and know something of the Asian people. You also ask me whether I would prefer to be flying to Singapore, and I said I would.'

Victor still didn't say anything for, somehow, it seemed a moment not to interrupt, and she continued.

'My father owned a small electronics business that imported material from Korea, Japan, and Taiwan. It was quite successful, and he wished to expand. His Korean supplier offered him considerable help by agreeing to ship greater quantities of products and lengthening the amount of time my father would have to pay, but, foolishly, none of this arrangement was formalised, and after two substantial shipments of goods that, without the extended credit terms, my father could not have paid for, a visit was received from Doo-hwan. He explained that he was the chairman of the organisation to which our Korean supplier belonged and that his subordinate had acted in error when granting us the extra credit. He told my father he had seven days to pay or he would sue for recovery. We did not have the cash available, and to avoid liquidation, my father signed over 70 per cent of the business. He had tried very hard to raise the extra funds, but men wiser than he examined more carefully the ultimate ownership of the Korean creditor and refused help.'

She stopped and took a deep breath, tightening her grip on Victor's arm.

'My father had a weak heart, and the stress brought on by this situation and the shame he was bringing to his family eventually brought on a heart attack from which he did not recover. I am his only daughter and had acted for some time as his assistant. I was familiar with the situation, and when my father died, Doo-hwan suggested to me that he take over the company and that I go and work for him. He would pay me a reasonable salary, and having taken 70 per cent of the business, he discharged the debt. He also suggested that 30 per cent was not a lot to be left with, and he made quite a generous offer for the balance to be paid in deferred terms over a period of three years.

'I had little option knowing that to try and hang on to my bit would only bring disaster, so I accepted the proposal. I thought that perhaps in joining the enemy, I might be able to avenge my father. Doo-hwan believes that because of the deferred payment terms, he has me in his control, for unless I meet the minimum conditions laid down and am a good and diligent employee, I will never see all the money. He was so supremely confident of owning me that he never thought for one minute I would wish to seek revenge. He was sympathetic about my father and did not believe he was responsible for his death. I did not share his view, and now I might be able to seek revenge.'

She relaxed and sat back but still gripped Victor's arm.

'Victor, you do believe me, don't you?'

It was a simple enough question, and her explanation was plausible, but both the explanation and the question still left doubts in Victor's mind. It was a question of whom to trust and then perhaps how much to trust them, or perhaps he was just getting too cynical in his old age, but in that case, why should this beautiful young woman welcome him into her bed and continue to act as though she were truly attached to him?

Perhaps he was wrong about the romance; perhaps she had not just been doing a job. He had to maintain an open mind. He didn't feel threatened by her and had formed a genuine liking for her as he now thought she had for him, though why such a delectable creature should want a liaison with a rather dowdy, staid, late middle-aged Victor Stanley, he could not fathom.

The great Rolls-Royce engines had lost their roar and were pushing north and west entering Russia and starting the long haul across Siberia.

'Veronica, so many things have happened to me in the last few days. I don't know what or whom to believe. I want to believe you because that's the way I would prefer things to be, but tell me why you haven't been to the police or consulted your lawyers.'

'What would I tell them, Victor? I haven't actually done anything against my will, I haven't been kidnapped, I am being paid for what I am doing, I have agreed to sell part of the company, and my father did get into debt. What action would the police take if I told them this story? They would probably want me to come back with hard facts. Our company lawyers, who were a small but reputable Singapore firm, told us that the supplier was acting completely within his rights and we should have protected ourselves by coming to them before the act rather than after it. It is a lesson to have everything documented, something I now do.

'I could ask the same of you, Victor. Why haven't you been to the police? You have been in Doo-hwan's presence. You know him to be dishonest, but he didn't harm you, and apart from being pulled in off the street, the treatment you have received at his hands has generally been completely courteous. The only hard fact we have between us is that we know about the intentions of Doo-hwan and his connections with your Dr Yoreen, and at the moment, that amounts to no more than industrial espionage. You have your own problem with the missing sample. You are not going to draw attention to yourself yet, so it suits both of us to stay quiet. I have no doubt that if Doo-hwan knew that I was playing a double game, I would die for it.'

All of that was logical. Victor was better off waiting on events. The police would find his story difficult to believe. NTI would think he had lost the sample under suspicious circumstances and blame him for it; he would probably lose his job. The whole situation was delicate and had to be handled as such; played right, he might win in the end. He might be the saviour of NTI—pigs might fly. To threaten Doo-hwan would be foolhardy, and like Veronica, he had no desire to 'become deceased'.

Veronica needed some sort of answer, though, just for the time being.

'Perhaps you and I have got to work together. If we do, perhaps we will solve all our problems.' He said it with more conviction than he felt.

She leaned closer and kissed him on the cheek.

'Thank you, Victor. I promise that you can trust me.'

He hoped he could. He had the long night for further thought on the matter.

Chapter 7

Beginning to warm towards the day ahead, Hipkiss dipped a toe tentatively into the bath water. The temperature suited him, and he placed the whole of the foot under the surface seeking the bottom delicately. He had once slipped when carrying out this manoeuvre, banging his head severely on the edge of the bath. Unfortunately for many, it had not rendered him unconscious and he did not slide below the surface and drown; so much trouble would have been avoided if he had. It was, however, a warning, and he had installed on the far wall a substantial handle that he now leaned over to grip as he raised his other leg and carried out a similar exercise. He turned and, placing both his hands on the sides of the bath, lowered his bottom towards the warm surface of the water, and as it enveloped him, he welcomed it with a contented little sigh and, having made a three-point contact with the bottom of the bath, felt safe.

As a small child, Hipkiss had been different from other boys, and rather than have sailing ships and small motorboats or even ducks on the surface of his bath had demanded a submarine. His father had diligently searched Hamleys for such a toy and, eventually finding one, had wondered why on earth his son should choose such a complicated plaything. It was only when his cousin James came to stay and bath time became something of a game that he realised that the submarine was to sink any other surface craft, thereby placing in the hands of his son a victory on every occasion, for despite the constant arguments of James, the whining Hipkiss insisted that no other bath-going boat or creature could go underwater, and therefore in all games of war, he was to be the victor. This attitude had carried him through life with only a few minor hiccups along the way, although whining had been replaced with an egregious sycophancy towards his betters who thought his ways a respectful interest in their superiority and well-being. Kevin exhibited contempt for his contemporaries and lesser mortals; the contempt occasionally had a veneer of friendship with it, which was soon to be discovered as shallow and meaningless.

Having wallowed long enough in the warm water and having soaped the available parts that he could reach without having to strain himself, he turned the shower selector to overhead and finished himself off under its powerful beat. He turned off the water and faced the room again, catching once more his fully naked reflection in the mirror. He was not proud of his manhood, which, in his opinion, had been placed there as a small joke by his Creator. Futile efforts with patent devices had not succeeded in extending by one millimetre this piece of flesh, which had all the makings of a fine weapon apart from the woeful lack of length. He cringed at the memory of the disparaging remarks of some of his near conquests.

He climbed from the bath with the same infinite care that he had entered it and towelled himself off before picking up a bottle that announced that if he applied this elixir to his face, it would make electric shaving easier; it did, the Remington gliding effortlessly over his less than powerful beard and smoothing his skin in the manner the company's tireless owner had suggested during his numerous television appearances. He took a solid stick of Sure and applied it liberally under his arms; he could not abide perspiration. There followed the powerful scent of Aramis aftershave and body cologne. He carried in his briefcase a small top-up spray for application during the day to maintain his fragrant state.

Still naked and feeling a little better, he walked from the bathroom back into the bedroom and to the dressing area, where he selected a pair of bright red abbreviated underpants, which were now a shade too small; some of the good living had allowed just a hint of slackness to appear in the belly. A white shirt, immaculately turned out by Clinton, a pair of fine black socks, a dark blue lightweight Christian Dior suit, a matching Givenchy tie, and black shoes from Churches completed his expensive ensemble. A quick comb and a brush through his modestly wavy hair and a fixing with Paul Mitchell Freeze and Shine sealed him into place. He smiled at himself once more in the mirror and proceeded towards the door. Just inside was a white bell push, which would alert Clinton to the fact that his master was about to leave for the office. He pushed it.

He stepped through the main door, and a momentary frown of annoyance creased his forehead, for despite the fact that his good fortune had left him with sufficient money to afford the luxuries of life such as Clinton, his company car, for which he had had to seek special dispensation for his own man to drive, was a Rover 75. Although it glistened in pristine black elegance, he was reminded that it complied with the general policy of purchasing British-built motorcars, a policy that had been introduced by his chairman and one that he had not been able to overturn. It stemmed from a lack of interest on behalf of his chairman in anything comprising a motor vehicle mainly because he didn't like to drive, but, secondarily, as an exceedingly wealthy man, he could buy whatever he wanted to keep at home, and the company vehicle was of little consequence therefore.

He entered the climate-controlled interior and immediately picked up the phone. It was a compulsive gesture, for by now, the status of the car phone had declined, and even the portable job of extreme miniaturisation, which he kept in his briefcase, no longer had people casting admiring glances his way. He had recently been asked to stop using it in one of his favourite restaurants; Kevin had not been pleased.

The offices of NTI sat between the West End and the City and took three floors of a purpose-built office block, the top most floor of which was reserved for the senior executives and for board and conference rooms. It also contained a self-indulgent kitchen and a number of highly efficient secretaries.

He was greeted by the doorman's salute and the bright smile of the receptionist, who received a condescending nod in return.

The lift took him to the executive suite. He entered through the outer door to his office, and his secretary, Marcia Payne, greeted him enthusiastically; it was something she had trained herself to do, and who wouldn't with a salary of £40,000 per annum and a rather nice Ford Escort on the company? She knew that apparent loyalty lay with the man who signed the paycheque, like him or not. She followed him into the office with three files in her hands and placed them in front of him as he sank into his comfortably upholstered armchair.

'The urgent mail is in the red folder, your papers for a chat with the chairman are in the green folder, and the blue folder contains the personnel details you asked for in connection with your meeting with John Joyce. He is due here at eleven o'clock.'

'Thank you, Marcia, and, by the way, Victor Stanley should be back from Japan today. I want a meeting with him. Get him in here as soon as possible, this afternoon if you can.'

Marcia left the office with a twist of her hips. *He really was a bastard,* she thought. Victor Stanley had been away on an arduous trip, and he wasn't really going to feel like a major meeting this afternoon, but then this was the Hipkiss's method—keep them tired and nervous and running.

She switched on the PC and inserted the disc. It contained a letter that had already been basically constructed to reflect the dismissal of John Joyce, whom she rather liked. He always had time to come and have a chat with her when he was at HQ, and with a commanding personality and a successful divisional operation, she wondered why Hipkiss was so intent on getting rid of him. She supposed he was a threat; Hipkiss did not like threats. John Joyce had recently made the cardinal mistake of proving, in front of a divisional board meeting, at which the chairman had been present, that a decision made by Hipkiss some time ago with regard to a manufacturing investment not only had been foolhardy but also resulted in losing the company several hundred thousand pounds. Hipkiss had argued that if the divisional board had felt that strongly about his original decision, they should have had the courage to stand up and say so. The chairman, always weak in the face of intercompany arguments, had not intervened. She wondered if John Joyce was aware of what was going to happen, and she wondered if there would be any fireworks; she hoped so.

Kevin went through the mail. There wasn't really anything that was of outstanding importance today; a couple of quite nice-looking invitations, some internal copies keeping him informed about what was going on in the divisions, for his information network gathered together all the copies of correspondence and memos from divisional managing directors, which were sifted by Marcia in order that he didn't miss anything significant. He didn't have time to read them all, and if he missed anything of importance, then he always had someone else to blame for not bringing it to his attention. On top of the pile was an inward fax from Kenezo Nonaka of Nonaka Corporation, which pointed out what an extremely interesting and productive meeting he had had with Victor Stanley and how Nonaka Corporation wished to continue these discussions with a view to forming a Japan-based joint venture to exploit the superconductive polymer technology. It went on to say that they regarded Victor Stanley as having been instrumental in bringing the two businesses together and looked forward to working with him to establish the new venture. The latter part of the message did not please Kevin; too many people liked Stanley, and that always made him feel vulnerable. Perhaps it was time he moved him on too.

Marcia went over to the small refrigerator in the corner of her office and removed a carton of orange juice and poured a glass, placing it on a try with a glass of sparkling Malvern water. Kevin did not drink coffee or tea at the office, as he had been told that caffeine was bad for him. She knocked politely on the door and entered. Kevin was on the phone, and she placed the tray on the right-hand corner of his desk and returned to her own office.

Kevin put the phone down, picked up the orange juice, and drank half the contents of the glass. He followed this with a drink of cleansing water. His internal phone rang softly. He picked it up.

'Hipkiss.'

'Ah! Good morning, Kevin. Chairman here.' Kevin waited. 'Er … I think we have a meeting scheduled.'

'Yes, Chairman,' said Hipkiss at last. 'I'll be right along.'

Sir Dennis Matchett had become a Knight of the Realm under a rather dubious set of circumstances concerning a government job. New Technology Industries was once a small and extremely impressive fast-growth company, and it was an undeniable fact that in those years, Sir Dennis had been the architect of its success. This had been noticed in government circles, and he had been sounded out about taking over as chairman of a government enterprise not noted for its sparkling success. The government had not realised that Sir Dennis's success had come from sitting behind a desk and using his brain. Never good with people, he only allowed his innermost group of management to get close to him and then not that close. Sir Dennis had been one of those people lucky enough to be born with a silver spoon in his mouth and had admittedly turned it into gold. He had done this with the help of that group of senior managers who had let his brilliance rub off on them and had been able to bask in the glory of his success. They did what they were told, were rewarded well, and would lick his arse when asked.

Most of the senior management group had now reached the peak of their ability, and the company growth was beginning to flatten out. It had been admitted that a talented chief executive would create a new driving force, and Sir Dennis had eventually presented them with Kevin.

Sir Dennis Matchett had been flattered by the approach of this very senior civil servant and, after a most satisfactory negotiation, had agreed to head up the Technical Improvements in Government Establishments Committee. This was to bring government departments kicking and screaming into the modern day with regard to how they handled and used advances in technology. It meant that Sir Dennis had to work with and help manage a large number of people and get on with them, leading from the front. Unfortunately, he was incapable of doing this, but the government did not discover the problem for some time.

Again, as luck would have it, the country was moving steadily away from manufacturing and replacing this hard-earned skill with service-based businesses that were only too keen to be at the forefront of technology, and with government grants to help them, Sir Dennis found a willing audience keen as mustard to modernize. Tiger, as the committee came to be known, was therefore seen to be a success, and improvements made during Sir Dennis's tenure were real.

After a period of three years at the helm, Dennis Matchett was again sounded out as to whether he might accept a knighthood; his answer was not long in coming. He joined that noble band of successful businessmen that needed to add stature to wealth and in so doing further distanced himself from his fellow men.

The complaints from government departments subject to his scrutiny started to come in shortly after Sir Dennis had decided that he should now embark upon the final leg of his ennoblement and go for a life peerage. He became a major donor to the Tory party using company funds and poured substantial amounts of his own money into a mixed bag of charities. Those with the highest profile benefited most.

After a year of substantially depleting his bank accounts, he inexplicably resigned as chairman of the committee and returned full time to a company that had stagnated during his partial absence. He gave as his excuse the need to get back to the main job in hand, but those in government circles who knew better had found that his rather able right-hand man had actually been the one to influence people and bring about the successful changes. He had protected Sir Dennis until he could do so no longer. A scurrilous document was being circulated with Sir Dennis as the subject matter. The document contained a number of unflattering opinions expressed by senior people he had come into contact with during his time as head of Tiger. The minister quietly interviewed some of his team and found to his horror that Sir Dennis was, in their opinion, the most unlikeable man they had ever met or wished to cooperate with. Added to this, he was told that in the event he was to continue in office, certain members of Tiger would resign within the year.

On a wet and cold Monday morning, the minister had asked Sir Dennis to call on him. It was an unscheduled meeting, and Sir Dennis wondered whether it heralded his greatest ambition. Regrettably for him, it did not, and he sat in stunned surprise as the minister told him that his government job was at an end. He thanked him for the excellent results and wished him well, handing over to him at the same time his letter of resignation, which had been thoughtfully prepared for Sir Dennis to sign, and so he did.

Chapter 8

It was an untroubled flight, and Veronica slept much of the way curled up in her seat. Victor slept fitfully, the problems that lay ahead refusing to let his mind close down.

Breakfast came and went. The imminent landing at Heathrow was announced and the seat belts fastened.

Victor turned to Veronica. 'I would like you to know that I have enjoyed our interlude. I know your motives might not be the same as mine, but whatever the circumstances, I feel flattered that someone young and beautiful should involve herself with me.'

'Oh, Victor, the pleasure was not all one way, you know. You underestimate yourself, and my mind is confused now about the future. You have restored my faith in businessmen, though. I thought all the nice guys had disappeared, but now I know I was wrong. I also know that it is inevitable our paths must part now, for we both have our own problems to solve, and that can only be done separately. If in the future we meet again, then fate will decide what happens then.'

Victor took her small left hand in his, and drawing it to his lips, he kissed it. 'You are a lovely lady. I wish you luck.'

The big Boeing bumped gently as the wheels hit the tarmac, and Victor's subconscious told him he was safely home, whilst his active mind was trying to understand just what it was Veronica was telling him. This diminutive and lovely creature was on some sort of mission that he had first supposed was to do with rescuing her father's honour and returning to the family fold a small company in Singapore that had apparently been stolen. On the other hand, here was an agent of Doo-hwan who clearly had a job to do escorting him to London and no doubt reporting that he was safely home. Beyond that lay something else, something she had to do to maintain her position in Doo-hwan's organisation, something that involved George Yoreen. It all left Victor unsure of where her loyalties lay. Time would tell.

The plane turned off the main runway and entered the taxiway towards terminal 4.

'I am aware', said Victor, 'that you have an objective other than just escorting me home. Doo-hwan will exert extreme pressure on George Yoreen, and somewhere in all this, you have a role to play. You will eventually be in direct opposition to my own objectives. Somehow, Doo-hwan has to acquire the secrets of the superconductive polymer, and someone has to carry them back to him. I know that I should inform the police, but for obvious reasons of my own, I cannot do that without incriminating myself. My other problem is that the evidence is entirely circumstantial at the moment, and I have to wait on events.'

'Wait and see what happens, Victor. It won't all be bad.' She gently squeezed his hand.

From where Victor sat, it did not look good, though; he had lost the sample, and that had sealed his lips as tightly as anything could. His plans to avoid detection for this crime and hang on to his job were forming in his mind and involved the return of what would be a bogus sample to laboratory stock. First, he had to acquire something that would pass casual inspection. He knew that checks would ultimately reveal a loss, but by then, he would have a better chance of survival. There were all sorts of reasons why small amounts of material were lost during routine tests and experiments.

Veronica interrupted his thoughts. 'Victor, I want to leave you at terminal 4. If our paths cross again, I hope the circumstances will be happier ones. Think of me sometimes.'

Victor would think of her often in the weeks ahead.

'When we are through customs', she said, 'I will make a telephone call and a car will collect me and I shall just walk away from you.'

In so saying, she leaned over to him and kissed him again on the cheek in the way a daughter would. Victor smiled at her.

They were slowing down now for entry to the gate and were not far off the scheduled arrival time as it was just coming up to 6:40 a.m., only five minutes out. An announcement came over the intercom to the effect that passengers should please sit down until the aircraft came to a standstill. Victor had never been able to fathom out why the minute one approached the gate, everyone sprang up and started to hurl things around the cabin and stand in the aisle, for it would be a good ten minutes yet before they would allow them off the plane. Veronica had gotten her hand baggage out and was sorting through it, apparently for small items of fragrance and colour, which she carefully applied to her person. Victor collected the various papers he had been looking at and also the other odds and sods that needed to go back into his briefcase. The plane came to a halt; the engines started to die, and the 'fasten seat belts' sign went out. Victor stood up and joined the queue at the top of the staircase to get out ahead of economy class.

They went up the ramp from the gate and entered the corridor towards arrivals. Terminal 4 has certain redeeming features about it, apart from the architecture, which appears unfinished as though someone felt that exposed tubes and girders were of great artistic merit. At least it was still relatively uncrowded. Passports were inspected, and they passed through into the baggage area. Veronica was still at Victor's side, although she hadn't spoken to him since leaving the aircraft. Victor saw their bags come up the chute and drop onto the oval carousel. He lifted first his and then Veronica's off and placed them on the two luggage trolleys he had collected. Victor left Veronica to push her own trolley and, without a backward glance, headed for the green exit.

Veronica had dropped back a few paces and followed Victor out. Surprisingly, there was only one customs inspector in the green area, and he was more interested in some of the wilder Oriental tourists who might be carrying more exotic items in their bags than tired businessmen. They were through and clear and walking one behind the other down the concourse. They turned left facing the information desk with the car hire cubicles to the left and the Bureau de Change to the right. There were a number of people waiting for loved ones and chauffeurs with unpronounceable names on small boards collecting their bosses and their bosses' bosses.

Veronica's trolley drew alongside Victor's and stopped. She reached over with her right hand and squeezed his left.

'Bye-bye, Victor,' she said and turned right towards the telephones. Victor was tempted for a moment to go after her but resisted. He would have to go in that direction anyway because the entrance to the Underground was there. Suddenly, he was tired and wanted to be back home again to feel the security around him and to be part of the real life where there was no worse a threat than the beloved Kevin invading his day.

He walked over to the Bureau de Change, stood in front of the Travelex Corporation information board, which informed him that the Japanese yen was being purchased at 192 to the pound, and handed over a considerable number to a girl who could even have come from Singapore. She handed him back £182.63p, and he put it into his pocket and, turning through 180 degrees, walked towards the three lifts that would take him and his trolley down into the Underground area to catch the tube. The green light on the left-hand elevator flashed. The double doors opened, letting out a geriatric couple in Indonesian embroidered shirts. Victor pressed the button marked Underground.

It was extraordinarily warm for the time of year in London, and the soaring eagle advertisement of Daikin, purveyors of air conditioning, which was fully illuminated for the travellers' consideration, seemed out of place but desirable in a city where an open window was the usual form of changing the office climate.

The trolley gathered speed down the gentle slope towards the Underground station, and Victor had to physically check it.

'Welcome to the Underground,' the sign said as Victor entered the fully lighted area. He went over to the ticket machines on his left and selected the fare for Sloane Square. As he walked through the gates, a train pulled in, and Victor boarded a carriage that had never heard of Daikin air conditioning or in any way bore any similarity towards the air-conditioned and pristine underground systems of Tokyo and Osaka. It was packed and about to disgorge most at the next stop, the main station for Heathrow. The nervous expressions of departure blues on the faces of most of the passengers sat happily alongside Victor's joyous expression of arrival. They were the usual mixture, businessmen, tourists, visiting family groups, and the rest ranging from wild bushy hiking couples to robed Africans returning to tribal lands where their word was probably law.

On the lengthy journey into the West End, Victor had time to wonder what form of transport Veronica was taking and whereabouts she was being taken to. She hadn't offered the information, and he had not sought it, but he had no doubt that Doo-hwan had arranged things for her in the luxurious style to which Victor had even become accustomed.

Victor stayed on the train to Knightsbridge rather than follow the tortuous route to Sloane Square via the Circle Line. His watch told him it was still early, but it was quite busy as he struggled up the steps with the case that was now getting ever heavier. The escalator took some of the load, and after only a few more stairs, he stood thankfully at the top of Sloane Street and looked at the imposing facade of the Hyde Park Hotel.

Victor crossed over at the traffic lights to the Harvey Nichols side and picked up a passing cab. He gave him the address and sank back in the seat, and he set off down Sloane Street towards the Square. They turned left into Sloane Square, went round past the Royal Court Theatre, and entered lower Sloane Street. Victor's home was at the bottom end of a row of elegant red brick houses on the west side of the street between the square and the Sloane Club. The cab slowed down, did a U-turn, and pulled up outside the front door. Victor paid him the minimal fee, got out, mounted the four steps into the porch area, and pulled a bunch of keys from his pocket, and selected the appropriate one and inserted it into the Yale lock.

He was fortunate enough to have married a lady in all senses of the word. He was doubly fortunate that their combined fortunes over the years had managed to acquire for them a rather nice first-floor apartment, which would now be termed 'extremely desirable'. It had been elegantly and tastefully furnished in a style that Victor and his wife both enjoyed. He entered the small inner hall, closed the door behind him, and went through a second set of doors and up the stairs where a part-stained glass window faced him on the return. At the head of the stairs, there was another door, and he selected the second key, this time a more substantial Chubb, and turned it in the lock. He pushed it open. Gloria stood there in the centre of the small hall.

'I heard your taxi,' she said simply. 'You should have phoned. I could have come and met you.'

'There was no point,' he said. 'It was a quick journey, and I just wanted to be off the plane and back here in the fastest way I knew possible.'

For another moment or two, they smiled at each other and then, like two veteran stars of the screen, came graciously together and embraced. She was soft in all the right places still and looked a million dollars. Her favourite fragrance of the moment, Obsession, filled his nostrils, and they kissed. He couldn't help thinking that this was a very different form of kiss from what he had so recently shared with Veronica Tan, and his conscience pricked but only momentarily. Just as he was conscious of her elegance and sweetness in his arms, he was conscious that he was unshaven, unclean, and generally offensive.

They drew apart, and Victor picked up the case and went down the passage to their bedroom. It was a large room with a big bay window and a substantial bathroom off it, big enough to contain a huge shower, a bath, and all the other essentials. He felt as though he needed each one of them for half an hour. The bed dominated the room, but, basically, it was two substantial single beds joined together to form one massive king-size domain. Visitors thought they must have spent a lot of their time in bed and had a highly active and adventurous sexual life. They might not have been wrong in the past, but it had entered a gentler phase, and the bed had become something of a retreat. Normally, they were fairly early birds in the sense that they didn't go to bed late when they weren't entertaining or being entertained, and they didn't stay late in a morning. It was a good place to have a conversation or watch the television or take early morning tea or, for that matter, still make love.

He lifted the three-tonne case on top of the bed and inserted the keys into the locks and undid them. He spun the combination to the correct number and, flicking the catches open, split it into the two parts that he so much liked about this old Samsonite. Gloria came and stood behind him and watched him take the things out of the case because, traditionally, he had always brought something back from every journey, and although she never expected it, there was always an eager anticipation to see what might be coming this time. He first unloaded his cigars and various paraphernalia of the journey, collected items of this and that; for the main part, useless mementos but things that reminded him in office and home of the journeys he had been on and the places he had visited, a sort of nostalgia for the nomadic man. There was also the usual amount of laundry, which he sensed she turned her nose up at but nevertheless resolutely tackled. Finally, in the bottom of the case lay a small package with the word 'Mikomoto' on it.

Victor was aware that he missed an anniversary whilst away, a not uncommon occurrence during his lifetime, and therefore not only had his conscience pricked him about Veronica but also it had made him doubly aware that something special was needed, a peace offering. He picked up the small pack and turned round and held it out to her. She looked into his eyes.

'You look tired, Victor. There is a tiredness about you this time that I haven't seen before. You really shouldn't have been worrying about bringing me gifts.'

'It never worries me, darling', he said, 'to seek out a gift for you. I missed our anniversary, I forgot the card, and you haven't even berated me for it, but I remembered before it was too late, and this is just to make up for that forgetfulness. Yes, I am tired, I am bloody tired, and I think I am getting more tired all the time, and this trip has certainly been no sinecure. The worst thing is that I have to be up again at the crack of dawn tomorrow and get out to the research labs before anyone else does.'

She took the pack and held it in her hands for a moment.

'Something's gone wrong,' she said.

'Yes, something's gone wrong,' he replied.

'Is it serious?'

'Yes, it's serious.'

'Do you want to tell me?'

'Yes, I want to tell you, but, first, let's just get this case off the bed, make a pot of tea, and I'll take a shower, and then I'll explain as best I can what's happened. Now, open your present.' She took off the outer wrapping, and there was a long, slim box inside. She carefully opened it. Inside was a perfect set of pearls, something Victor had wanted to buy for a long time but had always felt that it was overextravagant. This time, he had an excuse and a conscience working against him—a forgotten anniversary and a wild affair.

'They're beautiful, Victor,' she said. 'Put them on for me.'

She handed them to him, and he took each end in each hand as she turned and lifted her hair at the back of her neck. Victor fastened the gold clasp, and she walked over and stood in front of the mirror. He had always been told that the test of a good pearl was to place it on a piece of pure white paper, and if it was whiter than the paper, then it was a good pearl. If it wasn't, you were not buying a pearl. Set against her skin, they shone, and the lights picked up the inner colours and matched the happy sparkle in her eyes. He felt the familiar tug at his heart that said to him, 'Thank God I have got this woman.' He never really wanted any other except in the purely carnal sense of the word, and he guessed that would go on happening from time to time if an opportunity arose, but it was never where his heart was.

She turned round and came towards him with her arms open, and he walked to her again. She clasped him and kissed his mouth, saying thank you with her lips and voice and body, but Victor really was in need of a sleep. There would be time for the other later. He pushed her gently away and said, 'Go and make the tea. I'll have a shower.'

He stood there in the shower letting the hot water pour over him. The shower was driven by a powerful little motor that supplemented the weak water pressure and turned a trickle into a raging torrent. He copiously soaped every part of his body, poured shampoo over his hair, scrubbed his back, and turned it to cold. The shock to his system only allowed him to stand under the cold stream for a few seconds. He stepped out feeling altogether better and, taking the big bath towel, rubbed himself vigorously with it and walked naked into the bedroom. Gloria came in through the other door with a tray and two steaming mugs.

'You've put weight on,' she said.

'I always put weight on when I travel,' he retorted.

It was an everlasting battle, her gentle persuasion that he really ought to do something about it and his equally gentle response that it was very difficult living the sort of lifestyle he did, but she was right and he knew it, and one day, just one day, he would have to accept that, but not at the moment.

Gloria lifted the duvet, picked the pillows up, and propped them up against the headboard. She was still in her housecoat after Victor's early arrival.

'You have time for a rest, darling,' she said and patted the bed invitingly.

Victor ran a comb through his still damp hair and then eased himself into the comfort of the best bed he knew. God, he was tired.

Gloria put the mug of tea down on his bedside table and walked round to the other side, a journey of approximately ten minutes, and put hers down, and taking off her housecoat, she stood there in a very nicely cut black nightdress with a scalloped low-cut top and a flowing skirt that he could just see the shape of her legs through.

'Do you feel better now, darling?'

'Yes, I suppose I do,' he replied. 'The shower's made me feel a whole lot more alive,' and still he looked at her.

She leaned over and picked up the hem of the nightdress and, in one smooth movement, lifted it up to her waist. Her legs were slightly apart, and Victor could see the whole of her sex as though it were beckoning him.

'I think you deserve a little reward for those pearls', she pouted, 'so I am going to give you a quickie. You're not to do anything. You're just to lie on the bed and relax. Leave the rest to me.'

In so saying, she completed the act of raising the nightdress and lifted it completely over her head and dropped it on the floor. She got on to the bed and crept across it towards him until she was kneeling by his side. Despite the tiredness, he felt the arousal happening and slid down the pillows until he was almost flat on the bed.

'It's been quite a while, Victor', she said, 'and I'm going to enjoy this.' She lowered her right hand and took his now expanding organ by the shaft and gripped it firmly. It responded by going harder and tighter, and the circumcised head became bright red. With her other hand, she started to place her fingers inside her own sex and to gently rub it until they came out glistening, and changing hands, she put the now ample silky juices over him, and then raising herself slightly, she put one knee across the other side of his body and faced him; she was completely straddling him. She had that expression on her face that she always got when she was about to go into ecstasy; it wasn't beautiful, but it clearly indicated that she was enjoying what she was doing, and her pleasing features turned into an expression of what Victor could only describe as open lust.

She shuffled forward until her sex was directly over his organ, and taking her left hand and guiding him, she gently dropped herself onto him. The silken tube that led to the innermost parts of her body enveloped Victor completely, and their two pelvic areas came together briefly before she raised herself up as though she was almost going to leave him and descended again. Victor was lying there in a semi-exhausted state with this most wonderful sensation gripping him and knew that it was going to be better than any sleeping pill he could take to send him off into a few hours of total oblivion.

He had no way of controlling events in this position, and after what only seemed like a few minutes, he felt the sperm within him start its journey, and in a glorious crescendo, it spouted within her. She opened her eyes in surprise, and then they softened.

'Was that nice, darling?'

'You know it was, but I'm sorry you did not get the full thrill out of it as well.'

'That's for another time,' she said. 'That's just a little thank-you, and I can always do a bit of DIY.'

DIY was something Gloria was quite good at, and Victor supposed that she had developed a suitable technique over the many years of his journeying, and it quite excited him to think about it. He had tried to persuade her to let him watch sometime, but she always refused, saying it was too private for even a husband to view. He lived in the hope she would change her mind one day.

She sat on him for a few minutes longer and then gently released herself and went to the bathroom and reappeared a few moments with a small towel, which she had soaked in warm water and lovingly sponged him and then herself. It had been a very short and erotic experience, and now Victor could feel himself slipping away into sleep. The tea remained untouched on the bedside table.

Gloria stood by the side of the bed still looking at him.

'You were going to tell me your problems, Victor.'

'Later,' he said. 'Leave it until I wake up, but don't let me sleep too long. I have work to do.' It was the last thing he remembered for some time.

She shook him gently awake, and he found it difficult to respond, although it was still light outside.

'It's five o'clock, darling.'

Victor reluctantly sat up and looked about the room. It was good to be home. The hum of traffic came up from the street; people were going home from work.

Gloria sat on the other side of the bed; she had put on a pair of trousers and a light knitted cotton sweater.

'Before anything else happens, I want to know your problems,' she said.

'I've got to get out to the labs as soon as I can,' he said. 'During my journeying in Japan, I mislaid the sample that I took with me. That is the simplest explanation I can give you.'

'But that was terribly valuable, Victor. How on earth are you going to explain it?'

'I'm not quite sure, but I think I have a way around it that has a 50 per cent chance of succeeding, but I haven't time to tell you the complex tale that led up to its loss or what has happened since, but I will tonight as best I can, I promise you.'

'You're not in any danger or anything like that, Vic?' she said, using the diminutive that she did at times when she became slightly agitated.

'No, I don't think I'm actually in danger', he said, 'apart from the danger of losing my job if I don't sort this thing out. However, what I am going to do is go out to the labs and take some of the base material that is not fully reactive and is not kept in a secure area. I will make that up as my sample and hand it back in to George Yoreen in the morning in order that he can replace it in his sample stock, and with a bit of luck, no one will bother checking, at least not until the usual monthly assay test. We know that the product can deteriorate over a period, and because it is still experimental, I am just hoping that any losses of activity that they might come up with will be judged to be part of that experimental process, but I have to act now because I have to explain to Hipkiss how the trip went, and George Yoreen will have to confirm that he received the sample back again.'

'Vic, you're worrying me. There's more to this than you are telling me, so please be careful.'

'Of course, I'll be careful. I am always careful.'

'You weren't careful in Japan when you lost the sample, were you?'

'No,' he said, for that was the plain truth of the matter.

By the time he got downstairs, Gloria had prepared him a couple of pieces of toast, which he buttered and ate with some cold ham, and he drank a glass of cold skimmed milk. Time was passing, and soon, it would be safe to make the trip to the labs. Very few people worked late if they could help it at NTI, and Victor was sure he could go in, do what he had to, and be back before anyone was the wiser. He would need a car. They were lucky enough to have a garage for one car and had a street-parking permit for the other, and his company vehicle had therefore been in the garage during the time he had been away, or at least he hoped it had.

'Is the car in the garage, darling?'

'Yes, but I've been using it, and it's a bit low on petrol.' In saying that, she went over to a drawer in the sideboard, pulled it out, took the keys from it, and gave them to him.

'I don't know what time I'll be back, but I think it will be sometime around eight or nine. Hopefully, I'll have sorted things out by then, and I'll fill you in a bit more with the facts.'

'All right, darling. Now, remember, take care.'

Victor kissed her and went downstairs and out through the rear entrance of the building. He went over to the garage and unlocked it, and his old and trusty 190E Mercedes stood there waiting. Victor eased himself down the side between wall and car and had just enough room to squeeze himself into the driving seat. It started at the first touch, and he drove out into Lower Sloane Street.

It was now 6:30 p.m., and the traffic was thinning a little. He turned north and retraced some of the journey the taxi had brought him on. He went around Sloane Square and, cutting his way across to Cromwell Road, headed west and eventually picked up the end of the M4 and, putting his foot down, skirted Brentford, slowing only as the signs for Junction 3 came up.

He turned off at Junction 3 and headed north up the Parkway and left into North Hyde Road at Hillingdon. It was then just a matter of a few lefts and rights and there were the gates ahead of him. The setting was really quite pleasant and backed onto the Union Canal. It had not been a difficult run out, and Victor had enjoyed getting behind the driving wheel again. It was generally recognised by security that Victor put in some unusual hours because of the many trips he made and the antisocial times of departure and arrival, it was necessary for him to catch up on events when he could. It was no surprise to the gateman when he drew up and presented his pass.

'Hello, Mr Stanley,' he said. 'I haven't seen you for a while. Have you been travelling again?'

'Yes, Bert,' Victor responded. 'I've just returned from one of those wonderful Far East trips where you guys think I have a ball.'

'We know you have a ball, Mr Stanley,' he said. 'Leastways, you always look as though you've had a ball, but this time, I'm not so sure 'cos you look all clean and healthy. You should by rights be worn out. I'm told those girls over there are something else.'

'Don't believe all you hear, Bert. Besides which a young man like you could get into serious trouble.'

He laughed. 'Chance would be a fine thing, sir.' The gates swung back, and with a wave of his hand, Bert invited Victor through.

'I don't suppose Dr Yoreen is still here by any chance, Bert, is he?'

'Cor, no, sir, he won't stay much after 6:00 p.m. if he can help it, but I'll have someone let you into his office if you like.'

Now that was strictly against the rules. Victor could not believe his ears; what a piece of luck. It was something he hadn't banked upon.

'Won't that get you into trouble, Bert?'

'Oh, no, sir, it'll be all right. I'll have a word with Dr Yoreen, and if you'd like to leave a message on his desk, I'll explain how it came to be there. There won't be a problem.'

'Thanks, Bert. I appreciate it,' said Victor and drew away from the gatehouse and parked in the visitors' car park. By the time he had walked round the block and up to the main entrance of the number one research unit, there was a guy in a uniform with a bunch of keys.

'Good evening, sir,' he said. 'I'll just let you in. Bert said it would be all right.'

'Thank you. I appreciate it.'

He inserted the key into the outer door, opened it, and led the way through. There was an alarm panel mounted on the wall opposite—each block had its own individual system—and he keyed in the neutralising number, and they went through the next set of doors.

'You're all right now, sir. The alarm's off,' and with that, he opened the outer door to George Yoreen's suite and checked to see if the door to his office was open; it wasn't.

'That's funny,' he said. 'Dr Yoreen usually leaves his office open so his secretary can get in if she works late.'

'Ah! Well, he must be working on something particularly confidential at the moment,' Victor responded. 'Don't worry about it. I'll give Bert a call as soon as I have written up a short report and left in on his desk and you can lock it up again.'

'Thank you, sir. I'll just unlock it for you.' He did and left.

Victor went back into the secretary's office and walked on through into George Yoreen's. He walked round the desk and looked for the sample log. He located it and put it on the desk. Opening it, he found the date and time of allocation and checked against that the details to make sure what he put on the new label would match. He shut the book and returned it to its proper place. He then drew a piece of paper towards him and wrote a note to George explaining that he had wanted to get the sample back into safekeeping as soon as possible. He went through into the laboratory and, from the cupboard over one of the benches, removed one of the standard sample bottles. The base polymer, although valuable, was not protected, and there were numerous sample bottles all dated and batch numbered on the shelves; they had differing amounts in each. Victor undid several and poured a small amount from each until he had the 100 ml he needed to fill his bottle. He then tightly resealed it and returned to George's office and, sitting in front of the PC, typed and printed up a label. He stuck it on the bottle and rubbed it vigorously in his hands and rubbed it against his jacket sleeve to make it look used. Then he took the sample record book from the drawer in George's desk and signed it back in. He left the bottle with his note on the desk and left the office with a sigh of relief.

Chapter 9

Sir Dennis's immediate problem was to get back into gear. He had grown used to a three-day week, and the appointment of Kevin had bridged the gap for him. Now, he had to ease back in; not that it was now his intention to work flat out, just to be around when he was needed.

Sir Dennis Matchett prided himself on being a good judge of character; in truth, he was the most appalling judge of human potential. In his efforts to bring his thinking up-to-date, he had allowed old-fashioned values to take second place to thrusting ambition backed up by paper qualifications you could paper a wall with and an ability to talk but not to listen. He had become enchanted with the rapier-minded MBA whose experience was as thin as the paper his qualifications were summarised on. Sir Dennis took at face value the stated ability of such cloned individuals to run a company and manage the people within it; after all, hadn't they been groomed by their MBA course to do such things? The truth was they had not; they had been trained to think of self-first and all other things second but to articulate this so skilfully that it sounded commendably different.

Hipkiss was from such a background; the size of the opening employment package, the quality of the share option, and maximum participation in the senior management bonus scheme were the things he made his joining decision on. He had been educated to run a company; after all, he had been trained in one of the best chemical companies and had reached a very senior position in no time at all. Universally hated by his colleagues, he had taken the job at NTI to get away from them. Sir Dennis had been a pushover; Kevin had looked him in the eye and lied competently. Sir Dennis was taken in; Kevin appealed to him.

Following the Hipkiss interview, Sir Dennis refused to consider other worthy characters within the business who could have done the job standing on their heads and in so doing had alienated a number of very senior staff who were now keeping their heads down and coasting along, some towards retirement and others in the sincere hope that alternative employment opportunities would come and find them; some were to be lucky.

Kevin Hipkiss, however, had come as a great relief to Sir Dennis Matchett and had enabled him to walk away from his conscience; after all, with a young man like Hipkiss in charge of the business, he could concentrate on chasing his life's ambition, the life peerage. His knighthood was all very well, but it wasn't quite enough despite his sincere belief that it had elevated him above most of his fellow men and colleagues. Now that he had Hipkiss inserted between himself and the rest of the employees, he could grandly communicate his views to the troops without actually having to meet them. His place in the boardroom was assured as the founder of the company, and he supposed that on the whole, they were a tolerably good lot in there, particularly as he had chosen several of them from a careful selection of his business acquaintances.

Sir Dennis Matchett still preferred to keep even his non-executive members at a distance and, when asked by Kevin Hipkiss whether he thought it would be a good idea for the board to have dinner together on the eve of a board meeting, had replied,

'I think not, Kevin. I do not invite them to my home, so I see no reason to become overfamiliar by indulging them prior to a board meeting. However, if you wish to go ahead with such an arrangement, you may do so.'

Kevin had had to swallow that one, but he was, anyway, the exception to the rule. Kevin was fortunate enough to be persona grata in the household of Sir Dennis Matchett. Kevin had the distinct and uncomfortable feeling that his strange and distant employer fancied him, but that was preposterous.

Kevin made the short journey from his office to the outer door of his chairman's. The guardian angel awaited inside, for it was impossible to get past his secretary without a permit to enter, even for Kevin. She was a puffed-up blousy and substantial lady reeking of self-importance. Sir Dennis indulged her, some said he screwed her; whatever it was, there was a rather special relationship, and not even Kevin dare put her down. He smiled, she smiled, she picked up the phone, spoke briefly to her lord and master, and waved Kevin through. He pushed open the door and shut it behind him.

'Good morning, Chairman.'

'Good morning, Kevie.'

It was an annoying habit of his chairman to occasionally reduce the names of people he liked to the diminutive.

'Kevie' suited him very well; he would have been horrified to find that it had rapidly become his nickname throughout the organisation.

He waded through the thick pile carpet and sank himself into the chair facing the desk. Kevin had become very fond of the chairman; after all, he had been picked up from relative obscurity and planted in a job that only he knew he could do. The thin veneer that cloaked him with the qualities of a gentleman and his boyish good looks had appealed to Sir Dennis, and although it had worn a little thin at times, there was a mutual need that bound them together. Sir Dennis smiled as indulgently as he knew how.

'I'm hearing some good things, Kevie. It seems that Stanley's come back with something of a coup from Japan.'

He looked quizzically at Kevin, raising one eyebrow in the fashion that he had perfected over the years. An icy feeling close to jealousy immediately gripped Kevin's soul. Praise for Victor Stanley from Sir Dennis? This was praise indeed. Praise should be reserved for the feats of Kevin. He picked his words carefully.

'I have not yet fully debriefed Stanley, Chairman. He only arrived back a matter of hours ago, and, frankly, it amazes me how you found out anything at all.'

The eyebrow went up again.

'I am not badly informed, Kevin, as you know I have a long-standing relationship with young Nonaka's father. I received a brief fax from him yesterday telling me that his son's views were that we had a remarkable product worthy of development, and when Nonaka senior sends me faxes, I know something serious is afoot.'

'It would appear, Chairman, that Victor Stanley has done a passable job, but then that is what we pay him for—he is a marketing man. He is in our employ to put over the best of our technology to potential investors and customers, but I don't think his performance in Japan is any extraordinary feat.'

'No', said the chairman, 'but it is a feat, nevertheless, that Victor Stanley has achieved single-handedly, and it should not be lightly dismissed.'

Kevin could hardly believe his ears. Was this the uncaring, almost withdrawn Sir Dennis that he had come to know? What had happened to make these comments spring from his lips? Perhaps the stirrings of old memories of the days when he actually got on slow planes and flew to Japan and achieved great things.

'I don't want to take any of Victor's glory away from him, Chairman,' lied Kevin. 'He is a competent servant of the company, but he is getting on a bit, and this might be a time to make a change with the Nonaka relationship. If, as you say, he has set in motion a new deal, then it would be a good time to pat him on the back and replace him with a younger man who will be able to bring new energy to the challenge ahead.'

As always, Kevin had missed the essential features of dealing with East—the long relationships, the building of trust and loyalty, the establishment of friendship, patience, and even the getting drunk together.

There was a particular school of thought in industry that if you didn't succeed the first time you went out East, then you were obviously sending the wrong chap, and if you sent another chap more powerful, more intellectual, and louder, he was sure to succeed where the first one hadn't. When he also came back empty-handed, you probably sent two chaps of even greater seniority and drive and then you gave up.

Victor Stanley had had the great good fortune early in his Far Eastern tours to be allowed to set up his own programmes and form his own contacts. Sir Dennis still visited the area then but concentrated on the important relationship with Nonaka. It was through his visits that the two elder statesmen had become friends. Victor carried this on when his chairman took up his government job and had been unable to make regular visits. This special relationship with Nonaka and a host of others Victor had established had actually made him indispensable to both NTI and the Far Eastern contacts. Kevin needed to learn this.

'Kevin, pay and rations is your domain, and you have my complete authority to deal with these things as you see fit. However, I think you should consider matters most carefully. If you are intent upon changing the team, then you must change it in such a way that those leaving will not blacken our name because we have treated them badly. If you do go ahead with any changes, I would rather you do it without involving me.'

The chairman shuffled his feet in agitation and gazed steadfastly out of the window. After a few moments, he looked back at Kevin.

'The main point of our little chat today, Kevin, concerns my role in the future of things. As you know, I have decided to retire from my government post having achieved the main part of the work and to make way for fresh blood.'

This roughly followed the lines of the press release.

'This means that I am back again in the hurly-burly of NTI, and I want to work out a fair and equitable split of duties between you and me.'

Kevin almost gaped. He had been so used to Sir Dennis taking nothing but a casual interest in the business and to giving him occasional briefings as to how things were running; the thought that he would become more seriously involved horrified him. Would his ways survive full scrutiny from a reactivated chairman? Admittedly, the business was succeeding, but this was because certain of the key players had done rather a good job—in some cases, despite Kevin.

'I am sure, Chairman, that you will be more than welcome again in returning to a more active role, but perhaps now it would be better if you carried on in a non-executive capacity where your wisdom and seniority can be used with great effect round the group companies. You know how much the City is encouraging the split between chairman and chief executive.'

Kevin knew the minute he had shut his mouth that he had said the wrong thing, and Sir Dennis looked over the half-moon glasses in his most withering manner, a look that had been known to reduce the knees of lesser mortals to jelly. Kevin was grateful he was seated.

'I think, Kevin',—Kevin had noticed the change to the extended name form—'that I will be the judge of what is required in my company.'

Kevin was not going to argue.

'Well, Chairman, the first thing that we could usefully do is to get you involved immediately in the forthcoming planning cycle. We are working now on the budgets for 2004 and the update of the five-year plan. Because of our rapid growth, the long-term planning is becoming critical to our future if we are to have the resources to meet our expenditure and manpower needs. I have been thinking of introducing consultants to take us through a strategic planning process.'

The conversation rambled on and left Kevin very much where he had started—in charge of the day-to-day affairs. The chairman agreed he would deal with the more rarefied aspects of running the business including communications with the City where the parasites had to be continually fed with the blood of success or they would die on their host and poison their system. He would join Kevin in the planning process and agreed to consider his views about ultimately changing to a non-executive role, but not yet.

Finally, Kevin excused himself and, dragging his feet wearily through the pile of the carpet, went unsmiling and without communication past his chairman's secretary.

Back in his own office, he lowered himself into his chair and, for the second time that morning, felt mildly chilled. He looked at his diary; it was one of those that had times down the left-hand side of the page neatly divided into quarter-hour breaks. He liked to stick to a timetable, as it gave him a sense of achievement. Eleven o'clock was circled, and the name that stared back at him was John Joyce. *Pay and rations,* thought Kevin.

'That's what he said, pay and rations,' Kevin called out to no one in particular. At least those two pleasures were not to be denied him. He picked up the phone and pressed the little button that would summon Marcia Payne, as he had re-entered the office by the second door that allowed him to escape when he needed to avoid her attention. Marcia tapped discreetly at the door and entered. She stood looking at him with a vague expression of dislike.

'Is Joyce here yet?'

'Yes,' said Marcia. 'He's waiting in the outer office.'

'Send him in.'

She turned on her heel and left the interconnecting door open. He heard a murmured conversation outside, and John Joyce strode into the office without greeting. He walked almost up to Kevin's desk and waited, a technique that always put Kevin on edge; he hated to be the first one to acknowledge the presence of another. This morning, he had no option.

'Er … good morning, James. Thank you for coming.'

'I didn't have any bloody alternative, did I?'

'Quite, quite,' said Kevin. 'Sit down, please.'

Joyce took the most comfortable chair in the office and tried to look casual, but he felt far from it. He knew what the score was; he knew that he had undermined this man, insulted him, shown him up for what he was, been outspoken in his presence, and in all but words told him that he was a contemptible little shit. The words marched around his brain, and he savoured them knowing that he would actually be able to extract them this morning and put them into his mouth and watch the impact.

'This is not an easy task.' It came out rather like a squeak, and he did it again, lower octave.

'This is not an easy task.'

'I heard you the first time', said Joyce, 'and the only person it's not going to be easy for is me.'

'But you don't know what I'm going to say.'

'Let me try and add two and two together in the most simple form,' said Joyce. 'Ever since you walked into this outfit, I have disliked you. Ever since you set eyes on me, you've disliked me. I run a good ship, I run an excellent profitable division, and you are trying to take it away and give it to some second-rater whose company you have purchased with the idea that I might like to do something else, and I have told you that I don't like your ideas and I won't go along with them. Faced with these circumstances, you are trapped into the only alternative you have left.'

For the second time that morning, Kevin gaped; it was becoming a habit. It was only a momentary gape, but it annoyed him.

'I don't think there is any need to take that attitude—'

Joyce did not let him finish.

'I'll take any attitude I like, Hipkiss, so get on with what it is you have got to do and then we can all go back to enjoying ourselves.'

This was getting out of hand. Kevin felt his control was slipping.

'I think it would be better if we had the company secretary in here,' he said formally.

'Anything you like,' said Joyce. 'If you think you need a witness, then you get one.'

There was a knock at the door. Kevin looked up, startled. He had given instructions not to be interrupted.

'Come in,' he said.

Marcia Payne walked in with a tray of strong coffee and placed it on the desk, and without looking at Kevin, she poured James Joyce a cup and handed it to him. He smiled at her; she left. Kevin could pour his own.

Kevin dialled a number of the internal phone and spoke softly to it. He poured his own coffee and took a small sip, looking over the rim of his cup at the victim. Joyce said nothing. To Kevin's relief, there was another knock on the door, and Gordon Blossom entered with a file under his arm.

Blossom was a total neutral. He had everyone's interest at heart but was ultimately the servant of the company. He did what he was told without falling out with anyone. He was unambitious but clever. He was the company's memory; all events were noted and recorded by him. Everything was done within the law. He was also a man guaranteed to take any story told to him directly to either Hipkiss or, in his absence, the chairman himself. It was well known in the company, and he had often been the purveyor of tales that had turned out to be scurrilous rumours. It did not put him off, as he regarded himself as a sacred conduit even if some would say sacred cow!

'Good morning, Mr Joyce.'

Joyce grunted. Kevin cleared his throat. Blossom sat down at the side of the desk and placed the file primly on the corner.

'I think, Gordon, it would be better if you were here while I have this conversation with James Joyce, as there may be some matters we need to refer to of a legal nature. You can also record the events, for the record, so to speak.'

Gordon smiled encouragingly. Kevin continued.

'As I was saying, James, it appears that there is some incompatibility between your style and mine—'

Again, Joyce stopped him.

'Nonsense. There is no incompatibility. I just object to the way you do things, particularly interfering in the running of my division. You know damn well that my operations run well and produce above-average results, yet you continue to stick your nose in and upset my senior staff. If you call that an incompatibility, then I have another word for it.'

Gordon Blossom's eyes came out like organ stops; it was a long time since he had heard anyone speak in this manner, and to address his chief executive thus was clearly a bold yet stupid action. Again, Kevin found himself floundering. He wasn't used to people fighting back; normally, when he engineered someone into a defensive position, they just sat there and died. This man clearly wasn't going to.

'An attitude like that will get you nowhere. I consider your operations below par. They should be producing much better results. Furthermore, you constantly undermine my authority. I have told you several times it cannot continue, yet you ignore me. There is no point beating around the bush any longer, James. I just don't want you in the company any more. There is no mutual respect left, and under these circumstances, one of us has got to go. I am therefore dismissing you.'

'You contemptible little shit,' said Joyce. Blossom choked. Kevin gaped for the third time in recent memory.

'You contemptible little shit', repeated Joyce for good measure, 'you're not fit to wipe my arse, and you sit there and glibly discharge me after all my years of service to this company, and you expect that I'm going to take it lying down. Well, I've got news for you, laddie—I'm not.'

He turned to Gordon Blossom.

'It might not have escaped your notice, Blossom, that I have an exceedingly good contract—'

Kevin interrupted.

'How dare you call me a contemptible little shit,' he howled. 'You're fired, *fired*, do you hear?'

Blossom sprang from his seat; it had never been seen before.

'Kevin, please don't say any more. We have to handle this in a civilised manner. It must not deteriorate into a row.'

Perspiration sprang onto the upper lip of Kevin; his usual self-control failed him. He placed his hands flat on the desk to stop them shaking; the atmosphere was electric. Kevin slowly raised his right hand and reached out for the coffee pot. He poured himself a cup shakily and took a large mouthful. He realised it contained caffeine; he needed it, something he had sworn not to touch again. There was a time for change.

James Joyce sat back; he actually relaxed.

'Fired', he mused, 'fired for incompatibility of style. Nice one that, Kevin. I wonder how it'll look in the announcement.'

It was Blossom who replied.

'Mr Joyce, we have to work this out as amicably as possible. I know you feel aggrieved, but it is my job to produce a satisfactory settlement, and I can't do that if there is no communication, which seems likely if the two of you go on like this.'

'I've news for you, Blossom dearie,' said Joyce. 'It may be satisfactory to you, but it'll never be satisfactory to me, not even when I've accepted it, not even when it's five years old, not even when I go to my grave. This worm we see in front of us will never rest easy again. I swear on my mother's grave that I will not rest until he is destroyed in business. He is not fit to run a company.'

He could have sworn Blossom blushed.

The chairman's words of only a few minutes ago were remembered by Kevin. Sympathetic treatment was something he found very difficult to give, but he suddenly knew that across from him was an implacable enemy, someone who had the strength of character to actually frighten Kevin, someone who might actually stand up at an annual general meeting and foul-mouth him. He cringed at the thought of it.

'We are prepared to buy out your contract, James. You have a three-year term, and we will negotiate. A court of law would never award you three years, but I'm sure there is a figure that your lawyers and ours can arrive at. Furthermore, we will pay your legal costs.'

He wiped away an imaginary spec of fluff from his lapel using the movement of the head as a way of avoiding eye contact.

'There is nothing further to say now. The meeting is over.' Kevin shifted the papers in front of him to the side of his desk but made no attempt to get up or to re-establish eye contact.

Joyce thought he was mishearing.

'Pay my legal costs, what on earth for?'

Gordon Blossom came to the rescue.

'Mr Hipkiss is right. There is no point going on with this discussion. I suggest that you consult your solicitors and have them get in touch with me. It is better for the legal brigade to work things out between them. It is also better for you to deal through them, as that way, we will avoid acrimony. We would appreciate it if you would now relinquish your duties and return home. You will be maintained on the payroll for a further three months and have the use of your car and reasonable expenses. You will have no further executive duties, and you are barred from company premises.'

Joyce sat there for a few seconds at a loss for words for once. Paying all the legal costs was a novelty; it suggested to him that he was in a very strong negotiating position, which he would have to exploit as fully as possible. Finally, he stood up pushing the chair backward so violently with his legs that it flew across the thick pile falling onto its back. He took three steps forward and glared down at Hipkiss.

'I don't use words lightly, Hipkiss, nor do I want to give ammunition to your legal eagle here, but let me tell you this. There is no doubt that we will meet again, and if ever you give me the opportunity, or even half an opportunity, to get even with you through legitimate and legal means, I will do so, so keep looking over your shoulder. I curse you by all that is holy and all that is evil. May you rot in hell.'

'Is that a threat?' squeaked Kevin, feeling distinctly uneasy.

'Read into it what you like, you snivelling little ratbag. You don't need a threat from me to frighten you. You will fail anyway—people like you always do.'

John Joyce turned on his heel, leaving Kevin shouting incoherently behind him. He slammed the door with all his might; it rattled Blossom's teeth.

Marcia sprang up from her desk as he sprang through the door.

'What on earth is the matter?' she asked.

Joyce looked at her.

'I'm afraid, dearie, that today, even you are tainted with Hipkiss, and anything that is near to him is far away from me.'

He walked by her and out into the corridor; it was the last time she would ever see him at NTI.

'I'm sorry, James,' she whispered. 'I'm so sorry.'

'My god! How can he treat me like that?' yelled Kevin, addressing no one in particular.

Gordon Blossom agreed it was disgraceful; how anyone would have the temerity to treat his chief executive in that way, he could not imagine. However, the man had gone, and, thankfully, they could now get down to the task of arranging the settlement.

'I want him squeezed,' said Kevin. 'I want the least amount possibly paying out, do you hear?'

'Yes', said Gordon, 'but, unfortunately, James Joyce has one of the old-style contracts signed by the chairman when there was a threat of takeover and long before your time. I can tell you now that Sir Dennis will want to see the settlement on all those contracts, and I think it would be unwise to suggest to him that we do not honour it, at least in substantial part.'

Kevin had had enough.

'OK, OK', he said wearily, 'just see to it, but I want to be kept informed every step of the way, and I want to be involved, because if I can squeeze him, I will.'

'Is that all?' asked Blossom.

'Yes', said Kevin, 'and on your way out, tell that secretary of mine to bring me some decaffeinated coffee.'

Kevin usually enjoyed the challenge of getting rid of someone, but this morning, it had all gone horribly wrong, and it had left him feeling drained and out of sorts. He had not liked being called names, and being intensely superstitious, he was genuinely worried by Joyce's curse; it just wasn't his day.

Chapter 10

Dr George Yoreen sat at his desk in the small office off the main research lab. He was very pleased with himself; in fact, he positively glowed. Thoughts ran through his mind about little luxuries that he would soon be able to afford, little luxuries that he was positive he absolutely and totally deserved for the many years of research he had put in with companies such as NTI that, in his opinion, had been ill rewarded. A brain such as his was a prized possession, not just for himself but for anyone lucky enough to have temporary control of it. The reason for the exquisite pleasure was the bottle that stood on his desk; it was the returned sample from Victor Stanley, so thoughtfully placed there last night with his note of explanation.

Although he was aware that Stanley had taken a sample of the conductive polymer with him to Japan, for some reason, it did not feature positively in his memory at the time of his meeting with Doo-hwan, and now it was indeed manna from heaven.

He picked up the glass bottle that contained 100 ml of the highly valued product and casually inspected it to make sure that it was one of the original sample stock items; it was. He put it down and then took the sample log from the drawer in his desk marked 'Highly Confidential—Company Secret' and noted Victor had signed it back in. The log contained records of sample movements; any product leaving the laboratory had all details recorded with the reason for the movement; everyone had to sign out and in, including the chief executive and the chairman. With any major product, it was an essential feature of making sure that none of their material slipped away into foreign hands. He looked down the log headings to check the quantity, and there it was—Victor Stanley, 30th May, 100 mls SCP, and there followed a special reference number identifying the batch. The purpose for removal was given as 'Japan demonstrations'. He closed the log.

In his mind, Yoreen had already decided upon a plan of action that would hopefully satisfy his chief executive. Within any of his experiments, he was permitted a certain amount of loss because of spillage or degradation. The superconductive polymer was notoriously sensitive to heat in a certain part of its process, and to bring about the essential activity, it had to be brought to within one degree of this critical temperature. Occasionally, because of carelessness or errors in control equipment, this temperature had been exceeded, and small losses had been experienced in the laboratory. There was therefore a precedent that Yoreen hoped to capitalise upon.

He went from his small office into the private laboratory. This was the inner sanctum of the whole research complex, and only Yoreen had direct access to it. Anyone else requiring to enter this area needed clearance by Yoreen operating a security panel on the inside of the door. Hipkiss had even introduced a weekly password as an added safety measure. He placed the bottle on the laboratory bench and then returned to his office, made sure that the outer door was shut but not locked, and returned to the laboratory, closing the connecting door from his office and making sure that the security switch had automatically engaged. To all intents and purposes, he was now able to do anything he liked provided he did it by the rules.

He took from a cupboard above the bench a glass measuring cylinder and poured into this the 50 ml of the liquid contained in the bottle and resealed it. The rest of the material he took over to a large vessel in the corner of the lab marked 'Adulterated SCP Stock', removed the top, and poured the liquid in—if only he had known! Again, he picked up the measuring cylinder, and taking it over to the sink, he carefully washed it out and placed it on the drying rack with several others. Satisfied, he picked up the remaining sample, placed it in his pocket, and returned to his office after keying his pass number into the lock.

At his desk, he again took down the sample log and, against Victor's signature of return, recorded a positive entry of receipt for the sample. He then took from the top left-hand drawer a report form headed 'Losses due to experimental error', and he wrote that 51.3 ml of material had been lost because of thermal degradation and indicated that this was because of his personal error when he was interrupted at a critical moment during confirmation of assay before returning the sample to the temperature controlled bulk stock. When he was reheating it, he forgot to engage the temperature control mechanism and had answered a phone call; the temperature exceeded the safety point, and he lost activity. He knew that Hipkiss would be unhappy about such an entry, but it had happened before, and, after all, he was a trusted member of the team. It was not really sample losses within the laboratory complex that they were worried about anyway; it was losses of samples outside the laboratory that really worried everyone, and, so far, there had been none of these, or so he thought.

He took the bottle out of his pocket and placed it in the centre of his desk and turned his mind to thoughts of how he was going to remove it from the laboratory complex and through the outer gates. There were routine searches sprung on all personnel leaving the laboratory, and no one was immune from this. It was well understood that should anyone be caught with any material whatsoever on him, he would be subject to instant dismissal, whether it was the chairman or a laboratory cleaner.

In the past three months, George Yoreen had been searched twice, and he had once been stopped at the gatehouse and his car had been gone over in minute detail. There was no pattern to these searches, and it was therefore a risk that he was sure he had to take; he couldn't see any satisfactory way around it. He knew that later in the day, he had to report to Hipkiss to bring him up-to-date with the latest developments in the research programme and the state of commercial development for the new product. As the pilot plant was now beginning to produce this material in kilo lots, he knew that they were approaching their most critical phase, that of full market evaluation. Security would be at its tightest.

George Yoreen was a creature of habit, and rather than interrupt his day by going to the canteen, he invariably brought with him a small lunch, which was prepared by Sybil. This consisted of a plastic box that contained sandwiches, a piece of fruit, and a flask, which usually contained some soup. At the moment, these two items resided in the bottom right-hand drawer of his desk, and he pulled it open and lifted out the flask. It was one of the wide-necked variety that allowed one to put in it things that contained more body than just tea or coffee, and on this day, it contained some oxtail soup. He looked at his watch; it was near enough to oxtail soup time, and he took the large outer cap off, and, unscrewing the inner cup, he was greeted by a puff of steam and a most appetising smell.

He poured the soup into the outer cap, but having done this, he did not pick it up but instead picked up the sample bottle that was on his desk and tested it for size to see if it would go through the orifice and into the flask; it would.

The degradation temperature of the polymer was in excess of one hundred degrees centigrade, a temperature never reached by his soup. Releasing the bottle into the flask, he poured back into it enough soup to fill it and consumed the balance. The dark top of the bottle bobbed around just below the surface of the soup, but a casual glance would not necessarily reveal that there was anything amiss. He returned the inner stopper and, having wiped out the outer cup with some tissues from his desk, which he dropped into his waste paper basket, he then replaced first the inner cup and screwed on the outer cup.

He went over in his mind again the steps that he had taken, for it was essential that he did not make a mistake and that he was not caught. The fear of being caught was only outweighed by the absolute horror of foregoing £1 million, and he was as confident as he could be that the £1 million was coming his way and very shortly. He studied the box of sandwiches but really hadn't the stomach for them, as there was a small knot of fear and trepidation in his belly.

Instead, he picked up a packet of Benson & Hedges cigarettes, which he occasionally smoked, and lit one. He drew in the smoke deeply and exhaled it in a fine mist and repeated the exercise. He felt better; at this point in time, lung cancer was the very last of all his worries.

The phone rang, and he almost leaped out of his skin and took a few seconds to adjust himself to its strident tonal demand. He picked up the receiver.

'George', said his secretary, 'don't forget that your appointment with Mr Hipkiss is at three o'clock, and he doesn't like you to be late. Oh, and don't forget to take the sample log with you.'

'Yes, yes, I know,' said George, somewhat testily.

'Oh, and don't forget, George', said the secretary, 'that at two o'clock, there is a routine fire test, and we have to assemble at the stipulated assembly point.'

'Ah! Thank you, Monica,' said George, rapidly gathering his thoughts together.

A routine fire test, a routine fire test. What happened when they had a routine fire test? The alarm sounded, and everyone had to leave the laboratories and assemble at a collection point, and all this had to be done in a time scale that usually meant you dropped what you were doing and just got out. The dates and times of such tests were known only to the heads of department in order that they could be as realistic as possible, and it was the only time that laboratory fire exits were used without triggering the security alarm, which would have been neutralised at the central control. Dr Yoreen saw the opportunity and grasped it. The routine search system would be suspended to allow people to get out quickly, and if George had his briefcase ready, he could carry it out of the building with him. He took the flask and sandwich box and put them back in the case and closed the catches.

That left the car itself and the possibility of a search at the outer gate. George felt the risk was low. After a fire test, they would hardly stop the technical director on his way to see Kevin Hipkiss. He planned accordingly.

At exactly two o'clock, a klaxon-like sound ripped through the laboratory complex. People everywhere were conscious that this could be a routine test alarm, but, nevertheless, they were never actually sure. It could be a fire or it could be an escape of some poisonous chemical within the complex itself, and the rules were quite simple: if you didn't get a wriggle on and get to the assembly point on time, you were in trouble. Mistakes were not tolerated twice; they became a disciplinary matter and could result in dismissal. It was for their own good after all.

Staff everywhere virtually dropped what they were doing. Those in charge of specific key reactions threw the emergency switches on the apparatus, which would ensure that all heat and power was switched off. Several experiments would be ruined, but this was an acceptable risk. Those who were close to essential papers picked them up and tucked them under their arms. George Yoreen, now very adequately prepared, picked up his briefcase, walked through his secretary's office, and headed down the corridor to the main assembly point in front of the canteen. The chief fire officer talked over a handheld radio until he received reports from each of the groups that the full complement of people, as signed in that day through the attendance log, had been accounted for. He looked at a stopwatch in his other hand and went over to George.

'That was a pretty good exit, Doctor. You should be pleased with them, but we've got to keep them on their toes, and I think we need another lecture in a couple of weeks' time to go over the basic facts of survival.'

'Good, good,' said George. 'Now, you will have to excuse me, Mr Smith, but I have an appointment with the chief executive, and I am already hideously late.'

'I'm sorry, sir,' said David Smith. 'Allow me to escort you to the gate,' and walking with George, they rapidly covered the ground to the car park, and David Smith got in the passenger seat, much to George's delight. He started the engine and headed for the gate. Once there, the security guard on duty, a grim-faced man in a black uniform who would have been at home in the SS, held up an imperious hand. The car came to a halt, and David Smith got out.

'It's all right, Simpson. I can vouch for the good doctor here. The fire drill has made him late for an appointment with Mr Hipkiss.'

'I don't know about that, Mr Smith,' said the terrifying Simpson. 'I have to routinely inspect vehicles, you know, and occasionally the person in them.'

'Yes, I know, Mr Simpson', said David Smith, 'but this is the head of research, I am the chief fire officer, this is a company car, and it is hardly likely Dr Yoreen is running off with the company secrets on his way to London, is it now?'

'Well, I suppose not, sir', said Simpson, 'but, nevertheless, perhaps you'd just happen to open the boot.'

Exasperated, George passed him the keys. He was sure that the man would notice his nervousness, and he could feel colour coming into his face; his hands also felt clammy as he returned them to the wheel. David Smith accompanied Simpson to the rear of the car. The key was inserted, the boot lid opened, a bit of rummaging occurred, and a mat was lifted. Simpson reappeared at the door and handed George the keys.

'All right, sir, that'll be all. Thank you very much. Sorry to have delayed you.'

George felt that under these circumstances, servility was the best routine.

'That's all right, Mr Simpson. You are only doing your job, and I hope you continue to do it just as assiduously following any emergency. We have many secrets to protect in here, and we rely on you, you know.'

'Thank you very much, sir,' said Simpson.

David Smith made sure the passenger door was shut and tapped smartly on the roof with his hands to indicate that all was clear, and George pulled out of the exit and into the avenue and headed east for London. Fortunately, it was one of those fairly routine journeys without too much traffic at a sensible time of the day, and he was in the car park underneath head office at ten minutes to three.

He looked carefully around him in the gloom; there was no one evident. He took the briefcase off the back seat and, putting it on his knee, released the catches. Inside was the flask containing the sample, and he picked it up and fondly examined it; it was his passport to a fortune, and he smiled self-consciously. Leaning over to his left, he opened the glovebox and popped the flask inside and then took his ignition key and locked it. He put the sandwich box on the passenger seat, and taking his briefcase with him, he got out of the car and locked the doors. He walked across the gloomy parking area to the lift. There was a keypad at the lift in order that unwanted visitors could be kept out. He keyed the current access number, and a light came on acknowledging his signal and the lift was on its way. A few minutes later, he was letting himself out on the executive floor, and walking over to the reception desk, he announced himself to the young lady who sat behind it; he never knew who they were because they seemed to change so regularly, but this one was certainly an attractive addition to the premises.

'Mr Hipkiss is expecting me,' he said.

'And you are, sir?' she asked.

'Dr George Yoreen.' He smiled his most ingratiating smile; she returned it brightly.

'Thank you, Dr Yoreen. I will just get in touch with his secretary. Please be seated.'

George sat down and was sorry that the desk hid what he took to be a very good pair of legs beneath the excellent little body. Unfortunately, they weren't a very pleasant little pair of legs beneath the body; they were rather short and dumpy, and the regret of her life, George was never to find that out.

'Do you know where Mr Hipkiss's office is, Dr Yoreen? You are expected.'

'Thank you. Yes, I know,' said George and wandered along the carpeted corridor and into Marcia Payne's office.

'Hello, George. You can go straight in.'

'Thank you, Marcia,' he responded and walked through the half-open door into the presence.

Hipkiss got up from behind his desk and walked round towards George and held his hand out. It was a while since they had seen each other. Hipkiss believed in looking after and making a fuss of the technical brains in his organisation; after all, it was probably they who would make him glorious.

'Hello, George. Let's go and sit over there and make ourselves comfortable.'

Sitting 'over there' was the small area laid aside by Hipkiss for his guests. The chairs offered were extremely low and uncomfortable with an equally low and uncomfortable coffee table. Hipkiss had selected them personally; his taste was not always perfect in these things. George curled his long legs up as best he could.

'Something rather funny appears to have been going on last night, George,' said Kevin.

'What do you mean?'

'Well, I rang Victor Stanley's place yesterday only to find that he wasn't lying in bed after his long flight from the East but was in fact out at the labs, and there was no reason why he had to go there so soon after his return. I would have liked to have seen him first.'

George knew instinctively that Kevin would resent the fact that he had not been the first person to speak to Victor, but he had only seen his note and spoken to him briefly on the phone this morning. He would suspect, of course, that Victor had said things to him that Kevin could now no longer claim as his own words of wisdom. Kevin always liked to be a carrier of special news and views.

'What did he want, George?'

'Not much,' said George. 'He was just worried that the sample he had been carrying around with him should be returned safely into stock, and I think he felt it safer to get it to me to re-enter it into the log as rapidly as possible. Rather than bring them into the office here this morning, for them to be transported back to me later, he felt it would be safer to return them directly. Anyway, I understand he is seeing you immediately after me, so you haven't missed anything, have you?'

'No, not really, I suppose', said Kevin, 'but, nevertheless, I would like to have confirmed that those samples went back into stock.'

'Well, of course, they went back into stock,' said George. 'I am hardly likely to be sitting here and telling you that he delivered them if he didn't.'

Kevin scratched his nose, sniffed, looked speculatively at George, and said, 'Mm, I'd better have a look at the sample log, then.'

George dutifully opened his briefcase and handed over the sample log. Kevin looked through it. The last entry was quite clear—the sample logged back in by George Yoreen, code numbers were correct, and he had no reason to have any doubts about the situation, yet somehow, something niggled at the back of Kevin's mind; it just didn't seem absolutely natural. He dug a bit deeper.

'George, we have a wastage factor in connection with these samples, don't we?'

'Yes, we do,' said George, raising an eyebrow quizzically. What on earth was he going on about now?

'Well, what would you say was the normal wastage factor nowadays, based on the average since the start of the SCP project?'

George thought. He knew what the answer was, but he wanted a bit of time. He looked around him and then rummaged in his briefcase, took out a small notebook, and had a look at the last set of analysis figures he had in there; they were quite meaningless now.

'About 12 per cent.'

'Why do we lose such a high percentage?' asked Kevin.

'Well, you are bound to lose a high percentage when you are playing with lots of small samples. You get the stuff that sticks to the glass and spillage. There is evaporation and degradation because of heat. There is even destruction when we lay down material in the user state. It all amounts to a tidy sum. In fact, I think we do remarkably well to hold it at the present level and would not be surprised to see the figure rise next time we calculate the average.'

'What about the material that we incinerate?'

George started to get slightly worried. This was digging deeper than he had expected. He gathered his thoughts again.

'The material that goes for incineration is relatively straightforward. We start each month with good stock, which includes new product and old product that is uncontaminated. At the end of each month, the contaminated material is incinerated. The good stock varies in activity because of dilution and evaporation factors, but we can compensate for that when we use it.'

Kevin kept his own record of the figures each month. It was safe to trust no one. On his calculations, the actual loss factor was 11.7 per cent. Again, a small alarm bell rang in his mind.

'Surely, George, we can't be consistent on a 12 per cent loss?'

'No.' said George. 'It's an average, but for the past few months, it has been fairly consistent, but as I said, it is starting to shift as the experimental programme increases and we use more material.'

'How do you check to make certain there are no losses because of pilferage, George?'

The question was totally unexpected, and there was a straightforward and simple answer, but George was wondering whether this might not get him into extremely deep water.

'What do you mean?' he said.

'Well, there must be some sort of precaution you take to make sure product does not leave the premises apart from the security system.'

'Well, we're not having product stolen. We're a secure laboratory, we have searches on the gate, we have absolutely routine test procedures, and it would need collusion to move any significant quantity out of the laboratory. Besides which the log books quite clearly show you that there is no movement of material. Every experiment requires two signatures to sign on and off. All product issued must have my signature, and at the end of each experiment, I am responsible for logging back in unused product and agreeing the amount used with the team.'

'What if we did a calculation on the activity of the material taken back into stock, George?'

Kevin looked him straight in the eye. He didn't often do that to a subordinate, but every now and then, he summoned up the courage.

George thought frantically about the right response to this awful question. There was no doubt that if the activity of the redundant material was checked, it would reveal any discrepancy between apparent stock and calculated activity. No material had been stolen. George's explanation of losses would therefore cover any loss of activity.

'Losses are always explained, Kevin, for whatever reason. If we lose activity during laboratory experimentation, there is a procedure for logging that just as we log movement of product. Every month, we incinerate all redundant stock, and a regular assay is carried out to compare actual activity with the calculated activity, and that, too, is a matter of record. There has never been a material difference between the two figures.'

'All right, George, I believe you, but I would have been much happier if Stanley had returned the sample in a more conventional manner.'

George was only too delighted he had not.

The records having been inspected and George having reported progress, he was told it was not fast enough, but then he was allowed to escape.

On his way out, George asked Marcia the whereabouts of Victor Stanley.

'He's back in his office, George. I know Kevin wants to see him in a matter of minutes, so if you need him, hurry up.'

George went off down the corridor and knocked on Victor's door.

'Come in.'

'I hope you don't mind, Victor, but there were a few points I wanted to go over with you before you go and see the lovely Kevin.'

'That's fine, George. Draw up a chair.'

He did and lowered himself into it with a sigh.

'You sound troubled, old Doctor. What's the matter?'

'Hipkiss fired John Joyce just before I saw him. I can't think why. He was such an efficient man, so well liked.'

It came as a nasty surprise to Victor. He was on a similar level, and Hipkiss was getting through too many. It made him all the more vulnerable if any scandal should break following the problems in Japan.

'The bastard. Is there no end to the man's jealousy, to his inadequacy? He hates anyone near him to succeed, so now one of our most able divisional MDs goes too. It won't be long before you and me get hit, George.'

'I have no intention of that. I am planning an early retirement. He's not going to get me. You should do the same.'

'I prefer to hang on, George, in the hope I can see Kevin get his just rewards. If he wants to fire me, he can do so. I'll take the money and go, but not quietly. How come you can afford it anyway? You're always pleading poverty.'

'Maybe a fairy godmother will appear, Vic. Watch this space. Seriously, though, watch yourself with Hipkiss. He doesn't like the way you returned the sample—thinks there is something fishy about it, is there?'

'No. I wanted it back in safekeeping, as I said in my note. I presume you logged it back in?'

'Of course, I did. It didn't give me a problem, but Hipkiss put me through the hoop anyway worrying about activity of redundant stock. I told him there wasn't a problem. Did I do wrong?'

'Not as far as I am concerned, George. There was nothing wrong with my product.'

The phone rang. Victor picked it up and agreed with the caller that he would be straight along.

'George, you have got to excuse me. That was Hipkiss, so now it's my turn to be put through the hoop!'

Victor gathered together some papers as George left the office.

'Good luck, Victor. Let me know how you get on.'

'Yes, I'll call you.'

Victor walked to Hipkiss's office, and Marcia smiled as he entered the outer area.

'He's eating nails today, Victor, so be careful dear.'

'I'm a big boy now, Marcia. I can deal with most of what Mr Hipkiss can throw at me, but thanks for the warning.'

Hipkiss did not get up to greet his guest but merely pointed to a seat and carried on writing something on a pad while Victor settled himself. He was rounding off an aide memoir to cover the conversation with Victor, for, despite the chairman's warning about his views concerning senior staff, Kevin was going to have things done his way.

There was no welcome home, no praise for a job well done.

'I've been talking to the chairman about your sales role, Victor. I think it is time to bring in some new blood, get some young talent trained up, you know, while you are still here to guide them. Good idea, don't you think?'

Victor had had no time to think; his instant reaction was defensive.

'I hardly expected this when I had come to report to you about Japan. I heard you had fired John Joyce today, a good friend of mine and a good managing director. Is it my turn now?'

'Don't be so sensitive, Victor. You are doing a good job in your own fashion. I'm not going to comment on Joyce. I'll just pretend you never mentioned it.'

But he made a margin note nevertheless that Victor had mentioned it.

'It's time to think about the future, and I want to plan for orderly succession.'

'Well, I don't want to give up any part of my job. I am stimulated by it and do it well, and, furthermore, I have a good few years to go yet before I want to take it easy. You will have to push me. I won't volunteer to go.'

Kevin huffed and puffed for a bit, but either he had had enough of pushing people around today or he was prepared to wait. They talked on for a bit and reached some sort of general understanding that they would meet again to discuss matters in more detail and that Victor would, for the time being, be limited to his Far Eastern projects and one or two other minor commercial development aspects as well as the superconductive polymer project sales development.

He then turned to the sample.

'Why did you take the sample out to the research labs last night?'

'Because it seemed a sensible thing to do. I wanted to get it back into a secure area with George Yoreen and have him check it into the sample log as soon as he arrived this morning.'

'You could have brought it here,' said Hipkiss. 'I could have checked it in for you and saved you the trouble.'

This was Mr Nice speaking, and there wasn't any such thing, so he had to have an ulterior motive.

'Well, I didn't bring it here, but by now, it will be logged back in, and George Yoreen will have it if you want it.'

'I've already talked to George about it.'

'You have?'

'Yes.'

'Well, you know the facts, then.'

He hesitated.

'I have instituted some enquiries with George. I have asked him what the wastage of these technical samples is, and I have asked him how we can check this. You know how terribly important this project is to us and how disturbing it would be if any of this material fell into the hands of a competitor.'

Victor knew now why he'd wanted the sample back in his own hands. He had wanted to make damn sure that he hadn't lost any or given any away, and he breathed an inward sigh of relief.

'Well, none's got to any competitor from me. You can see that it was logged back in and there was no problem anywhere. George will have completed his tests on it, so they must be good too. Otherwise, you would have heard. What exactly have you asked George to do?'

'I have asked him', said Hipkiss, 'to keep a log of the material that goes for incineration and to determine the activity of that material immediately prior to incineration. This way, we will be able to make sure that any reduction in activity can be spotted and reasons investigated in case a non-active dilution has taken place. I have asked him to start this new check with the current disposal batch that is due for incineration in a week's time.'

This was riveting stuff! Victor had hoped George would come up with a rational explanation to cover any discrepancies; he hadn't mentioned this bit of his conversation with Kevin.

Victor looked at his watch; it was nearly five o'clock. He was tired; he wanted a drink and to go home.

'Is there anything else?' he said.

'No, not really,' said Kevin. 'I'll be in touch.'

He was dismissed.

Chapter 11

The window overlooked a particularly expensive sector of Hyde Park; it was a deep bay. There were window seats within the bay covered in a rich orange-and-gold fabric with a fleur-de-lis design. Seated in one corner, her legs resting on the surface of the cushions, was Veronica Tan. She was dressed in a loose-fitting black silk trouser suit, and she watched with interest the activities in the park and the horses that carried a certain class of person that she would never be.

When she had left Victor at the airport, there had been a momentary feeling of intense loss, as though something good had left her life forever. She had a mission to carry out; her loyalties were stretched rather like a double agent, and she wasn't quite sure at the moment just whose side she was on. Allegiances formed too quickly could affect the final decisions that she would have to make; she'd liked Victor, of course, and his gentility and concern and even his lovemaking, which had quite surprised her. He was a far cry from Doo-hwan, whose instructions had been clarity itself. She had gone to the apartment as instructed. The fax that had arrived for her had said simply, 'Stay there and await my call.' She was doing exactly that.

The sumptuous luxury with which she was surrounded was a product of Doo-hwan's illegal activities and was owned by a man of some importance in local and government politics. On occasions such as this, he withdrew to a small house in the country and left important visitors in the hands of a manservant who doubled as a very adequate bodyguard, housekeeper, cook, and chauffeur. It was he who brought the silver tray into the room and placed it on a small table close to Veronica. She looked at him speculatively wondering at the sort of exercise that had to be undertaken to keep his body in the shape and state that it was; she wondered what he would look like without any clothes and shuddered a little. She had not been overimpressed by muscle-bound men; in her opinion, they were short in brain and in other areas too, and she smiled to herself.

'Will there be anything else, madam?' It wasn't quite a sneer.

'Yes. I am expecting a call from Doo-hwan. I would appreciate it if I could have the portable phone. It will save me having to use the one in the hall.'

He went in search of it and a few minutes later brought it to her. She put it down beside her and turned once again to look out into the park; it was a dismissive gesture. The sun was shining as it had nearly all this English summer; the grass was turning brown. Two children walked a dog, which seemed capable of carrying them both on its back. How differently the world reacted to dogs, she thought, here, they were worshipped, while in China they were eaten. She turned back and picked up the elegant Georgian silver pot that contained the coffee and poured it into a Royal Worcester cup to which she added a little cream. She had to admit that she liked the style. She raised the cup and took a sip of the highly roasted brew that the flat's master kept as his standard offering.

In Singapore, it was the end of the day. It had been an unremarkable day, hot and humid like almost any other. Doo-hwan had remained at his desk, in offices close to the exclusive Goodwood Park Hotel, all the working hours except for a short break to take lunch with a client. The client had been in a nervous state; he was short on his purchase quota of a certain forbidden item that he was contracted to take from Doo-hwan. He feared that this lucrative source of income would be cut off to him and had been at pains to explain to Doo-hwan, while little trolleys of dim sum plied their way between the tables, that it was not entirely his fault. Doo-hwan knew this but felt that it was good to keep him nervous whilst giving words of encouragement. Nervousness in the presence of Doo-hwan was not difficult; almost everyone who came within the orbit of his terrifying smile knew that. Doo-hwan had gently let it be known that failure to catch up with the backlog would perhaps result in the client being cut into as many little pieces as there were in the dish of rice he stirred idly with a chopstick. The client had lost his appetite, and Doo-hwan had gone home amused at the power of the spoken word.

The office was in a corner of a new business centre built for small users of space who liked luxury with discretion; it was on the third floor. Unpretentious from the outside and only moderately luxurious by Singapore standards on the inside, it created an impression of normality. The nameplates that were screwed to the wall outside these offices proclaimed them to be the headquarters of several entirely legitimate enterprises; they were also a cover for other undisclosed activities. Clients were reassured by the surroundings; they had the right balance and feel about them, for Doo-hwan had discovered a long time ago that the particular type of businessmen he wished to attract into his web had a deep resentment at the display of too much luxury, which was viewed as being directly proportional to the prices he would be paying for his product, whatever the product might be. Doo-hwan pressed the world time button on his organiser and keyed in London; the digital display told him it was two minutes to ten in the morning. He picked up the phone and dialled a number.

The strangulated electronic sound that indicated the portable phone was ringing made Veronica jump. She picked it up and pressed the receive button. The voice at the other end identified itself and proceeded to give her instructions with regard to the next stage of the job. She listened carefully and made notes on a small pad she had recovered from the table. It was time for the good doctor to deliver.

At last, she was released from the need to remain in the flat, and she set about planning her meeting to pick up the sample and to make arrangements for the delivery of the money. The operation was now entering a critical stage, and a sixth sense told her that there was danger and even death in the air.

Later the same day, Sybil Yoreen received a telephone call at home politely asking that when Dr Yoreen returned that evening, perhaps he would be kind enough to telephone a London number. Sybil carefully noted it down and assured the caller that he would. When she replaced the receiver, her hand trembled a little, and there passed through her mind thoughts of substantial wealth and tranquillity, a retirement present undreamed of and one that was surely free of danger. She hardly suspected what could go wrong, and had she done so at this moment, things might have been different.

The sample that Dr Yoreen had spirited away from the laboratory had been carefully hidden in a corner of his apartment and was now ready to begin its long journey of conspiracy and treachery.

Sybil Yoreen recovered this sample from under the floorboard in the corner of the dining area and put it in her small suitcase that she used when they went to their little house in Cirencester at the weekend. She carefully locked up the apartment at the appropriate time and drove her car to the research laboratories, where she parked outside the security gate. The guards knew her well, for this was a ritual that had been going on for a good many years, and she got out and went over to the gatehouse to talk to them while she awaited the good doctor.

People were now beginning to stream away from the complex looking forward to their weekend of relaxation. Some would spend it in hard physical activity; others would spend it eating and drinking. Some would spend it miserably in the company of wives and husbands they had come to detest, and some would have what they referred to as a normal existence, if that word could ever describe anything anymore.

George suddenly appeared in the crowd and walked purposefully towards the security exit. Every now and again, one of the security guards signalled to a member of the crowd leaving the establishment, and they went into a small room where a random search was carried out. George was today one of those people.

'I am sorry, Dr Yoreen, but you are on the list today,' said the guard.

George smiled expansively.

'That's no problem, Harry,' he said, and he went into the search area where the guard apologetically made him turn out his pockets, inspected his briefcase, and gave him a perfunctory body search of the sort carried out at some of the world's airports you would rather not travel through.

'You're clean, Doctor,' said the guard Harry, and George went on his way emerging from the outer door of the security office and kissed Sybil warmly on the cheek. She returned to the passenger seat of the car, and George eased himself in behind the wheel for the relatively short run to Cirencester, always assuming, of course, that the M4 was not snarled up with an accident.

As the car moved away, Sybil could not contain her excitement any longer.

'It's happened, George,' she said.

George glanced briefly towards her and then back to the road; he knew instinctively what she meant.

'You mean they want the sample?'

'Yes. The money's ours.'

George could hardly contain his own excitement. It was what he had always dreamed of—creating the perfect product and getting handsomely rewarded for it. He would have preferred it if the company would have come up with a similar package, but there was no way that they recognised his genius in the way he did. There was no way that they would reward him in the way that Doo-hwan would, and he argued with himself that it was, after all, only a commercial development and he was only embarking in a bit of industrial malpractice. It was done all the time. He supposed that it was also vaguely criminal this stealing the secrets of the company, but, again, his own morals suggested to him that as the product was his invention, he could hardly steal it. Anyway, it would take NTI some time to realise that another organization had something similar, and it was unlikely that they would connect it with treachery of their director of research.

The journey to the small house in Cirencester was a light-hearted affair, and they talked much of the need now to have a break and the fact that, almost immediately, they would have the sort of funds available to them that would permit such a break. George had holiday due, and they decided that if all went well, they would fly to Nice for a few days next week, if they could get in. Sybil would go down to the travel agent in the town tomorrow morning and make appropriate enquiries.

They turned off the M4 at junction 15, and it was then only a short journey to their weekend retreat. George parked the car in the street and, having recovered the small suitcase, locked it. They went over to the bright yellow door, inserted the key, and entered. There was an immediate sounding of the security system alarm, and George keyed the code into the little box on the wall; it stopped.

Sybil disappeared into the kitchen and set about opening windows and switching various devices on that would be needed for their weekend comfort. George took the suitcase upstairs, opened it, and took out the box containing the stolen liquid. He opened the wardrobe and placed the box behind a pile of shirts on the top shelf. He straightened them self-consciously, looked in the mirror, winked at himself, and went downstairs to the kitchen, where Sybil was struggling with a bottle of wine. He took it from her and opened it; it was icy cold from a week in the fridge, and he poured them each a glass, handing one to Sybil and raising the other to his lips.

'Well, old girl, it looks as though we can plan our retirement now,' and he put his arm round her shoulders and squeezed. 'Won't that be wonderful? No more hassle, no more worries, just a life of idleness doing what we want to when we want to do it. I might even give the odd lecture, always provided someone pays my expenses, of course. However, first things first, I suppose I had better make the telephone call.'

Sybil opened her handbag and took out the piece of paper with the number scrawled on it. George took it from her and went into the small sitting room. He picked the phone up from the bookcase in the corner and dialled the number.

The phone rang three times before Veronica Tan picked it up for the second time that day and pressed the receive button. She recognised instantaneously the nervous tones of a dishonest man.

'This is Dr Yoreen. I have received a message to call this number.'

'Thank you, Dr Yoreen. My name is Veronica, that is all you need to know. You have in your possession a certain article that I am required to pick up and transport. You can also confirm, please, the reference for that article. Do you understand what I am talking about?'

George Yoreen understood only too well; his instructions had been crystal clear and had included in the detail a reference number for the time when he was contacted. He now articulated the coded reference number into the mouthpiece and received back the correct reply.

'How shall I get this to you?' asked George. 'Do you want me to bring it up to London, or will you come here?'

Veronica had also received clear instructions from Doo-hwan and told George that she would leave immediately for Cirencester and would pick up the sample during the hours of darkness that very evening. She expected to be in the area at 9:00 p.m., and she would visit the back door of his cottage, where he would hand over the sample, and she would depart immediately.

'As far as I know, Veronica', said George, 'you don't even know where I live or the local geography or the layout of my house to enable you to get to the back door easily. This is a little terrace block, and you have to go around the back and down a small passageway before you can find me.'

'I am fully familiar, Doctor, with the geography,' she said. 'I have studied the route for quite some time in order that I am not conspicuous. Please don't worry about how I'm going to get there. Just be ready with the sample and make my job easy. In return for the sample, I will give to you an envelope, which will provide the necessary information on how to obtain the money, which will be your fee for stage one of this transaction.'

George heard the change in tone as the line went dead; she had hung up. He looked at the receiver and put it slowly down.

In London, Veronica pressed a small bell push, and the muscular John Lawson appeared in the doorway in a surprisingly frilly apron, which she assumed must belong to the lady of the house. How wrong she was.

'John, I want to be in Cirencester at about nine o'clock. I will give you instructions how we'll locate the man I wish to see when we get there. When do we need to leave?'

John looked at his watch and made a rough calculation. 'I think, to be safe, we should leave right now, Ms Tan, for even if we travel fast, we'll not be there before nine thirty.'

'OK', said Veronica, 'let's get moving. I'll just grab a jacket, and you get the car out. I'll meet you downstairs in the garage in five minutes.'

John gave a small bow and withdrew. He unfastened the bow at the back of the apron, folded it up, and put it carefully away in a kitchen drawer that contained several others. Had she seen into his bedroom, she would have been surprised at the range of other outfits that pleased John Lawson and his employer, whose particular predilections encompassed many forms of sexual deviation.

She went into her bedroom and picked up from the bed, where she had left it, a black silk blouson that would make her almost invisible in the dark. She took the lift down to the basement garage, where the black Rolls-Royce awaited her with the engine purring quietly. John sprang out and went round to the back door.

'No, I'll travel up front,' she said and climbed into the dark interior and snapped shut the safety belt as John closed the door. They drove up the ramp and into the night air and turned west. As soon as John was clear of the town, he put his foot down, and the large machine gathered speed at a surprising rate. He turned off the M4 at exactly nine o'clock. Being late didn't particularly worry Veronica, for she knew that George Yoreen wasn't going anywhere, and she took a certain pleasure in the agitation she knew would build up as the clock passed 9:00 p.m.

George Yoreen looked at his watch for the hundredth time. It was now twenty minutes to ten, and he was becoming extremely nervous.

Seated across from him, even Sybil was beginning to look worried.

'Where the hell is she?' said George. 'Surely something must have gone wrong. She wouldn't be this late on purpose, would she?'

'What did she say exactly, George?'

'She said she'd be here at around nine.'

'Well, stop worrying, then. It's only twenty to ten, and that's not far from nine. She'll be here. The stakes are too high for her not to be.'

Another ten minutes passed very slowly, and, suddenly, there it was; the small bell that was attached to the back door burst into life. To George, it sounded as though a fire alarm had started, and he shot out of his seat as though jet propelled and raced into the kitchen with indecent haste.

A few hundred yards from where George Yoreen's house was located, the black Rolls-Royce stood at the side of the road. The driver sat behind the wheel, and the engine was running; the car displayed no lights. A policeman emerged from a small alley further up the street and, stepping out, looked first one way and then the other. He saw the large black car. He withdrew into the shelter of the alley again and took out a packet of cigarettes and, stepping backwards into a recessed doorway, lit one of them and thought about his girlfriend, with whom he would rather be passing the evening than on a routine patrol in this very quiet little town that had little crime. He smoked the cigarette in a leisurely fashion, and when he emerged again from the alley, he saw the black car was still there. He thought it strange at this time of the evening that such a vehicle should be parked there, and his curiosity aroused. He walked over the street for a closer look; it was a Rolls-Royce.

The policeman then noticed that a man was seated in the driving seat and that the engine was running. Not wishing to expose himself unduly, he retreated again into the passage having noted the registration number. Using his small radio, he now put out an enquiry as to the pedigree of the car and received back the information that the car belonged to a gentleman whose name was known to him; he was advised to leave it alone. Leaving it alone was one thing; waiting and watching, another. He waited and watched.

George tore open the back door and, looking ahead and slightly down, saw a small figure all in black with a pale face glowing in the reflected light from the kitchen. The face spoke.

'I am Veronica, Doctor. Have you the sample?'

George had left it in the sitting room.

'Just a moment, just a moment,' he said and rushed back into the house and picked up the box from the sitting room before returning to the back door, holding it in front of him, right arm extended, as though it was a bomb about to go off. He thrust it into the hands of the girl, and she turned and vanished down the passageway.

Surprised, he looked at his other hand and found in it an envelope; it was anonymous and brown and had no lettering on it. George carefully locked the door, and returning to the sitting room in a state of extreme nervousness, he thrust the envelope into Sybil's hands.

'You open it, Sybil.'

She put her finger under the flap and tore it open along the top and withdrew from the envelope a sheet of paper with typing on it. This revealed the name and address of a bank. Looking again into the envelope, she found a small key in the very bottom. She handed the two items to George. He was surprised that the bank was in London. He thought it would have been a Swiss bank, but closer examination made him realise that the number was not an account number and that the key must be to a safety deposit box.

Veronica walked quickly down the passage and, after a couple of turns, emerged into the street where the car was parked. The policeman did not notice her until she was virtually inside the Rolls-Royce because the black costume and black hair was as good as a camouflage outfit, and she had moved without sound in her black trainers. He could not tell from this distance whether the figure that entered the passenger seat of the Rolls-Royce was male or female. The lights came on; the driver indicated his intention to draw out into the road and did so. The policeman having seen nothing suspicious lost interest and resumed his lonely walk through the town.

The car moved back to London at a more pedestrian pace, not wishing to attract unwelcome attention.

Back in the apartment, Veronica put the box in her room.

In Singapore, it was 8:00 a.m., and despite it being Saturday, Doo-hwan was at his desk. He was there ten minutes later when the phone rang, and his great face turned into a smile of genuine pleasure at the news that was imparted to him. The sample was secure.

George Yoreen was too excited to sleep, but beside him, his wife, Sybil, sibilantly snored while he imagined cavorting through the surf of a desert island accompanied by a bevy of nubile maidens intent upon acceding to his every whim. He felt an urgent need to possess one of them, but reality being what it is, he had to satisfy himself with the considerably less nubile wife, who nevertheless gave up on the snoring and was surprisingly compliant for the hour. It was only then that George finally lost consciousness.

On the other hand, Veronica Tan, having delivered the good news to Singapore, slept soundly all night knowing the following day, she would have to take the thirteen-hour flight back home, acting as the courier.

Sybil went down to the travel agent the following morning and secured for herself and George a flight to Nice on Wednesday and booked a double room for them at the Hotel Westminster. To her disappointment, she had been unable to get into the famed Negresco as some international congress had filled nearly all the rooms between Cannes and Monte Carlo. She returned to the small house and gave the good news to George.

Early on Monday morning, they took their usual drive back to London, and she dropped George at the research centre and returned to the flat.

George went into his office and rang Kevin Hipkiss to inform him that he was having a short break from tomorrow, Tuesday, to the following Monday. Hipkiss was not pleased; he had had a weekend of indifferent entertainment and had actually had to tolerate sitting next to a table where several Californian gentlemen were smoking large Havana cigars, still illegal in USA, which had given him a headache and put him in such a bad mood on the Sunday evening that he had been completely unable to accomplish an act of seduction on a young lady he had been pursuing for some time. She had told him in no uncertain terms what she thought about his bad-tempered efforts and his lack of prowess as a lover. He had no doubt that a further attempt would be futile. He therefore took his anger and frustration out on George Yoreen point-blank, refusing his permission.

Normally, George would have accepted the bad-tempered refusal, but today was different. Today, he had a substantial sum of money in the bank and he didn't actually need the job anymore, and he therefore told Kevin that as he was entitled to his break, he was taking it, and if he didn't like it, it was just too 'bloody bad'.

Hipkiss was incoherent with rage but was as impotent to stop it as he was impotent the last evening to accomplish the simple act of seduction. He needed Dr Yoreen for the completion of the tricky work that was required to establish the full commercial process for the invaluable polymer, and he informed his long-suffering secretary to let George know later in the day that he had thought over his decision and reluctantly acquiesced to his request. He also took a small book from the locked drawer of his desk and looked up a telephone number and dialled it on his private line. A female voice at the other end of the phone answered, and an appointment was made for that evening when Kevin's sexual prowess would not be questioned.

For George, it was a long and tedious day, and each minute seemed to last an hour. He could not concentrate his thoughts on anything in particular, and his surprised staff agreed behind his back that a holiday was long overdue.

At eleven o'clock on the Tuesday morning, George entered the doors of the bank, and at the enquiries desk, he was guided to the section that dealt with safety deposit boxes. A young man asked him for his name and his identification number.

George wrote this down on a piece of paper and handed it to him. He was shown to a small private room where he was left alone. George took out a large and rather grubby white handkerchief and wiped away the moisture that had gathered on his upper lip. The room reminded him of a prison cell; it was not a nice room.

The young man returned with a large steel box and placed it on the table in front of George.

'I will need your key, sir, as well as my own,' he said as he inserted his into the lock on the left of the box. George handed over his own key, which the young man inserted into the other lock and turned. He did not lift the lid but discreetly withdrew, leaving George with the ultimate responsibility. He pulled the box across the table towards him and sat looking at it for fully five minutes. He was almost reluctant to open it, savouring the moment above almost any other in his life to date. Finally, he lifted the heavy lid, letting it crash down noisily onto the tabletop. Inside the box was a briefcase. He took it out and snapped the two locks at the side and raised the second lid. The sight that greeted him brought tears of joy to his eyes, and the grubby handkerchief was deployed again, for inside the case were high-denomination Swiss and American banknotes, which he knew would add up to £250,000. He could hardly believe that so much money could be contained in such a small area, but first things first, he was more worried about its transportation and resting place than he was about counting it or the space it occupied. He lowered the lid again and snapped shut the locks. He had removed from an envelope on top of the notes a set of keys, one of which he now inserted into the briefcase locks and turned them. Standing up, he held the briefcase in his right hand and pressed a small bell push by the door with his left. He locked his lock on the safety deposit box and put the key in his pocket. A few seconds later, the door opened, and the young man who had shown him to the room enquired whether everything was satisfactory. George assured him it was, and carrying the case to the door, he walked out onto the pavement.

He hailed a passing taxi and gave him the address of his flat. The taxi took him straight there. Sybil was waiting patiently within, and, together, they emptied out the notes onto the dining table and counted them. At the current exchange rate, they amounted to a little over £250,000, and they sat there looking at it and discussing how on earth they were going to deposit such sums of money without arousing too much attention. In the end, it was decided that they would keep it in cash at the same bank whence it had come and where they would be able to draw from it and eventually distribute it into a number of accounts on their travels. George felt it safe to remove the equivalent of £50,000 immediately, which they would bank when they were in the South of France, and having done this and entrusted it to Sybil, who was instructed not to leave the apartment under any circumstance without him, he returned to the bank and surprised his young friend there by redepositing the locked briefcase.

The flight to Nice was uneventful. It was a beautiful clear day over the whole of France, and for once, no one was on strike. One hour thirty-seven minutes after taking off from Heathrow, they touched down on the main runway at Nice Airport. They disembarked and took the short walk to the immigration area, where they had to queue for ten minutes or so while passports were examined, and then proceeded to the baggage hall, where they collected their two suitcases and walked without further trouble to the row of taxis, and twenty minutes later, they were checking in to the Hotel Westminster.

Chapter 12

Veronica Tan had travelled first class to Singapore and arrived on the Sunday evening. She was met there by Voire Africa, who drove her to Doo-hwan's apartment. She handed over to him the precious box.

The great hand of Doo-hwan enveloped the carton.

'You have done well, Ms Tan. Now you may return to your home and your work while we analyse what the good doctor has sent us.'

He shook the packet containing the sample as if expecting it to rattle. He looked pleased when all he could discern was a faint noise of liquid in motion.

'Hopefully, all will be well and we shall be able to proceed about our business without the threat that this invention will put a stop to some of our more commercially sensitive activities. He will take you home.' He indicated to Voire Africa again, who nodded his head. 'I will be in touch with you in the next few days.'

The greeting had been formal, the thanks almost non-existent, and she could not escape his presence soon enough. Doo-hwan seriously frightened her yet, at the same time, held a strange fascination, and she thought, not for the first time, that evil corrupts. She had to admit that she had quite enjoyed the intrigue. She had certainly enjoyed the luxury and the lifestyle of the last few days; it was something alien to her, and returning to her small apartment in a state-owned block of flats with all the noise and populace that surrounded her was very much second best. The hot tropical night was stifling, and she was glad of the air-conditioning units, which had been such a luxury to buy at the time. She undressed and, naked, admired her slim form in the mirror and thought of Victor Stanley. She touched herself gently where he had touched her and then, with a shrug of the shoulders, walked into the bathroom and turned on the cold tap of the shower and stood there until she had washed herself completely clean of the dust and experiences that had so filled her life of late. Why Victor Stanley?

She dried herself, put on a voluminous robe, and made a cup of tea in the tiny kitchen. She took it with her into the only bedroom with the large double bed that seemed to fill almost the entire space, and propping herself against the headboard, she sipped the tea and tried to imagine what was yet to come.

The foyer of the Hotel Westminster is a reflection of former glories when Nice was one of the favourite playgrounds of the rich; now there is an air of decadence about it, but it was a luxury that Sybil was unused to, and as George registered, she looked about her at some of the old paintings of Nice that adorned the walls. The lift took them to the third floor, and they were shown along the corridor to room 309. The porter placed the bags on the beds where George told him and showed them the bathroom and the minibar and how the air conditioning worked. George overtipped him as a guarantee of future deference and aid; he might as well not have bothered.

Sybil stood in the middle of the room and looked about her. It was smaller than she thought it ought to be and was completely covered in a flowered wallpaper that went up and over the ceiling, giving her the impression that they were in a large box that was perhaps tied on the outside with ribbons, something to give away. The twin beds were side by side with one headboard joining them. Opposite was a small television, a fridge that was unnecessarily noisy, and a table. The window looked over the Promenade des Anglais onto the beach, and there was a small balcony on which there were two chairs. She walked over to it and, with some difficulty, opened the door and stepped out. The afternoon was beautiful; the sun was shining from a clear blue sky. The private beaches opposite were full of people, and everyone appeared to be having a good time.

'Oh, George, this is wonderful,' she said. 'We're going to have a lovely few days.'

George put his briefcase down on the table and opened it. There was not a lot inside, just a few papers a book and a large cardboard filing pouch secured with rubber bands. He took the filing pouch out and opened it; it was packed with money.

'First things first, Sybil,' he said, 'I'm not going to leave this amount of money lying around the hotel. I'm going to deposit it in a bank and leave us enough to have a truly marvellous holiday with.'

He counted Swiss francs to the equivalent of £5,000 and put them in his pocket. He left the rest of the notes in the pouch and placed them back in the briefcase. He then went over to the small bedside stand where the telephone directories were piled and looked up 'banks' in the Yellow Pages. George had a basic mistrust of foreign banks and preferred, where possible, to have his money in what he regarded as absolutely secure organisations. He regarded the Swiss banks as the main objective for his funds, but this would necessitate a visit to Switzerland on several occasions, and for the moment, he felt that £45,000 could be placed without too much question in Barclays Bank on the Rue Alphonse Karr.

It was some time since he had been in Nice, but he knew he could find the bank if he and Sybil walked into the town, and as they had been cramped up in an aeroplane and an airport for several hours, they needed the exercise anyway.

First, they unpacked the two cases and put their clothes away. Then with George carrying the briefcase, they descended once again to the foyer. George stopped halfway to the door, and Sybil almost collided with him. There was something niggling at the back of his mind, something about sums of money in an English bank—traceability, responsibility, Inland Revenue officers, and a host of other things. What if by placing the money here in Barclays, news was to get back to unfriendly ears? People might start asking questions, and that was the last thing he wanted. Why not some other bank, a bank that would be grateful for the funds and wouldn't really care that George Yoreen had deposited cash? He walked thoughtfully down the marble steps to the glass doors with Sybil following him now at a safer distance. By the time they got to the pavement, she was aware that he was not entirely happy.

'What's the matter, George? Are you nervous about carrying the money?'

'No, Sybil, it's not that. I'm … I'm not nervous at all. It's thoughts going through my mind, thoughts about traceability, thoughts about what would happen if anyone found out that large sums of money had suddenly gone into a new account in an English bank overseas. How would I explain it? How would I explain it to the Inland Revenue? I just think we have to be a bit more cautious, perhaps take a few more risks.'

'Then use another bank, George. It's simple enough. There are plenty of them. We can deposit other sums in other places and in different banks in the future as we travel. No one will know anything about it if we keep the sums to sensible amounts. We can have mail sent to a mailing address in London. If the tax man ever catches up, we will probably be dead.'

Sybil put her arm through his, and he carried the briefcase in his right hand. They turned left along the Promenade des Anglais. After only a short distance, George stopped suddenly again. Sybil's momentum carried her on another pace or two, disconnecting her arm from his and spinning her back to face him.

'What have you stopped for now, George?'

He raised his left hand and pointed. A sign on the wall announced the presence of a Middle Eastern bank with French associations.

'It's an omen,' said George.

'Don't be daft,' said Sybil.

'It is, Sybil, I tell you. I express my worries, we walk a few hundred metres, and there facing me is the answer to the problems. The Arabs know all about money. They don't need to question it, and here we have a perfect place to deposit funds.'

The manager in Barclays Bank on the Rue Alphonse Karr had a sudden feeling of loss that he could not explain. It was as though a mild depression had come over him, and he took it home to his French wife that evening and disappointed her, but he was unable to explain why. It had passed the following day.

George Yoreen took hold of Sybil's hand, dragged her across the pavement rather unceremoniously, and opened the door of the bank.

A dark-skinned young man sat at a desk to his right. He wore an immaculate blue suit and a white shirt that clearly was an advertisement for a detergent company. A neat polka-dot tie completed the picture. George went towards him. The young man rose from the desk, walked around from behind it, and said in immaculate English, for no one could take George Yoreen for anything else,

'How can I be of service to you, sir?'

Sybil stood two paces behind George, a fact that impressed the young man.

'I want to discuss the possibility of depositing some money.'

'Certainly,' said the young man. 'Please, be seated, sir.'

He drew a chair towards the desk for George, and George sat down. He went back round his own desk and sat down also. Sybil was left to drag the only other available chair close to George; she sat down. The young man looked expectantly at George and moved a few pieces of paper around the desk, picked up a small notepad, and withdrew from his left-hand inner breast pocket a gold Cross biro.

'First, sir, can I take your name?'

George looked at him. 'Is that absolutely necessary? Can't I deposit money anonymously using a numbered account?'

'No, sir, it is never possible to deposit money without a name. Certainly, we can make the account as anonymous as possible, but we are not a Swiss bank, and there are a certain number of formalities we must go through here in France.'

'Our name is Yoreen,' said Sybil, refusing to be left out or intimidated by this chauvinist and spelt it for him. 'He is George, and I am Sybil,' and for good measure, she spelt those names too. 'Have you made a note of that?'

Her tone was abrupt; she had not liked being left to draw up her own chair, and she did not trust men who still regarded their female consorts as second rate.

The young man wrote down the names.

'Thank you, madam,' he said.

Further details of a form-filling nature followed with assurances from the young man that these were entirely confidential. They then came to the amount.

'Do you have a cheque or bearer bond, sir, or some other negotiable instrument that I may deposit?'

'No,' said George. 'I just have cash.'

The young man's eyebrows rose as far as they could go but rapidly descended. He was assuming the sum to be substantial from the nature of the conversation, and a man who could deposit substantial sums of cash having walked in off the street was either a gambler or, as the bank termed it, an 'illegal'. It was the bank's policy that they accepted deposits with the minimum of fuss and the maximum of security provided there were no known reasons why they should not. The young man's eyes again were in motion, this time looking at the briefcase. George picked it up and put it on the table. He turned it towards the young man and invited him to open it. The young man placed his thumbs on the two buttons at either side of the case and drew them outwards. The locks snapped and sprang open; it was an enthusiastic sound. The young man raised the lid of the case and removed the pouch and opened it, taking rapid note that there was a mixture of US dollars and Swiss francs within it. He closed it again. He informed George that it would take only a short time to verify the amounts and would he please wait where he was. He then took the pouch and, having pressed a small security button, was allowed behind the teller's desks and disappeared from view.

There was still no one else in the bank, and the two tellers had a bored and resigned look upon their faces. They were staring at George and Sybil.

'Do you think this is all right, Sybil?' whispered George in his stage voice.

'I suppose it's as good as anything you're going to get, George, at short notice and acting impulsively like this, but this bank and the young man make me feel uncomfortable. It will have to do for the time being, though.'

George smiled at her and was somewhat comforted.

After some ten minutes, the young man returned with the briefcase and a piece of paper that had noted on it the exact amount of Swiss francs, the exact amount of American dollars, and their conversion rate into euros. For good order's sake, he had placed against this the equivalent in English pounds, and allowing for the various small charges associated with the transaction, it was near enough to the sum that George had in his mind. A conversation then followed with regard to the sort of investment that George might be persuaded to enter into, as the young man felt that it was entirely unnecessary to lodge the money in their safety deposit; he should set it to work immediately and, at the very least, put it in a secure deposit account. A rate of interest that George thought was reasonably acceptable was proposed, and he promised to consider it and return to the bank to let them know his decision.

A coffee was brought, and some surprisingly sweet cakes were served with it. The young man gave some further details of the bank and wrote down for George the address of their London branch but assured him that this was only for emergency communication and that they would not be made aware of any transaction that took place in France.

After the coffee, George gave instructions for the money to be placed in their strong room and signed a form and was given a box. The young man took George into a private room, and there, the money was put in the box and the box was locked.

George then made his excuses for departure, and after a respectful shaking of hands, the young man informed them politely that he looked forward to their future visits with considerable enthusiasm.

They stepped out of the bank and onto the bright sunlit pavement. George felt a surge of relief; at least he was rid of the large sum of money, and the treatment he had received had at least been courteous, if not a little suspicious. Sybil was less satisfied and wondered what would happen in the event anything happened to George—would she be able to easily recover the money? She felt him relax, though, and put her arm through his, and they walked towards the centre of the town.

Burning a hole in George's pocket, there remained the relatively large amount of Swiss francs that he still desired to convert, and having looked up on the handy street map provided by the hotel the location of Barclays Bank, this having been his first but unwise choice for deposit, he decided that they could at least have the privilege of changing the money for him.

There was a pretty blonde girl at one of the teller's desks in Barclays, and George approached her. In halting French, he asked if he could change some Swiss francs, and in English, she informed him that he could speak to her in the language they mutually shared.

George brought out of his pockets the large denomination of Swiss franc notes and placed them in the little tray in front of the girl.

'How do you want this, sir?' she asked.

'I'd like it in one hundred euro notes, please,' said George, and the young lady filled out the appropriate form and did the conversion. She counted out the notes and, in small bundles, handed them over to George, who put them back into his pocket.

A short while later, the manager, going through the pile of paper on his desk, noted the conversion of a substantial amount of Swiss francs. For some reason, it made him feel uneasy, but he had no idea why but made a mental note of the name.

George and Sybil left the bank feeling considerably elated. They now had more spending money than they had ever had in their pockets before and were rid of the burden of carrying around substantial quantities of cash. They headed for a small pavement cafe in the pedestrian area and, sitting down, ordered coffee and cognac, large cognacs. Half an hour later, they returned to the hotel in a relaxed and happy state. George telephoned the Negresco and booked a table for two at eight o'clock in the Chantecler Restaurant to round off their exciting day in a perfect manner.

In Singapore, Doo-hwan was seated at his desk. He was in a towering rage; almost every muscle in his body was tensed. His massive right hand hit the desk, and every article upon it leapt into the air. The small man in front of him was terrified, for he had clearly displeased his master, and he was now in fear and trepidation of his life as the voice boomed out.

'What do you mean the product doesn't work? Are you some sort of Oriental cretin? I do not pay you to fail, Dr Tan. I expect you to reproduce the formulation and match it against the sample we have. Why have you failed to do this?'

The fist came down again, and Dr Tan saw all his life pass in front of him in one short moment of time. He was rendered almost speechless and started to stutter an answer, painfully aware of the fullness of his bladder and his lack of ability to control its function when faced with rage such as he was being subjected to now.

'B-b-b-but you d-d-don't understand, master,' he blurted.

Again, the fist descended. 'Of course, I understand, monkey brain!' Doo-hwan shrieked. 'Your laboratory has failed to match the sample.'

'N-n-no, th-that's n-n-not r-r-right,' wailed Dr Tan.

A black thought occurred to Doo-hwan. He raised himself from his chair and placed both of his massive fists on the desk as though he was going to break it in two.

'What do you mean that's not right?'

'It wa-wa-was the incom-ing sample that failed to … to … work, master. It wa-wa-was not our incompetence in its use.'

Dr Tan could have sworn he could see steam coming out of the nostrils of Doo-hwan as he subsided once again into the chair.

'Failed to work?' the voice interrogated, softly now.

'Ye-es, master, it f-failed. There wa-wa-was no way we could make it p-perform. There was n-no conductivity.' Dr Tan's confidence was coming back as the terrible cloud that had hung momentarily over him was passing away, and with it the blame.

'What does it mean, Dr Tan?' Doo-hwan queried.

'It m-means, master, that we will n-not be able to m-match the product that has been produced by NTI in England, for we ha-have no reference s-sample for matching, and the amount of information we are able t-to obtain through analysis and f-formula breakdown is not adequate.'

The huge man behind the desk had about him the air of a volcano about to erupt. The small scientist in his employ knew the signs and cringed. He was actually tempted to raise his arms in front of his face to protect himself, so physical was the presence in front of him. Doo-hwan stared at him for what seemed like a lifetime.

'What is it you need, Doctor, to provide us with enough of this material to avoid catastrophe?'

'I-it's q-quite simple, master. We need an exact f-formula and a re-reference sample of the real product if we are to make p-progress quickly. Possibly just the real p-product would do if we are p-prepared to w-wait a little longer.'

Doo-hwan was past waiting. He needed the active material to prove to the authorities that it was no longer a secret formula and that others could copy it and reproduce it, which would buy him time in the part of his empire that was imminently capable of collapse in the face of such a new invention should it come into use before he was ready. It now appeared that he had been double-crossed. He ran his hand absent-mindedly over his face and found to his surprise that there were beads of perspiration brought on by his near physical onslaught; he forced himself to relax. Across from him, Dr Tan saw the loosening of the muscles in his system and also lowered his defences; he waited expectantly.

'It would appear, Dr Tan, that we have been seriously double-crossed, and this matter is now out of your hands. However, I want to understand quite clearly once more what it is we have in our possession. Tell me.'

Dr Tan withdrew from his pocket a small notebook and opened it. He referred to the notes that he had made earlier.

'It a-appears, m-master, that the sample we were provided with wa-was an extremely weak version of what m-must be the real product. Its composition will tell us some of the s-story we want to know, but there is no way we can use it in an effective way to m-make demonstration s-samples to prove that we, t-too, have a similar product to NTI and th-that the adoption of such a p-product by the authorities would therefore be useless.'

'In your opinion, Dr Tan, how could we have come to be in possession of such a sample? Why would this doctor Yoreen, who is a man so full of greed and with so little moral virtue that he would sell his own grandmother to a tinker for a fart, would he wish to double-cross us? What has he to gain from it? We did, after all, offer him a very large sum of money. and he had already received a down payment. For all I know, the money may not now be recoverable.' The thought was not a nice one.

The doctor could think of several explanations why such a situation would have occurred. He had no vested interest in protecting his unknown supplier, but he had to share with Doo-hwan the perplexity as to what the real explanation might be; perhaps there was some rational and honest explanation.

'Whether or not Dr Yoreen has double-crossed the organisation, master, is not for me to judge, and the only reasonable explanation I can offer as to why we should have received something that was incomplete is that through some English bungle— this is not unknown, you understand—the wrong sample has been dispatched to us, and if that is not a reasonable explanation, then our supplier or the courier is dishonest.'

Doo-hwan sat there quite still looking speculatively at Dr Tan.

'I don't suppose it really matters, Doctor, why the mistake occurred, but in our business, there is no place for mistakes and no place for dishonesty. The two things are almost as bad as each other. I have no option but to make an example.'

He stood up on his short and powerful legs; it was a sign that the interview was at a close. Dr Tan thankfully stood up, bowed respectfully towards his employer, and, turning about, left the room as rapidly as he could politely do. As the door closed behind him, Doo-hwan picked up the telephone. After a few seconds, he said some words into it and replaced the receiver. A short time after that, there was a knock at the door, and Voire Africa appeared. There followed a conversation that ended with Doo-hwan giving the instruction that the girl was to be brought to him immediately; could she be in it?

Lee Doo-hwan admired Veronica Tan. Ever since he had taken the business off her father, who was in his opinion a fool, he had wanted to involve her in the inner workings of the organisation, but there had always been a feeling that she was not yet a part of it, although a servant of it. She had been very compliant after what she felt she must have thought was a generous offer by his organisation to take over her father's business and to save the family honour and indeed to keep her in a job, but he was not yet confident enough that she was totally loyal, and he had not tested her with anything other than the simple escort and courier responsibility. He was reluctant now to become too angry with her, but he had to find out whether she had switched the sample, whether indeed she would have had the time or the knowledge, whether perhaps she had taken up with Victor Stanley and that between them they had conspired to prevent him obtaining what he had paid for. Common sense told him, however, that everyone had too much to lose in this affair, and most of this loss was also concerned with lives, not just possessions and reputations. Dr Yoreen had been informed about 'becoming deceased', and he was heading down precisely this path.

The lift took Doo-hwan to the basement car park, and once there, he walked over to the far corner and inserted a key into a metal door that was marked 'pumping station'. He walked into the small room beyond and pressed a switch on the wall. The light revealed a mass of pipes and pumps of one sort and another to serve the building, but the left hand wall had another steel door in it marked simply 'stores'. Doo-hwan inserted another key into this and again turned the lock, which moved noiselessly. Again, he opened the door and turned on a light. It revealed a short passage comprising a concrete floor, walls, and ceiling with one bulb hanging on a flex to illuminate it. He shut the door marked 'stores' behind him and walked down the passage to the final door, which had no name on it at all. He inserted the same key that he had used for the stores door and opened it. Once more, he turned on the light, this time to reveal a rather different interior.

The concrete passage he had passed through was his entrance to a nuclear shelter. The shelter was very substantial and capable of surviving a nuclear blast and maintaining the people within it for a considerable period. There were various hydraulic devices operated from within that sealed off the corridor that he had just come through and closed down all the external vents, allowing them to survive on an internal air system. At the moment, the air within the room was cool, as it was connected directly to the building's air-conditioning system.

The suite comprised the large central room with a small kitchen and bathroom off it. At the far end an archway, which was curtained, led into a sleeping area where bunks were piled naval fashion, one on top of the other. Within the central room itself, there was a substantial bed that folded out of the wall; this was reserved for the master himself should he ever be unfortunate enough to have to use the shelter for any serious purpose. He could also escape here in the event of a major problem with the authorities, for apart from the original construction crew, there was no knowledge of this area, for it had never appeared on any official plans. The construction crew were part of the organisation and had been dispatched to far corners of its empire, one of them who had shown a tendency to talk too much anyway had met with a messy end. It had proved a wonderful example to his colleagues.

Veronica was still in bed when the bell rang, and although not asleep, she was luxuriating in the fact that she had no immediate job ahead of her and that she could allow herself a day of relaxation after her recent ordeals. The bell came as a surprise to her, for she wasn't expecting anyone. Pulling a light robe around her naked body, she looked through the peephole and, with surprise, saw Voire Africa standing there. She had no premonition that anything was wrong and opened the door. He stepped quickly inside and shut it.

'Get dressed,' he said. 'Doo-hwan wants you, and he wants you now.'

'Why, what's the matter?' she said. 'Has something gone wrong?'

Voire Africa studied her. 'You might say that, but surely you know what's wrong.'

'I don't. All I know is that I did what I was told to do and delivered what I was told to deliver, and now I am trying to recover from all that has passed in the last few days, and you come and tell me I have got to go back to the office. If something's gone wrong, it's not my fault.'

'Don't complain to me, Ms Tan,' said Voire Africa. 'Just get dressed. I've a job to do. Don't make me do it in an unpleasant way.'

Frightened now, Veronica quickly pulled on some jeans and slipped her feet into a pair of blue jogging shoes. She took a silk blouse with a tie waist out of the cupboard that served as a wardrobe and slipped into it. She could feel the heavy silk material against her nipples, for in her fright, they had become hard, and she was uncomfortably aware of this.

Voire Africa waited in the small living area where he had been sent, but he didn't have to wait long. The door opened, and Veronica came out still pulling a brush through her hair.

'Let's go,' she said.

When they arrived at the office, Voire Africa parked the car in the underground car park and took her over to the steel door in the corner.

'What on earth are you doing?' asked Veronica as he inserted the key into the pump room door. He opened the door and pushed her through.

'Never mind,' he said. 'Just keep your mouth shut and do as I tell you.'

For an awful moment, she thought that she was going to be locked in the pump room, but he came in after her, closing the door behind him. He then went over to the other door and opened that. She saw the lighted passage beyond and went down it. As she did so, the door at the other end opened, and Doo-hwan stood squarely in it, blocking off almost any other light. It was obvious that he was not a happy man.

'How nice to see you again so soon, Ms Tan. I trust that you have had a good night's sleep and are at least partially recovered and able to answer some quite critical questions that I have as a result of examining the sample you brought me.'

He showed her to a chair, and she sat down. He drew up another one in front of her and lowered his large body onto the reinforced seat. He instructed Voire Africa to stand behind her. Doo-hwan picked up from the table to his right a riding crop; it was a particularly thin and vicious-looking instrument.

'Do you know what this is, Ms Tan?'

'Yes, it's a riding crop,' she whispered, her voice had deserted her.

'Do you know what is going to happen to you, Ms Tan, if you do not answer my questions truthfully?'

The question didn't really need her to answer, and she paled, for she knew exactly what would happen to her.

'No,' she whispered.

'Then I will tell you, Ms Tan. Our friend Voire Africa here will remove all of your clothes and lay you out on the table over there in the corner.' He pointed with the crop to the table in question, which she now saw had some restraining straps at each leg. 'I will then proceed to thrash you with this riding crop starting with your buttocks and working slowly up to your shoulders, and I shall, after every stroke, invite you to become more honest. If I don't believe you, you may never leave this room again.'

Veronica had no doubt that he would do exactly as he said, and she felt weak and defenceless, and tears started to fill her eyes.

'Now, Ms Tan, tell me exactly what happened when you picked up the sample and whom you met between the time you picked the sample up and its delivery here to me in Singapore. Do not miss anything out.'

Veronica haltingly began to describe the journey from the moment she had left the darkened passageway behind Dr Yoreen's house to the time she had boarded the aircraft the following late afternoon. She assured her employer that she had not spoken with anyone other than the manservant in the apartment and that the sample had been in her possession and, in her view, apart from the time she was asleep, at every moment. She explained that even when she slept, the sample had been in bed with her.

Doo-hwan listened appreciatively, taking in every detail. He could see that the girl was quite clearly terrified and that it was very likely that she was not telling him the truth. He turned to Voire Africa.

'Bend her over the end of that chair,' he said, indicating the vacant armchair next to the one Veronica was sitting in at the moment.

Voire Africa reached out rapidly from behind her and grabbed her hair. Veronica screamed, but he had it tightly in his grip, and raising his right arm, he brought her to her feet and encircled her upper body with his left. She was contained in a vice-like grip and frogmarched to the chair Doo-hwan had indicated. Still standing behind her, he pushed her up against the chair, and releasing her body but not her hair, he quickly changed his position to stand at her side and clamped his hand across her waist and bent her double. Veronica started to scream as Doo-hwan picked up the thin crop from the table and walked round to stand behind her.

'Ms Tan, I am going to ask you again to describe the events from the time you picked up the sample to the time you delivered it here, and I want you to tell me exactly what happened just as you have already done. As you know, I have an excellent memory, and I need to determine whether you are telling me the truth. If I feel for one moment that you have deviated, you will feel a taste of what is to come. Watch.'

Voire Africa twisted her head to one side in order that she could see Doo-hwan move to the chair back that he had just vacated. He raised the riding crop in his right hand and, with all his force, brought it down on the fabric cover. The fabric split, and the fine cotton stuffing that was its interior sprang out.

'I needn't tell you, Ms Tan, the effect that this crop would have on that very pretty behind of yours.'

Veronica started to cry seriously now, thoroughly terrified that he would do exactly as he stated and that she, like the chair, would be split apart.

She haltingly went through the story again between sobs, trying to miss nothing that she had said the first time. From time to time, Doo-hwan brought the crop down on the chair at her side, shredding it to ribbons; each time he did it, it was as though he had struck her, but the story remained intact.

'Release her,' said Doo-hwan, and Voire Africa reluctantly took his arm from the clamped position over her waist and let go of her hair.

She virtually collapsed onto the floor but, gripping the back of the chair, just managed to avoid it and instead pulled herself up and stood there trembling and sobbing quietly, her face blotched and tear-stained.

'I believe you, Ms Tan,' said Doo-hwan. 'Much as I would have liked to use this riding crop on you, I cannot. What a pity.' He turned to Voire Africa. 'Take her home.'

George Yoreen had had a bad night, for, despite the simply exquisite meal in the restaurant at the Negresco, the various noises alive in his room at the Westminster Hotel had kept him awake. First, it was people next door who had come in too late shouting and thrashing about. Then they had turned on their air conditioning, which had vibrated against the wall, and when this went off, he was aware that his own fridge was running and still there was traffic outside. He got out of bed and turned the fridge off and then got back into bed and fell asleep. He was awoken by a police siren and got up again to have a look out of the window, got back into bed again, fell asleep again, and after what seemed only like a few minutes, daylight started to filter through the shutters. He lay there wondering why, despite all this, he didn't really feel too bad, and then he remembered the money and he smiled. He looked over at Sybil by his side, who was still snoring gently. He reached out a hand and shook her. She opened first one and then her other eye and looked bleakly at him.

'For heaven's sake, it's still the middle of the night,' she said.

'No, it's not. It's time to be up. Don't you realise we have got money burning a hole in our pockets? We are going to enjoy today. We are going to have some real fun.'

At the same time, Thursday evening in Singapore, Doo-hwan was once again seated in his office. He had given instructions to his secretary to get in touch with New Technology Industries plc in England and to enquire as to the whereabouts, using one of his many legitimate company names, of Dr George Yoreen. Margaret Chan had been informed that Dr Yoreen was taking a few days' holiday, and although the informant was not absolutely sure, he thought it was somewhere in the South of France; he was sorry he couldn't be more helpful, but the doctor would be back in the research department the following week.

This was not good enough for Doo-hwan, and he placed a person-to-person call to a man in Marseilles. The gist of the conversation was that he wished to use the services of this man and his organisation to locate a certain scientific gentleman and his wife who were staying somewhere in the South of France. This would require a certain amount of legwork, but he wanted the job accomplished as swiftly as possible. The man at the other end of the telephone conversation in Marseilles was eager to please Doo-hwan, for they had carried out illegitimate exercises together that had been to their mutual advantage in the past, and each time they had worked like clockwork. Furthermore, the money that was due had been there exactly when promised, and nowadays, this was rare, even in the criminal world; he was eager to earn more of this.

The transaction completed with satisfactory swiftness. A further series of telephone calls were made by the man, and his associates to people in various towns spread out along the French Riviera. It was a surprisingly short period later, a few hours to be precise, that a contact in Nice informed the Corsican, for that is what he was, that a couple by the name of Yoreen had registered at the Westminster Hotel the day before and had been out around the town that very day spending what appeared to be a not-insubstantial amount of money.

The Corsican thanked his contact and, replacing the receiver, looked at the clock and made a rapid calculation of the time in Singapore. He decided against calling Doo-hwan for the time being and instead went out for a few drinks with friends, returning to his flat at 2.00 a.m. on the Friday; in Singapore, it was 9.00 a.m. A further conversation took place on the telephone, this time of prolonged duration. The face of the Corsican slowly lost colour while this conversation was going on but started to gain it again when sums of money began to be spoken about that were clearly of interest in Marseilles. In the end, a further deal was concluded, the outcome of which would be a satisfactory state of affairs for both parties. Doo-hwan asked to be informed when the job in question had been completed.

George popped another piece of croissant into his mouth and chewed upon it enthusiastically. He added a mouthful of coffee to it and produced the croissant soup so popular with Frenchmen before swallowing the resultant masticated mess.

'I think a day on the beach would be nice,' said George.

'So do I,' said Sybil, who was still sitting up in bed sipping her coffee. They selected one of the expensive private beaches that lined the Promenade des Anglais and decided to go down there mid-morning and spend the rest of the day, including lunch, in the sunshine. The heat had now gone out of the summer sun as autumn unfolded. There was little danger of being burned to a cinder, and this suited George nicely. There were some technical papers he wanted to read, which he had brought with him. These would not occupy all the day, and he had promised himself that before he was too much older, he would like to try one of the beach activities. There were various things to do such as jet-skiing or being towed behind a speedboat on a parachute; it was this latter event that rather appealed to him.

It came as something of a shock to George to realise that he had just paid out somewhere in the region of forty-five pounds for himself and Sybil to lie on a mattress on a pebble beach for a whole day. Admittedly, this included a beach umbrella and some rather worn and grey towels as well as the free use of the more basic facilities of the beach, but he was under no illusion that by the time they had had lunch and enjoyed some of the other activities, it would be a very expensive day indeed. The thought was momentary, and swept away by his new affluence, he didn't really need to worry about £45 or even £450 anymore, and following the beach attendant to the two mattresses, he gave him a twenty-euro tip.

They spread around them their collection of books, sunglasses, and sun preparations and eased themselves down onto the mattresses for a day of comfort. George summoned the same beach attendant that had shown them to their mattresses, who was now in a very agreeable mood, and ordered coffee and some mineral water to drink. George slipped off his shoes and undid the voluminous shirt, which served as half jacket and half shirt for such occasions as this. Sybil unbuttoned the front of her beach dress to reveal her ample figure encased in a surprisingly modern high-cut one-piece swimsuit, which George had not seen before. He looked at her appreciatively, for despite her growing bulk, she still had a handsome face and excellent legs and the boning in the suit was obviously doing its job well. He looked around the beach and noted that several of the more elderly women were there without tops. Surprisingly, the younger women wore more clothes than their mothers, which he couldn't quite work out. He turned to Sybil and whispered, 'I do hope, Sybil, that you are not going to join this crowd of elderly matrons in making a public display of yourself.'

'Oh, George, you are a prude,' she said, but to his relief, the top stayed firmly up.

Across the other side of the Promenade des Anglais, the phone rang in a Middle Eastern bank. The young man that had been attending to George and Sybil only shortly before spoke to the voice at the other end. The conversation was brief, and he put the phone down again; the face gave nothing away. A short while later, he made an elaborate excuse to his boss and left the bank and, walking up the street, entered a public phone box where he placed a call to a number in Marseilles. There followed a much longer conversation.

Chapter 13

Since signing the sample back into the laboratories and completing that tricky part of his mission, Victor Stanley had spent the next few days completing the report work necessary following the visit to Japan. Several conversations had taken place with Kenezo Nonaka, and there was now a very real prospect of putting together a substantial Japanese deal. The idea was that NTI would form a joint venture company in Japan by putting in the technology to date and with Nonaka putting up the essential manufacturing equipment and providing the onward development team for the Far East with the appropriate marketing backup. Nonaka would enter into an arrangement with regard to technology exchange, and whereas NTI would hang on to its original intellectual property rights, Nonaka would be able to participate in these through licence, and the two companies would share any subsequent development ideas.

Several conversations had taken place between the chairman, Sir Dennis Matchett, and Kenezo Nonaka's father, the chairman of Nonaka Corporation. Kevin Hipkiss had been involved little in the whole of this process, as he was by now convinced that this was a chairman's folly and, moreover, it was something Victor Stanley was likely to bury himself with. Hipkiss had almost gotten to the point now of ignoring Victor, and he began to wonder whether the man was running scared. He certainly believed the technology had been compromised but could not prove it; because of this, he was in some doubt as to whether it was a good idea to continue with the project. A bit of standing on the sideline suited him for the moment, and he had left Sir Dennis to champion the cause. As a result of this, Victor was finding more work directed at him from the chairman.

It suited Victor quite well, for he knew that if a confrontation was going to occur, and he was convinced it would. He would be in a position of strength within this operation and might be able to salvage something for his own protection. The fact that John Joyce had been so unceremoniously whisked out of the organisation had come as a terrible shock to Victor and to many of his colleagues. Already, there were rumours spreading that Kevin Hipkiss had overstepped the mark and that he was being carefully monitored by certain non-executive directors and that if his performance on a day-to-day basis didn't improve fairly rapidly, then it might be the lovely Kevin himself who might be looking for alternative employment. Some wishful thinking at work here.

There was no doubt in many people's minds that clones such as Kevin, for he came from a common stock, would stay only a short time in any particular working environment, and during that time, they would bring about substantial change that, at first, might appear extremely beneficial; they called this the management of change. Such changes were exemplified in Kevin's case by introducing into the organisation a formal strategic process carried out by highly paid consultants who came up with a form of operation promoted by Kevin in the first place. The chairman, who had never adopted a company strategy, went along with it. This accomplished, job vacancies at senior levels were filled by sycophants from Kevin's previous jobs with little talent other than to take their higher than average salaries and say yes when asked to do so. Change attracts attention, and with the right PR presentation, which Kevin also managed, the City started to pay attention to him. Oh, glorious day.

The analysts came to love him. He was an able presenter and quoted modern management techniques at them that came straight from the very best theoreticians. They believed in each other, feted each other, and held hands through all the good times. The friendships were built flimsily, one sustaining the other, but no one could afford a mistake, and when a mistake came into view, the hand-holding and backslapping stopped to be replaced by criticism, which damaged individual and company alike. Kevin did not believe the hand-holding would ever stop, not with him in charge.

Victor's problems were more immediate, however, and he was going to gain nothing from speculating on his future now, nor of daydreaming about the chief executive, his rise and fall. Victor was convinced that somewhere in all this, there was the perfect way of running NTI, but he didn't really know what it was; it certainly wasn't Kevin's techniques, nor Sir Dennis Matchett's, who, although he had been brilliant in his earlier days, had now so delegated the business that he no longer had a grip on day to-day-events and did not have the hearts and minds of the employees.

The way forward for Victor at this point in time was not precisely clear, and he had a conflict going on inside him because of the knowledge he possessed. On the one hand, he was fully aware that George Yoreen was selling the secrets of the company; on the other, he was aware that he had unwittingly placed in someone's hands a free sample of the vital superconducting polymer. He was completely unable to prove the complicity of George Yoreen, and the risk of exposing himself in the process would mean a precipitate end to a career without the privileges that an engineered end might bring. He was fed up and worried. Enjoyment was going out of his job; he did not like working for the egregious Kevin and no longer cared if he had lost a bit of SCP. He doubted, anyway, that alone, NTI had the basic technology to take it on to greatness. Perhaps a quiet end to his ambitions was the best way out.

It was Thursday night, and tomorrow, Victor could look forward to the weekend; dammit, he could look forward to it tonight. He looked at his watch and found, to his surprise, that it was time he should have been on his way home. He picked up the papers on his desk and put them roughly in order for the morning's work. He looked in his diary to see what events might thrill him tomorrow; there were none. Finally, he picked up his Samsonite briefcase and walked out of the office, turning off the light and closing the door behind him. To his surprise, Hipkiss was descending the stairs from the executive suite on the floor above. He was dressed in what Victor could only refer to as a more casual outfit than he would usually choose, and it was certainly not the suit that he had come in this morning. He was not unduly late; normally, he prided himself upon working long hours. Arriving early and leaving late impressed the troops, or so he thought; it certainly impressed Sir Dennis Matchett. Tonight, he was early—why?

Most of the staff had gone home by now, and Kevin was clearly not expecting to see anyone on the stairs. He registered obvious surprise at Victor's presence.

'Ah! Victor, you're working late tonight, I see.' He was ill at ease and had coloured up.

'Yes,' he said. 'Occasionally, I do, you know. It's a question of getting the things finished for the day,' and Victor turned towards the lift.

Kevin positively scampered round the corner saying nothing more and continued on his way down the stairs; less energy was required to go down.

Victor beat him to the foyer and fully expected to see Clinton and his car awaiting, but it wasn't. Hipkiss came out of the door that hid the entry to the stairway.

'Not using your car tonight, Kevin. That's unusual for you, isn't it?' enquired Victor again.

Kevin looked right and left as though looking to see if anyone else was listening.

'No. I've got a private engagement of a less formal nature this evening. Now, goodnight, Victor.' Clearly, Victor was not intended to respond, and Kevin walked purposefully out through the doorway.

Something in his demeanour, the embarrassment and hesitation, made Victor wonder just what he was up to, and when he was a reasonable way down the street, he started to follow him. Kevin walked as far as the tube station and abruptly disappeared from view, descending the stairs to the booking hall. Victor quickened his pace, thankful that it was a cloudy evening and that the light was already deteriorating. As he rushed into the booking hall, he saw Kevin walking towards the westbound platform already through the ticket barrier. Victor put coins in the automatic ticket dispenser and took the ticket. He then followed Kevin through as a train pulled in. Victor let him get on the district line train and boarded the same train two carriages behind.

At each stop, Victor got up and hovered in the doorway, but it was not until Earls Court that he emerged and headed off into the tangle of small streets, confident that he was now anonymous judging by his now much less furtive walk. He was not aware that anyone had an interest in him. Eventually, he stopped outside a house in Pembridge Gardens and pressed one of a number of bells by the door. Maintaining a sensible distance between them, Victor could not see who opened it, but Kevin stepped quickly inside, and the door closed. Victor waited five minutes and walked the remaining two hundred yards to the same door and looked at the names on the bell pushes. For the most part, they looked innocuous enough until he came to the name that indicated the occupier who had the basement flat. The small card was red, and in black writing was the name Valerie Stern, Governess.

This part of the town had a number of establishments where gentlemen of a particular predilection could take themselves and, in return for parting with a substantial amount of money, could enter any sort of fantasy world they wished. Victor speculated that if he just used the first initial of Valerie, the words would turn into V. Stern, Governess. He removed the comma as well, V Stern Governess, of course, 'Very Stern Governess'.

Well, well, did Hipkiss have a secret that Victor had unwittingly stumbled upon. Was he at this very minute undergoing some horrendous ordeal that he would describe as ecstasy and others would describe as torture? The mind boggled.

Victor walked further down the terrace of houses until he was able to get to the back. There was a narrow service lane shared with a number of similar villas on the next street, and counting off the houses, he walked down this until he came to the appropriate number. He was hoping, he supposed, that being a basement flat, there was some way he could get a look at what was going on. By now, it was quite dark, and opening the gate, which gave a hideous shriek and stopped him in his tracks until he was assured that no one had reacted to it, he walked as silently as he could over the paved area. He was horribly aware that anyone looking out of their windows could see him, but London being what it is, he doubted they would, or if they did, they would mind their own business.

Immediately to Victor's left, there was a large bay window, but although light was coming from underneath the curtains, they were carefully drawn. To the side of the bay window was a door, obviously a garden door from the kitchen or utility area, and he moved over to it and unenthusiastically turned the knob and pushed. To his utter amazement, it opened, and he walked carefully forward into a dimly lit passage.

A few paces further on was another door, which opened into a small kitchenette. Victor entered with infinite care, wondering all the time what the hell he was doing there; he was no Sherlock Holmes or James Bond, and although his life had altered dramatically in the last few days, none of their qualities had suddenly been bestowed upon him. All he really wanted was a return to normality, and this wasn't the way, or maybe it was!

It was then that he was able to pick up the distinct voice of what must have been Valerie Stern acting sternly. The door to the room with the bay window was firmly shut, and there was no way that he dare open it. There was a convenient keyhole, and Victor looked through it, but to his disappointment, the view showed him a blank wall. The voices, however, were quite clear, and there must be a way of capturing them for use later.

Victor had with him the light attaché case he sometimes took papers home in to read. He had put it firmly under his arm, and the slight bulge in it reminded him that he had in it his Sony recorder. He returned to the kitchenette and put the case carefully on the bench and undid each fastener silently by putting his thumb over the snap mechanism and easing it slowly open. From inside, he took the handheld recorder, and making sure that the tape was in and it was ready to go, he closed the case and returned to the hall.

Going up to the door, he held the recorder against it and pressed the switch to 'dictate'. From within the room, a voice suddenly shrieked out; it was female and was the sort of designer voice cultivated to strike with terror a cringing male supplicant.

'Kevin, you are a filthy little bastard. You have been a bad and wicked boy, and Nanny is going to deal with you. What do you have to say to that?'

The voice that replied was clearly that of Kevin Hipkiss, who had apparently receded into a more youthful personality.

'Please don't punish me, Nanny. Please … please don't punish me. I am terribly sorry for what I've done.' The lisp was pronounced, the whine genuine, and it continued until interrupted once again by what Victor now knew to be a fantasy nanny figure.

'But, Kevin, I distinctly told you to behave yourself, and while Nanny has been out, you have wet your nappy.'

Victor doubled up; this was so howlingly funny that he could hardly hold the small recorder against the door without rattling it. Kevin had wet himself! Oh my god, what would Sir Dennis think about this?

'You know Nanny's got to punish you, Kevin, because big boys like you should have completed their toilet training by now.'

Valerie Stern seemed to be enjoying herself; a note of enthusiasm was contained in the latest harridan-like delivery. Inwardly, Victor was convulsed with laughter. Could this be the Kevin Hipkiss that all at NTI knew and feared?

It was Kevin's turn to plead.

'Oh, Nanny, no … no, Nanny, no. I promise to behave, I promise, I promise.'

'But that's not good enough, Kevin. I think you know what we have to do now. You have got to learn your lesson. Otherwise, it will have to be the big stick.'

'No, not the big stick. Please, Nanny, anything but the big stick.'

'Well, then, I think it will have to be an enema. That will teach you to control your filthy habits, you pathetic little boy. I shall go to the bathroom to prepare it. Don't dare move until I get back.'

My god, thought Victor, *that must mean she's coming out.* He lurched backwards, almost colliding with the half-open door to the kitchenette and just managing to get round it and out of view. Through the crack between door and frame, Victor saw emerge from the room opposite a startlingly attractive young lady in a short blue dress with a white pinafore and white nurse's hat. Across the front of the white pinafore, it had the legend 'Nanny Stern'; Victor could understand the attraction of being at her mercy. She was made of stern stuff.

Nanny Stern went to the door next to the kitchenette and opened it, and Victor could hear some preparations being made; the recorder was still running. Victor had outstayed his welcome. Any minute, she might decide to leave the bathroom and join him in the kitchenette. He really dare not stay any longer. Anyway, he had obtained fortuitous, if almost unbelievable, evidence, and it was time to escape with it if he was ever to use it. He would just have to leave Kevin to the none-too-tender mercies of Nanny Stern.

He went back down the small hallway and let himself out of the door into the back garden and scurried across the small distance to the gate. Halfway down the service lane, he could contain himself no longer and started to howl with laughter. It was just too funny for words, and his mirth was fuelled by imagining now the antics that were being gone through in the bathroom—Kevin undergoing a semi-medical situation, which would put him in the most excruciating pain ending in total humiliation as the forces of the body unsuccessfully fought those of the enema.

Gleefully, Victor pocketed the little recorder and set off on his journey home to enjoy with Gloria the whole sordid episode. He had enough evidence to ruin Kevin now if he needed it, and he suspected he would.

In Tokyo, it was Friday morning, and Kenezo Nonaka was in a meeting with the head of the Chemical Analysis Department and his two assistants. In front of them was a complicated report about an analysis carried out on a sample of polymeric material that had surprisingly come into their hands; it had no reference number and was stamped 'Company Secret.'

The sample had actually come to the Analysis Department by the hands of Kenezo Nonaka himself. Nonaka had a high regard for the relationship with NTI in London; that regard had been built up almost entirely through his long-term friendship and association with Victor Stanley. When Victor had told him about the small problem that he had, Kenezo Nonaka had instantaneously seen a major opportunity. It had been careless and foolish of Victor Stanley to leave the sample hidden in that way, and it was his duty as a good Japanese citizen to have a look at it in case it would be of substantial value to them. He was aware that his father and Sir Dennis Matchett had been talking about a deeper and longer-term relationship and was aware that it was built around this new area of chemistry. However, he was sure that if he could go to his father with the formula for such a product that had been obtained directly from NTI itself, it would save them a great deal of money and put them in a powerful position, for, whereas he respected the technology of NTI, he was convinced that with that technology in the hands of Nonaka Corporation, they would be able to make progress more rapidly. He doubted whether NTI's new chief executive, Kevin Hipkiss, would be up to coping with an Anglo-Japanese joint venture anyway, and now that might not be necessary.

The head of the Analytical Department was explaining that they had carried out a substantial and detailed analysis of the product, and he was convinced that from this, they would be able to produce a matching material. He was surprised at some of the materials that he had found in the sample, as much of it was novel chemistry and quite advanced, but having worked now with NTI for such a long time, the information file built up contained many of the secrets; the British had loose tongues. Nonaka had, anyway, already been told the formula for the inert carrier, and this had provided Dr Nobura with a deep insight into what materials it was designed to carry. He was convinced that he knew the method that was being used to manufacture on a small scale, and he had therefore placed in the hands of his colleagues in the development laboratory the instructions to proceed further.

Kenezo Nonaka smiled grimly. He would beat NTI at their own game. He took a small stamp from the table in his office and, pressing it to the document in front of him, left his identifying mark alongside of that of the Analytical Department chief and his two assistants. The next phase was under way.

In Marseilles, the Corsican had assembled all the necessary facts with regard to the whereabouts and activities of George Yoreen. He had imparted all this knowledge to Singapore and had received back the appropriate instructions. In turn, he had sent one of his trusted couriers to Nice who had interviewed a young Middle

Eastern man with a growing reputation in his particular skill, and the courier had negotiated a most satisfactory financial deal with regard to the employment of that growing skill.

The young Middle Eastern man sat and looked at the piece of paper that was in front of him. He had brought it with him from his small apartment to the office that morning to compare with a name that he was sure was similar—a name that he had done business with only a few hours ago. He drew the file across his desk marked George Yoreen and looked at the piece of paper attached to it, giving his hotel and room number, and knew that by an amazing coincidence, it was one and the same. The young man was the very same that had deposited the money for George in the small Middle Eastern bank.

It was George's bad luck that on an impulse, he had decided to use this bank instead of taking the more conventional route because he thought it might be less secure.

Mr Alii's full Europeanised name was Alphonse Alii, a pleasing association of letters he had chosen after a brief spell in England, for it had the advantage of appearing at the beginning of any telephone directory, and he rather liked the idea of his clientele calling on 'AA' when they needed service. On such occasions, Alii was usually able to plan without indecent haste the commission given, but today was different, for the message received had been quite clear and had given him twenty-four hours to act and report. He picked up the telephone and rang his immediate chief, who granted him an interview. Five minutes after that, he left the building, having made an appropriate excuse about a serious problem at his small apartment that had to be attended to immediately. The bank was never overstretched at the best of times, and a few hours off were commonplace amongst members of its staff. As Alphonse Alii had not yet passed through the Yoreen file for registration, he took it with him. It contained the bank's key for the deposit box, and Alii was of the opinion that a little extra added to the fees he was to receive for the job he was about to embark upon would always come in useful; it was unlikely that the bank would ever find out.

Placing the file in his briefcase, he walked the short distance to the bus stop and then picked up a number 9 bus that took him the ten-minute journey to the area in which his flat was situated. He had particularly chosen a middle market area in order that he was surrounded mainly by flats that were permanently occupied by the natives of Nice rather than one of the more expensive areas where flats were often shut up for months on end and where an individual living comfortably all the year would be noticed. Being noticed was not good for his health.

He took the stairs two flights up to the door, which was on a small landing shared by one other flat whose occupier was the twice-divorced owner of a beauty salon frequented by tourists. The lady had a particularly amorous nature that occasionally suited Alphonse Alii. She held another fascination for him too, as almost monthly, she changed the colour of her hair. She was a perfectionist in this matter, and it was the change in the colour of the hair normally hidden by her knickers that held Alii's interest. He put the key into the security lock on the door and turned it. Entering the flat, he neutralised a complex alarm system, a system not normally associated with a small urban flat. He had to take into account, however, that he kept confidential bank papers there and equipment of an altogether different and illegal nature. The system gave him a comfort factor he would have been unhappy without.

He put the briefcase down on a low table in the small sitting room, and proceeding into the bedroom, he took another key from the bunch in his hand and inserted it into a very strong steel cupboard that was fastened onto the wall. When the cupboard was opened, it revealed a number of items that would have been better off in an armoury than a Nice apartment. There were handheld communication devices, a number of handguns, some with silencers, and two collapsible rifles with telescopic sights. He selected the lighter of these two and took it out of the cupboard together with a short carrying case. He relocked the door and took the rifle back into the sitting room and put it alongside his briefcase on the table.

The carrying case was designed to look like an innocuous sports bag capable of holding a squash or tennis racquet. The rifle broke down into three handy parts, barrel, stock, and telescopic sight. He minutely examined the instrument of death to make sure that all the parts were in perfect working order and then took it to pieces, placing each part carefully within the carrying case. He took the box of ammunition he had also taken from the cupboard and made sure that there were enough rounds for him to complete the job; it was unusual for him to require more than one bullet. Satisfied, he then changed into a pair of lightweight trousers, an innocuous T-shirt, and a lightweight blouson jacket. He put a pair of well-known trainers on his feet in order that he could move silently and with adequate grip under any conditions.

Having composed himself with a short prayer to his God, he left the flat unobserved and, returning to the street outside, picked up a bus that would take him to the Promenade des Anglais. He alighted close to the Hotel Negresco and crossed the road when the traffic allowed and walked along by the private beaches. He was convinced that at this time of the day, 2:30 p.m., George Yoreen and his wife would be sunning themselves probably just having partaken of a pleasant lunch. He was right, for having searched for only fifteen minutes, he saw the bulk of the two persons close to the waterline. Having located them, he moved back from view and, turning away from the beach, faced back across the Promenade des Anglais and looked at the buildings opposite.

Ideally, his position of access to the target should be from the roof of the Hotel Westminster itself, he thought, but almost next door was a block of flats under construction, and this would be less risky; he was further attracted to it because of a strike of building workers who had halted production for some weeks now, and there was an air of abandonment about it. He crossed over the Promenade again and inspected the front fence of the block. It was impossible to gain access, and taking a side street, he walked down towards a multistorey car park that lay between the building and the next street. He walked along the edge of the site, inspecting the fence carefully. He discovered that there were several areas of access probably caused by local youths or casual thieves intent upon stealing the smaller items of builders' hardware.

The buildings overlooking the area were not of particular importance, and he doubted that anyone would take a lot of notice of him with his generally anonymous appearance; this would help, too, in preventing an accurate description later for the authorities. He had little time in which to work.

Alii slipped through the nearest gap and walked rapidly and confidently across to the building. Most of the internal stair work had been completed, including the emergency stairs, which had the advantage of being enclosed in their own stairwell, and he started his journey up to the sixth floor.

He arrived at the top without being out of breath and stood there for fully five minutes, listening intently for any noises within the building itself. He had not seen any evidence of anyone else being within the building on his walk up, and it was essential that when he gained access to the roof itself, he was not overlooked or seen in action. The fire stairs finished on the sixth floor, and although the roof had been mainly completed, there were still some gaps for the unwary. He went over to the opposite side of the building, moving through what must be the luxury penthouse apartment, and found a small staircase giving access to the roof. He went up the staircase and opened the small door onto the roof. He stood in the doorway and looked about him. He was not actually overlooked by any building in the immediate area, and it was unlikely that anyone able to look down on him from a distance would be able to identify him or know what he was doing. His training and natural instinct told him that he must have some form of protection to disguise the nefarious nature of his activities.

Several small buildings sat on the roof itself, and one of them housed the engine for the lift. He walked over to this and found that if he faced to the south, he could lie within the shadow cast by the building and have access through the parapet to the beach. Conveniently, various piles of bricks and other building supplies cluttered the roof, and by the time he had tested his prone position, he found that he was able to blend himself in amongst the miscellaneous collection of building materials and become almost invisible to anything other than direct aerial observation. Although there were aircraft flying in the area, these were mainly small planes towing advertising slogans out beyond the beach or the helicopter service moving between Nice Airport and Monte Carlo; these offered no serious problem.

Going back into the shade of the lift building, he knelt down and opened up the sports bag. He took out the three pieces of the rifle and assembled them carefully. He was particularly careful that the telescopic sight was aligned and secured correctly. In judging his distance between the target and the building, he had measured the number of metres as he walked from the edge of the beach to the building and from there to the back of the building by using what was now a trusted pace. He added some more metres by guesswork and knew that over this distance, even a few metres of inaccuracy would not move the bullet enough to change the final impact from fatal to non-fatal.

From within the carrying case, he took out a lightweight polyester cover measuring three metres by three and having a strange mottled pattern of greys and browns giving an excellent urban camouflage effect. Remaining in the shadow of the building and out of view because of the pile of building materials on his right, he laid down the sheet on the ground and close to the parapet itself. Having done this, he settled himself down into the prone position and shuffled forward, taking care not to jar or bang the rifle. He placed the barrel of the rifle through the opening in the parapet and focused the telescopic sight on the waterline. He searched diligently in the area of contact where he had seen George and Sybil Yoreen and found George sitting up apparently reading a book, while Sybil continued to sun herself in the fully stretched position. He noticed what really excellent legs she had. The telescopic sight was extremely powerful and revealed details in stark close-up. He swept it further afield, picking up even more desirable targets but not in the sense that he wished to destroy them, merely to possess them. His thoughts turned to the twice-divorced lady of variable hues; he would need her later, and he wondered what effect green dye had had this month.

Down on the beach, George had had a short snooze and, having come round from this, continued to be enthusiastic about his paraglide. He nudged Sybil.

'Sybil, do you think I'd be an absolute idiot if I tried going up on that parachute thing that the speed boat is towing out from the beach?'

Sybil looked at him for a moment in surprise.

'George, if you want to risk life and limb, please leave any keys to the appropriate money boxes here with me.'

He laughed. 'Oh! I don't think anything untoward can happen, but if it makes you feel happier and if that means I have permission to try it, I'll leave anything with you.'

He placed by her his small handbag that he carried on such occasions and also took out of the back pocket of his shorts a credit card case that might part company with him in mid-air. By now, Sybil had sat up and began to take notice; George was actually serious.

'George, I don't want to put you off, my darling, but don't you think you are just a bit too old to be embarking upon this sort of thing, particularly now with all our newfound comforts stretching ahead of us?'

'Sybil, there has got to be a little bit of adventure in life as we well know, and this ride, in comparison to other recent events, is really very safe. I have spoken to the man who drives the boat, and they have never had an accident, so why should they start with me?'

'Oh, well, I suppose you're going to do whatever you want in the end, but just be careful. I'll stay here and guard the treasures.'

George stood up and stretched himself before walking over to the little jetty that stuck out into the Mediterranean to seek out the young man who was organising the paragliding. He made an arrangement to go on the next but one launch and handed over to him a not-insubstantial sum of money. The cost of spending time on this beach had started to escalate seriously. In order that he could study the technique, George sat down on the sand and watched the next two launches. It appeared that the individuals merely fastened the harness onto themselves and waited for the rope from the boat to go taught before walking forward a few paces and then literally being plucked from the water's edge by the ascending canopy of the parachute. There appeared to be nothing to it. He was a bit more trepidatious about the landing, as this was not quite as easy, and he had noticed earlier in the day that several of the birdmen had actually ended up face down in the water. However, no one seemed to have come to any major grief, and he dismissed the fact that he might end up with a broken leg or an arm.

On the roof of the block of flats, Alphonse Alii of AA Services had observed George Yoreen's walk along the beach and his conversation with the man in charge of water sports. He guessed that something interesting was about to happen and suddenly realised that George Yoreen was going to make an ascent by parachute behind a speedboat. A spectacular opportunity opened up before him; the thought of assassinating his target whilst suspended in mid-air appealed to Alphonse. It was something that had never been accomplished before; it would go down well in the history of assassination! Furthermore, if he took the opportunity early on during the run, then by the time George Yoreen's body was returned to the shore, Alii would be down the stairs and out of the block of flats and probably be able to observe the chaos that would ensue. He took careful aim with the rifle at George Yoreen and again adjusted the sights. He added another one hundred metres to the distance to anticipate the ascent by parachute and the distance the boat would move out from the shore before any sort of height was achieved. Then he waited.

The young man in charge of water sports summoned George to the launch site and carefully went over with him the essential features of ascending and descending and enquiring from him as to whether he suffered from vertigo or any other physical or medical problems, as the last thing they wanted was somebody panicking at the top of the ascent and particularly someone of more advanced years who might have a heart problem. George assured him that there was nothing wrong with his physical condition and that he would be perfectly capable of making the ascent, and even if he fell on the descent, it was not going to harm anyone but himself and he would only get a bit wet and have his dignity damaged. They all smiled and had a little Gallic chuckle about his bravery and courage, and he was helped into the harness. He put his arms through it rather like a jacket. The garment was elongated to wrap around the body, and straps also ran round the upper part of his thighs. It was impossible for him to slip out of it.

George walked forward a few metres to the position indicated by the dispatcher, who held the line in front of him. He signalled to the man in the speedboat, who instructed the driver, for there was an observer and a driver. He asked George whether his wife would like to go in the speedboat as a passenger. George waved to her and gestured for her to join them but received a negative shake of the head.

'No, I don't think she would have the courage. She hardly wants to be in at the death.'

The dispatcher indicated to George that the boat was about to move and would he please watch the observer, who would indicate whether he was going to take him up or down by signals of the hand and showed him what the signals were. He also indicated to George the hand signal he was to give if he felt unwell or wished to return immediately to the shore. In the absence of any hand signals from George, they would complete the ride in some five minutes and return him gently to the beach.

So George Yoreen was ready; the boat was ready. George lifted his right hand as a signal that he was able to be lifted off and out in the boat. The throttle was pressed down to its full extent. The boat quickly gathered way, and the rope in front of George tautened. He felt the jerk and ran three or four paces forward. The canopy behind him filled with air, and to his absolute amazement, he was lifted at a quite frightening rate of knots upwards on the end of the cable. It was just like he imagined flying would be; it was extremely exhilarating. If death can be exhilarating too, then George Yoreen was only seconds away from the ultimate thrill of his life.

AA Services on the roof of the temporarily abandoned apartment building adjusted the rifle again. He reached to his side and picked up two bricks and moved them in front of him. On these, he placed a folded damp chamois leather and rested the barrel of the rifle on it. He settled down with the butt tucked securely into his right shoulder, a bullet already in the breech. He felt the cold steel of the neck of the stock against his cheek as he looked through the telescopic sight. He moved fractionally to pick up the figure of George Yoreen on the end of the line, and as he focused the sight more accurately, the back of George's head became almost as big as a football.

The boat was heading straight out from the shore and had not yet commenced some of the manoeuvres that would make George's trip more interesting. George looked about him; it was a magnificent panoramic view, and he gained confidence in his ability to fly.

He turned his head to look back towards the beach, but it gave him some discomfort, and he looked down again at the boat. Alphonse Alii took the first pressure on the trigger. It was at this point that he was at his most deadly; it had never been known for him not to progress from this point with a clear view to the target. Entirely without nerves or pity, he made a first-class killing machine. The cross hairs of the telescopic sight neatly bisected the back of George Yoreen's head. He lowered the barrel slightly until he was at the very top of the neck at the point where the skull curves inwards. He took the second pressure, and with a slight thump, the rifle recoiled into his shoulder. The roar of the traffic below absorbed the relatively small noise that the weapon produced, and he quickly readjusted his position to view his target in case a second shot was required.

George's last memory as he soared out from the shore was one of great contentment; he was a man of substance. There was no conscience in his make-up rather like there was no pity in Alii's. He was temporarily enjoying his newfound wealth, but he could have done without the momentary irritation as the bullet hit the back of his head. After that, there was nothing.

The bullet entered the back of the head and tore around inside the skull of George Yoreen, mashing it to a pulp. The brain was scrambled; a massive haemorrhaging took place. To those watching on the shore, there was no apparent change with the exception that George dropped his arms down to his side.

Alphonse Alii again sighted the rifle on George. He noted then the position of the boat and readjusted the sight on the driver. The features of the man sprang to life in the telescope, and he could almost count the bristles in his moustache. He looked bored; it was probably the twentieth run of the afternoon, and despite the fact that copious amounts of money were flying into the coffers, it was not exactly a lot of fun to continuously drive round the bay and deposit fare-paying passenger back on the shore. Alii's actions were about to change all that, but for the moment, it suited him that the crew was bored. A lack of hand signals from George would not alarm them, and he would complete his ride even if most of it would be wasted.

Alii adjusted the rifle again and could quite clearly see the entry wound; this and the posture that George had now adopted in the harness convinced him that the man was dead. Without rising, he snapped apart the rifle and, reaching out, picked up the carrying case and slipped it inside. He squatted down and picked up the polyester sheet that he had been lying on and, folding it rapidly but carefully, put it inside with the parts of the weapon. He pulled the zip and then shifted backwards in the shadow of the lift machinery building and quickly re-entered the apartment block. He walked across the top floor of what was to be an exotic penthouse and descended the stairwell provided for emergency purposes. *How appropriate,* he thought.

By the time he had reached the ground floor, the driver of the boat had started to take a great curve to bring the body of George Yoreen parallel to the beach and to give him a view to the west. Alii walked over to the fence to the same small gap that he had entered through and, peering quickly out, ascertained that there were no people immediately observing him, slipped into the small street behind.

The boat having travelled the prescribed distance to the west turned again further out from the shoreline to bring the flyer back in the opposite direction. The driver reduced speed and brought George lower. He was skilled at bringing his passengers down to dip their toes in the water before lifting them rapidly again to maximum height at full speed.

'I don't think I've ever seen anyone so relaxed on this ride,' said the observer. 'Do you think he's all right?'

The driver looked over his shoulder at the dangling form.

'He isn't giving any hand signals to the contrary, Albert', he said, 'so I suppose he's OK. Let's just finish the ride. We'll find out soon enough if there is a problem when we drop him on the shore.' And with saying that, he accelerated the boat again, lifting George back from the toe-skimming position to full height and started the curve back towards the launch point.

Alphonse Alii walked out onto the Promenade des Anglais and, as luck would have it, found a bus approaching the stop that he normally used. It didn't really matter whether it was the right one; he just needed it for his quick exit from the scene. His luck was in, however; it happened to be the one that took the route right past his apartment.

The boat headed back towards the shore, making the necessary manoeuvre to bring the flyer gently down towards the beach. By this time, the observer was beginning to get a little worried about the totally relaxed nature of George Yoreen. He could see no sign of animation.

'I think he's fainted,' he called to the driver.

'Well, if he has, there isn't anything we can do about it. We've got to bring him in. We can't leave him flying there all afternoon, so give me a hand.'

The observer, looking out the back of the boat, would advise the driver at the exact point of turn. This was a question of angles and speed in order that the boat could turn out towards the sea whilst leaving the flyer to drift gently into the shoreline. He gave the usual command, and the driver turned and drew back the throttle. The boat settled in the water, and the body of George Yoreen came serenely down and collapsed into the surf.

The attendant on the shore didn't move for a few seconds, as this was quite a usual happening; people often stumbled and fell. Closer observation suggested, however, that something was wrong, and he raced down the beach to George.

Sybil, watching the descent, had also become unnerved by it, as George had seemed altogether too still, and when she saw the attendant run into the surf, she abandoned her place on the beach and ran after him. The attendant reached George Yoreen, whose face was pressed firmly into the sand. He grabbed the harness and pulled, lifting him bodily from the water and dragging him up the beach. Sybil arrived at the scene only seconds after. George's eyes were wide open in surprise. The attendant eased him further up the beach and withdrew his hand from the back of the harness; it was covered with blood. Sybil saw the blood and screamed.

'George, George …' she cried, 'what's happened?'

The attendant, by now seriously worried, looked at the back of George's head, and there he discovered the gaping wound.

'Mon Dieu!' he said. 'I think he's been shot!'

Alphonse Alii got off the bus and walked to his apartment. He knew that a job had been well done, and he knew that $50,000 would be deposited in a particular bank account in Switzerland.

He rapidly ascended the two floors to his apartment, and letting himself in, he locked the door securely. It was always his first task after such an adventure to thoroughly clean the rifle, and he took the pieces from the case and, placing them on the table in the small kitchen, put on a pair of disposable surgical gloves and meticulously went over it, removing all traces of recent use together with any fingerprint evidence. He lightly oiled the machinery and reassembled the gun in its full form and returned it to the secure cupboard. He put the polyester sheet in the washing machine together with all his clothes, and, naked, he then went into his small bathroom and took a long shower, scrubbing himself all over.

Alphonse Alii, having completed the washing that always followed the ritual killing, made himself an omelette and ate it with some crusty bread.

He heard the door of the apartment across the passage open and shut, and he knew that the divorcee had returned. The colour green sprang into his vision.

He let himself out of the apartment, and leaving the door open and carrying a small jug, he rang the bell of the divorcee. In only a few seconds, it was opened, and the slim middle-aged person stared out at him.

'Why, Alphonse', she said, 'can I help you?'

'I'm sorry to disturb you, madam, but I have foolishly run out of milk, and I wonder if I could borrow some.'

She looked at the jug he was holding and smelled the aftershave on the young muscled body. There was a stirring within her, as it had been some time since she had had Alphonse; it had been in her purple period, if she remembered correctly. Now, here he was clean and bright and without milk.

'Do come in, dear,' she said and stood aside for him to enter the small apartment that was the mirror image of his own.

'I was about to have a glass of wine, as I have just returned from the salon. Would you care to join me?'

Alphonse said he would, and the divorcee, having excused herself to slip into something a little more comfortable and have a quick wash, left him sitting in the best of her chairs and went into the bedroom. She removed the working clothes and replaced them with a tight white sweater and for her a very short skirt. She removed her panties, knowing that the effect she was likely to have upon him would be electric. Going into the bathroom, she used the bidet carefully, and drying herself and reapplying her make-up and perfume, she came back into the living area, smiling winningly at Alphonse, and went into the kitchen, where she took from the fridge a bottle of good Macon and opened it. She picked up two glasses, put them on a small tray with the bottle, and took them back into the living area.

In front of Alphonse was a round glass table, and going between him and the glass table, she bent forward and placed the tray upon it. Sitting back relaxed in the chair as he was, Alphonse was subjected to the most amazing view. The long slim thighs disappeared up into the very short white skirt, and between them was a mass of green hair, which matched almost perfectly what the beauty salon owner was sporting up top. She remained leaning forward as she filled the two glasses with wine. It was not until sometime later that those glasses were actually drunk.

Chapter 14

The problem, as Victor knew, in having a tape of such incriminating evidence as that just collected from the Kevin Hipkiss indiscretion was getting someone to do something about it.

Victor returned to the flat with the small cassette burning a hole in his pocket. He couldn't wait to share its contents with Gloria.

As soon as he got home, Victor poured a decent-sized drink for them both and recounted the tale, using it as his explanation as to why he was returning so late from the office; dinner was spoiled. Placing the Sony dictating machine on the table, Victor pressed the play button. The sordid noises came over quite clearly, and Gloria hid her wide grin partially behind her hand.

'What do you think to that, then?'

'It seems to me that you have got a tiger by the tail, and your problem, Victor, is a simple one. It's whether the tiger is going to get round and eventually bite you or whether you can swing it fast enough and far enough to hurl it into oblivion.'

'You mean Hipkiss as the tiger, I take it?'

'Who else, my love?'

There was a lot of truth in what she had said, and perhaps studying this in the cold light of day might alter Victor's views about how he should use the evidence. At the moment, he was of the firm opinion that an interview with Sir Dennis Matchett should be sought at the earliest possible moment and that a duplicate of this excellent recording should be played to him.

'The question is, darling', said Gloria, 'whether you want to run the risk of exposing the horrible little Kevin and at the same time exposing yourself, because as the potential instrument of his downfall, you may easily be the potential instrument of your own.'

Victor was not quite sure how to react to that. He took a contemplative sip of the drink and leaned back in the chair, putting his left arm out along the armrest and clutching the substantial glass firmly to his chest with his right. He looked down into the golden liquor, but there was no answer there either.

'I suppose I am prepared to take the risk,' he said. 'The problem is whether we have enough in the financial kitty to exist without immediate employment prospects. Our lifestyle would certainly be altered if I fail, and we would probably have to give up the flat. On the other hand, if I can bring about the eventual downfall of a man I have come to hate and detest and of a man who is in control of a business, which he will ruin, it might save me. It is a gamble.'

'Darling, there will always be a way forward for us. I have seen what has happened to you over the last few years, and I have lived the dreadful hurt that you have lived, and I don't ever want to see it happen again, and if you want truly to be vindictive and to get even, then I will always support you even if it means having to sell this property and go somewhere else or even if it means you taking a lesser job. I have enough money to see us through to pension time, and we have been wise in that department, at least.'

Victor took another drink from the glass and looked over it levelly into her eyes. They were still beautiful eyes; they were large and expressive, and you could sink into them like sinking into a pool. Victor had come to trust those eyes, and often they read for him situations that he could not read for himself. Gloria was much more perceptive than Victor, who was much more trusting and gullible. The female is the more deadly of the species; equally, she is often the more rational. When the male instinct was to strike out and kill, the female would withdraw and protect. When Victor's instincts drove him towards a dangerous situation, Gloria's drew him back from it; it was one of the reasons why he loved her so much.

'Let's sleep on it,' he said. 'I'm sure there is a lot more to talk through yet, but I do want Dennis Matchett to hear this tape, and I do really want him to know what that horrible little shit he hired is like.'

It was already eight o'clock, and Victor had had nothing to eat for hours, so Gloria prepared pasta and salad with some French bread, and they sat at the kitchen table with a bottle of red wine, which they finished off with the cheese. By the time they finally sat down in front of the television, it was nine o'clock, and the news on BBC 1 was just coming on.

The first two items on the news were of minor international importance, something about the Americans failing to win hearts and souls in Iraq and Tony Blair lying yet again about tax increases. The third item, however, transfixed them both; it started quite simply.

'We bring you now a short news item from Nice in the South of France where a British industrial scientist has been murdered under most peculiar circumstances. Dr George Yoreen was today shot through the back of the head whilst paragliding behind a speedboat off the beach outside the Westminster Hotel in Nice, where he was staying. There appear to be no immediate reasons for the murder, but the French police have mounted a huge investigation. Dr Yoreen was accompanied by his wife, who could shed no light on his death.'

Victor looked at Gloria.

'Did I just hear correctly?'

'Yes, of course, you heard correctly. George appears to have been shot.'

'Oh my god, this is absolutely terrible,' moaned Victor and felt almost immediately that he knew exactly why George had been disposed of. The thoughts went rushing through his mind about the sample, the fact that he had been unable to return the proper one, and the even worse fact that he had returned a dud that should have been placed with the rest for incineration. Victor knew that George must have taken the dud sample and used it for his own nefarious purposes, and if that was the case, then whoever tested that dud sample would find it to be useless.

Instructions must have been passed out from Doo-hwan to eliminate George Yoreen, and Victor was an unwitting accessory.

He sat there stunned as Gloria prattled on about what a tragedy and what an awful thing to happen and how was Sybil going to cope and other remarks that rather floated by him.

'Are you listening to me, Victor?'

The sound of her voice changing tempo finally got through to him, and he looked up to find Gloria staring at him with a puzzled expression.

'Yes, of course, I'm listening to you. It's just that this has come as rather a shock.'

Victor then told her in as few words as he could the general outline of the sorry tale and how he felt in some way involved directly in George's death.

'I'm sure, darling, that whatever happened, George Yoreen would have sold NTI down the river, and under such circumstances, he deserved to be punished. I admit this was rather drastic, but when you are playing for high stakes with dangerous men, you know the odds. George lost.'

There wasn't a lot Victor could do to argue with the logic of that statement, but it didn't remove that uneasy feeling that maybe if he had handled things a bit differently, George would still be alive, but he hadn't planned for these things to happen and had not known that when he took his particular course of action, it would affect George. How could he know George would use the very sample he had returned? It was his bad luck.

Kevin Hipkiss was wearing a blue dressing gown over grey silk pyjamas and was sitting with his feet up on a comfortable footstool. He had had a light meal on his return from the encounter with Nanny Stern, and the well-upholstered chair was now his retreat of comfort. He had showered and changed into his night attire after inspecting carefully the damage that had been done to him earlier in the evening. The examination sent a thrill through his small mind. Kevin was an exceedingly complex character, for whilst being a cruel bastard with those around him, he liked to be treated by a cruel bastard himself from time to time. Another few degrees right or left of his particular brain patterns and he would almost certainly be in permanent care, but as it turned out, he was sane enough to deploy all his limited talents and use as his escape valve his perverse evenings with Nanny.

He wriggled a little to get himself into a more comfortable position and, picking up the remote control for the television, turned on the ITV programme; it was three minutes to ten.

The newscaster looked solemnly at the camera.

'Earlier today, Dr George Yoreen, the chief scientist of NTI plc, a well-known company dealing in speciality chemicals, was murdered whilst on holiday in Nice. The circumstances of his death were dramatic, as Dr Yoreen was at the time being towed behind a speedboat whilst hanging from a parachute, and the murderer shot him through the back of the head. No other facts are yet known, but police have started an immediate investigation, as Dr Yoreen was thought to have been working on some extremely important and confidential projects for his company, which had far-reaching potential for fighting fraud.'

Kevin blinked. Kevin did not wish to take in what had just been said, as it was obviously some awful dream; he must have momentarily dropped off to sleep in front of the television, but there was no mistaking the fact that the screen was still speaking to him, and a moment or two later, the telephone rang. He picked up the cordless receiver from the side table and pressed the receive button.

'Matchett here, Kevin,' said the voice at the other end.

Kevin clenched his sphincter, and an exquisite liquidity seemed to overtake him. The voice continued. He really needed Nanny now.

'I wonder, Kevin, whether you have just seen the news and, if so, what sort of initial impact this has had on you.'

Peerless twit! thought Kevin. *What sort of fucking reaction do you think?*

'Yes, Chairman, I have seen the item. I just couldn't believe it. I was hoping that it might have been a bad dream and that I'd dropped off here in the chair, but it isn't. I was about to leave for the office when you telephoned,' he lied smoothly.

'I'll meet you there', said Sir Denis, 'and I think we'd better quickly get together one or two other senior managers to determine how we should handle this. As a matter of fact, I had received a call from the British consul in Nice to let me know what had happened. Fortunately for us, he is an old friend of mine and knew where to get hold of me. The consul seemed to think there was something extremely sinister about Yoreen's death that might have ramifications in government circles, not just in NTI. I didn't want to bother you immediately until I'd had time to think about it and to see what sort of tone the television channels gave to the news item. At the moment, this seems fairly bland, but by the morning, there will be a lot more news, and by then, I would imagine they will want to interview me and possibly you, Kevin.'

Kevin removed a small speck of white cotton from the sleeve of his dressing gown; it was a reflex action arising out of the possibility that he might be interviewed on television. This was a thrill for Kevin, as he had wanted to get his face in front of the public for some time, but not under these circumstances. He had been having some training from a consultant who claimed to build the right image for a person when facing a television camera. Kevin had paid privately for this and was now ready to be launched. He could have chosen a better time, but Sir Dennis, being the more interesting and well-known character, might do the interviews at the start, and Kevin could come on later as the caring boss; he had taken lessons in that presentation as well.

Sir Dennis was talking again.

'I'll get on to our legal people, Kevin, and will you pull in Yoreen's number two and anyone else you want? Oh, yes, I think it would be a good idea to have Victory Stanley in, in view of the delicacy of the negotiations with Japan.'

'I don't think that's necessary,' said Kevin. 'He's not a member of the board or anything, Chairman, and I don't think there is much he could contribute at this point in time.'

'Just do as you're told,' said Sir Dennis testily. 'At least Stanley is articulate and knows how to deal with the sort of political situation that might arise from this. He is, after all, as our sales director, our senior diplomat.'

Kevin resented this, as he resented having to have Victor Stanley around, but this was not the time to argue.

'As you say, Chairman. I think I'd better get on now. I'll see you at the office as quickly as possible.'

'Yes, do that.' The phone went dead.

Kevin pressed the bell push, and a few moments later, Clinton appeared. Clinton was not best pleased, as he had also been watching the television and, following the announcement of the death of George Yoreen, had quite correctly surmised that he might be summoned for night duty. His plans to continue his relaxation in front of the box were sadly dashed.

'I see you've got a bit of a problem, sir,' he said. 'It looks as though our evening's going to be messed up a bit.'

'You have surmised right, Clinton, for once, so might I suggest you go and put something more appropriate on, and I will do the same. I'll see you downstairs in ten minutes.'

Clinton cleared away the various items Kevin had scattered around and took them out to the kitchen. He put them on the side and then went back to his room and changed into his grey suit, stuffing the tie into his pocket for later if needed.

Upstairs, Kevin gave himself a quick run over with the electric razor and, selecting a white shirt and conservative tie, put on a lightweight blue worsted suit and a pair of highly polished Bally shoes. He combed his hair carefully and sprayed it with Freeze and Shine to stick it down and to help cover the little bit that was thinning and where he had to be a bit more careful with regard to the draping of his thicker and more copious locks. He took a quick look at himself in the mirror, declared himself fit for action, and went downstairs to join Clinton.

It was not Clinton's idea of fun to be dragged out in the middle of the night to take his smart-ass boss on an urgent and mysterious mission, but, unfortunately, it was all in the line of duty. He opened the door as Kevin appeared and waited until he was nearly inside and shut it briskly, getting some satisfaction from the curse on the other side. He went round to the driver's door and opened it.

'What the hell do you think you're doing, Clinton, shutting the door before I was in the car? You could have caught my hand.'

'I'm very sorry, sir,' said Clinton. 'I'm sure it won't happen again.'

He started the engine and, switching the air conditioner to cool, pulled out into the almost deserted street. At this time of night, it was no particular difficulty to get to the office. As he drove, he wondered about the effect George Yoreen's death would have on the company and the exact circumstances surrounding it. It wasn't until the first editions of the morning papers were printed that he saw the peculiar and horrific circumstances surrounding that death.

Sir Dennis Matchett's Jaguar was parked in the chairman's slot, and next to it was a car Clinton didn't recognise filling the spot of the managing director. Normally, Kevin would have raised hell about such an incident, but clearly, tonight, his mind was elsewhere, and pulling into the next available parking space, Clinton got out and opened the door for his boss.

'You need to get that bloody heater seen to, Clinton. It's freezing in that car.'

'Yes, sir,' said Clinton.

Kevin pulled his jacket down and straightened his tie. He removed the slim briefcase from the back seat and headed for the entrance.

'Will you be requiring me any more tonight, sir?' called Clinton.

Kevin looked over his shoulder and, not being a man of compassion under any circumstances, said, 'Yes, you'd better hang around, Clinton, and keep within earshot,' and disappeared through the doors. Clinton cursed him.

Kevin pressed the button for the executive lift, which was parked on the executive floor, and waited for it to come down. He looked at his himself in the small glass panel in the lift door, but even that didn't give him any particular satisfaction this evening. The panel moved aside, and the reflection disappeared with it. He stepped into the lift and pressed the red button, giving the lift the authority to bypass all other floors and go straight to the executive suite. It amused Kevin to do this when other people were in the lift with him.

Emerging from it, he first went to his own office and, placing his briefcase on a table, opened it and took out the various papers that he might need, and then going to the filing cabinet in his secretary's office next door, he removed a set of keys from his pocket and unlocked it. He pulled out the bottom drawer and removed from the penultimate section a file simply marked 'Yoreen'. He placed it with the other papers, picked up a notebook and a spare pencil, and headed for Sir Dennis Matchett's door. He knocked and went straight in. There was no one in the secretary's office, but he could hear voices in the chairman's. He pushed the door aside and entered.

'Ah! Good of you to come so quickly, Kevin,' said Sir Dennis Matchett. 'You know Max Fiddler, of course.'

Sir Dennis gestured sideways to a dapper little man in a blue-and-white striped suit with a face that told you nothing. He was the senior partner of Fiddler, Gloat, and Penworthy, a firm of city lawyers whose thoroughness was reflected in the size of their fees.

'Of course. Hello, Max. Pity you have to come here under such circumstances.'

Max grimaced, or at least Kevin took it for a grimace because it could equally have been a smile, but the circumstances not warranting a smile, he took it for the former.

'Very disturbing state of affairs,' said Max. He studied closely the fingertips of his right hand and, turning them round, looked again as if making sure that the nails were still there, and apparently being satisfied, he returned the hand to the arm of the chair and looked enquiringly towards Sir Dennis; so did Kevin.

Sir Dennis cleared his throat. 'It looks as though we've got a very delicate problem facing us, one that we have to handle with the utmost care. You both know that George Yoreen was working on a most interesting and confidential project representing for NTI a breakthrough in a new field of advanced chemistry. We have made various noises in the city about the ultimate success of that chemistry. Much of our ability to generate large future profits will be damaged if the technology has been compromised in any way. We cannot avoid either a short-term drop in the share price while we clear up the matter of Yoreen's death. However, we must not let that affect our confidence in the project or how we continue to present that confidence to the press and analysts. None of this is going to be easy, and by dawn, we have to have an appropriate press release and suitable responses to radio and television enquiries, because this is quite clearly going to be a sensational story, which is likely to run and run.'

Sir Dennis looked at the two men in front of him with a tired expression, not just born by having to abandon his sybaritic pastimes but of something much deeper; he was weary of the game.

'I've telephoned my secretary to come in, and she is going to bring Marcia with her too, Kevin. They should be here in half an hour or so. They are going to bring some coffee and sandwiches with them, and between the five of us, we'll get the appropriate work done and be in a position to field the various enquiries as soon as the telephones start ringing in the morning. I've left instructions at home that no one is to put any calls through here, and I have had the night watchman made aware that any calls that he answers will be met politely with the simple statement that the office is closed and that there is no one here to answer any questions. Now, let's get down to business.'

Despite his growing antipathy towards work, Sir Dennis still commanded attention, and once embarked on a course of events, he organised it well and drew on the skills of his subordinates to present a committed response to a problem. It had been quite some time since Sir Dennis had been presented with such a difficult set of circumstances, and he was determined that he was going to get the best out of it. This was not a little affected by the fact that as the chairman of NTI, he was the one who was going to get it in the neck now, and at the next shareholders' meeting, he was already beginning to realise that Kevin Hipkiss was going to run a mile from any confrontation that presented him in any other form than the perfect chief executive.

They worked tirelessly on the presentation, trying to miss nothing and trying to anticipate all the awkward questions that were going to asked. Sir Dennis wanted NTI to appear a caring employer, and therefore arrangements were also put in motion that would result in the return of George Yoreen's body. They even tried to contact the distressed widow but had failed to do so, being informed in halting English that she was 'under seduction, plees call back.'

To his horror, Kevin, as the most junior company person present, was left to take the minutes of the meeting, and for the first hour and half, he seemed to do nothing but write furiously and only found relief when Sir Dennis's secretary finally turned up an hour after the promised time and relieved him of his duties. It was after this that Kevin was able to think for himself again as he listened to Sir Dennis going through the wording of the press statement for the umpteenth time with Max Fiddler to make sure that they had gotten everything just right with the very limited information available.

Kevin's thought process started to consider the security procedures to protect the new polymer technology, and he recalled again his last conversation with George Yoreen concerning the assay of the sample stocks and of the materials destined for incineration. He had the horribly uneasy feeling that somewhere in all of that, there existed the reason for the death of George Yoreen. Kevin also knew that this was not something he could keep from his chairman; it was pertinent to the whole set of circumstances they were studying. He hoped his intuition would not let him down.

'Chairman, there is something else I think we ought to consider in this whole sad set of circumstances, for despite the fact that we are sitting here getting our stories right for the questions that will inevitably come from the media and the shareholders tomorrow, we have not yet looked deeply enough into the real reason for the death of George Yoreen. I hardly think that the spectacular circumstances of his demise were brought about by some lunatic taking a pot shot at a bloke being pulled behind a speedboat on a parachute. It must have been something much more sinister.'

Sir Dennis looked at him over his glasses and made Kevin squirm; stating the obvious did not always win points.

'If you have facts, Kevin, that you are not yet revealing, then it's about time you did so. We cannot afford to miss anything that will make us look fools later, so spit it out.'

Kevin felt sweat run down his left-hand side as though a small waterfall had suddenly started to work in his left armpit, and he clamped his arm to his side for the cotton to absorb it. He didn't like being put under pressure; it was a new experience for him. Kevin was used to situations where he had other people under pressure, and now that he was the one under interrogation, he momentarily saw a situation where his own career and his growing reputation might be severely damaged if he was wrong about what he was going to say. The waterfall continued, and he thanked God that he used a good-quality, ozone-friendly deodorant. He looked across at Max Fiddler, but all he got was a bleak expression in return and a slight raising of the eyebrow. There was going to be no help there; he cleared his throat.

'I assume you know—'

'Kevin, at this point in our analysis of the situation, don't assume anything,' said the chairman.

'I have always protected the technology surrounding the new superconducting polymer, and it was stipulated right at the beginning of the programme that every gramme of waste material was to be collected in a receiver and a record was to be kept of every sample that went out and every sample that was returned. Because we know the strength of the various batches that we are developing and because we record each of these, the amount of material going into the collecting vessel is known. We are able to determine the active content of the waste material, and we know the acceptable loss factor associated with the experiments. From time to time, we have assayed the contents of the receiver, and they have always been within the acceptable percentage loss of the calculated active content.'

He cleared his throat again and continued with his tortuous explanation.

'However, we do not do this on a daily or weekly basis but on a three-monthly cycle, and the next assay is now slightly overdue, as George Yoreen had insisted on taking his holiday before completing the work on the current batch. I had an argument with him about this and had given specific instructions that the work was to be carried out forthwith and his deputy should have gotten the figures together by now and this will tell us whether there has been any loss. There are no outstanding demonstration samples with any of our people, and if there is a loss against the theoretical and actual calculations, then we know that it must be Yoreen who will have diverted an amount for his own purposes, and as a result, he has met his untimely end for circumstances we can yet only guess at.'

'Good God, man, that's dynamite,' said Sir Dennis. 'If it's true, we have a catastrophe of the greatest proportion. If our security has been compromised, then we will suffer permanent damage and our position as a major government contractor will be jeopardised. What a wonderful front-page news story that will make in every serious paper in the world.'

Max Fiddler tapped his pencil idly on the table, and in the silence that followed, it sounded like the drum roll prior to an execution. Fiddler retained his bleak expression, but behind it, his mind was working to protect his client and increase his fee.

'I think it highly unlikely', said Fiddler, 'that anyone is going to believe that an eminent scientist was the subject of a bit of target practice off a beach in the South of France, so we must anticipate that the press and television are not going to be the only people that are going to express an interest in our affairs. We're going to get enquiries from government departments and the police. Furthermore, Chairman, as you state, something very nasty is going to happen to the share price. There are going to be rumours spreading around the market that somebody's out to stop us in our tracks, and for those reporters that have a keen nose, they're going to start asking just how secure our establishments are. Kevin's already mentioned that there may be an outside chance that we were being robbed of material, and if we were, then where on earth is that material now?

'It's highly unlikely that anyone in the laboratories will have kept an eye on George Yoreen because he was above suspicion and he knew it. The security of our organisation is only as good as those at the top, and if they are corrupt, then they can get away with murder, but not apparently from being murdered.'

Max Fiddler allowed himself a dry chuckle.

'The security of the organisation, if my memory serves me correctly, did not allow any person to be by himself in a secure area, but that is too trite a statement. There would be exceptions, wouldn't there, Kevin?'

Kevin nodded, not trusting himself to speak.

'I thought so. So Yoreen was able to have access at all times to his lab?'

Kevin took out a large white handkerchief with the name 'Cardin' woven neatly across one corner and blew his nose gently. It was a technique he used to remove perspiration from his upper lip without other people noticing that there was any there. Max Fiddler noticed.

'We have to accept', whined Kevin, 'that George did have access. We had to let him have access, as he was the original eccentric scientist, but I don't mean by this he was unreliable. I mean he would get ideas at all times of the day and night, and if he did, then he had to go and put them into practice. This meant he had to have access to the labs, and the guards and security people got used to this.'

There was a discreet knock at the door, and Kevin's secretary, Marcia Payne, entered carrying a welcome tray of coffee.

'It's time for a break,' said Sir Dennis. 'I think we've made ourselves aware of the critical nature of our problem. It remains to draw up the action lines about who is going to do what because I want this handled sensibly and systematically and with purpose.'

Marcia poured coffee for Kevin and Sir Dennis and looked towards Max Fiddler.

'Black, please, Marcia,' and she poured again. She could sense the tension that was in the room and hoped that Kevin was under pressure. As many secretaries do, Marcia Payne probably knew the business as well as her boss, and she knew the characters much better because she'd been there longer. Marcia had a reputation for being a sympathetic listener, and people came and talked to her; they talked to her about things that they hoped would get passed on to Kevin or even to Sir Dennis.

'May I say something, Chairman?' she said.

'Of course, you can, Marcia. Anything that can shed light on this terrible state of affairs we're in will be welcome.'

'I think it might be a good idea to talk to Victor Stanley, sir. He is the man who has recently been out to the Far East, and he did carry a sample with him. I know this because I put the travel plans together, and he mentioned to me the fact that he was not looking forward to carrying material and would not be happy until it was back safely here in the labs. I know that Victor is as honest as the day is long, but it might be that something happened while he was away that he regarded as trivial but that might in fact be material.'

Sir Dennis had listened to this short delivery with something verging on amazement, and now he turned towards Kevin.

'Is it correct, Kevin, that Victor Stanley carried a sample with him?'

'Yes, of course, it is. He had to talk to Nonaka Industries, and we had to demonstrate that we had the product to a number of other interested parties.'

'But surely that wasn't necessary, Kevin. We have credit cards containing the polymer that we can perfectly adequately demonstrate. Why did he have to carry the polymer itself?'

'It was a matter of judgement,' said Kevin.

Bad judgement, thought Fiddler.

'I really felt that at this stage of the development in our relationship with Nonaka, they would want to see that we had something that was more than just a working model, and I authorised Victor Stanley to carry a small sample with him, but this was returned and logged in. I told you that I keep a very careful check of all sampling procedures.'

'There is one thing for sure,' said Sir Dennis. 'You'd better get down to those labs and talk to Yoreen's number two—what's his name?'

'Dr David Frome,' said Kevin. 'If you've finished with me, Chairman, I'll get down there and start checking and phone him to come in.'

'I think you can leave Max and me to sort out the final detail with regard to the statements we've now got to make. The only thing that's outstanding is whether there has been a real loss, and if so, is the company under some sort of threat either from industrial espionage or just plain piracy of our product? And you're the only one who can find out, Kevin, so on your bike!'

'Oh, and, Kevin, don't forget to have Victor Stanley come and see me at the first available opportunity.'

Kevin strode purposefully and thankfully towards the door. Conversation resumed behind him, and he knew that by the time he got back, there would be a number of statements suitable for different parts of the media that would partially whitewash the company and be borderline acceptable in the city. He was less sure that they would survive a full investigation by the police, and he was sure that this would ultimately come.

Kevin had forgotten to call Victor Stanley; now he would have to do so.

Although the lights burned in the building, it was still the middle of the night, and rain had started to hit the glass in increasing force as it was driven by a strong westerly wind that had blown continuously for the last few days. The building had an empty and unloved feeling about it, and Kevin was glad to be doing something that he knew was under control. He got to the reception desk in the main hall and sat down on the corner of it and took from his pocket the small black book that contained the numbers of key personnel throughout the company. He looked up the home telephone numbers of Victor Stanley and Dr David Frome before setting off for the labs.

Chapter 15

It was early afternoon in Singapore, and Doo-hwan had taken his habitual lunch at the Mandarin. A nightclub during the evening, the Mandarin was turned over to an endless procession of dim sum at lunchtime. Trolleys of delectable little snacks were wheeled around by attractive girls in tight dresses. The method of ordering was to signal a particular trolley, and when it pulled up at the table, the girl would serve you with whatever you fancied, marking each item off on your bill and moving on to the next customer. It was colourful, busy, and anonymous. No one really paid much attention to who was there; it was just a noisy place to go and have a rather good, relaxed meal. It was a place that some Singapore businessmen would take their visitors to, and if it was the first time they had eaten dim sum, then they came away feeling that they wanted to do it again. Today, Doo-hwan had with him Veronica Tan. He had telephoned her that morning and told her that a car would collect her for a lunch meeting. Doo-hwan had formed the view that Veronica Tan had carried out his instructions to the best of her ability. He believed, whatever the circumstantial evidence might suggest, that she had not, either wittingly or unwittingly, double-crossed him. He knew that there would be other opportunities to use Veronica, and he had not given up the idea altogether that he still might be able to rescue what was now a disastrous situation for him.

Veronica had not even considered refusing the invitation to lunch; besides which she was hungry. She had taken particular care to dress simply and traditionally and looked as though she had been poured into the red dress with a silver dragon motif running diagonally from her right shoulder to just above the left knee. In a city full of beautiful girls, people had still noticed her entry to the Mandarin and speculated upon the sort of girl that would allow herself to be the companion of such a gross and ugly man.

Always to the point, Doo-hwan said, 'I have decided, Veronica, to forgive you.'

She looked at him from under lowered lashes and said nothing. It was better to say nothing; there was nothing to forgive, but if this was Doo-hwan's way of rehabilitating her and restoring her comforts, then who was she to argue?

'You must understand that it is very important for me to obtain this new product that will be used by the authorities of this country and others to prevent me pursuing successfully my more profitable businesses.'

Veronica was aware that Doo-hwan and his seedy empire were heavily involved in illegal gambling rackets and counterfeiting. His tentacles went out into Japan, where he had formed a very useful laundering operation with a number of Japanese gentlemen who moved substantial amounts of money out of the shady pachinko industry. He was into Hong Kong, where credit card fraud was a major business.

The Japanese government had recently announced that it was going to use a new form of monitoring within the industry and all the pachinko parlours were going to be converted to a new form of payment system. Detailed enquiries by Doo-Hwan had revealed that it was the intention of the government to clean up its act; certain ministers were alleged to receive huge payments from pachinko operators, and another major scandal could not be afforded. All sorts of ideas about protecting currency, credit cards, and gambling chips were being examined, and experimental work with NTI's superconducting polymer had proved very encouraging.

Further investigations had revealed that Nonaka Corporation had made a proposal that would result in all money that passed through the pachinko pinball industry machines being in the form of a plastic coin. The plastic coin would, in turn, be drawn only from special government outlets against a cash advance and would duly be exchanged for cash at any time by the government on demand. To protect itself, the government had asked Nonaka Corporation for a device that would protect the plastic article. Impregnation with SCP would work well, and it was this rumour that initially made Doo-hwan aware of NTI. It was then that he decided to act.

He imparted all this detail to Veronica, who understood only too well that if gamblers could only draw government coins and if those same gamblers could only exchange those coins with the government for money, then if there was no ability to counterfeit those coins, the government could not lose. What she was hearing was a gross oversimplification of the whole system, but she understood well enough that this was a new form of gambling currency, and the government would make money from it by charging a premium on issue and a discount on cash-in. The plastic coins were to contain the new superconducting polymer and would therefore be readily identifiable until someone was able to copy them.

There had been a number of tests conducted by Nonaka and by nominated government-controlled scientific departments, and they had satisfied themselves that there was no known substitute for SCP. Further work showed that not only could the SCP work in one problem area but also that by further careful development, all sorts of crime could be controlled. Outside this highly specialised area, a number of other uses were now being looked at.

Fear and consternation was running through the Eastern criminal world, and plans were afoot to capture the technology and copy it. This activity had been the focus of Doo-hwan encouraged by international contacts. It was sad that the efforts so far mounted by Doo-hwan had come to nothing, but through his contacts in Japan, he was quite sure that at some stage, he would penetrate Nonaka Corporation if he drew blank at NTI.

'I have been wondering, Veronica, what might have happened to Victor Stanley, that man that you appeared to be so fond of. My information is that he is very well connected within Nonaka Corporation, and it might be that he is visiting Japan again shortly. I have told my people that a close watch is to be kept on the activities of Victor Stanley, and I think it might be a very good idea, should the opportunity arise again, for you to be available when next he visits this part of the world.'

It was true; Veronica had, in a strange sort of way, felt protected by Victor and had enjoyed the physical side of their relationship. She closed her teeth on a particularly scrumptious morsel of prawn. Still, she remained silent.

'You are very uncommunicative today, Veronica,' said Doo-hwan in his precise way. 'I should remind you that it might be dangerous to defy me in any way, for despite your extreme beauty and the fact that I am very fond of you, it is only a fondness that a child might have for a doll, for it can be pretty and attractive but can be quickly discarded or crushed if it ceases to please and be replaced by another one so easy to purchase.'

It was not a pleasant comment; to be disposable was not part of Veronica's plans for the future.

'I admit to a certain fondness for Victor Stanley, Mr Lee.'

She had taken to addressing him by his first name with the formal prefix, as she had seen the effect it had had on him the first time she had tried it. Now, all around his personal office, it had become an accepted form of address, rather like the retainers of English private companies who would address the owner in a similar way. Lee Doo-hwan enjoyed it. Lee Doo-hwan would very much like to have been surrounded by English-style retainers. He had, in his wilder moments, considered investment in an English stately home but had finally decided that a combination of snobbery and racism would not permit him to genuinely enjoy it, and his natural inclination to have such inconveniences removed from the local community would not exactly meet with joy in English rural police forces.

'The fact that I'm fond of Victor Stanley, Mr Lee, also means that I would not like any harm to come to him. You know as well as I do that when he came to Japan and you decided on your elaborate scheme to get hold of the new technology, he was an innocent party to all that.'

Little did she know that within twenty-four hours on the other side of the world, Victor Stanley was going to be facing a confrontation that would set in motion a chain of events that would lead to the questioning of that innocence.

The snake-like power that Doo-hwan held over Veronica was not all to do with the eyes; he still controlled the only thing in her life that she truly wanted—her father's old company. Her only means of support came from Doo-hwan, and while that lasted, she had no alternative but to go along with his illegal schemes whilst trying to keep herself as far away from the real criminality as she could. It was true he appeared to have genuinely developed a liking for her, and so long as she carried out the so far simple tasks he had set her, she would be rewarded and would eventually be presented with the opportunity for revenge.

Her pattern of thought was again interrupted by Doo-hwan.

'I take it, Veronica, that you will have no objection to being available, then, for another meeting with Victor Stanley?'

He wiped away a morsel of food from his chin area and presented his best winning smile, the face opened like the entrance to a gigantic cave and the teeth were an uneven set of stalactites and stalagmites set almost at random in the jaw; it was not a pretty sight. Some had been known to give way to Doo-hwan without a struggle when similar displays of bonhomie had been taken as some sort of fatal grimace, which would be followed shortly after by instructions to do gross harm to the recipient. Veronica had seen it before and returned the gesture with her perfect lips and teeth, but not the eyes, never the eyes.

'If you need me to pass your messages to Victor Stanley, I will be pleased to do so, but I am certain it will get you nowhere.'

'We shall see, my dear,' said Doo-hwan and started to remove from around his neck the linen napkin that had protected his massive front and, more particularly, his new silk tie, a present from a Japanese visitor, from the general detritus of his eating habits.

He ponderously moved the chair back a few inches before he was assisted by what seemed like a small army of undermanagers who fussed around him like worker bees around a queen, steering him towards the entrance so that by the time he reached it, he had been brushed down and tidied up, his hat was on his head, and his car was drawing up at the door. Veronica brought up the rear unattended. Strangers asked who the man was but looked at her; it was enough.

Seated in the back of the big Mercedes, Veronica was dwarfed by her companion. Voire Africa was at the wheel and followed the instructions to take 'Mr Lee' back to the office and drop Veronica where she wanted to go.

'Remember to let me know what you are doing on a daily basis,' said Doo-hwan. 'I might need you at short notice, and I don't want to waste time finding you.' His hand vanished inside a huge trouser pocket and emerged holding some folded money; he thrust it into Veronica's hand. 'Go and buy yourself something nice,' he grimaced. She took the money and, opening her handbag, placed it in a side pocket.

'Thank you, Mr Lee. You're very kind.'

It was only a fraction of what was owed, but she had learned a long time ago to take everything she was given; there was no shame in it and no loss of pride. Most of it was put away for the future, for it did not matter whether she purchased something expensive or not; everything looked good on Veronica Tan.

The car stopped in front of Doo-hwan's office building, and Voire Africa got out and opened the door for him. It took time to extract himself from the rear seat, but, eventually, he emerged and exposed himself momentarily to the strong sunshine before making for the comfort of his office air conditioning. He gave no backward glance, and Veronica was left alone. She asked to be dropped off by the Dynasty Hotel.

The lift took Doo-hwan to the third floor office; he was expecting a visitor. His secretary brought him an iced coffee and put some mail and a few emails and faxes in front of him. Doo-hwan had been the first person in Singapore to install a fax machine. He had regarded it as the greatest office invention since the computer, but he had never been able to master the computer, which he sported on his desk. On the other hand, the fax had given him hours of pleasure. A sort of faxual satisfaction had arisen from his ability to keep in close touch with his subordinates by issuing personal handwritten instructions. He had asked his technicians if they could devise a way of sending an invisible fax that could only be activated by the receiver using a special piece of equipment. He had been told that they had heard rumours about some sort of chemical coating that might permit this but had not seen it in action; he had issued instructions to track it down. Email was all right but not secure, and he did not like it.

He looked through the messages. One of them informed him that Mr Yoshinori Oku would be visiting him as arranged at 3:00 p.m.; it was now 2:45 p.m. He looked at the rest, but there was nothing needing his immediate attention.

At exactly 3:00 p.m., his green desk phone rang. Doo-hwan was in the process of lighting a large cigar and completed the act of ignition to his satisfaction before he reached for the instrument through the cloud of fragrant smoke. Too many people could afford good cigars today and had driven the prices up and made the best of them scarce. He sincerely hoped that the USA did not normalise relations with Cuba or there really would be a major problem.

'Mr Oku and another gentleman are here to see you, sir,' said Margaret Chan.

'I will be right out,' said Doo-hwan. 'Put them in the boardroom, Margaret, and give them some of that awful Japanese tea you keep for such occasions.'

Margaret Chan replaced the receiver and took the lift down to reception. She was amazed to see that the Japanese visitors were dressed like American gangsters from the days of Prohibition—black suits, white shirts, and ties and highly polished black shoes with white spats. She knew also that many of Doo-hwan's visitors were not what could be described as normal businessmen. These two were small even for Japanese and, although exquisitely polite, had an aura about them that was unnerving. She introduced herself and showed them into the boardroom on the first floor, informing them that Doo-hwan would be with them shortly.

The boardroom was traditional English style as interpreted by a Singapore interior designer. The table was capable of seating twelve in supreme comfort and was made from mahogany, as were the leather seated armchairs. Gilded wall lights illuminated the room when necessary. Now, there was enough light from the two large double-glazed windows. Air conditioning hummed quietly in the background; it was pleasantly cool without being refrigerated. On the walls hung a mixture of modern views of Singapore painted by a well-known local artist and some truly hideous modern art of significant value but of no appeal. The carpet was Chinese silk with an intricate design of snakes and dragons; the snakes were red with bright silver eyes. The whole thing was a discordant visual symphony. The ring on the middle finger of Yoshinori Oku was distinctive and similar to the carpet, a red snake with diamond eyes, the same ring as worn on the left hand of Lee Doo-hwan.

The second Japanese, a man called Shimada, took from his briefcase an electronic device not unlike a small portable radio. He turned a knob, and a small red light came on followed by a high-pitched whine. He adjusted another knob, and the volume of noise reduced. He then walked slowly around the room several times, pointing the device in all directions. The noise level remained the same. He said something in Japanese to Oku, who nodded, and the device was switched off and returned to the briefcase apparently having satisfied the visitors that there was no hidden surveillance that would record any conversation that was to take place this afternoon.

Doo-hwan gave the visitors enough time to satisfy themselves that the boardroom was free from bugs. It would have been unthinkable to walk in on them while they were scanning, as there would have been loss of face all round and the meeting would have been blighted from the start. Trust had to be established. His cigar well lighted and with his best grimace in full view, he strode into the boardroom. The two Japanese bowed to him, and he made the effort to return the compliment.

'It is with pleasure that we greet you, Doo-hwan San,' said Yoshinori Oku. 'This is my close colleague, Shimada, whom I don't believe you have met before.' Doo-hwan inclined his head in the direction of Shimada.

'We are here on a mission of some delicacy and importance,' said Oku. 'We have become aware of certain facts that might interfere with our business relationship, and we must study these and decide how to act.'

'Please be seated, gentlemen,' said Doo-hwan. 'We can at least conduct our affairs in comfort.'

The Japanese went to the side of the table opposite Doo-hwan, who had strategically placed himself in front of the windows to have his back to the light. Long experience had shown him that the light shining on the faces of others often revealed half-truths and lies, while he who sat in the shade could often get away with less than all the truth.

Chairs were drawn out and papers taken from briefcases and put on the table just like any ordinary business meeting. There was little difference anyway between the criminal and the nearly criminal, so Doo-hwan had adopted the ways of the so-called legitimate businessmen and had raised the standard of his criminal colleagues. So much now was legitimate anyway; only parts of his empire were the subject of interest by the police, and he was careful not to live alongside those. His activities in Singapore were straight; it was only the planning that took place there for matters that were outside the jurisdiction of the Singapore authorities, and despite these activities, he had so far remained only the subject of deep suspicion.

Yoshinori Oku was a member of a select criminal syndicate from Tokyo, and his speciality was gambling, credit card fraud, and prostitution. He had come into contact with Doo-hwan as a means of laundering money through South Korea and had channelled that money into some very profitable business as a result of Doo-hwan's advice. Tainted funds had therefore been turned into blue-chip holdings, and the money arising had been ploughed back into building more criminal activities and in providing funds for politicians who would then close a blind eye to those criminal activities. The government was cracking down hard on this bribery now, and many of the political allies were running as fast as they could away from their former friends. A hard core of corruption remained, and as long as it did, Oku was safe.

There were few niceties to exchange; they were not nice people. 'It is in the field of gambling that my greatest worries exist,' said Oku. 'You are aware of the government's intent to introduce a scheme whereby the highly lucrative areas of my gambling empire are in danger of collapse because of our having to accept their new plastic currency. If this is the case, then our operations will be the subject of the closest scrutiny, and many of our cash businesses will be turned over to a currency, which is readily identifiable and which cannot be changed for cash except at government offices, where they will take their percentage by discounting the sums that we bring to them. It will drive gambling underground, and our main cash generators will be severely curtailed. The numbers of people using our legitimate gambling parlours will increase, and with that, our percentage of the skim will decline to nothing. We cannot live on what the government leaves us. It will place in question the whole viability of our operations. You have mentioned to us that you are within reach of acquiring a technology that will enable us to counterfeit the government coin, and it is essential for us now to start planning how we might be able to use this. Can you inform us of the progress that your organisation has made with regard to bringing this about?'

This was an unusually direct approach for the Japanese. Normally, circumlocution was the way in which any serious business discussion started. It was an indication of the extreme urgency of the situation that Oku had come straight to the point.

Doo-hwan was painfully aware that his recent experience with regard to the testing of the superconducting polymer could jeopardise the relationship between himself and the Japanese.

'Oku San, I have acquired the first of several samples, and my chemists are even now embarked upon a thorough investigation of their capability. As you are aware, Nonaka Corporation in Osaka has developed a close relationship with the British company NTI and is negotiating a licence for this material, which your government is so interested in developing. There have been a number of most unfortunate incidents surrounding our examination, but I am confident that with the forces at my disposal, I will ultimately have in my hands perfect examples of their technology and that I shall be able to deliver to the syndicate a material that will enable you to produce a perfect copy of the new government countermeasures and open up new possibilities in credit card fraud.'

Oku sucked his teeth; Shimada did likewise. It was an indication of discomfort, something Doo-hwan had realised about the Japanese.

'It was our impression', said Oku, 'that you had acquired a sample of perfect material and that apart from your investigation into its chemical construction, you had at least been able to prove that it worked and that the investigation you are embarked upon would bring results.'

Doo-hwan blinked slowly and adjusted in front of him the few papers that held closely typed and irrelevant information. His mind was working in top gear, and the various probabilities were being measured one against another. He had to keep the confidence of his Japanese colleagues and at the same time lie to them about the progress that was being made.

'There has been a most unfortunate incident. I learned through my intelligence gathering network of the superconducting polymer of NTI and became convinced that my technicians could work with it and eventually match it if I had a sample of the original. I dispatched an envoy to England to obtain a quantity from NTI's senior scientist whom I had persuaded to part with some by way of a debt repayment. This involved careful planning and the payment of a not-inconsiderable additional bribe.'

Oku sat absolutely still opposite him. There was no change in his facial expression. It was Shimada who interrupted.

'We are already aware', he said, 'that a senior scientist of NTI has been assassinated while on holiday in France. It is this particular circumstance we wish to investigate with you today most carefully.'

Doo-hwan felt distinctly warm despite the air conditioning. The trust that had been established so carefully between his organisation and that of Oku was something that had been worked upon for many years. They had a mutually satisfactory business arrangement, and many billions of yen had passed through his hands successfully and resulted in the generation of considerable wealth both for him and the Japanese.

'The death of the scientist you refer to was a most unfortunate circumstance but one that I directly engineered.' He looked from Oku to Shimada; they said nothing. Doo-hwan was tempted to run a finger between his ample neck and his even more ample shirt collar but desisted; it would have been a sign of weakness and alarm.

'I had obtained from Dr Yoreen, for that was his name, a sample of the new superconductive polymer. It is this material that your government has in mind to use, and, indeed, it is also under investigation by several other government authorities within the region. You are aware, I am sure, that it is not just your gambling activities that are under threat but those of several other of my business partners. This material, when used on anything from plastic gambling chips and coins through credit cards into folding currency, can quickly reveal by a very simple investigative process whether those items are counterfeit. The system works, as I understand it, by placing a small instrument on the locator box on any genuine article. This instrument then passes a small electric charge, and if the article is genuine, then the circuit between the two contact points on the instrument is closed and a confirmation signal is received, which the examiner recognises. When the instrument is placed on any counterfeit item in the locator area and it is unable to close the circuit satisfactorily, the test signals a negative response. Worse still, the microchip technology enables individual articles to identify themselves with unique codes. The sample we were so willingly provided with turned out to give a negative result. There was in fact no reason to suppose that Dr Yoreen would have double-crossed us, for he had nothing to gain and had so much to lose as he proved when he lost the most important thing he possessed—life. A set of circumstances must have developed whereby either wittingly at the hands of a third party, or unwittingly, he gave to us a material believing it to be genuine when in fact it wasn't. I have therefore instructed my colleagues that the genuine article is to be acquired without further ado.'

Oku spoke. 'This is a most unfortunate position for you to be in, Doo-hwan San, for I have given certain reassurances to my people in Japan that, within the foreseeable future, we will be able to create a response to any of the government's anti-counterfeiting measures. What you tell me now means that the assurances I have given may be less than satisfactory.' The Japanese wrote something on a piece of paper and passed it to Shimada. He read it and said nothing.

In adversity, there is often strength, and Doo-hwan was quick to realise that the two faults, his of not being able to deliver the product on time and the statements made by the Japanese to their colleagues, had come together to bind them into a situation from which they must both recover; one had no strength without the other. The loss of face and reputation by the Japanese would place them at risk within their own criminal Yakuza just as failure on Doo-hwan's part would place him at risk.

'I do not regard this as a failure. It is merely a problem that has arisen along the path to acquiring the information we want,' said Doo-hwan. 'It was important that the failure of Dr Yoreen was seen clearly to be a failure, and I therefore issued the instructions that resulted in his death. It will serve as a lesson to others that we approach that broken promises do not end in glory.'

Shimada passed the piece of paper back to Oku. Oku read carefully and looked up.

'My colleague and I are disappointed in the turn of events today. This was not the meeting that we had expected. We had looked forward with some pleasure to strengthening the relationship that exists between our two organisations today, and we find that we are having to return to Japan with news of little comfort. It is important that we now understand between us how we are to proceed, and we would like to hear from you on this matter.'

Doo-hwan took from his pocket a large white handkerchief and blew his nose copiously; it gave him a few moments for thought. He refolded the large handkerchief and put it back in his pocket. He had removed from his lip beads of perspiration so surprisingly formed there.

'Oku San, I must express my deep regret in the failure of the first part of our plans. However, it is very rarely that any business development runs straight and true, and this appears to be no exception. During the period that I discovered with certainty that NTI was developing this new chemistry, I had the pleasure of talking to a certain Victor Stanley, who was the envoy from NTI talking to Nonaka Corporation in Osaka. I must admit he was not a willing guest, but the circumstances that followed this placed him in close proximity with one of my junior colleagues, a Ms Veronica Tan. I am reliably informed that Mr Stanley and Ms Tan formed a relationship that was not altogether platonic, and because of his close involvement with Nonaka Corporation, I feel that we should be able to use him as a suitable provider of the information that so unfortunately went astray when I used Dr Yoreen.'

'But how long will this take?' asked Oku. 'The government is working rapidly with Nonaka, and if they come up with a substantial lead on this technology, the damage will already have been done.'

'With the greatest of respect, Oku San, I think that your government and the governments of other interested countries still have some way to go before they can find a suitable process to use the product, and I think the time to develop this technology exceeds the amount of time we require to lay our hands upon the real product. Indeed, if that were not the case, there would seem little point in my continuing the search.'

'Back in England, I have mounted a twenty-four-hour watch on Victor Stanley, and I am awaiting the opportunity to use my knowledge of his relationship with Ms Tan effectively. He has a marriage I am sure he wishes to protect. His wife is, fortunately, a woman of some modest circumstance, which in, the event that Mr Stanley was to be found to have compromised himself with the technology of NTI, would undoubtedly be of immense importance to him. This lady has no idea of his brief association with Ms Tan, and I do not believe for one minute that he will have told her about it.'

Doo-hwan stopped and again removed the unwanted beads of perspiration from his upper lip.

'If the facts were revealed to NTI that Mr Stanley had unfortunately been in conversation with people of criminal intent, then I would not give much hope for him maintaining his position there. Under those circumstances, he must become a pliable object, and as we know he has carried samples before for NTI to appraise Nonaka Corporation of the efficacy of their product, he will know intimately the way into their technology and how to acquire the missing sample for us. The late and unlamented doctor Yoreen was excited by a large amount of money, the majority of which I hope to recover. I am sure Mr Stanley, whilst not necessarily being motivated entirely by money, will wish to protect the relationship with his woman. He might not be averse to an approach that would make his retirement a long and happy one either.'

Oku was sucking his teeth again; they were very large, very yellow teeth and protruded slightly in the grand tradition giving him the appearance so often depicted in British films of World War II. Had Oku been old enough at that time in his life, he would undoubtedly have been marked down as one of the more cruel persecutors of Western soldiers.

'You place me in a position where I have no option but to continue to support your activities,' said Oku. 'I am reluctant to do this, as it means I will have to reassure my colleagues in Japan that everything is on course when in fact it is not. You understand, I am sure, that in putting me in this very difficult position, a failure to deliver what we both require could place both our futures in grave danger.'

He made a gesture with his right hand by drawing it from left to right across his throat. Shimada, who had sat silently by his side, shivered visibly. Doo-hwan was not too delighted either. They all knew the risks that they were taking; the stakes were extremely high.

'I am indebted to you, Oku San, for your patience, and for my part, I assure you that no stone will be left unturned to bring about a satisfactory conclusion to our affairs. Because of the circumstances surrounding the death of Dr Yoreen, I am sure there will be a protracted investigation. Equally, I am sure that at NTI in England, there will be a tightening of security. It is not the time now to actively pursue our dealings with Mr Stanley, but as soon as those circumstances change, I will inform you.'

Oku pushed his chair back from the table and stood up; Shimada did likewise. He shuffled the few papers in front of him into a neat pile and placed them in the slim attaché case he had brought with him. Doo-hwan moved his chair back and stood up. His legs were not as strong as they had been at the start of the meeting, and it was with considerable relief that he realised it had come to a conclusion without any serious threats to his present well-being having been issued. He was not so sanguine about the future. He also knew the strength of his own organisation and took some comfort from the fact that if there was to be a battle, he would not succumb easily. This was all negative thought, however, and he had no intention of being thwarted in his desire to remain in his lucrative business and to have the necessary countermeasures to fight the legitimate forces ranged against him.

'I will deliver back to Japan', said Oku, 'the message that our talks have proceeded well but that the timing has unfortunately been upset because of the unfortunate death of Dr Yoreen as a result of his apparent double-cross. I can buy at least some time on the understanding that I deliver as well your assurances that you have another line of investigation that will ultimately deliver the goods.'

Oku bowed deeply to Doo-hwan; as did Shimada. Doo-hwan unsuccessfully tried to do the same; it was not that he was unwilling but just unable. The interview was at an end.

Chapter 16

Kevin pressed the appropriate buttons on the telephone. The phone started to ring, but it took some time before a voice answered; it was a woman. The voice was somewhat detached, full of sleep and not a little irritable. All this Kevin managed to realise from just listening; he was a perceptive sort of person.

'Hipkiss here,' he said by way of introduction.

'If this is the start of a dirty conversation', said the voice at the other end, 'I don't think you've picked a very good time for it. Goodnight.'

To his utter amazement, Kevin found himself holding the telephone receiver with no one any longer at the other end. It had not occurred to him that the utterance of the word 'Hipkiss' in the middle of the night to a strange woman might seem like an unwelcome invitation.

'Stupid bloody bitch!' he yelled at no one. He pressed the buttons for a second time. The phone rang again; he let it do this for several minutes before a man's voice answered.

'I think I should warn you', the voice said, 'if we have any more trouble from a caller like you, we shall immediately ring the police.'

Kevin was not going to be outdone this time. 'David, it's Kevin!' he yelled down the phone.

At the other end, David Frome, who was sitting on the side of the bed holding the receiver to his ear with his back to his wife, put his hand over the mouthpiece. 'Oh, fuck', he said, 'it's my boss.'

Judith Frome was by now also sitting up taking notice. She was naked from the waist up showing off a pair of large but well-formed breasts with big nipples.

'I'm sorry, Kevin. I hadn't realised it was you, and it is the middle of the night. My wife is always a lighter sleeper than I and got to the telephone first,' he added lamely. 'What can I do for you?'

'I am sorry to have alarmed you, David', said Kevin, against his better judgement, 'but there has been a major news item on television that has focused on George Yoreen. I am surprised you didn't see it on the news earlier this evening.'

'We were out for dinner with friends and didn't get back until half past eleven. After that, we didn't put on the television, so I am in ignorance as to anything that might have been announced involving George. I thought he was on holiday in the South of France.'

'He was and is in a sense', said Kevin, 'but very unfortunately, his holiday is now somewhat permanent—he's dead.'

David Frome could have sworn that Kevin had said that George Yoreen was dead, but he couldn't momentarily take it in.

'Did you say 'dead', Kevin?'

'Dead, yes, dead, dead, dead,' said an increasingly exasperated Kevin.

'My god!' said David Frome. 'How? What happened to him?'

'This is neither the time nor the place, David, to go into the circumstances of George's death. I will explain that to you at the laboratory. Get dressed and meet me at the entrance to the research block. I suggest you prepare yourself for a very long day. Now, I really have to go.'

David Frome put down the receiver and continued to sit on the edge of the bed staring at the wall ahead of him. His wife moved across the bed and put her arms round him. The tips of her large nipples touched his back; it was cold.

'What on earth's happened, David?' she asked. 'Calls in the middle of the night, the chief executive on the telephone, and now you sit staring at the wall as though transfixed. Talk of death as well. Who's dead, David? Come on—give.'

Judith was the stronger of the two, adaptable and ambitious, slow to shock. She saw David was shocked, though, so badly that he remained staring at the bedroom wall unmoved by her gesture; not like him at all, and it worried her. What events had made this happen?

'George Yoreen has died', said David slowly, 'somewhere in the South of France apparently, and I have to go to the labs now. There must be some very strange circumstances surrounding all of this.'

'Strange?' said Judith. 'It's bloody well amazing.' She let go of David and slumped down on the bed. 'That means you are likely to be head of research. Yippee!'

Judith always had an eye to the main chance, and here was one to ram home in no uncertain terms. If it was left to David, he would probably just coast along burying his nose in research and not looking for the main opportunity. Judith was looking for the main opportunity.

'I don't know how you can react in such a way, Judith,' said the honourable David. 'It's terrible to immediately be on the attack, to take advantage of George's death. You know that I worked very closely with him, and it's come as a great shock, and, frankly, I can't understand your attitude.'

She really couldn't care a dam whether he liked the attitude. It was a common fact that when a personnel disaster occurred, it created an opportunity somewhere else. She knew that it was important to push David, as he would never push himself,

179

and she also knew, from the comforts she had seen George and Sybil enjoy, that anyone in the head research spot at NTI would live very well indeed, certainly better than she lived now. There was the nagging little thought at the back of her mind that her reaction to the chief executive's opening remark on the telephone might be held against her. Perhaps she would have to do something about that. She regarded herself as a very attractive and sexy woman. She was feeling extremely sexy now at the prospects that lay ahead of her. David still had his back to her, and she drew up her right leg until the sheet fell over her knee. She then pushed it down with her right foot, revealing the matching parts to the rather good breasts.

'David.'

He knew from the tone of her voice what she wanted. He looked over his left shoulder and saw her now spread-eagled naked behind him.

'David, do some research on me,' and she winked lasciviously.

Normally, he would have been quite attracted by the prospect of such an invitation, as their marriage was still new enough for it to hold certain fascinations for him, and he was quite sure that he hadn't yet plumbed the depths of the sexual possibilities that presented themselves on a very regular basis, but at the moment, he could only feel disgusted at her immediate and brazen attitude towards his obviously enhanced prospects; she was turned on by it.

'You're sometimes an uncaring and dirty bitch, Judith. If you think I am going to climb on top of you because the prospects for my future have suddenly been enhanced by the death of a close colleague, then you're beyond hope.' He got up and, without a backward glance, walked through the bedroom door and down the short passage to the bathroom. She called after him.

'If I don't push you, David, no one will. You only get a few opportunities in life, so, for goodness's sake, take this one …'

He closed the door behind him and cut off the rest of what she was saying. Careful about his appearance at all times and wanting to present the best now, he ran a bowl of hot water and shaved quickly but meticulously. He turned on the shower over the bath and stepped into it, drawing the curtain around him, and washed himself as quickly as possible. He stepped out of the shower and almost measured his length stepping into a pool of water on top of the tiled floor. In his haste, he had not closed the shower curtain properly, and part of it had deposited enough water to cause a hazard. He picked up Judith's bath towel and threw it into the pool knowing that it would annoy her and feeling a momentary glow of satisfaction, which he couldn't quite explain. He towelled himself vigorously down, applied a squirt of antiperspirant under both arms, and splashed his face with the last remaining drops of his Aramis. He combed and parted his quite luxurious auburn hair, patted it into place, and, apparently satisfied, left the bathroom.

On returning to the bedroom, he found that Judith had taken on one of her customary sulks and was now curled up in a small ball underneath the covers; he was glad. It would take her some time to come round again now, and he was relieved at not having to face the prospect of another interrogation on his weaknesses.

When Kevin had put down the receiver after his complex exchange with Judith and David Frome, he was not in the best of moods. How dare the wife of some trumped-up little scientist think that he, Kevin Hipkiss, was some sort of pervert calling women in the middle of the night to get some sort of vicarious thrill. He made a mental note that the next time he saw Judith Frome, he would make her aware of his displeasure. Now was not the moment; it was more important to have her husband firmly on his side, as without his help, Kevin would have a task ahead of him that he could not complete.

It was still pitch-black outside. He stood just inside the doors in the expectation that Clinton would see him. His expectation was not fulfilled. Rain came slanting against the glass and, despite its thickness, was audible. He had no raincoat or umbrella with him, and the prospect of making a dash for the car did not please him. *The bastard's fallen asleep again,* he thought and continued to stand there. The rain did not relent, nor did the car move; he could see it clearly in the floodlit part of the executives parking area.

Finally, he pushed open the door and, at the top of his voice, yelled, 'Clinton!' Still, nothing happened. He tried several more times without effect.

Clinton saw and heard and grinned to himself, keeping his head lowered as if asleep.

At last, glancing at his watch, he decided he could wait no longer and, stepping out into the downpour, ran as quickly as his fit body would allow him to the car. He reached for the rear door and pulled the handle sharply. He let out an exclamation; it was locked.

'Clinton!' he screamed. 'Open the bloody door!'

Clinton looked up and rubbed his eyes and, feigning surprise, pulled the handle of his own door, which released the central locking system. Hipkiss threw himself wet and dishevelled through the door onto the back seat. He was beside himself with rage.

'Clinton, the company does not pay you to sit around comfortably in a motor car sleeping while the chief executive stood a hundred metres away behind a glass door clearly in view and clearly wanting your services to avoid an unnecessary journey in foul weather. Already, tonight, you have attempted to shut my hand in the door, and now you apparently want to drown me. Well, hear this and hear it well. If I have reason to reprimand you again, I shall instruct personnel to provide you with a written warning as to your conduct. Now, drive me to the research labs.'

Fuck off, thought Clinton. *You're a bastard, Hipkiss, you always have been, you always will be, and the last thing you are actually going to do is fire me because I am sure you know that I know more about your activities than I should. There are not many chauffeurs and manservants who would stand the pace as I do. Even your simple mind must have taken that in.* Then he reverted to company form.

'I am sorry, sir, no excuses.' The car reversed smoothly out of the parking space and set off the short journey to the research labs. Clinton glowed with satisfaction.

It was early afternoon in Osaka, and Kenezo Nonaka was talking to his father.

'We have carried out a number of experiments on the misappropriated sample that Victor Stanley so unhappily misplaced. I have entrusted this task to Dr Nobura.'

The great man nodded. 'He is a good choice, my son. I knew when we appointed him head of R & D, we would not regret it, and now he has his ultimate opportunity.'

'I have told him, Father, of the great honour bestowed upon him and the serious responsibility that goes with that. I have even indicated that a successful outcome to the analytical programme will enhance his standing and seniority in the company.'

Nonaka senior inclined his head towards his son. His face was yellowing now with age, but his eyes were older still; hooded and elongated, they stared at his son with interest. He maintained his silence for a few moments.

'You realise, my son, that we have obtained a piece of priceless research for which we have not paid, and we have obtained it if not dishonestly, then without honour. We are all aware of the importance of this invention. We are aware that our government and the governments of other friendly states would gain immeasurable benefit from the use of it, and, furthermore, the criminal fraternity would be put in turmoil. This, in turn, means that any product developed by ourselves, whether with the help of NTI in England or through our own technical resources, will be the prime target for terrorists and criminals throughout Japan. We place ourselves through this act only a little above those people, for it is greed and not honour that has motivated us.'

The old head looked down at the desk in front of him and apparently read something that was placed there. He looked up again. Kenezo had not moved. He knew that when his father was finished, he would be told.

'There was a time', he said, 'when New Technology Industries and our own company worked closely together for our mutual benefit. A subtle change has taken place within that organisation over the last few years, and my old friend Sir Dennis Matchett is not the man he was. I have looked on with some dismay since the appointment of Mr Hipkiss, and I can only say that this man is not one with whom we will ever form a lasting relationship. I cannot therefore feel that our activities at the moment are altogether wrong. I want it to be understood clearly, however, that in all this, there is one name that must be protected, for it is this man who has, above all, strengthened the relationships between our companies at a time when, if he had not applied his considerable skills towards that event, they could have deteriorated and perhaps even collapsed.'

He looked down again at the piece of paper and read two words, 'Victor Stanley.' He continued. 'If Dr Nobura feels that we have a chance of completing a successful analysis of the NTI material, then we will submit a sample to our government contact within the Ministry of Trade and Industry, and through their good offices, we will seek a comparison with the English samples already submitted for approval. In the event that our material is comparable, then we will face NTI in open competition if necessary. It is the skill of our company to take an idea or an invention and to develop it to the point of commercial success rapidly and to market it successfully. It is a fact that these English, who are so inventive, place too much trust in the development of that inventiveness with others. It has become so commonplace that when a company such as NTI has taken its materials to the first point of commercial examination, they then provide samples to close working partners such as ourselves to further assess them. There lies the danger. Once assessed and with the ability in our hands to manufacture, we will make progress more rapidly than they, and the first shall become the last.'

Kenezo Nonaka received his instructions in the statement from his father. He was in agreement with what had been said; even if he wasn't, it would not be possible to go against what his father desired. He was pleased that the name in front of his father now was that of Victor Stanley, for despite the differences of East and West, he looked upon this man as a friend. When close relationships are formed between honourable people, they should not easily be torn apart.

'I hear what you say, Father, and I will act honourably with regard to your thoughts and views and seek to protect Mr Stanley as well. Now, if you will forgive me, I must have a further meeting with Dr Nobura and develop the working timetable. As soon as I have any clear evidence that we are succeeding in the analytical process and that we are in hope of being able to match the NTI product, I will inform you.'

The old man inclined his head once more across the big desk. His son bowed slightly towards him and, turning on his heel, walked through the door into the corridor. In front of him was a painting by Constable, a tranquil English country scene. Turning right down the corridor towards his own office, he would pass several more works of art collected not so much for their beauty but for appreciation in value. They were impressive to foreign visitors, many of whom coveted them. It was a source of satisfaction to the old man to possess such treasures from the art of the West. His own Japanese treasures of an altogether different pictorial nature were contained in a private viewing room at his house in Kobe; not even his son had been allowed to see these.

Victor Stanley just could not sleep. The news of the night before had been so stunning in its magnitude that it had driven every bit of fatigue from his body. His mind would not stop working on the problem of George's death. Every question that it put up, he found an answer to; but when he asked himself the question again, he found a new answer, and so it went on. Gloria was not much better, and knowing of his discomfort, she, too, lay there wide awake. Eventually, she turned on the light.

'It's no good us just lying here pretending to be asleep. darling,' she said. 'We might as well accept the fact that this is just not going to be a good night, for there are too many events in our minds, and I can understand the thoughts that are going through yours at the moment.'

'I still can't believe it,' said Victor. 'I can't help feeling that my activities in Japan recently may have contributed directly to George's death and I have become embroiled in what could turn out to be a horrific and continuous nightmare.'

Gloria knew better than to force the pace at this moment. She dearly loved her husband, and although she knew he was not perfect, she equally knew that in most of the things he did, he sought to protect her and to shelter her from the more unsavoury events that took place at NTI.

'I am going to get up and make us a cup of tea.'

It was usually Gloria's solution to a problem in the middle of the night, and it wasn't a bad idea anyway if Victor was going to talk, and she suspected he was. She went out of the bedroom and walked into the kitchen and, turning on the light, went across to the electric jug, filled it with water, and placed it carefully back in its holder and depressed the switch. She took from the cupboard two large mugs and placed in them two Marks & Spencer Extra Strong tea bags with two Hermesetas for Victor and nothing for herself. She watched the jug boil slowly. Finally, the automatic switch clicked, and lifting the jug from its holder, she poured the boiling water into the mugs and stirred them vigorously to release the strong full flavour of the tea. She added skimmed milk and, putting them on a tray, returned to the bedroom. Victor was sat up in bed with a frown on his face.

'Come on, darling,' said Gloria. 'I am sure it's not the end of the world.'

Victor forced a smile. 'Well, I agree with you there. It might not be the end of the world, but on the other hand, it might be the end of world as we know it. The events of the last few weeks may be such that it will alter our lives immeasurably if that little shit Hipkiss has anything to do with it. I am afraid none of it will be for the better.'

'Victor, we have been married a long time. We've gone through a great deal together. You started with nothing and I with a little, and together we have managed to improve upon that, so if the worst really happened, then we shouldn't have any regrets and we're not going to starve. Whatever the circumstances, I will still love you.'

Victor was extremely touched by the statement, but he wondered how far that statement would be stretched if Gloria knew about the startling little affair with Victoria Tan. That was something he couldn't really get out of his mind either, for at his advanced age, to be suddenly thrown into what was a deeply exciting, if momentary, relationship with a totally exquisite young lady was nothing short of a wonder to him. He still couldn't believe some of the things she had done to him and the extreme and exquisite pleasure he had derived from that. Perhaps now was the time to bring Gloria more fully into the Japanese picture, and although he had told her many of his problems on return from Japan, he now needed to fill in the gaps, so he did.

As dawn was coming up, light started to fill the window of their bedroom, which faced away from Lower Sloane Street, and across the grounds of the Territorial Army Headquarters, it was yet too early for there to be any activity there, but Victor had gravitated to the window during his long discourse on the Japanese saga and finished it whilst staring out into the dawn of a new and momentous day.

Gloria was sitting up in bed and had listened without interruption to everything that Victor had told her. His only omission was the full content of the relationship with Veronica Tan, but she suspected that it might have been something stronger than he had indicated, but it was really of no consequence. It wasn't that she didn't resent the possibility that Victor had screwed someone young enough to be her daughter; it was rather the fact that it was far more important to her that the relationship they had built up should not be destroyed at this point by her anger and resentment over what was, after all, a liaison that would not be sustained. She dismissed it from her thoughts; he was a very lucky man.

'I really don't see that you have done anything wrong, darling. If, as you suspect, George Yoreen double-crossed this man Doo-hwan unwittingly, then it was his own funeral, quite literally as it turned out. In double-crossing Doo-hwan, he was selling the secrets of his employer anyway for a large sum of money, so whatever the circumstances, the fact that he died because of it was not your fault. If he had succeeded and placed in the hands of this criminal the material that you have been developing, then it would have been a disaster of the first magnitude. As it is, it would appear that the world has had removed from it a rather greedy scientist. Indeed, if the theft had been discovered, he would anyway have spent a considerable time in one of Her Majesty's prisons, and that would have been the end of him anyway. As a matter of interest, what do you suspect happened to the sample that you had hidden?'

'I don't even dare speculate on it,' said Victor. 'I have been friends with Kenezo Nonaka, as you know, for a long time, and we have worked together on many projects. These have not only been successful for Nonaka Corporation but also been successful for NTI. This latest project, despite its secrecy, was one that was going to create great wealth for both of our businesses, and the only thing that I can suspect, and I don't even like doing that, is that knowing my predicament at the time, Kenezo took advantage of me and stole the sample. If that's the case, this now means that lying in a laboratory somewhere in Osaka, probably under the careful analysis of a gentleman called Dr Nobura, is the NTI prototype. Because of the amount of information exchanged between our two companies, I believe that Nobura is quite capable of filling in the missing pieces when he has completed all the analytical processes available to him. If this is so, then NTI, who has so far only developed the prototype but has admittedly had it tested and approved in its first stages by the various authorities, will have to move extremely fast to build a production unit.

'The Japanese are particularly good at taking original ideas and scaling them up to full production. In my estimate, they would do it at least three times faster than any UK company or indeed any European or American company, come to that. If this is the case, then our own invention may well come back at us in another form, and we would then be placed in a position of weakness with regard to negotiation about the income from the technology itself.'

'None of this is going to look very good on the record of your friend Kevin.'

'He's no friend of mine,' said Victor.

'You know what I mean,' said Gloria. 'If all this comes to rest on his plate, then Sir Dennis isn't going to be delighted with his little blue-eyed boy. Maybe that'll do you some good.'

'Despite your confidence in me, darling', said Victor, 'I don't think that when those circumstances arise, I will necessarily be a part of NTI.'

The phone rang.

David Frome stopped his Rover at the gates of the R & D Centre in Hillingdon. He took from his pocket the special pass that allowed him access to the laboratories during normal working hours and handed it to the guard who approached the car. It was not someone that David recognised, as his hours of business did not usually require him to be around the R & D Centre at night and they had an altogether different crew on. There was a photograph that was a good resemblance of David on the pass, and the guard took it, consulted a clipboard he held in his right hand, and said, 'Good Morning, Dr Frome. I have been expecting you. If you will just sign the log, sir, I'll let you through.' He handed the clipboard through to David, who saw his name and the entry time written down and signed against it. The guard checked the signature against that on his security pass.

'Thank you, Dr Frome. You're clear to proceed.'

The gates opened, and David drove through and parked in the senior staff car park. The rain had abated somewhat, and dawn was beginning to appear in the east, or at least there was a change in the density of the night. He turned off the engine and the lights, and picking up his attaché case from the back seat, he shut the doors of the car and locked them. He walked across the car park and under the covered walkway to the lighted entrance of block number one. He had noticed the chief executive's car in the car park, and his driver had raised a hand in greeting. He could never remember the fellow's name. *Something like Hinton,* he thought; he didn't pursue it. Standing on the other side of the glass doors in all his glory was Kevin Hipkiss.

'God! You took your time,' said Hipkiss as David Frome entered. 'What do you think, this is some sort of Sunday afternoon tea party?'

'As you have not yet told me exactly what is going on—apart from the death of poor old George, that is—I don't know what to expect,' said David. 'I guess, however, it's not a Sunday afternoon tea party.'

'Don't be flippant with me, Frome,' said the egregious Hipkiss. Never at his best with staff anything below director level at the best of times, he was positively objectionable at the moment. David Frome knew that it was unwise to pursue this line of conversation; after all, he was talking to the chief executive, and he was mindful as well of the words that Judith had forced upon him, even if she thought he wasn't. There was undoubtedly an opportunity going to be opened up in front of him, and now that he was back in R & D block number one, he really very much wanted it to be his kingdom.

'I'm sorry,' said David. 'It's just that I'm not used to being dragged out of bed in the middle of the night for a dramatic situation such as this. Please let me know what it is you want me to do.'

Kevin signalled him to follow and, opening the door onto the central corridor, walked smartly down it until he came to the door of the late George Yoreen's office. He inserted a key that he had taken from his pocket into the lock and turned it. He opened the door and walked inside. When George had left, he had made a half-hearted effort at clearing his desk for his holiday; however, to anyone else, it still looked as though a localised whirlwind had deposited a heap of papers across it at random.

'I just don't know how he ever worked in an atmosphere like this,' said the ever-neat Kevin. If Kevin had more than three pieces of paper on his desk at any one time, then it was his standing instruction that they had to be placed in clearly identifiable piles. Each of these piles had to be as geometrically perfect as possible; otherwise, he felt compelled to adjust them.

'It was just the way George always worked,' said David. 'It wasn't that he was untidy. It was that he just used the surface of his desk as a filing cabinet, and generally speaking, he could usually place his hands on the papers he wanted.'

'Yes, but no one else can,' said Kevin.

It was true, thought David. Certainly, he didn't know where to start looking for anything even if Kevin knew what he was looking for. With a grimace at the mess in front of him, Kevin walked round the desk and sat behind it in the somewhat battered and comfortable chair that George had so enjoyed. He could have sworn the seat was mildly sticky. David Frome drew up a chair on the other side of the desk and also sat down. Kevin looked steadily across the cluttered desk at him.

'I suppose this might be an opportunity for you to better yourself,' he said.

'Would you like to clarify that statement a little, Kevin? I'm not quite sure how I should read it.'

'What I mean is', said Kevin carefully, 'that the death of poor old George places you in a key position within NTI. As the deputy head of research and as George's right-hand man, you are the only other person who has full knowledge of the chemistry of the superconducting polymer project. It is therefore of the utmost importance that we carry out a careful investigation as to why George Yoreen was murdered. I might as well say right now that I have my own suspicions, but, undoubtedly, the press and the police will be on to us within the next few hours, and if possible, I want the company to at least be ahead of them in the investigation.'

David sat there listening. Kevin was obviously going to reveal all to him, so he shifted into a more comfortable position on a very uncomfortable chair. Kevin continued.

'George Yoreen wasn't the type of person who would normally have developed many enemies, I think. He was at heart a boffin. He was very good in this particular field of polymer chemistry. A number of people knew of his skills, and a smaller number knew of the technology that we were working on. Our friends in Japan, Nonaka Corporation, are therefore under some suspicion, and the envoy working between UK and Japan must also come under suspicion of being involved one way or another—namely, Victor Stanley.'

'I can't believe that,' said David Frome. 'Victor is a man of the highest integrity, and I don't think for one minute that any of our technology would ever be compromised by him or that he would have one evil thought in his mind. It is laughable to suggest that he be involved in George's death.'

'I am not asking for your opinion,' said Kevin nastily. 'I am merely telling you what my thoughts are. It is your job to listen to them and then act upon my instructions. Do I make myself clear?'

'Yes, sir,' said David.

'That's better. As I was saying, Victor Stanley is also a suspect. On his last trip to Japan, a sample of the active material was logged out, and on his return, the same sample was check weighed and logged in. In both cases, George Yoreen signed the log, and I authorised the original carrying of the sample. I now want you to tell me what would happen to the sample that had been returned by Victor Stanley.'

'Normally, George would have taken back the sample from Victor, and he would have added it directly to the returned material vessel. As you know, we take no samples back into main stock but put them back into the receiver where we are able to determine by assay the general strength of the active material present. This must reflect the actual solids content of total material produced and used within a very small error factor.'

'How often do you carry out an assay on the returned and used working sample flask?'

'Normally, we would do this once every two weeks, but as George and I have to check this jointly and as he has been on holiday, it is now overdue.'

'Just as I thought,' said Kevin. 'It is therefore important that we carry out an immediate assay on the strength of the active material in the receiver. I presume you are able to calculate what it should be taking into account the fact that the returned sample from Victor Stanley would have been added.'

'Yes, in theory, this is perfectly possible, and taking into account the acceptable error factor, it is generally very accurate.'

'How quickly can you get this done?'

'If I start work now and have the right number of assistants there to help me, it can be accomplished by mid-morning, always assuming that you are prepared to accept my figure in the absence of any corroborative evidence.'

'Yes, of course, I am prepared to accept your figure,' said Kevin. 'It is just important that we get it done because we are going to have to make some sort of statement concerning what's been going on. I suggest now that you get your team assembled, but don't tell them what the problem is until they get here, and even then, I don't want anything said about Victor Stanley. I just want a straightforward investigation following the death of our chief research scientist. I take it you have the appropriate telephone numbers of the people you need.'

'Yes. I can get on to them straightaway,' said David.

'Then do it. Let's just get on with the job.' Kevin looked up at David Frome as if still surprised to see him there. 'You can leave now,' he said dismissively.

David was relieved to get out of the office and into the laboratory proper. He went to his own office, which was carved out of a corner of the working area. He put his attaché case on a side table and sat behind his desk. He picked up the phone.

Left alone, Kevin also picked up the phone. He dialled Victor Stanley's number. He had been looking forward with some anticipation to this call, and it was now late enough in the morning to ring him but early enough to wake him from a deep and sound sleep, always assuming, of course, that Victor Stanley had not heard the news the previous evening and had not been on the telephone half the night to his friends in Japan.

Victor Stanley answered himself. 'Hello, Stanley here.'

There was no apology from Kevin for the earliness of the hour or the abruptness of the message; his only disappointment was that he couldn't see the expression on the face at the other end of the phone.

'Ah, Victor, I have some rather bad news, I am afraid,' said Kevin. 'I don't know whether you know, but George Yoreen was murdered yesterday in the South of France.'

'Yes, of course, I know,' said Victor. 'I do try and keep up with the news, you know.'

'Well, in that case, you will also probably be aware that we have had to start an immediate investigation within the company as to why this might have happened, and I'—self-importantly—'have been up most of the night with Sir Dennis addressing the problem.'

Kevin waited for a response from the other end of the phone; there was none. He continued. 'Sir Dennis has asked me to instruct you to be in his office as soon as you can reasonably manage it. I would suggest seven thirty.'

'And I would suggest eight o'clock,' said Victor.

As Kevin had mentioned the earlier time, he had looked at his watch and had rapidly determined he would be hard-pressed to make it by seven thirty, as the morning was now advancing. For this particular interview, he did not want to arrive flustered or dishevelled.

'I said seven thirty,' said Kevin.

190

'And I said eight o'clock', responded Victor, 'and eight o'clock it's going to be if I am going to turn myself around in suitable time and gather together the information I need for a meeting with Sir Dennis.' Victor had spelled it out syllable by syllable, and Kevin hadn't liked that, nor had he liked the tone, but because he was going to achieve the ultimate satisfaction, he thought, from this particular meeting, he gave in ungraciously.

'Oh, all right, then, Victor, if you must insist, eight o'clock, but make sure you're there.'

'I will,' said Victor and put the phone down. At the other end, Kevin was left holding the receiver. He placed it back none too gently in the cradle.

Sir Dennis and Max Fiddler had also spent a very long night. They had together created and agonised over a number of statements for internal and external consumption. They had addressed every conceivable problem that they saw arising in the next few hours and in the next days and weeks. They were preparing themselves for an in-depth investigation, not only by the police over the circumstances of George Yoreen's death but also by the press, who would undoubtedly latch onto the fact that George had been working on a top-secret project. Once the press were aware of this, their talent for investigative journalism would no doubt produce more information, some of which would be true and more which would not. They would speculate wildly on what NTI had to hide.

There would be speculation on how this product, whatever it might be, would be of use to the world and, more particularly, why it should result in the death of their top scientist. It was going to be a testing time for NTI, and Sir Dennis did not savour the fact that he would be the main contact for press and television. They had discussed the role of Kevin Hipkiss in all this, and Max Fiddler had been absolutely adamant that he should be kept out of the television lights as much as possible.

'You may not be particularly good in front of the cameras, Dennis, but at least you are not going to be there for your own self-glory and aggrandisement,' said Max. He didn't pull his punches when it came to making statements of a material nature, and he felt that his analysis of Kevin Hipkiss had been fairly accurate. He had decided some time ago that Kevin was there to score big marks with his friends in the City. It was important to Kevin to be talked and written about. Just so long as his name kept on appearing, then his path to the top was made more certain. Max did not want this to be a time when Kevin would benefit.

Max was convinced that Kevin was only at NTI until such time as something bigger and better turned up. Offer him more prestige and more money, and Kevin would be off like shit off a shovel. In short, Max Fiddler had gotten Kevin about right. It was now his main job to protect his client, and he would deploy all his skills

191

to accomplish this. He would have to remain within the realms of what was honourable and basically honest, but then, today, that didn't mean a lot. He had already anticipated the sort of fees that were going to flow into Fiddler, Gloat, and Penworthy and taken some considerable satisfaction from this.

Max Fiddler and Dennis Matchett had finally come up with the draft statement that they felt would reassure the various people that would be looking for answers today. After much agonising and the throwing away of many drafts, the following now lay in front of them.

PRESS STATEMENT

NTI plc has, for some time now, been working on a highly confidential project that will revolutionise the battle against crime and introduce into the world the first truly conductive plastic. Tragically, the chief scientist, Dr George Yoreen, was murdered yesterday in Nice. We are not aware yet of the reasons for this dreadful act, but we cannot rule out the possibility that his murder was a means of removing the leader of the development team. There may even be more sinister implications.

An immediate internal investigation has revealed that no samples or confidential papers are missing. The main work surrounding the development of the superconductive polymer has been completed, and the research unit is fully able to complete the process development and launch the product with only minor delays to the original schedule. We wish to reassure our shareholders, government agencies, and trade contacts at home and overseas that we are able to live up to all our obligations.

Dr David Frome has been appointed chief scientist. Dr Frome has worked with George Yoreen on the project from its inception.

There then followed a couple of more items about whom to contact for further comment. Sir Dennis was nominated, with Max being the alternative. Kevin's name was left out and, in Max Fiddler's view, with good reason.

Sir Dennis Matchett reread the press release for the fiftieth time; he still wasn't entirely happy. It was his view that anything released to the press was a building block on which to build an unsafe structure, and therefore the less that was said at this stage, the better. On the other hand, he also realised that they were going to be interviewed by so many people in the next twenty-four hours that they must have something to fall back on, and this was the very least that they could produce. They were working anyway in an area where they had little real knowledge and had to leave themselves free to manoeuvre in future statements. They would start to learn things from the police investigation, and Max Fiddler would send off immediately one of his junior colleagues to Nice to dig around there and see what he could come up with independent of any official enquiry that might be taking place. Max had already telephoned the person in question and given him precise instructions as to what he would be doing over the next few days. He had instructed him to be at their offices first thing this morning in order that he could be given precise details of what to look out for.

'I am still not happy with it,' said Sir Dennis. 'It seems to me that we are giving too much information away to our competitors via a simple press release.'

'It is nothing that the press won't be learning anyway,' said Max. 'By the time they have completed their own investigations, the whole world is going to know something about superconductive polymers. Let's face it, most of your competitors will know about them anyway.'

'I suppose you're right,' said Sir Dennis reluctantly. 'You usually seem to be when we get into a fix. That's why I have come to rely on you so much over the years.'

Max looked at him carefully. *He really was losing his balls,* he thought to himself. He went on to think what on earth would happen to this interesting company once Sir Dennis had decided to leave control to the likes of the Kevin Hipkisses of this world. At least he would not be around to see this; it would then be the responsibilities of those in his own organisation who were rising to the top, and he sometimes wondered about them.

'For heaven's sake, Dennis, don't start going sentimental. That can wait for later. I'm here, first, as the paid servant of the company, and, second, as your friend, and what I am doing now is what I perceive as my duty to the company and to the shareholders. I might remind you also that I am one of those.'

Sir Dennis took a large white handkerchief from his right trouser pocket and blew his nose copiously to hide the temporary embarrassment of this exchange. He had always found close business relationships rather offensive. It had been one of his lifelong practices to distance himself from his senior colleagues.

Once in an unguarded moment when Sir Dennis had been asked by a fellow director why he never joined them for dinner on the evenings prior to a board meeting, he had intimated that he chose his friends with care and didn't see any reason why he had to share his social moments with colleagues. It was this attitude that had led him to be a poor judge of men as he only saw in them what he wanted to see and so studiously avoided contact outside the workplace that he never saw the whole employee.

In the days before his involvement with the Technical Improvements in Government Establishments Committee, he had devoted enough time to the business for this not to matter entirely, but in the last year or so, his chairmanship of that committee had seriously eroded his 'hands-on' control, and he had closed a blind eye to the activities of Kevin Hipkiss and some of his more outrageous actions with regard to the manipulation of people and the inhuman way in which he was achieving his objectives. The City appeared to like him well enough, however, and admittedly, since Kevin had come on board, things had gone along very nicely. There had not been any particularly spectacular acquisitions or any really newsworthy achievements apart from the superconductive polymer, but the share price had been going up quite steadily, and the general reporting in the financial press and by the City analysts had, on the whole, been favourable.

Why should this all have been blown away now? Just when he was beginning to think that he could leave go entirely; after all, his doctor had urged him to do so if he wished to live to a ripe old age. Now, here he was having to marshal all the resources to fight what was going to be a particularly bloody battle. There must be somebody who was responsible for all this; he needed a sacrificial manager. Once identified and placed on the altar, the focus would go from him and from NTI; the villain of the piece could be roundly blamed, and having been identified and sacrificed, everyone, including Sir Dennis, could get back to the job of running the company.

He shook his head as if to clear it of these distracting thoughts and picked up the telephone to his right. He pressed the button marked secretary and spoke briefly into it.

The door opened, and Kathryn Goodbody came into the room like a flagship in full sail. It had been an unfortunate circumstance that had given her the name of Goodbody and then proceeded to fashion her in the shape of a Russian weightlifter. She had been with Sir Dennis almost since the beginning of time and was his last line of defence. She was frankly horrified by the events that had taken place in the last twenty-four hours and had formed already her own opinion as to what had happened.

'Is there something I can do for you, Sir Dennis?' she enquired.

'Yes, Kathryn. Max and I have been working most of the night on a statement that will be issued immediately to all the grade-one names on the press release list. I want you to type this up and get in touch with the PR Department and make sure that you are happy that their list complies with your category one. The most important is the stock exchange. If you can also prevail upon Marcia Payne to fix us some more coffee and perhaps some bacon sandwiches or something, I am sure Max and I would be eternally grateful.'

Max nodded his head enthusiastically.

She remained standing in front of the desk. Sir Dennis knew well the particular expression on her face.

'It appears, Kathryn, that you have something to say, so say it.'

'You know, don't you, Sir Dennis, that you have an interview with Victor Stanley first thing this morning?'

'Yes, I do, Kathryn, and I presume, between you and the chief executive, you have done your usual good job in making sure that he'll be here. However, what's this got to do with our immediate problem?'

'It seems to me, sir, that if he has been to Japan and has had a sample on his person, and if Dr Yoreen is the individual responsible for logging in and logging out samples, then there just might be some connection. For instance, could Victor Stanley have taken a sample out of the country and brought back something entirely different? Could George Yoreen have accepted that entirely different material as being the real thing, and could the circumstances that have arisen since be as a result of that?'

'Kathryn, that's very perceptive of you, and thank you very much, but I have already thought of that. Now, please get on and see that this material is released through PR, and make sure that you handle it all personally. When we start to get the enquiries coming in, I will be the first line of defence. Make sure all calls are put through to me. Meantime, I don't want you to put any of your thoughts into the ears of anyone else in the organisation, do you understand?'

'Yes, sir.' She turned ponderously and somewhat moodily on her heel, causing a physical draught with the movement of her voluminous skirt and left the room.

'Had you really thought of that?' asked Max.

'No, not really, but I couldn't let her think that I hadn't. She might just have something.'

'Indeed, she might,' said Max.

Chapter 17

Chief Inspector Pierre Dupre was a taciturn individual. He had been attached to the regional police headquarters based in Nice for the last two years and had a number of credit-worthy cases to his name. He had tackled many different types of crime ranging from murder and prostitution to drug running. He found all crime totally distasteful and felt that God had placed him on this earth to rid it of as much as he possibly could in the time allotted to him. He was a faithful follower of the commandments, although he had to admit, from time to time, he had a little trouble with coveting.

As soon as his department had been informed of the death of this tourist Yoreen on the beach in Nice, he put into action what he now knew to be his well-oiled investigative machinery. He had summoned his crew, who were ably managed by his deputy, Alain Rochet, and had given them instructions as to how to start what would almost certainly become a rather delicate investigation. He was not fond of tourists, and he certainly wasn't fond of tourists who became deceased on his patch.

The initial explanation of the death of George Yoreen over the telephone from the beach front to police headquarters had been, to say the least, extremely dramatic. The first policeman on the scene indicated that this tourist had been shot through the head while being dragged behind the boat on one of those dreadful parachute things. The policeman had immediately decided that the perpetrators of the crime must therefore be the people in the boat or those connected with the boat and had informed Chief Inspector Dupre that he had arrested the lot of them. Dupre was not pleased. He spoke quite gently to the policeman at first and then shouted a lot. He couldn't undo what had been done, but, clearly, his presence was needed.

He picked up Alain Rochet on his way out of the building, and they got into the car and were followed by two more cars of alerted policemen. The sirens screamed continuously through the thick holiday traffic and seemed to make little impact. *It would almost certainly be quicker on foot,* he thought. He had, at one time, thought of using a police motorcycle as his means of transport around the area but had been persuaded that his dignity would suffer as a result. Instead, he had to put up with the delays that gave to the criminal such a serious advantage.

They eventually arrived at the beach, and Dupre was gratified to see that a policeman was stationed at the entrance stopping people from entering or leaving. There were a number of angry and distressed individuals who wished to leave. There was also quite a crowd of those who had gathered to speculate on the cause of death and the events that would follow. Chief Inspector Dupre did not like crowds.

His team of police officers were now tumbling out of the cars. He gave them immediate instructions to have the area cleared of all those who were not immediately connected with the case. He issued further instructions for all people on the beach to be briefly questioned and their names and addresses taken. If they were unable to prove their identification, then a policeman must accompany them to a place where that would be possible. This might take some time, he pointed out.

It is amazing how cold people can become after an event such as murder on a hot and sunny afternoon. At one moment, they are lying in the sun enjoying themselves and sipping alcoholic drinks; the next, they are wildly excited and hysterical at the chain of events that has occurred. Then once the excitement has begun to wear off, the sun loses its heat, and they start to feel nervous and agitated and want to get dressed and go away. Today would be no exception; many were in a mild form of shock. However, the investigation had to be carried out with thoroughness, and Inspector Dupre was nothing if not thorough.

'Rochet, I want you to take all the visitors to the beach, and beach staff, and assemble them in the dining area and take statements from each. Link each statement to a positive identification, and we will go through them back at headquarters. Take the boat crew and dispatcher away and question them in more detail.'

Rochet nodded and turned away to carry out his task. Dupre went down to the sea's edge where the police surgeon was already present and where the chief suspects, as identified by the police patrol that was first on the scene, were standing nervously in a little group. Dupre identified the driver and observer within the boat and those on the beach responsible for water sports; some were known to him. Others were itinerant workers who came in to work through the summer and then returned whence they came richer in pocket and very probably the fathers of bastards.

Albert Leroux had been a police doctor for thirty years, but he could not recall ever having seen such a spectacular shooting, and it was with some fascination that he speculated on how this had been achieved. He had hoped to have a little more time before Pierre Dupre descended upon him, but he had already decided that it couldn't have been carried out from the beach itself or from anyone driving the boat.

'What have you found, Doctor?' asked Dupre.

'What I have found, my friend, is an entry wound almost dead centre at the lower part of the back of the skull. The bullet in question was soft-nosed and, having entered, broke up and tore around in the skull, mashing everything in its path to a pulp. Death was instantaneous. In my opinion, it is the work of a marksman, and the shot certainly didn't come from the boat or the near shore.'

197

'So you are satisfied that these people operating the boat and working on the shoreline are free from blame?'

'I am as sure as I can be at this point, but it is your decision, Inspector Dupre, what to do with them. I will speculate further if you would like.'

'I would like that very much,' responded Dupre.

Albert Leroux took him by the arm and drew him apart from the policemen and their temporary prisoners. He walked to a quieter part of the beach. Leroux stood with his back to the ocean and pointed towards the buildings on the other side of the Promenade Des Anglais.

'It is my opinion', he said, 'that a high-velocity rifle fired from one of those windows ahead of us, or even from the roof, killed the victim. To use such a rifle with such accuracy, we would need to have a highly trained and experienced assassin at work. I will know more when we have carried out a post-mortem, but I would not expect to find very much from the fragments of the soft-headed bullet. It may have come to your attention that the block of flats opposite us has been neglected for some time now because of a strike, and the obvious place that the assassin would choose would be the top floor.'

Pierre Dupre looked carefully at the building in question and instinctively knew that Leroux was correct. The buildings on either side would have been very difficult to use, as they were hotels, and the numerous staff would have noticed the comings and goings of strangers and would have been able to trace anyway, through the registration system, anyone taking a room for a short period. It would not be a normal chain of events for an assassin of this calibre to use a place where there was any chance of being traced.

'I appreciate your thinking, Albert,' he said. 'I will have our forensics people do a thorough check of the building and see what we can find. Now, you must excuse me because I note that the most distressed person on this beach who is being comforted by my sergeant is a lady, and she is presumably the wife of the victim.'

'You are right,' said Leroux. 'Good luck, my friend. I will talk to you later.'

Pierre Dupre was never particularly happy when having to comfort the partner of a murder victim. He was of the general view that the murder victim's partner usually blamed the police for the circumstances that brought about their death. Starting with such a negative attitude, it was difficult to turn it into a positive contribution to a murder investigation. Certainly, this lady was making a great deal of noise; at least he could sympathise with the very real loss she had experienced. He strode over to her and introduced himself.

'Madam, I am Chief Inspector Pierre Dupre. I am in charge of the investigation into this murder. I do not wish to add to your distress, but I need you to identify the body. I understand that it is your husband.'

Sybil looked at him through her tears. She was normally quite fluent in French, but although she knew what he was saying, she hadn't the words to reply.

'I am sorry, I do not speak French.'

Oh, merde, thought Pierre Dupre, *I am going to have to carry out this whole dammed investigation in English.* His English was very good, but like many French people, he resented having to use it. It was national pride not to do so. He believed that the French language should have been the language accepted throughout Europe, but it wasn't, and now, not only had he got what appeared to be an English victim but also he was going to have to carry out the investigation as though he were an English policeman, which was another aspect of England that he didn't really care for. Inspector Dupre didn't care for much at all about England.

'I am sorry, madam. I will repeat the statement in English,' and he did.

Sybil still couldn't believe it. How could something like this have happened? George was just enjoying himself, admittedly a little dangerously, but she had never felt that the danger was so acute. Why would anyone have wanted to shoot her George and shoot him in such a very final manner and so dramatically as well? The whole sad event was being played out on a stage, spectators were gathered everywhere, and now here she was the centre of attraction herself at a time when all she wanted to do was turn the clock back a few hours and relive those precious moments in a different manner. She broke down again and cried copiously into her handkerchief. Pierre Dupre waited patiently for a break in the hysteria. Finally, she apologised and declared herself fit to talk.

Dupre led Sybil gently to the body.

'Is this your husband, madam?' he asked formally.

Another howl of anguish rent the air and was accompanied by a vigorous nodding. Dupre again waited until the spasm had passed.

'I must ask you to tell me formally, madam, is this your husband?'

'Yes,' sobbed Sybil.

'You must forgive me, but I know little about you or your husband, and there are a number of essential questions I must ask you. Please tell me your name and why you are in Nice.'

The interview went through all the routine questions that he had to use to identify people and to put them in the right place at the right time and ultimately to determine whether they were involved in the crime or whether they were merely victims of it.

In view of the obvious distress of the English lady, the interview moved rapidly from the beach area to the Hotel Westminster.

Pierre Dupre found out on the way to the hotel that she was Sybil Yoreen and that she was the wife of George Yoreen, that they were on holiday in Nice as a perfectly normal event during the year. No, she had no idea why George should have been shot, and she did not believe that he had any enemies.

'I know this is very trying for you', said Pierre Dupre, 'but can you please tell me what sort of work your husband did?'

Sybil did not feel like answering any more questions at the moment. She was still in a state of shock and liable to burst into fits of tears, but she knew that there would be little option but to face the interrogation at some stage, but being made of the stuff she was, she went ahead with it.

'My husband was a research scientist,' she said. 'He worked with a company called NTI in England and was in charge of their most important project. He was a man of considerable intellect and an important part of the scientific development team. He was the team leader.' She dabbed at her eyes with a handkerchief and sniffed copiously.

This was something interesting for Dupre. He had already realised that this was no ordinary murder, and now there came into the picture the smell of a motive. He pursued the point.

'Madam, if your husband was working on a major research project with this British company, are you able to tell me anything about it?'

He was treading here on delicate ground. He wasn't sure whether such things were covered by governmental contract undertakings or the Official Secrets Act, as it was operated in England, or whether this was just a commercial venture, but if he was going to get anything out of anyone, this was the time to do it. Madam Yoreen was at her weakest now, and if only to be released from the pressures of questioning, she was liable to give away information that she might withhold later. He would worry about the consequences of that later.

'It is vital', continued Dupre, 'that as soon as possible, we are able to determine why your husband was murdered. You are a visitor to Nice, so it is likely that any plans were formed elsewhere, perhaps back in England. The murderer might have followed you. If we are to pick up his trail, we need facts now.' Sybil understood completely the nature of her husband's work. She was involved in the dishonesty that had given rise to his death. She suspected now that something had gone terribly wrong with George's plans and that there had been a need to silence him as a result. So many thoughts were raging around inside her head that she could no longer rank them in immediate importance, but if there was a way of avenging his death, then at least helping this French policeman could be part of it.

'You must understand, Inspector, that I am not a scientist, and although I have taken a great interest in my husband's work throughout his life, much of it has been too complex for me to understand or even to describe in detail. I can tell you, however, that the project he was working on was something of great value to the British government and, as I understand it, to several other governments and was something to do with combating crime, particularly in the area of counterfeiting.'

Dupre was starting to become mildly excited. The case was rapidly developing an international flavour.

'Have you any idea at all, madam, what this material was that your husband was so involved with? Was it, for instance, something that the layman would understand if he had it described to him? Is it something that he could see demonstrated?'

Sybil thought about this. Certainly, George had brought home the samples, and she had seen him demonstrate it using the little electronic device that indicated whether the product was present or not.

'Yes, it is certainly something that anyone can readily understand once they have been shown how it works. It is not the function of the product that is complex but the chemistry that is involved in its construction. George always used to refer to it by its initials—SCP, but apart from knowing that these initials stand for "superconductive polymer", I can't tell you anything else about its function, only that when it is present on a piece of paper or in a piece of plastic, you are able to detect it with a small electronic device.'

The effort had been too much for Sybil, and she buried her head in her hands and sobbed uncontrollably. There was a soft knock at the door, and Alain Rochet came in together with a policewoman and another gentleman who carried a small case. He was the hotel doctor who had been summoned by the management at the request of the police.

'I am sorry to distress you so much, madam. I very much appreciate the help you have given, and I believe the information will be very valuable in allowing us to get on with the task of apprehending the murderer. I am now going to leave you in the good hands of this policewoman and the hotel doctor, who I am sure will make life a little easier for you.'

Pierre Dupre turned on his heel and left the room with at least enough information to start piecing together a picture.

Between them, the doctor and the policewoman persuaded Sybil that a sedative would be the best way of calming her down. The policewoman explained that she would stay with Sybil until a nurse was found who would stay with her through the night and be there when she awoke in the morning, which, in her experience, was the most difficult time of all. She did not add that her boss, Pierre Dupre, had told her that when Sybil dropped off to sleep, she was to look around for any evidence that might cast light upon the crime.

Sybil was grateful for the company, and she accepted the recommendations of the doctor. She also knew in the back of her mind that she was going to have to act as soon as possible, even with the tragedy weighing heavily upon her, to recover the money that was here in Nice and to get back to London to salvage what George had laid his life down for. Now, all she wanted to do was rest with her sad thoughts. She would have a night's sleep and could rest in her bed in the knowledge that she had protection, for she was by no means sure that she was not also a potential victim.

Sybil took her dressing gown and nightdress into the bathroom. She undressed and put on the nightdress. She looked in the mirror at the not-very-attractive face that somehow didn't seem to belong to her anymore. There was no one looking over her shoulder. There was no one to rub her back. The tears started to roll down her cheeks. She ran a rather brown stream of cold water into the basin and, dipping a face flannel into it, wiped her face and held the flannel over her eyes, allowing the cool to combat the swelling caused by distress. She could feel the sedative starting to take effect, and she returned to the bedroom, where the policewoman had turned down the bed. She climbed in, pulled the covers around herself, and lay back on the pillow. Already, night had fallen, and the roar of traffic on the Promenade Des Anglais was muted by the double glazing. It had a soporific effect on her, and with the events of the day beginning to go through her mind like a nightmare, she dropped off into sleep.

After Sybil had been asleep for some time and the sedation had taken hold completely, the policewoman had a leisurely investigation of everything in the room. She systematically went through suitcases, drawers, and, finally having found nothing of immediate interest in her search, settled down to go through the more intimate detail of Sybil's handbag.

She removed in order every item and put it on the table in front of her. Most of the stuff were the normal contents of a woman's handbag, but tucked into the side pocket was a substantial brown envelope. It had no markings on the outside, and she opened it and drew out several sheets of paper together with a key that had the number 237 stamped on it. The papers informed her that George and Sybil Yoreen had deposited with the bank, using a personal security box, the sum equivalent to 450,000 French francs. The policewoman's eyes opened wide in surprise. This was not an insubstantial sum of money and certainly not one that a couple on holiday would be moving about with. She took out her notebook and made entries in it, providing the essential detail that Pierre Dupre would need.

Well pleased with herself, she put everything back into the handbag in the exact order she had taken it out, taking care even to put the papers back into the envelope with the key exactly the way she had found them. It was later during the night that she handed over her tour of duty to a qualified nurse and returned to police headquarters.

The nurse who had replaced Nicole Lambert during the night understood the problems of police work and the needs of people such as Sybil. She knew that when she awoke, she would be at her lowest point and be in the greatest need of sympathy.

Pierre Dupre and his staff were still at work. They were pouring over the statements taken from the people on the beach and identifying and eliminating those they felt were of no immediate interest to them. They had not come up with any interesting leads. There were no apparent villains present on the beach that day, and the beach owner and the operator of the recreational activities were members of the local community with no police records. Dupre was frustrated, but having identified the profession of Dr Yoreen, he knew that this was no ordinary killing. It was too early yet to have a prime lead. He looked up with interest when the policewoman walked into the room.

'Well', he said, 'did you find anything?'

'Yes, sir.'

'Well, don't keep me in suspense, woman. Share your secrets with your superior.'

She had always liked Pierre Dupre, as, indeed, all his staff did. His taciturn manner hid a caring policeman, someone who valued his crew and, what's more, gave them credit for their successes. A true team event was rare with many chief inspectors taking all the glory and sharing it out little by little as they needed to. With Dupre, it was different, and perhaps that's why he achieved more.

'There is a very large sum of money lying in a small branch of a Middle Eastern bank here in Nice,' she said. 'It's not the sort of sum of money that two people on a short holiday in the South of France would have brought with them. Here are the details.'

She had transferred from her notes to a police report form the salient details. It was this that she passed across the desk to Dupre. He took it, read it, and whistled.

'Well done, Nicole. This is excellent.'

She glowed with satisfaction. It was a mark of high merit to be called by your Christian name, as Pierre Dupre used Christian names sparingly and only at times when he was very pleased. Nicole Lambert had only known him use her Christian name once before, and she was sure that this little bit of sleuthing would go down as a positive point in her record.

'I need to know more about this. It's important therefore that we follow Mrs Yoreen tomorrow morning if she leaves the hotel. I have informed the manager to let me know immediately if she decides to leave early, but I think that is unlikely, as she will be seeking our help with regard to the return of her husband's body for burial, and there will be a natural opportunity to question her further therefore later tomorrow.

'It might be that having deposited this money, she might now wish to recover it, as the circumstances surrounding her husband's death will almost certainly have affected her thoughts with regard to what should be done with it. They may have had specific plans, but almost certainly, her natural inclination at the moment will be to return home and think carefully about her future before she does anything with such a substantial sum. I will talk with Alain Rochet, and I want you to be back here in the morning at eight o'clock. Now, go and get some rest.'

'Thank you, Chief,' she said. 'The rest will certainly be welcome, short, though, it will be.'

Pierre Dupre studied the neatly printed police report form and took note of the receiving officer at the bank, a Mr Alfonse Alii. He knew of the bank; it was one of several small Middle Eastern banks operating in the South of France, some of which had a less than wholesome reputation. However, in this case, he knew of no particular irregularities, nor did he recognise the name Alfonse Alii. He would be some junior employee, no doubt, who had received the deposit gratefully; nevertheless, he must be investigated.

Alain Rochet came into the room and wasted no time in bringing Pierre up-to-date with the activities of the forensics team, who had been hard at work identifying the point from which the shots would have been fired. They had discreetly investigated the potential for those shots having been discharged from either of the hotels with a direct line of sight to the beach in question. No clues had been immediately forthcoming, and they had therefore concentrated on the block of flats where the best line of fire was to be had and where the assassin would have been able to enter and leave without arousing any undue curiosity.

'There's no doubt, Chief', said Alain Rochet, 'that the weapon was fired from the block of flats. A minute investigation of the scene indicates activity on the roof area, and we have identified that a rifle was discharged recently, and the point of discharge lines up accurately with the path the bullet would need to take to hit the victim. In the immediate area, there is evidence that a cover was placed on the ground and the assassin lay on the cover and may even have used that cover as well as some sort of camouflage wrapping. Although, because of the height of the block and because of the fact that the point where the weapon was discharged was in the shadow of the structure housing the lift machinery, it would have been extremely difficult for anyone to have seen him. I have nevertheless instructed two teams to make enquiries in buildings that would have a direct line of sight to the block of flats, and we might be able to pick up some evidence of someone seen entering or leaving. The fence to the rear of the block has holes in several places, but there has been too much general activity around the base of the flats and shifting builder's sand to clearly identify any particular set of footprints. There are, however, some reasonably clear prints in cement dust on the small flight of steps that leads from the penthouse apartment to the roof, and these have been carefully photographed, and by morning, we should have some idea as to the footwear that was used, although I suspect that this, too, will be relatively anonymous. There is no doubt we are dealing with a professional.'

'Well done, Alain. At least we have been able to identify the scene of crime. Meantime, while you have been active with the forensics boys, Nicole Lambert has come up with a particularly interesting piece of evidence in the form of a substantial deposit of money in that small bank on the seafront, and there just could be some link there with the case. I have asked Nicole to be back here first thing in the morning, and I will ask her to tail Sybil Yoreen in order that we can see what she does and whether she rescues the money so recently deposited. I will need to talk to her anyway in the morning concerning the return of her husband's body to England following the post-mortem, which I assume is under way.'

'Yes, the doctor is poking around now,' said Alain. 'It's interesting, too, that you've have found money is involved. I take it you have found out a little more about the activities of this George Yoreen.'

'Yes. He appears to have been some sort of high-level scientist and, quite surprisingly, was working on a project to fight crime, so I think the next thing we need to do is get in touch with London and talk to them about their part in the investigation that will ensue in England, but I will leave it until first thing. Now, I think it sensible if we both try and get a couple of hours' sleep, as tomorrow is not exactly going to be a relaxing day at the office.'

Routine overnight information had informed Scotland Yard about the death of George Yoreen. It was currently outside the jurisdiction of London, but, nevertheless, the murder of a British citizen was of interest to them, and when that citizen happened to be a high-ranking scientist in a company working on government contracts, then it caused more than casual interest. This information had landed on the desk of Supt Roger Schofield, who would have the job of coordinating any business between the French police in Nice and his London crew.

Coincidentally, Roger Schofield had also been one of the senior policemen that had been consulted about the potential for the product being developed by NTI to counteract fraud and counterfeiting, and he therefore had more than a passing interest in the case in question.

The telephone beside him rang softly. He picked it up and listened.

'Superintendent Schofield?' asked the voice at the other end in an unmistakably French accent.

'Speaking,' said Schofield.

'This is Chief Inspector Pierre Dupre of the Nice Police. I have been passed through to you as the person who would be interested in the murder of George Yoreen, is that correct?'

'Yes,' said Schofield. 'I have just been bringing myself up-to-date with the brief information available to us concerning his murder.'

There then followed a long discussion between the two policemen, where Pierre Dupre did most of the talking and Roger Schofield did most of the listening whilst making notes rapidly in a form of shorthand that he had devised as a young policeman and which had stood him in such good stead during the development of his career. He was blessed with an almost photographic memory, and with his concise note taking and quick grasp of a situation, he had risen to his current rank at a surprisingly early age. He had what his superiors called a 'nose' for crimes that were now referred to as white collar frauds. There were a number of quite senior British businessmen languishing in gaol because of his detailed investigations of their activities and subsequent prosecutions. He was feared throughout the City.

By the end of the exchange, Roger Schofield was very much wiser and had agreed with Pierre Dupre that an investigation would be set up immediately whereby he and senior officers would interview the appropriate people within NTI and that they would pool the information gathered. Schofield had suggested to Dupre that as soon as his investigations in Nice had reached the point where it would be sensible to meet face to face, then it would not be a problem for him to travel to the South of France. Pierre Dupre, always eager to increase his knowledge of the workings of the English police, had been equally enthusiastic about travelling to London. An understanding had been reached, and Schofield had agreed to discreetly pursue enquiries at his end.

Pierre Dupre put the receiver down and, turning to Alain Rochet, said, 'Superintendent Schofield in London is already aware of the problems we have here, and I have just persuaded him to provide us with information concerning George

Yoreen's activities at his place of employment. It is likely, then, that we will pool our knowledge and see if this sheds any more light on the case.'

A short while after the death of George Yoreen, the Corsican in Marseille received a telephone call telling him that the job had been done. He smiled to himself; the fee had been easily earned. He gave instructions that a fax message was to be sent to Singapore. It read as follows. 'Your uncle has been laid to rest. Sorry you could not be here. Your wreath was much appreciated by the family.' It was signed, 'Your cousin Alphonse.'

In Singapore, Doo-hwan was interrupted during a late-night meeting with colleagues and handed the message from Cousin Alphonse. He did not smile; he had nothing to smile about. He folded the piece of paper and put it in his inside pocket to transfer later to a place of security.

It was 7:00 a.m. before Sybil finally opened her eyes and lay there for a few moments looking at the ceiling. Across the room, the nurse noticed the movement of the eyes and immediately felt a wave of sympathy go out to this poor woman. She watched as Sybil's hand reached out and found an open space where there should have been the comforting bulk of George. She continued to watch as understanding came into those sad eyes. Anguish swiftly followed, and Sybil pushed herself upright and cried out.

'George, my god, George, what have they done to you?' Turning as her eye caught movement, she saw the nurse.

'Who are you?' she asked.

'I am the nurse who replaced the policewoman after you had gone to sleep, madam. I have been here during the rest of the night. I am so sorry about your poor husband. You have my sympathy, madam. I hope you will let me provide as much comfort as I can for as long as you need it.'

Sybil started to cry. Tears poured down her cheeks, and she set up a terrible wailing that could be heard for some distance outside the room. The nurse came over to her and sat beside her on the bed, taking Sybil's left hand in hers and patting it fatuously. It did little to help. She waited patiently until the spasm had passed.

'Coffee, I think,' she said.

Sybil nodded. The nurse rang room service, and with an alacrity not common to French seaside hotels, a waiter brought coffee and breakfast rolls. There was also a newspaper on the tray. The nurse picked up the paper and walked briskly to the dressing table to keep it from view.

'Please let me see that,' said Sybil.

The nurse reluctantly returned with the guilty piece of paper, which she handed to Sybil. The banner headline was a clear statement of fact. 'British Scientist

Murdered while Paragliding in Nice.' Sybil read the lurid details the reporter had managed to get into the story at such short notice. Despite the horrors of the story and the vivid memory she carried of the events in her mind, there was a hardening resolve within her to face the facts and to deal with them head-on. She was made of stern stuff, and these Frogs had to be shown that dealing with a woman like her was a rare privilege. There would be plenty of time for grief later. She put down the paper and, to the amazement of the nurse, drank some coffee and ate a large croissant in the French style before once again addressing her.

'It is very kind of you, nurse, to have spent so much time with me, but I am afraid that only I can cope with the problems that are ahead of me. I know that the police will be back here again shortly, and I will face more questions about my husband and, no doubt, be told about the cause of death, as if I do not already know. I also have the transportation of his body back to the UK to sort out, so I would like you to leave me now.'

The nurse was surprised. These English indeed had stiff upper lips. 'Madam, I understand entirely, and I don't want to be in the way if you do not need me, but I will leave you my card in case you feel the need for my services again. Call me anytime.'

With that, the nurse picked up her large handbag and removed a scruffy card and gave it to Sybil. She took her coat and straightened her uniform, and taking a head scarf from her handbag, she put it on and quietly left.

Sybil sat there for a few minutes letting the grief pour over her again before she felt fit enough to stand up. She realised that the death of George was just the start of her problems. She also realised that there must have been the most extraordinary circumstance that had led to his untimely end.

George was dishonest; it was something she had come to live with, but on this last occasion, he had done what he described as the deal of his lifetime. As it would set them up for the rest of their lives, she had no doubt that he would have done nothing to jeopardise it. Someone else had interfered; this had led to his death. The money had, however, been paid, or at least a substantial part of it had, and the necessity of recovering it was what immediately forced her into action. If George had laid his life down for it, then the least she could do was recover it and live in comfort until her time came to join him.

She went to the bathroom and looked in the mirror; the reflection was that of a stranger. She dropped her nightdress on the floor and manoeuvred her comfortable body into the shower. It was not true to say she felt better, but she was clean again, and with the application of a little make-up, she resembled once more the wife of George Yoreen.

The telephone rang in the bedroom, and wrapping herself in a towel, she went over to it and picked it up. The hotel manager asked her if Nicole Lambert could come up to her room. She said yes but asked for a few more minutes. Sybil put on an ill-assorted collection of clothes, and she was seated at the dressing table brushing her hair when there was a knock on the door.

Sybil was not really surprised to see the young policewoman again. She knew there were many questions yet to be answered. They talked over the events of the last twenty-four hours again, but this time like recounting a bad tale. Sybil felt as if she was outside the event hearing it from a distance. For her part, Nicole gathered no additional information, and she told Sybil that as far as the police were concerned, she was free to return to England. She asked for and received Sybil's address and telephone number, and for good measure, she also got from her the address of NTI. They then discussed the problems associated with the return of George's body. The phone rang.

Sybil picked it up. 'Sybil, this is Gordon Blossom speaking. I am terribly sorry to hear of George's death. Please accept my sympathy.'

There would be a lot of that, she thought, *some of it well meant and some of it not.*

He continued. 'I have been asked by Sir Dennis ...'

Greedy, self-opinioned bastard, she thought.

'To call you and offer every assistance both financial and administrative. The company regards George's death as a supreme tragedy, and Sir Dennis insists that you must be helped as necessary during the harrowing days ahead. All expenses will, of course, be picked up by us.'

Gordon Blossom, as company secretary, was used to dealing with a multitude of problems, often involving senior executives, but he had never, in his wildest dreams, thought that he would have to return the murdered body of their senior scientist, who had been so strangely gunned down, quite a long way down as it happened, to England in a coffin. He tried to conjure into his mind the picture of George being towed behind a boat on a parachute; his ordered existence did not allow him to do so.

Sybil knew when she was on to a good thing.

'Gordon, it's very kind of you to call. Thank the chairman for me when you see him. At this very moment, I have a young policewoman with me who has just brought up the question of the return of George to England. Perhaps when I have finished talking to her, I can call you back.'

'Of course, you can, Sybil. Please make any arrangements necessary, and if you let me know the outline of them, I will take over from this end and smooth the path, so to speak. I have already spoken to the hotel manager, and there will be no formalities concerning your departure. Just pack up and walk out whenever you want to.'

It was no less than she deserved, of course; she was the wife of the senior scientist.

'Thank you, Gordon. I will speak to you again in a short while.' She put the phone back and turned again to Nicole Lambert.

'That was one of the people from my husband's company in England,' she said. 'He has kindly suggested that I can organise the return of George's body and myself and let him have the details. The company will be responsible for all charges. I wonder if this is something that your department might be able to handle for me?'

'Of course, madam,' said Nicole. 'If you will let me have your contact in England, I will make sure the department provides all the information necessary concerning the return of your husband's body, and we can coordinate everything with your return home too.'

'I really do appreciate it very much, young lady. If at all possible, I was hoping that we could catch the evening flight today.' It was so easy to say 'we'; it caught Sybil by surprise, and tears came into her eyes again. She wiped them away with a small handkerchief.

'I will do my very best for you, madam. I just hope we can clear all the formalities in time. Don't worry about it, though. I will talk to you again later in the day.'

Nicole Lambert left the hotel room shortly after this exchange. She returned to the foyer and called headquarters. Pierre Dupre listened to her and promised immediate action. He would give her the details later. The result of his action would allow Sybil and George Yoreen to return home together.

'Now, I want you to stay as close as possible to this Yoreen woman, Nicole,' said Dupre. 'I don't want to lose contact with her until she boards the flight home to London, whether that is today or tomorrow. Phone in when you can and report events to me. In the meantime, I will ask Alain Rochet to take care of the details concerning the corpse. All being well, she will be on tonight's flight, and we will provide a car for her to go to the airport. I will let the hotel know that. The necessary paperwork will be done here, so you can devote your time to the lady, and she need not worry about a thing. Are you happy with this?'

'Yes, Chief,' said Nicole. 'Leave it all to me at this end.'

As soon as Nicole Lambert had left the hotel room, Sybil set about packing the two suitcases; it was not a happy experience. When she had finished the task, she picked up her handbag, and making sure she had the papers and the key she would need for the bank, she left the room and walked down the corridor to the lift.

Nicole was waiting patiently across the two carriageways of the Promenade des Anglais, waiting for Sybil to come out. She did not have to wait long. Sybil walked into the bright sunshine and descended the steps, and on reaching the pavement, she turned left. Nicole remained on the other side of the Promenade and kept pace with her. Sybil crossed over a small side street and, after a few more yards, turned into the doorway of a Middle Eastern bank.

On entering the bank, Sybil went to the enquiry desk and asked for Mr Alii.

Alphonse Alii was seated at his desk. He had expected Sybil to return to the bank, and now he watched her carefully as she was shown over to him.

'Mr Alii, I hope you remember me from yesterday when my husband and I deposited some money with you.'

'Yes, of course, Madam Yoreen,' said Alii. 'I cannot tell you how distressed I was to read in the paper this morning of the tragic and terrible death of your husband. Please accept my deepest sympathy.'

The face across the desk showed only compassion. Compassion seemed to flow from every pore of Alphonse Alii; it was one of his great skills to adapt to any situation presented. Sybil accepted the words of condolence with the tightly controlled expression she was to use many times in the weeks ahead.

'This is very difficult for me, Mr Alii, but as you are aware, we left with you a substantial sum of money. Under the present circumstances, I would prefer to have it back in my possession.'

Alii steepled his fingers in front of him and pondered her words; it was indeed fortunate that he had had second thoughts about misappropriating the sum entrusted to him. He had been persuaded when he had been informed by his Swiss bank, when he had called them on arrival at work, that a large amount of money had been credited to his account late the previous day; after all, his needs were modest. It would have been a foolish thing to do anyway at this stage of his career when he was building up a good client base that trusted him with these delicate little tasks.

Alii took from the drawer of his desk a file marked 'Yoreen', and taking a small envelope out of it, he withdrew a key marked 237. The file had not been processed the previous day because of Alii's brainstorm; the formalities to return the money to this woman were therefore few. He took a form from another drawer and filled it out. It would discharge the bank from responsibility once the money was outside their doors and enable Alii to deduct a modest standard charge for the temporary use of a security box.

'Please sign here, madam,' he said, pushing the form to Sybil and holding his finger against the place where she was to put her signature. Sybil signed. Alii stood up and disappeared behind the counter. A few minutes later, he reappeared and, going over to Sybil, said, 'If you will come with me, madam, you can take away your property.'

Sybil followed Alii to a small room to the side of the main bank counter. On the table in front of her was the box with a key in one of the two keyholes.

'I have turned my key, madam,' said Alii. 'If you will insert yours, you will be able to take out the contents. Please call me by pressing the bell here on the wall when you are ready to leave. There is a small charge for the safe custody amounting to fifty euros. How would you like to settle that?'

Sybil opened her bag and took out her wallet and withdrew the exact sum and handed it to Alii.

'I will have a receipt ready for you when you leave,' he said and, turning round, left the room.

Sybil inserted the other key and opened the box. The money lay there exactly as they had put it yesterday, but there was little comfort in it without George. There was some comfort, however, in the knowledge that in London, there lay a much more substantial sum. It was so very unfortunate for her that Lee Doo-hwan was also aware of the money that lay in London and being the planner he was had left open the possibility of recovering that money. Even at this moment, one of his envoys was removing from the vault the sum that Sybil was counting on for comfort in her old age. It was going to be a sad fact of this whole saga that the only money that finally ended up in the pocket of George Yoreen's widow was £50,000 less holiday expenses.

She took the money out of the box and placed it in the large leather handbag she had brought with her. It was really quite surprising how little room such a large sum took up. She shut the handbag and pressed the small bell push. In a few moments, Alphonse Alii returned to the room.

'Thank you Mr Alii for your help and sympathy,' she said. 'I have completed my transaction, and I will now take my leave.'

Alfonse Alii led her out of the room, passing to her the bank's receipt in an envelope, and saw her to the door. As he showed Sybil Yoreen out, he noticed a young woman who had about her the bearing of the local police department. In his training, Alfonse Alii had been instructed in the art of people identification. The most innocent-looking people were often the most dangerous to the likes of Alii, and now the danger signal was very loud in his ears. Sybil stepped through the doors, and he stepped back. The advantage was with him, as the doors were of darkened glass to reduce the glare of the sun. He watched as Sybil walked down the street, the young woman in question also moved in her direction. It was time for Alphonse to go.

Nicole Lambert, having followed Sybil to the bank, had waited outside while her transaction was completed. She saw the young man accompany her to the exit and noticed nothing remarkable about him; her interest was more particularly directed towards Sybil's activities, and she followed her on her route back to the hotel.

Chapter 18

Dr David Frome sat at his desk and scratched his head. The theoretical volume in the vessel where all working samples were returned tallied, within experimental error, with the figures in front of him, yet the active content varied. The series of experiments that he and his group in the laboratory had conducted had apparently produced evidence that someone had misappropriated some active material. The only conclusion he could come to was that someone must have added inert liquid to the vessel to bring the volume back to the level that a casual observer would accept as satisfactory. Only the careful analysis they had carried out would reveal that the active content was unacceptable.

He had no doubt that the material that had been added to the vessel was the carrier itself free of active content. He had checked carefully the sample log that George Yoreen had maintained and where samples had been signed in and out by George and the chief executive. The last entry was the returned material following Victor Stanley's trip to Japan.

On going back through the records, the last routine calculation had been carried out immediately before Victor Stanley's trip to Japan, and everything had been in order. Again, the only conclusion he could come to was that the loss had occurred between Victor Stanley leaving for Japan and now.

It seemed inconceivable to him that his own boss would take material out of the laboratory, and therefore something must have gone wrong with the sample returned by Victor. He was aware, of course, of the detailed nature of the discussions that had taken place between Nonaka Corporation and NTI and the fact that they had gone into some detail about the manufacturing plant that might be required in Japan should production there ever be contemplated. He further knew that these discussions had kept the Japanese in ignorance of the material that they had developed that turned the simple polymer carrier into the highly secret and highly commercial product that was now evolving.

There had been no particular secret about the carrier itself, and they had gone into detail as to the equipment that would be required by Nonaka to carry out stage one of the manufacturing process. Frome had been directly responsible for briefing Dr Nobura, under secrecy, on this part of the process. Was it possible therefore that while Victor Stanley was in Japan, the sample had been switched for some material that looked like the original but in fact was not?

The normal procedure required that when George Yoreen checked the sample back in, he would carry out a routine test to determine that it was the same material that went out and that it must be fit for purpose, and George's initials appeared in the sample log indicating that this test had been carried out and that the sample was acceptable. Could it be therefore that George Yoreen, for some inexplicable reason, had retained the active material for his own purposes? Tests would routinely be carried out by George or, in the unlikely event that he was not available, by David Frome. Under normal circumstances, the loss could have been covered up, but these were not normal circumstances. George could easily have altered the volume to avoid anyone noticing apparent loss in the graduated holding vessel; this way suspicion would not be aroused. It was only under the present circumstances that anyone would have checked the assay between the last official test date and the next scheduled test date.

Frome reluctantly transferred his calculations onto a clean sheet of paper and presented it in such a way that it was a simple statement of fact; he was not there to draw any conclusions.

Kevin Hipkiss had been waiting impatiently for the result of David Frome's tests and jumped up from his seat as David knocked and entered George's old office.

'Well', he said, 'what have you found?'

David walked over to the desk and put the piece of paper in front of Kevin. It took only moments to take in the significance of the figures. Kevin sat down again quite suddenly. His face had gone very pale.

'We have lost some product,' he said unnecessarily.

There followed a close and detailed post-mortem that involved the chief executive and David Frome going through every aspect of the calculations and tracking the movement into and out of the laboratory of the various samples over the past few weeks. The only conclusion that could be drawn had been drawn. The loss was directly related to the removal of a sample from the laboratories that had subsequently travelled to Japan and had apparently been returned and had been signed in good order. There were only two names that could be involved in this process, and one of those names was now in a police morgue in the South of France. The other name was shortly to appear in the office of Sir Dennis Matchett. Kevin knew his duty.

'Well done, David,' he said. 'That's a good piece of work carried out neatly and confidentially. It is now important that the confidentiality aspect is maintained. You are not to speak with anyone concerning the actual loss. It is particularly important that should any outsider contact you that you refer such contact to myself or the chairman. Instruct the members of your staff that have been working with you this morning that we were bound to carry out this assay following the tragic death of George Yoreen. You have found nothing amiss, do you understand?'

'My people aren't fools, Kevin,' he said. 'They know that routine assays follow a careful timetable for very good reasons. Furthermore, they know that any assay that was carried out outside the normal timetable of events must have been done for some very good reason, and the reason is plain for them all to see—George is dead. Whatever I tell them, they are going to draw their own conclusions, and it would be better therefore if you tell them directly of the necessity of confidentiality in this matter.'

'How many are involved?'

'Only two,' said David.

'OK. You'd better wheel them in.'

David left George's office and returned to the laboratory, where he collected the two assistants. They had worked hard to produce the results required and were interested anyway to know why the sample analysis had been carried out. They obviously knew by now of the death of George Yoreen, and speculation would soon be widespread in the company as to why he should have been murdered in such a manner. David warned them that the discussion with the chief executive was likely to be very one-sided and that they should listen carefully and act accordingly if they wanted a long career with NTI.

They returned as a small group to George's office to find Kevin standing by the window, hands in pockets.

'As you know, we have had to carry out an analysis of the material in the receiver,' he said. 'You probably know by now that certain amounts of the active material are missing. It is imperative for the security of this investigation that this remains a secret between the four of us. I have instructed David Frome that nothing is to be said elsewhere in the research group, and I am relying on the two of you as well to keep your mouths shut. Let me put it another way,' he lowered his eyes shiftily. 'If I receive any information from a source that I have not directly revealed it to that any active material has gone missing from this laboratory, all three of you will be looking for another job.'

This brought home to the small group in ways that no other statement could the necessity of keeping their mouths shut; at least for the moment, their lips would remain sealed.

Kevin dismissed them and once again picked up the telephone and dialled the chairman's office. He recounted on the direct line to their headquarters the outline of his findings at the research laboratories.

After his somewhat restless night and rude awakening by Kevin, Victor had arrived at the office early enough to comprehensively review the situation and to write down all the salient points in order that he could make a straightforward presentation to the chairman. He had been hard at work for some two hours when Marcia Payne, Kevin's secretary, tapped at the door and walked in.

Marcia Payne had always had a soft spot for Victor; the feeling was mutual. She had been on duty continuously now since summoned during the night and, despite that, was still looking smart; her make-up was carefully modulated to reflect the pastel tones of her outfit. Marcia had always believed that any good secretary must present an image to the outside that was in keeping with the seniority of her boss whether she liked him or not. Marcia had no particular love for Kevin, but as the senior secretary available when he was appointed, she had been given the job. She had maintained it because the pay was good and there was a high degree of interest in what they were doing. She also knew that things could change; secretaries, particularly good ones, often outlive their bosses. There was a feeling of impermanency about Kevin; even his name was of that nature. His self-promotional style, his restless energy, and his bad judgement of people would eventually get up someone's nose, she thought.

She pulled down the red jacket over the straight navy-blue skirt. Her blonde hair, now with the occasional grey one showing, was tied at the back of her neck with a black bow, making her look younger than her forty-two years.

'Can I talk to you for a while?'

'Of course, come in,' he said. It was the first friendly face that he had seen this morning, and as she could undoubtedly shed some light on the present feelings in the company since George's death, she was an ally.

'Victor, we have been friends for many years, and we have seen this company go through some strange times. We have seen some strange people come and go, and although I wouldn't say it to anyone else, you know my views about Kevin. You must realise that the events of the last twenty-four hours have been staggering in their dimension, and I have spent almost the entire night with the chairman, Kevin, and Max Fiddler helping them to come to a conclusion about what might have happened and what could have brought it about. When I say helping them, I mean typing the endless drafts that have appeared concerning press releases and internal statements for the senior staff.'

'None of this can look very good for me,' said Victor, and he self-consciously ran his fingers over his now thinning hair. 'I have no doubt that the knives are out and that some sacrificial process is being considered.'

'I think you're right about that,' said Marcia. 'It seems that there has to be some scapegoat for the activities, and, certainly, you are in a position where they can easily make you that scapegoat.'

Marcia had seated herself opposite Victor in the somewhat worn and battered visitor's chair. She took from the box on the desk in front of her a cigarette; Victor always kept a box for visitors, usually with Dunhill in it. It was characteristic of the trust that passed between them that she didn't ask, and he didn't expect her to. He picked up the onyx lighter that stood by the box and, leaning forward, lit it for her with a hand that was not exactly rock steady.

'What worries me', said Victor, 'is the form that the sacrifice is going to take. I have gone over in my own mind everything that has happened to me, and some of the things that occurred on the last trip to Japan were bizarre and frightening. I haven't dared tell them to anyone yet, and I don't think the right thing to do is to reveal all those events to the chairman or indeed to Kevin.'

In Marcia's opinion, Victor appeared to have aged considerably since his trip to Japan, and there was a nervousness about him now that she had never seen before. Normally a quiet, calm, and thoughtful individual, he was now quite clearly agitated, his body would not stay still, and he made many small and unnecessary movements, which revealed his nervous state. Gestures of the hand that had never been there before, movements of paper and articles on the desk that normally would have stayed in their place—all added up to a man with a deep-seated worry; she could understand it.

'I dare not stay long, Victor,' she said. 'I know that Kevin is out at the research labs in Hillingdon, and I know that he had David Frome woken up during the night and brought in. I hope that information helps.'

'That can only mean one thing,' said Victor. 'He must have brought Frome back to analyse the flask containing the returned samples and working residues of the superconductive polymer. I can understand that there are forces at work that would like to acquire this material because of the potential it has for crime busting, and during my trip, I felt more than vibrations concerning this.' He leaned forward across the desk, placing both his hands on the surface, and looked earnestly into Marcia's eyes. She could see the strain in his and the little bloodshot lines that normally wouldn't have been there. She caught the rank odour of his breath as he came closer to her, again something that she had never known before.

'Despite all the problems I had on my trip to Japan, I was never out of possession of the sample that I took with me.' He needed someone to believe this; Marcia could fulfil that role.

'Victor, I have never known you to do anything other than that, which was straightforward and honest. You're too nice a man to work with the people you do and even to do the job you do, and I believe that you believe everything you tell me, but somewhere down the line, other people have other thoughts, and they are going to use them against you to save their own skins, and you have to understand that.'

The main problem in Victor's mind was questioning the honesty and integrity of his friend Kenezo Nonaka. It seemed inconceivable to him that Kenezo would have switched samples when he rescued for him the original material in Osaka when his room had been changed. He blamed himself anyway for the fact that he had forgotten to take the sample with him when he switched rooms, and he knew that in not declaring this problem, he had made things worse for himself. He had gone on to consider whether Kenezo Nonaka could be involved in any way with Doo-hwan and had then dismissed this as being ludicrous. In his dealings with Nonaka Corporation, he had always felt that they had a relationship that, whilst not totally open, was at least based on mutual trust and honesty, and he would have always maintained that there was no way that Nonaka would compromise him by stealing the sample that, in effect, they were going to be the manufacturer and seller of in the Far East. Now he was no longer sure.

While these thoughts were going through his mind, Marcia had taken the half-smoked cigarette and stubbed it out in the ashtray. She stood up and looked down at Victor, who remained seated behind his desk.

'I want you to know, Victor', she said, 'that whatever the circumstances in this company, you can rely on me as a friend. I can't do anything officially for you, but at least I can keep you informed about things that are happening if and when you want to know them, and therefore please ring me at home any evening.'

There was nothing left to say. Victor rose from his desk as though he was going to start to say something; he even raised his right hand and then let it drop back by his side. He just looked at her appreciatively, and she smiled and, turning, went out of the office as quietly as she had entered it.

Victor resumed the work that he needed to do to make sure that the interview with Sir Dennis Matchett went as smoothly as it possibly could. Lying in the right-hand pocket of his jacket was the copy of the small Sony tape that he had made of the meeting that Kevin had had with Nanny. He opened the top right-hand drawer of his desk and drew out of it the old Sony M-88V in order that he had something to play the tape with to the chairman. He was still in two minds as to whether this was going to be a conclusive and satisfactory end to Kevin's career, but at least he was going to put these unsavoury facts on the table; they were some form of weapon, and he had few enough of them.

At 8:25, he picked up the sheaf of papers in his hand, inserted the small tape into the Sony machine, and, leaving his office, took the lift to the chairman's suite.

He walked through the door and into the impressive presence of Kathryn Goodbody. She, too, had been on continuous duty now for over twelve hours and, unlike Marcia, was beginning to look like it. Her voluminous garments appeared as though she had slept in them, and strands of her never-too-tidy hair had parted company with the bun-like structure on the top of her head that was used to imprison them.

'I think I am expected, Kathryn,' said Victor. 'I hope the chairman is not suffering too badly because of his nocturnal meanderings.' He tried one of his crooked little smiles and failed.

Kathryn was not in a mood for pleasantries. She had, together with Marcia, been preparing the copious notes, both public and private, emanating from the chairman's office. Those concerning the private sector she had read, questioned, been told not to, and then reread. Amongst them were notes about the suspected involvement of Victor Stanley. Always a keen supporter of her well-beloved Sir Dennis, she naturally sided with him against those that he perceived to be his enemies whether or not the day before they had been her most devoted friends.

'If you take a seat, Victor, I will see if the chairman is ready.' She sniffed copiously and got up from behind her desk, and moving ponderously around, it allowed her surprisingly small feet to carry her across the few feet of deep carpet to the chairman's inner sanctum. She knocked quietly and went through.

The television screen in the corner of her office, which monitored the stock exchange movements and more precisely their own share movements, blinked at him. The early market was generally down, but the rather surprising aspect was the degree of fall in the share price of NTI. The reaction to the death of George Yoreen had been quite surprisingly dramatic.

Kevin, on his many sorties into the City, had so extolled the capabilities of George Yoreen that the parasites had come to believe that he was the only generator of new products within the company, and because of his current activities, they had been led to believe the next great leap forward in profit generation was about to take place at NTI. The fact that George Yoreen had been murdered and murdered so dramatically, coupled with the current wild speculation that maybe Kevin Hipkiss might not survive the crisis, had resulted in a sudden and savage lack of confidence, which had taken the share price down from 374p to 310p. The only satisfaction that Victor could get out of it was the fact that it had fallen below the option level at which the chief executive had been granted his recent bonus issue. It was going to take a long time for them to rise again.

Kathryn reappeared in the doorway and, holding it open, said to Victor, 'The chairman will see you now, Mr Stanley.'

Victor stood up and walked with more confidence than he felt into the chairman's office. His first surprise was the fact that Max Fiddler and Gordon Blossom were there too.

'You know Max Fiddler, I think, Victor,' said the chairman. He didn't bother to say anything about Gordon and pointed him to a chair that appeared to have been placed so that it was the natural focus of the three people already assembled.

Victor was used to working against the odds in his job; he was equally used to presenting to the other side an image that looked confident and calm when it was not, and he drew upon his last reserves of strength and determination to do just that now.

'Good morning, gentlemen,' he said. 'I am sure George's death has come as much of a shock and surprise to you as it has to me.'

He put his hands in his jacket pockets as if to make sure that the flaps were not trapped inside, lifted them both self-consciously out again, and smoothed them down. He walked over to the chair and sat down. He crossed and then uncrossed his legs. He felt as though he was back at his first interview.

'Victor', said the chairman, 'I have asked Gordon and Max Fiddler to be here with me because of the grave nature of the discussions we are about to have. I do not intend at this point in time to question particularly why George Yoreen met such a very tragic and untimely end. I suspect that the police are at this very moment starting their investigation into that matter and that they will end up here before too soon.'

Sir Dennis, never able to look people in the eye at the best of times, shifted his gaze continuously around the room, almost as though eye contact with Victor would turn him to stone. He appeared to look at his fly, his left hand, his right index finger, which he was about to raise but didn't, the view out of the window, and at the tie pin, which secured his conservative blue-and-white knotted tie to his equally conservative blue Oxford shirt—anywhere except at Victor himself.

'We can only assume that poor George met his death because he was not altogether honest. This is a conclusion we have come to most reluctantly. It is possible that this could be connected to something George was meant to give to a contact, such as a written formula or even a sample. If this was the case, then something must have gone wrong for him, but why he should have been killed is a mystery.'

There was a short silence then as if they expected Victor to speak up; he remained silent. It was Max Fiddler who spoke.

'Please understand, Stanley, that everything that is being said in this meeting is of a confidential nature and that no accusations are being made. We are trying to get at the truth. It is not our job to question any criminal element that is undoubtedly at play in all this, but it is our job to protect the company and the interests of the shareholders.'

Max Fiddler, despite his night-time activities, remained razor sharp and pressed. He smiled encouragingly at Victor.

For his part, Victor sat quite still in his chair and contemplated the others; still, he made no reply. The chairman spoke again.

'The chief executive this morning instigated tests on the superconductive polymer residues flask. You are fully aware, Victor, that all working samples of the superconductive polymer are placed in a special flask when they have been used and that all samples allowed to leave the research laboratories are added to the flask on their return.'

Victor didn't need to say anything; he merely nodded in the direction of Sir Dennis, who continued.

'The purpose of putting these samples into a holding flask such as this is in order that we can analyse the active material present and provided this is within an acceptable margin of error against a calculated experimental loss percentage we are satisfied. If the activity of the material has declined outside that level, then there have been other forces at work. Do I make myself clear?'

At this point, Sir Dennis was looking out of the window, but Victor knew that this time, a response was required.

'I am fully aware of the procedure, Chairman. Indeed, I was one of the people who suggested that we should protect ourselves in this manner.'

'Ah! Just so,' said the chairman, not having realised that Victor was in any way involved in such a decision. It was not the sort of thing that his chief executive would have revealed. In fact, from memory, he recalled that the chief executive had presented to him a confidential report about that particular procedure and claimed it to be his own original thinking. Perhaps Stanley was lying, but Sir Dennis, for all his faults, was also aware that his chief executive often claimed others' work as his own; it was one of his less desirable habits.

'The analysis carried out this morning by David Frome, whom, incidentally, we have just announced will take George's position, revealed that a substantial amount of active material was missing.'

The appointment of David Frome came as no particular surprise to Victor, although he realised that this had probably now closed off a friendly relationship, as, undoubtedly, David would do anything and say anything that coincided with the required views of his immediate superior now that he had suddenly become NTI's chief scientist.

'I find it difficult, Chairman, to understand how any material could have gone missing. You are aware that on my recent trip to Japan, I carried a small sample of material with me with the full permission of everyone concerned, and that material was duly logged back in and signed for by George Yoreen himself together with the required countersignature of the chief executive. There is no way that I could have substituted any other sample for the one that went out, and I can offer no logical explanation as to why the analysis should have revealed a missing amount of active ingredient.'

Now it was a fact that everyone in that room, with the possible exception of Max Fiddler, was aware of that the fact that the superconductive polymer was commonly referred to as the carrier. The other ingredients were placed with the carrier and then subjected to a process that binds them all together chemically to form what the layman would know as a compound. Once in this form, the compound becomes the highly valued product that would generate so much of NTI's future profit. Nevertheless, the so-called carrier looked, smelled, and felt exactly similar to the finished product. If the carrier had been added by itself to the flask, it would have mixed happily with the other contents without changing the appearance, and it would only be careful analysis that would reveal a dilution had occurred. It was rather like adding just a little drop more water to a glass of whisky; everything seemed normal, but it wasn't quite the same as before the little drop of water had gone in.

'Reluctantly, the only conclusion we can come to', said Sir Dennis, 'is that the sample that was returned from Japan was in fact not the one that you left with. We must assume that George Yoreen returned that sample to the flask and the analysis revealed the problem. We have therefore concluded that in some way, the sample that you removed from these premises was not returned as such, and that, either wittingly or unwittingly, you have been instrumental in its loss. I would like to hear what you have to say on this matter.'

So now they had said it. The real accusation lay out in the open. Either Victor had stolen outright the sample that he had taken to Japan or someone else had stolen it either in Japan, which Victor suspected, or George Yoreen had stolen it and added carrier to the flask. These thoughts went rapidly through Victor's mind and fell into a reasonable degree of order.

If the sample had been stolen from him in Japan, then whatever was substituted could not have been exactly the same as the material that had left England. If victor had returned that sample and that sample had been added to the flask, then not only would the activity have been reduced but also there would have been other problems when it came to analysis. The only conclusion therefore that Victor could rapidly reach was that he did return a sample and that George had stolen the sample and had added carrier to the flask to make up the volume. Unfortunately for George, the sample that he had taken, thinking it to be the superconductive polymer itself, was a fake. Wherever that fake went, someone else had become aware of its non-conforming nature, and Victor knew exactly who that someone was. Now was not exactly the time to reveal all this, and once more, he kept his mouth shut.

Sir Dennis was again looking at his flies.

'I have talked to my colleagues here about the delicacy of this situation, and whilst we are not accusing you of any malpractice, we do believe that you have been extremely negligent in your work, and this negligence has led to the problems that now beset us.'

Sir Dennis drew towards him a piece of paper that appeared to be a prepared statement. Sir Dennis was not generally capable of original thought at times such as this and would write down and subsequently read what he was going to say to the party he was talking to. The image Sir Dennis had managed to promote through the clever use of PR was that of an able communicator at one with his audience. This was far from the truth. If he could have gone through life without having to communicate at all, he would have been much happier.

The statement of negligence was something that Victor could not deny if, indeed, it was the case that he had lost the sample and that Kenezo Nonaka had stolen it. The fault lay with him. He knew as well that he should have revealed his suspicions when he returned; the facts would eventually become obvious, but he had not stolen the sample and he was not actually aware that, in the short time the sample was missing in Japan, it had been switched.

'It is with regret, Mr Stanley', continued Sir Dennis, 'that we are suspending you immediately, on full pay, from all your executive duties. You will leave the company immediately without returning to your office, and you will leave the premises. You will continue to be entitled to the use of your car and all other reasonable expenses whilst at home. We are aware that you have a contract with NTI, and we suggest that you talk to your lawyers about this. In the course of the next few days, the full board of NTI will meet and consider what further steps must be taken with regard to your continued association with this company. Do you understand?'

Victor was visibly shaken. The colour had gone from his face, and his right hand had gone inside his jacket as though feeling for the beat of his heart. Gordon Blossom, who had remained quiet throughout these exchanges, wondered whether he might actually have a heart attack. He continued to say nothing, however, as he was there merely as an observer, just another witness.

Victor, who continued to sit there, had various thoughts racing round his mind, but he could not put them into words; he was suffering from shock. Finally, he managed to speak, much to the relief of those seated near to him.

'I think what you are saying, Chairman, is totally unjustified. I have been a loyal servant of this company over a long period, and I have never done anything but my best for it and for you. Many of our overseas achievements have been in no little way because of my activities.'

Sir Dennis looked steadfastly at the notes in front of him, said nothing, and just shook his head wearily from side to side.

'I am sorry, Victor. Truly, I am sorry,' he said.

'I don't believe a word of it,' retorted Victor. 'No one around here is sorry. The things you should be sorry about you seem to close a blind eye to. The incompetence is not in me. It is in the clown you have as a chief executive. As you so rightly point out, I have a contract, and, indeed, I will consult my lawyers. Neither you nor anyone else will ever prove that I was negligent with the company's products or with its affairs, and in the end, you will regret what has happened here today. Not only are you going to damage me, but in so doing, you will damage yourselves as well.'

It was quite a mouthful, but Victor was not finished yet.

'There is one small piece of company property, however, I should like to leave with you.' Victor stood up and removed from his pocket the small Sony instrument. He clicked down the play button and placed it on the desk of Sir Dennis. The little speaker suddenly came alive.

The unmistakable voice of Kevin Hipkiss could be heard.

'Please don't punish me, Nanny, please … please … don't punish me. I am terribly sorry for what I have done.'

Victor had the exquisite satisfaction of seeing the faces around him fall into various forms of amazement and incredulity. The tape went on.

'But, Kevin, Kevin', said Nanny quite clearly, 'I distinctly told you to behave yourself, and while Nanny has been out, you have quite clearly wet your nappy.'

Gordon Blossom actually burst out laughing. The chairman leapt up from his desk faster than anyone had seen him do in years and closed his hands around the offending instrument, depressing the stop button and closing off the sound. Max Fiddler had his hand over his mouth and nose, and no one could quite determine what he was trying to hide. Victor Stanley looked at each separately and, turning on his heel, walked towards the door. As he went, he said,

'I would like you all to listen to the full tape. It doesn't start there and it doesn't end there, and what comes before and what comes after is equally pathetic and hilarious and is a clear indication of the sort of man that is running this company down. You might have me as your scapegoat, gentlemen, but you are not going to enjoy it.'

Victor reached the door and opened it, slamming it smartly behind him. Kathryn Goodbody, who was starting to rise from her chair, was so surprised she sat down again involuntarily. There was a loud snapping noise, which Victor did not wait to investigate as he forcibly slammed her door as well on his exit. It was as though he was closing doors on a part of his life, for he had no doubt that this was not a place he would be returning to in the immediate future.

Sybil struggled through the day in Nice. Inspector Dupre had asked her a few more questions, and she had told him as much as she could about George's work and had withheld nothing except, of course, his criminal tendency. Even in death, she wished to protect George and could not bring herself to reveal the connection with the strange people in the Far East.

There was a degree of self-protection in all this. With George being dead, there was no immediate breadwinner, and if she was to continue her lifestyle, she needed to collect the remaining funds in London. This was essential because George had never believed in a pension, as he was convinced that one day he would make a killing. What a pity it had been someone else who had done that. There was, of course, a little money put away, but not enough to live on in comfort for long. She thought, not for the first time, of the £450,000 lying in the London bank and knew that her primary objective was to recover that as soon as possible. No thought ever went through her mind, even momentarily, that Doo-hwan and his colleagues would have similar views.

Inspector Dupre had told her that by the late afternoon, he would be able to release George's body and that arrangements had been made through Gordon Blossom in London for its transfer to England on the same flight as Sybil.

Nicole Lambert had again appeared on the scene and helped Sybil through the brief formalities of arranging her flight home. She told her that the police in Nice had contacted Supt Roger Schofield in London, and she expected that the British police would want to interview Sybil as soon as possible after her arrival in England.

The arrangements with regard to checking out of the hotel had been taken care of by Gordon Blossom at NTI, and despite the misgivings in London about the activities of George Yoreen, it was felt generally they must make her homecoming as sympathetic as possible, as there was no evidence to suggest that she was involved in anything that George might have been a party to.

Sir Dennis Matchett had therefore instructed Gordon Blossom that she was to be met at the airport and taken either to their small London flat or to the house in

Cirencester. Gordon Blossom made all the arrangements and personally went to the airport.

Chief Inspector Dupre and his deputy, Alain Rochet, continued their investigation into the murder of George Yoreen. A forensics team was moved into the abandoned building immediately across the Promenade des Anglais and opposite the beach, and it was examined in minute detail. Fragments of the soft-nosed bullet had been removed from George's head, and they had been able to identify the make; they had no evidence yet as to the means of delivery.

The team confirmed where the firing position had been and also found that the ground cover used had been a polyester material. The two fibres that had led to this analysis seemed to suggest that they were unevenly dyed, which led them to suspect that it was of a mottled pattern or perhaps even a camouflage sheet.

They had meticulously looked for any new fingerprints in the vicinity of the firing position but had found none, nor had they expected to. The site itself was covered with many old prints from the activities of the building workers, but there was nothing to link with the assassin apart from the distinctive pattern of his shoes, which had left an imprint in the dust. Again, they were of no particular help, as they were from a common variety of trainer produced by High-Tech. There were thousands of similar pairs in Nice, and there appeared to be no particular imperfections in the imprint that would differentiate this set from any other.

Sybil had not seen George's body since the time of the death and could not bring herself to look upon his face. A French undertaker therefore took care of the boxing up of George and placed him in what he described as a suitable travel case and, having prepared the necessary documents with the police for the repatriation of George's body, had had it loaded into an anonymous-looking black van and transported to the airport.

Sybil had taken the money that she had collected from the bank, and apart from a small amount for her necessary expenses, she had put it into a large brown envelope supplied by the hotel and placed it in the bottom of her hand baggage.

Alain Rochet, on the information supplied by Nicole Lambert, was making arrangements now to interview the personnel of the small bank on the Promenade des Anglais, and a discreet watch was being kept on the premises to see if there were any unusual comings or goings. The cooperation of the manager would be sought with regard to explaining what sort of activities had been going on in connection with George Yoreen's visit to the bank, and he had no doubt that he would receive a truthful statement from them. The bank had already been contacted to supply a list of all employees at the branch, and this had been collected by a member of the police department, and the checks had started with regard to background of those employees and the location of their homes. Particular interest was being paid to any resident foreign workers. At the top of the list, as it was in alphabetical order, appeared the name of Alphonse Alii.

Arrangements had been made for Sybil to catch the British Airways flight BA 345 at 4:20 p.m., and Nicole Lambert had provided a police vehicle to take her to the airport and accompanied her on the journey. The driver had put both her luggage and George's in the boot and drove to Nice Airport in the heavy traffic westward down the Promenade des Anglais. Nicole sat in the back with Sybil.

Sybil turned in the seat and faced Nicole.

'I have still not come to terms with the fact that George has been killed. It will take a long time yet for me to return to a near normal life, if ever,' she said. 'This was going to have been such a wonderful holiday, and now only days after our arrival, I am going home alone.' She drew from her handbag a small handkerchief and dabbed her eyes. She didn't want to break down again, but the thoughts that were going through her mind made this almost impossible.

'Madam Yoreen', said Nicole, 'you know that the police department here will do everything in our power to find the murderer of your husband. Inspector Dupre has explained to you that we shall cooperate with the police in England, and although it won't help you now, I hope that when we do apprehend your husband's killer, it will at least give you some comfort and provide all of us with an explanation as to what happened and why.'

Sybil knew that in finding the murderer, they may well also reveal George's involvement in spiriting away a sample of the material that he had been working on for NTI. This was something she would have to face if and when that happened. 'You have been very kind to me, young lady,' said Sybil. 'I am very grateful for all the efforts you have made to enable my swift return to my home together with the body of my dear husband. If there is anything, anything at all that I remember that will shed more light on this terrible affair, I will, of course, communicate it to the police in London.'

By now, the car was entering the outer limits of the airport, and in a separate area, the anonymous black van was unloading a plain but substantial box.

Nicole Lambert leaned forward and gave the driver some instructions, which Sybil didn't understand. In effect, she had told him to go to the entrance for VIPs, as it had been arranged for Sybil to go directly to the plane from the VIP lounge to avoid having to mix with the other passengers. Gordon Blossom had arranged a business class ticket for her and had requested British Airways to do everything in their power to see that the seat next to Sybil was left free having explained the situation. The captain of the aircraft was aware of this, and as he did not have a full load that day, the appropriate seat number had been blocked off.

'If you let me have your passport, Madam Yoreen', said Nicole, 'I will take care of the necessary exit formalities and will join you in the VIP lounge. We have made arrangements for you to go straight there and from there to the plane.'

'Thank you very much,' said Sybil. 'It will make life a little easier.' She again dabbed her eyes with the handkerchief.

The driver drew into the kerb, and the door was opened by an airport official who spoke rapidly to Nicole. She gave him the necessary information he was seeking, and turning to Sybil, he said, 'I am very sorry, madam, to hear of the terrible events that have befallen you. However, we are seeking to make your passage through the airport as discreet and easy as possible, and if you will follow me, the policewoman will take care of the passport formalities, and I will see to it that you are undisturbed in our VIP lounge.'

Sybil got out of the car and followed the official. The driver unloaded the suitcases from the rear, and these were taken to check-in. Nicole Lambert accompanied them and had them checked through to London and went into immigration to have Sybil's passport cleared.

The box that had been deposited from the anonymous black van was put with the other freight goods that were to be carried on the British Airways flight.

There was only a short delay in the lounge before Sybil was escorted onto the aircraft. All the other passengers were in position, and she was the last to board. The stewardess in business class showed her to her seat and saw that she was strapped in.

Almost immediately, the doors were closed, and the captain received permission to start up.

As they left the crowded waterfront of Nice behind them and climbed up through the blue sky on their heading to London, Sybil enjoyed the luxury of her business class service while George travelled anonymously in the hold. It was not the sort of return that they had expected.

Supt Roger Schofield had received a telephone call from Chief Inspector Pierre Dupre of the Nice police telling him that Sybil was on her way back to London and filling him in on the recent detail concerning the forensic examination. A report had been faxed to Schofield's London office. Roger Schofield had arranged for Sgt Millicent Bywater to work with him on the investigation. Schofield's specialization was in company-related crime; this did not often involve murder, but, nevertheless, when he had been appointed to the case, it had been felt that there were more sinister implications than just the murder of George Yoreen. His team of people consisted of a number of very bright policemen and women, all of them nowadays with good degrees and specializations.

Millicent Bywater held a degree in chemistry and had then gone on to study law before joining the police. She was tall at five feet ten inches and would have been described by some as statuesque and by others as athletic; she preferred to think about herself as the latter. She had short natural blonde hair and blue eyes. She was broad across the shoulders and, seen from behind, had an almost masculine shape with a narrow waist and slim hips. She kept her figure by constant exercise, and it had developed for her a fine physique and a skin glowing from healthy living. From the front, she lost the masculine look; her face was attractive with good lips and high cheekbones. Her breasts were small and muscular; her long and excellent legs reached all the way to the ground. She was the nearest thing to perfection the Metropolitan Police possessed.

Millicent had been delighted to be drawn in as Roger Schofield's number two on the case, as not only did it have the makings of a most spectacular investigation but also she suspected it would reveal some most unsavoury facts relating to the activities of NTI. She wondered whether this might include such things as industrial espionage or sale of company secrets. She would soon discover how good her basic instincts were.

Roger Schofield had not thought it likely that Sybil would do anything other than return to her flat in London this evening. He had put a routine tail onto her as she arrived at the airport and had received a telephone report that she had been collected by someone. He had subsequently found this to be Gordon Blossom of NTI, together with a driver. Arrangements had also been made via the company for George's body to be collected and taken to a chapel of rest. The report from the French police was quite comprehensive with regard to the cause of death, and the forensic evidence concerning the type of wounds and the bullet used made it unnecessary for further examination of the body to be carried out. Based on the evidence of the French police, it had therefore been decided to allow George's body to go for burial the arrangements for which would be left to the widow.

The plane touched down in London two hours after leaving Nice at 5:20 p.m., UK time. Again, Sybil was escorted from the aircraft and taken via the VIP lounge to the waiting car. Gordon Blossom came to greet her as she came through from the custom-controlled area.

'I can't tell you, Sybil, how shocked everyone at NTI is about George's terrible death. I know when we spoke on the phone yesterday that you were in no state to receive anyone's sympathy, but the message now is heartfelt. Sir Dennis Matchett has asked me to have you taken wherever you require to go, either to your London flat or to your house in Cirencester.'

Sybil had taken Gordon's hand in hers when he offered it and was still holding it when he finished talking. She reluctantly released it; it was something familiar to hang on to.

'All I want to do is go home to the flat. I desperately need be alone tonight and to try and come to terms with what has happened and sort out in my own mind a reason for it.'

Gordon Blossom, who suspected by now that they knew the reason, did not feel that it would be diplomatic to embark upon any explanation as to the preliminary findings of the company, nor did he suspect that such a statement would be welcomed by his chairman. Instead, he concentrated on the minor details and told Sybil about the arrangements that had been made for George's body and that they had tentatively planned the funeral to take place in Cirencester two days from now, if that was satisfactory to her.

'I think he would have liked to have been buried in our local parish church,' said Sybil. 'I will talk to the funeral director myself tomorrow and make the necessary arrangements.'

'We are perfectly happy', said Gordon, 'to do all that for you, Sybil, if you would like.'

Gordon Blossom fervently hoped, however, that his role in this affair was now rapidly coming to an end and that she would take over the wifely duties. Never at home with dramatic circumstances, Gordon was beginning to feel distinctly uncomfortable and wished that the short journey into London was already over. Apart from anything else, he had missed his evening meal, which he usually took at precisely seven o'clock, as he was a creature of habit. He much preferred the orderly aspects of life that surrounded his job as company secretary. This stint of duty was something he didn't wish to occur again.

It was a pleasant evening in London, and people were going about their business as though nothing had happened. It seemed unreal to Sybil, and it was with relief when they turned into her street and stopped outside the flat. Both Gordon and the driver got out and helped Sybil in with the cases. There was barely enough room in the small hall for them to turn round.

Gordon took his leave as quickly as possible. He was not a drinking man, but on this occasion, he did feel that a stop at the local pub on the way home would certainly be welcome, and he therefore had the driver drop him off at the Crown & Anchor, where he took two large gin and tonic and speculated on what was going to happen next.

Sybil left the cases in the hall, and going through the living area into the small kitchen, she filled the electric jug with water and switched it on. She took from the cupboard a china mug, and placing a tea bag in it, she waited for the kettle to boil. When the tea was ready, she took it into the living room and put it on the table and took out from her hand baggage her passport and the various other papers that she had accumulated since George's death. These included a death certificate and cause of death together with the official release papers from the police department in Nice and the envelope containing the money. She sat and looked at the envelope for a while.

'Well, George', she said aloud, 'it's awful enough, my darling, that you are dead and I am sitting here looking at this paltry sum of money in exchange, but at least there is ten times more awaiting me for the pension fund.'

She took another sip of tea before putting the mug carefully to one side. She lowered her arms onto the table top and let her head rest on her right forearm and started to sob quietly, and then with ever greater volume, the tears dropped one by one onto the polished table, leaving little marks as they did so. She cried until she could cry no more and, finally getting up from the table, went through into the bedroom with the large double bed and flung herself on it exhausted. On the dressing table was a picture of George in his academic robes. He was smiling, pleased as punch, but not anymore.

The policeman sat in the unmarked car in the street outside the flat. He had reported in to Roger Schofield that Sybil Yoreen had returned to the flat and had stayed there. He now had a long vigil ahead of him until his relief arrived sometime the following morning.

Sybil awoke from her exhausted and tearful sleep at around 2:00 a.m. and, getting off the bed, removed her clothes untidily and, going to the small bathroom, brushed her teeth and splashed cold water onto her face. She looked into the mirror and drew no comfort from the image that stared back at her. She went back to the bedroom, and this time, turning down the bed covers, she slipped her bulk into it naked, and drawing the two pillows from George's side of the bed, she put them down alongside her and once more cried herself into a fitful sleep.

The following morning dawned bright and sunny. Sybil had cried herself through the night and was now dry eyed. She had still not come to terms with the events, but for the time being, she was not going to dissolve into tears again. She had something to do of great importance, and therefore she took a bath and towelled her large body down and applied a deodorant and a liberal sprinkling of eau de toilette Coco by Chanel. Perfume was a weakness with Sybil. She liked to smell nice, and this morning, she overdid things. She put on a good old-fashioned corset, which pulled her waist in uncomfortably reducing or redistributing some of her bulk. To the suspenders, she attached a new pair of chocolate-brown 30 denier stockings and stepped into a pair of voluminous French knickers. Realising what she had done, she then removed them, replacing them with a less ornate pair. She sat at the dressing table and, as carefully as possible, applied make-up to her ravaged face. When she had completed the task, she really started to feel that she could present herself to the world again. She put on a smart blue suit with a white blouse and blue shoes and went through into the small kitchen and, rinsing out the mug from last night, made some more tea, and taking two Ryvitas from a box in the cupboard on the wall, she put some marmalade on and ate them.

At just after 10:00 a.m., Sybil walked into the bank. The policeman on duty outside the flat had called Roger Schofield when Sybil had left and informed him where she was. Schofield dispatched Millicent Bywater, who arrived before Sybil had concluded her business and relieved the duty policeman.

Inside the bank, Sybil was explaining to the manager, whom she had insisted in dealing with and had been kept waiting until he could find time to help an unscheduled visitor, that she had come to collect the contents of a deed box that had been deposited with them the previous Tuesday. She produced the document that identified her and her ownership of the box and also put down beside it her key.

The manager was extremely confused. Only the day before he had released the box into the custody of another key holder.

He took Sybil off to his office. 'Mrs Yoreen, I don't know how to explain this to you without offence, but yesterday afternoon, the deed box in question was removed from our safekeeping.'

Sybil was struck dumb. She opened her mouth, but no words came out. She tried again.

'This is impossible!' she bellowed. 'The box was the property of my husband and myself, and my husband hasn't been for it because he's dead.' Tears poured once more down her face as she pounded the desk with her large fist.

The manager leaned back to avoid the onslaught of fist and tears and waited for the outburst to subside. He pressed a small button on his desk, and a secretary entered.

'Bring me the papers on the Yoreen deed box,' he said.

The secretary departed and, while Sybil continued to sob, returned with the papers.

'Mrs Yoreen, please compose yourself,' pleaded the manager.

'Compose myself, you halfwit. You give away £450,000 that is rightfully mine, and you ask me to compose myself. I will not compose myself. I have just lost my husband, and now you have lost for me my pension. What am I to do?'

Sybil opened her bag and pulled out a handful of tissues, which she rubbed her face and eyes with.

'I can understand your distress, Mrs Yoreen, but I do not deserve your abuse. The papers here are quite clear as is the document that gives you custody together with your husband and a Mr Lee Doo-hwan, or his nominated representative. Yesterday, Mr Doo-hwan's legitimate representative called with a letter of authority and the correct key. We did issue two keys when the money was put into safe custody at the special request of the depositor, one for Mr Lee Doo-hwan and the other for your husband.'

'But I don't know this man!' shouted Sybil. 'He had no right to come in and collect the box. The box was our property.'

'Mrs Yoreen, the bank was quite within its rights to discharge the box to the gentleman who collected it. Your husband might well have had joint custody, but there were no instructions that only he, or yourself, had the right to withdraw the box. There were three names to release it to.'

'You mean to tell me that if we had taken all the money away the first time we visited you, this other man would have not been able to collect it.'

'I am afraid that is exactly so,' said the manager. 'And now, Mrs Yoreen, I must ask you to leave. There is nothing more to be gained for either of us in prolonging this conversation.' He stood up and walked round the desk to Sybil and handed her the papers in question. There was no doubt they were genuine.

'I have never even seen these pieces of paper before,' said Sybil and started to feel distinctly nauseous.

'I assure you, madam, that the depositor was quite adamant about the method of withdrawing whatever was in the box, which you now tell me was a large sum of money. These written instructions are quite clear, and there are three names here as you can see.' He pointed them out to her. 'Provided you or your husband or the third signatory was able to produce positive identification such as a passport and the key, then under the terms of the deposit, any of you were free to remove the contents, and the bank has only acted in good faith in allowing that to happen.'

'But I don't know this man!' shrieked Sybil again. 'The name doesn't mean anything to me. Does it to you?'

'Whether it means anything or not to me, madam, doesn't matter. It is merely for identification purposes, and I am very sorry to tell you again that the contents of the box have been removed.' He shifted uncomfortably from one foot to the other, while Sybil remained seated. 'I really am very busy, and I must ask you again, if you have no more business to conclude with the bank, to leave.'

Sybil sat there stunned. Quite clearly, whoever was behind all this had played a much shrewder game than either she or George would ever have suspected. She was quite convinced that she had been robbed, but at this moment in time, she was unsure what she could do about it.

There was no point in carrying on at the hapless manager. He appeared to have done his duty. There was just one final thing she required.

'I need to check into the background a little more fully on this,' said Sybil in a much more reasonable tone of voice. 'Would you be kind enough to let me have a photocopy of the authorisation, and then I can study it more fully and see if there is any other action I can take.'

The bank manager considered this request for a moment or two, studying Sybil over his half-rimmed glasses, and finally felt there wasn't really any harm in it; at least he would be rid of her, and taking the original papers back from Sybil, he had his secretary copy the appropriate sheets.

Sybil sat there waiting for the world to end. Life was a shit. In a matter of minutes, the secretary returned, and holding out the copy of the document, instructing who could and could not enter and leave with the contents of the box, she gave it to Sybil, who inspected it and, too choked to talk, further handed it back with an affirmative nod of her head. The manager put it into an envelope and placed it back in her hand.

'I am very sorry, madam, if this has come as a shock to you, but I am sure you understand that the bank has only done its duty.'

'Yes,' sighed Sybil. 'Yes, I suppose you have.' She turned her back on him and walked from the office and out of the bank. She never wanted to see it again or him or anyone associated with it. She found herself once again on the pavement outside.

From the other side of the street, Millicent Bywater saw what appeared to be a quite smart but extremely agitated lady. She was holding a white envelope in her right hand and banging her left continuously with it. She seemed to do this for a matter of minutes before making her mind up what to do next. She strode of in the direction of the tube station, and Millicent followed.

Chapter 19

Philip Galsworthy had been the British consul in Nice for some years and, following the death of George Yoreen, had immediately interested himself in the sad affair. He had, unbeknown to Sybil, smoothed the way for the repatriation of George's body. He had spoken to the police and obtained what facts he could to inform the Foreign Office in London.

It was a strange coincidence that Philip Galsworthy had been at university with Dennis Matchett, and he had followed with interest the rise of his company, NTI. It was true that they had not been particularly compatible characters, but Philip maintained a sneaking respect for what the man had achieved. Because of this, he had paid particular attention to a chance remark the previous evening when he had been dining with John Ashdown, who was the manager of Barclays Bank in Nice. They met occasionally with their wives for dinner, and John Ashdown happened to mention George Yoreen.

'This affair with the British scientist is a strange carry-on,' John Ashdown had said. 'Have you got any ideas Philip why a man such as this should be gunned down here in Nice?'

'No, I haven't', said Philip, 'although I'm sure even the Nice police are going to find out the reason.' And they had sniggered like schoolboys.

'I do not know whether it's relevant,' said Ashdown when they had gotten over their fit of expat humour, 'but the day before this chappie Yoreen was shot, he was apparently in the bank.'

'Was he indeed?' said Galsworthy. 'That's an interesting coincidence. Was there anything unusual about his visit?'

'Well, I didn't actually see him,' said Ashdown. 'It was only when I heard the news of his death that the name registered with me. Apparently, he had called in with a reasonably large sum of mixed US dollars and Swiss francs and had exchanged it for euros. The amount was somewhere around £5,000, although that's not unusual by any means. The girl who did the transaction brought it specifically to my attention because our standing orders require that all amounts of foreign exchange over £5,000 in notes are notified to the manager, and this was all in used notes.'

'You know, I was at school and university with Dennis Matchett. He's the chairman of the company Yoreen worked for,' said Galsworthy. 'I am sure he would be very interested to know the details.'

'I don't know about that,' said Ashdown. 'I wouldn't normally have told you this. It's only because of our close friendship that I happened to mention it, but I suppose there wouldn't be any harm in you letting him know, provided that the source of your information was protected.'

'Oh, I assure you', said Galsworthy, 'that I would just let him know informally that this doctor Yoreen had changed a substantial sum of money. I will tell him through my official duties that I had come by the knowledge confidentially and leave it at that. I would imagine anyway that the police either here or back home are going to be looking into his financial affairs in fine detail.'

The conversation ended there, and they moved onto other matters.

Sir Dennis Matchett had given very careful instructions to his secretary that only the most important of telephone calls were to be put through to him under the present circumstances. Ever since the information had become public property, the switchboard of NTI had been jammed. These calls had come from all sorts of different sources, and a considerable number were from shareholders who had anxiously been watching the decline in the value of their stock and wanted to speak to Sir Dennis personally. At the best of times, he did not like shareholders and avoided talking to them as much as possible. Now, they were just a bloody nuisance.

Kathryn Goodbody was thoroughly frustrated. Despite the fact that the switchboard had very specific instructions, the phone on her desk rang constantly and interfered with the other work she had to do. Much of the detail she had been forced to pass on to Marcia Payne, and it was Marcia who had typed up most of the information destined for the general public and, more particularly, for the stock exchange and shareholders.

The phone rang again, and the flustered Kathryn picked it up.

'Kathryn Goodbody, here, Sir Dennis Matchett's private secretary.' It was her standard form of response; she had a certain status to maintain.

The voice at the other end of the line said, 'Good morning, Kathryn Goodbody. This is Philip Galsworthy telephoning you from Nice.'

Galsworthy never knew nowadays whether to address secretaries as miss or missus and therefore compromised by using their full name when he knew it. It often had quite gratifying results, as he had an easy and fluent style on the telephone. Kathryn Goodbody was one of those who reacted pleasantly to that form of address.

'Yes, Mr Galsworthy', she said, 'what can I do for you?'

'I would like to speak to Sir Dennis, if that's possible. I know how busy you will have been since the death of George Yoreen, but I hope he has a minute to listen to me. As the consul here in Nice, you will understand that I have had some minor involvement following Dr Yoreen's murder, and it just so happens that Sir Dennis and I were at university together. I think I have some information that might be useful to him.'

This was a call she was going to have to put through.

'If you will wait just one moment, Mr Galsworthy, I will try and locate Sir Dennis.'

She didn't wait for an answer but put him on hold and buzzed Sir Dennis.

'Yes, Kathryn, who is it now?'

'It is a gentleman called Philip Galsworthy who claims that he is the British consul in Nice and that you and he were at university together. He says he has some information concerning George's death.'

'Goodness me,' said Sir Dennis, 'yes, I do remember him. What a strange coincidence. Put him through.'

'Matchett here,' bellowed Sir Dennis into the telephone when the call came onto the line.

'Dennis, how good to talk to you again after all this time. I hope this is not an inconvenient moment.'

Sir Dennis took the receiver away from his ear and stared at it quizzically. It had been a long time since anyone had had the temerity to address him as Dennis; it was well known that he liked his full title to be used or, within the company, to be referred to as chairman. He was unused to such informality from relative strangers and found it mildly offensive.

'Ah, Philip, these are peculiar circumstances under which to make contact again, and I therefore assume you must have some particularly interesting facts about Dr Yoreen's death that you think I ought to know about.'

'I don't know whether they are of immediate interest to you, but I think it's something that you ought to be aware of,' said Galsworthy. 'I happened to be having dinner last evening with the manager of Barclays Bank here in Nice, who has been a friend of mine for some time, and he told me that a transaction had gone through the bank wherein your doctor Yoreen changed a mixed amount of Swiss francs and American dollars. The total was £5,000.'

So much for maintaining his promise of confidentiality!

Sir Dennis's reaction to this was one of incredulity. George was well paid, but it did not seem to him that he was the sort of man who would, under any circumstances, be carrying around mixed currencies in cash of that amount. It was another mysterious piece of the jigsaw; perhaps it would eventually fit with the others.

'That's very interesting, Philip. Dr Yoreen was on holiday in Nice, and, of course, he would have needed to change money on his arrival. However, the sum is generally larger than I would have expected. I wonder if I can ask a favour of you.'

'Ask away,' said Galsworthy.

'The sort of information you have given to me is going to be extremely sensitive in the wrong hands. We are having a few difficulties over here since Dr Yoreen's death with the share price, and the market is already worried enough without having this extra titbit of information supplied to it. I am very grateful indeed for the information, but I would ask that you keep it to yourself. It would worry me considerably, for instance, if this was mentioned in any report that you might make to the Foreign Office. It would also be difficult if your banker chum was forced to reveal these facts.'

Sir Dennis knew that he was asking a man to withhold important information for no very good reason and to influence others to do the same. He was not hopeful that he would get 100 per cent enthusiastic reaction.

'There's no problem keeping this sort of information to myself,' said Galsworthy. 'I don't know about the manager at Barclays, but I very much doubt whether it's an amount of money that he would refer to specifically in any report to his head office in England. I don't want to put too much pressure on him, Dennis, but I am sure we will do our best to keep things quiet here unless, of course, we are asked the direct question by the police.'

Sir Dennis knew that this was the best he was going to get, and even if it gained him a few days, they could, meantime, concoct a suitable story to explain why George had such a large sum on him.

'I am very grateful to you, Philip, and thank you very much for calling. I hope sometime when you are passing through London, you will take the opportunity of looking me up. You can always drop in and have a spot of lunch with us.'

'I'd be delighted to,' said Galsworthy, wondering who the other people would be. 'I wish you luck with your current problems. Goodbye.'

'Goodbye, Philip, and again, thank you very much.'

Sir Dennis sat there for a few moments thinking about what he had just heard. He then picked up the phone again. 'Kathryn, find Kevin Hipkiss for me, please, and get him to call me, or if he is in the building, I want to see him.'

Kevin had been mounting a damage limitation exercise to the best of his abilities. His part in this sorry tale was to keep the City contacts sweet. This was something that Kevin had been practicing to do for some time using his programme of self-aggrandisement and his private tutorials on aggressive communication. The various bankers and brokers he now claimed as his friends had been contacted personally following the press release and the announcement to the stock exchange concerning George's death.

Kevin had expressed some surprise to the brokers over the slippage in the share price, as he felt this was a gross over reaction to the situation. He had been told in quite simple terms that the market was already nervous, and when a company had been building up its potential to such a degree on a future invention, then the base upon which that building was being done had to be substantial; cracks were now appearing. Kevin knew that a lot of the hype in the share price was due to his efforts backed up as well by Sir Dennis. If the story was unsustainable, then there was no doubt that the current price was not an overreaction but a reasonable statement about the real value of the stock.

All this made Kevin a very nervous person. Kevin did not like being a very nervous person. Kevin was adept at passing on much of the pressure to his subordinates, but, nevertheless, he was aware that he was becoming increasingly exposed, and just as Victor Stanley had been selected, on fairly minimal evidence, as the scapegoat, he could well represent the ultimate sacrifice. He was unable to talk about his problems with anyone, as he was not a man who confided in others, and because of that, he had few friends. He counted his man Clinton as one of this small band; alas, even there he was wrong.

The telephone beyond his right hand rang. He reached for it, but his chair was too far back from the desk, so he stood and leaned forward. The seam of his trousers tore.

'Kevin, this is Kathryn, could you come along to the chairman's office as soon as possible, please?'

'I will be along immediately, Kath-rrr-yn,' rolling her name around as if it were the barrel of her body; she liked that, and this was one person Kevin cultivated. He was still smarting, however, from the fact that he was not invited to the Stanley meeting when he was sure he had something to contribute. He would have liked Kathryn to have let him know it was happening, but she had not. Now he would have to learn of events from the chairman. He put the phone down and picked up from the desk the increasingly thick file concerning the current problems, which contained as well the general background information on George Yoreen and Victor Stanley.

Chapter 20

Chief Inspector Pierre Dupre was in conference with Alain Rochet and Nicole Lambert. It was an oppressively hot day in Nice, and Nicole was aware that not all of them were wearing deodorant. Dupre had spent some time on the telephone to Supt Roger Schofield in London, but Schofield's investigation was only just beginning, and there was no useful news from that quarter yet. There had, however, been a whisper from Marseille. The police department there had picked up a rumour that a contract had been accepted for the death of George Yoreen; the source of the information was unusually reliable. The problem was the inability of his colleagues in Marseille to pinpoint who had been hired. Dupre was optimistic, however, that it was probably someone already familiar with the geography of Nice. The timing would not have allowed a stranger to learn where best to place himself and then to vanish into thin air. Forensics also felt a local was at work. So the contract man was in Marseille, and the assassin was living in Nice. Until there was evidence to the contrary, this was how he would play it.

Nicole Lambert had gone over in detail with her boss the contents of Sybil Yoreen's handbag, which she had inspected so carefully during Sybil's sedated sleep. The papers she had found identified the Middle East bank. It was decided that the manager of that establishment should be interviewed.

For some reason, maybe a sixth sense, Alphonse Alii had felt uncomfortable ever since he had spotted Nicole Lambert as a tail on Sybil Yoreen, but to act precipitately and leave the bank in a panic would blow his cover, so he remained nervously on duty.

The manager at the bank received a discreet telephone call from Alain Rochet concerning the deposit made by the Yoreen's and the subsequent withdrawal of the money by Sybil. The manager had refused to speak openly over the telephone, and an appointment had therefore been made. Alain Rochet had requested that he did not speak to members of his staff before they had had the chance to talk in detail; the manager had agreed.

The police driver made good time to the bank despite the heavy traffic on the seafront of Nice. He was a large man with a heavy black moustache and glimpsed through the rear-view mirror of a vehicle in front was able to strike fear into the innocent motorist; it was his only asset. There was therefore no need to use the klaxon available to him, and he stopped the car quietly in one of the side streets close to the bank. Alain Rochet got out and walked the short distance in the heat. The holiday crowds were going about their earnest pursuit of pleasure, and the beach cafes and waterfront bars were busy.

Alain Rochet went through the doors of the bank and entered the air-conditioned interior with relief. Seated at his desk to the right of the entrance, Alphonse Alii looked up as Alain Rochet walked over to the enquiries desk.

The dark-skinned young lady with eyes you could sink into looked up from the pile of paperwork in front of her.

'Can I help you, sir?'

'My name is Alain Rochet, and I have an interview with the manager. Would you be so kind as to let him know I am here?'

'Certainly, sir. Please wait a minute.' She stood up and smoothed down her skirt. Alain Rochet had the good looks associated with a certain class of French policemen written about by oversexed thriller writers. These looks generally encouraged young women to smooth their skirts. She turned on her heel and, with a wiggle of her not-unattractive hips, went through the door to the rear of the bank. Within a minute, she was back, and walking towards him, she went to the security door to her left-hand side and, pressing a button at the side of it, released the electronic lock. She opened the door and stood back for Alain Rochet to go through.

'If you will be kind enough to follow me', she said, 'I will take you to Mr Mohammed.'

Turkal Mohammed had been manager at the branch for five years. He was a man who took his banking duties seriously and in the overseas department had a growing reputation. He had managed to encourage depositors to have confidence in his bank, and as a result, his business had been growing steadily during his period of tenure. He had always followed the principle of behaving in France as the French should and had become an accepted member of society. He knew a large number of people and was welcomed, with some reservation, in the European banking circles of Nice. He had no record with the police, and it was the first time that he had ever had to talk with them about any of the activities of the bank.

The young lady knocked and opened the door for Alain Rochet and, smiling sweetly to him, asked him to enter. As he walked through the door, she closed it quietly behind him.

Turkal Mohammed was a short, rotund, and balding figure who got up from behind his desk and walked round to shake hands with Rochet. His suit was a regulation dark blue lightweight affair that would have hung more easily on a man with a few kilos less weight to carry. His black shoes shone as though recently polished. He wore half-rimmed glasses in gold frames, which sat just short of the bulbous end of his rather large nose. He shuffled through the carpet rather than lifting his feet up and gave the impression of sliding towards Rochet. He held out his right hand, the back of which was covered with dense black hair. He affected a gold bracelet on his wrist.

'Welcome to our modest bank, Monsieur.' His voice was deep and mellifluous as though generated by the substantial gut to which he pressed his left hand as though trying to contain it.

Alain Rochet took the furry offering and shook it briefly; it was as though he had a small lively animal in his hand. Rochet took from his inner breast pocket his identification card and held it out to Turkal Mohammed.

'Thank you for seeing me, Monsieur Mohammed. I appreciate you accommodating me on short notice. I am Chief Inspector Dupre's deputy, and we have been assigned the investigation concerning the death, of which I am sure you have heard in full detail, of the English scientist Dr George Yoreen, who was so spectacularly gunned down on the beach just across the Promenade.'

'Of course, of course,' said Turkal Mohammed. 'We were all terribly shocked by the incident.'

His French accent was good if not perfect, and he looked Alain Rochet directly in the face; no shiftiness here, no apparent wish to be immediately somewhere else.

Alain Rochet sat down in the comfortable chair to the side of the desk. The sunlight coming through the window was softened by the tinted glass, and the air conditioning held the office at a comfortable temperature. There were various certificates on the wall concerning financings that the bank had been responsible for and extolling the virtues of the manager. A picture of a man in flowing robes proclaimed the bank's service to a royal house, a large bookcase contained publications on finance in at least four languages, and there was a small conference table with four chairs. From his seat behind the desk, Turkal Mohammed pushed across a silver cigarette box and offered Alain Rochet one of the oval Turkish cigarettes within; Rochet politely declined. Turkal Mohammed sat back in the chair and waited.

'The enquiries we are making', said Rochet, 'are naturally of a confidential and delicate nature. Dr Yoreen was a British citizen, and we do not like foreign visitors being murdered in our country, nor for that matter do we particularly enjoy our own people being gunned down.'

A small smile crept into the corners of his mouth, though he did not feel particularly humorous.

'I am concerned here with catching the criminal responsible for Dr Yoreen's death. The establishment of the motive behind it will take more time, and the cooperation of our friends in England will be needed. We believe there is a conspiracy afoot. These enquiries have therefore taken on an international flavour, and they are already being reported in a number of newspapers around the world. Because of the spectacular nature of the death, the story is likely to get larger and more embellished before we have completed our investigation. It is extremely important for us therefore to gather the facts together as quickly as possible and to have them in a clear and lucid form. I am mentioning this to you because I know that banks have certain reservations about revealing the activities of their clients, but in this case, my department expects your full cooperation. I hope we might have it.'

Steepled fingers were pressed more firmly together. Turkal Mohammed leaned forward with some difficulty and continued to examine Alain Rochet's features frankly. Rochet felt mildly uncomfortable.

'It has always been part of our reputation, Inspector, to protect our clients. However, the circumstances concerning Dr Yoreen's activities with this bank are somewhat unusual. He was in fact a client for less than forty-eight hours and never actually opened an account here. I have spoken with the employee who handled Dr Yoreen's enquiry, a Mr Alphonse Alii. He has supplied me with details about the deposit he made and the subsequent withdrawal. I think under the circumstances, I can provide any information you require, but please understand that had the gentleman entered into a more comprehensive relationship with us, my hands would have been tied.'

'We have evidence that Dr Yoreen's wife was in possession of a key to a deposit box here at the bank and the number of that key was 237. Apart from this information, we have nothing else, and can you therefore fill in for me the missing pieces?'

Turkal Mohammed now leaned back in the well-upholstered chair. The steepled fingers were gently parted, and he drew towards him a pale yellow folder on the desk and opened it. Inside were two or three pieces of paper. He lifted one of these sheets and looked over the top of it at Alain Rochet again.

'Dr George Yoreen and his wife made a joint deposit with us of mixed US dollars and Swiss francs amounting to about €60,000. It was apparently their intention that this money would be put to work for them, but the initial instruction was to hold it secure. We knew this because our new money laundering rules require us to be aware of deed box contents. Mr Alii accepted the money in good faith, and as you will appreciate, it is not abnormal for banks to receive relatively large sums in cash. We are not generally in the habit of questioning our depositors unless we feel that there is something particularly strange about the amount or the type of deposit they are wishing to make.'

Alain Rochet knew that this was an understatement. It was rarely that a bank would ever question a depositor who was willing to place with them substantial funds, and nowadays, even some of the world's most respectable banks had passed through them huge sums of money that were quite obviously laundering exercises despite the best endeavours of the authorities.

Rochet did not suspect, however, that this was anything of that kind. He made some notes in his book about the form of deposit and confirmed the general details.

'I wonder if you would be kind enough', he said, 'to ask your Mr Alii to join us for a while in order that I can ask him whether he saw anything unusual during his meeting with the Yoreens. Perhaps also you could tell me how long Mr Alii has been with you and anything you have about his background.'

For the first time, Alain Rochet spotted a momentary uneasiness in the man opposite. The full and frank looking into the face technique momentarily lapsed. Rochet pressed on.

'It would appear that the last person to actually talk with the Yoreens before the doctors death was Mr Alii. It might be that he picked up some feelings about the state of mind of the Yoreens, and that is important to us.'

'Mr Alii has been with us now for almost eighteen months. He comes with a first-class recommendation and has carried out his bank duties assiduously. His personnel file gives a number of accredited qualifications but does not give a lot of background detail into his earlier career, but then, of course, he is a young man. He did, however, spend two years with the bank at home previous to his appointment here in France. Often in businesses such as ours, it is whom you know and not what you know that acquires some of the better postings.'

Again, Rochet detected the slight unease of the man opposite.

'What are you trying to tell me, Monsieur?'

'Mr Alii has as his patron, as I believe you would call it, the president of the bank himself. Apparently, the president and Mr Alii's father were business friends, and when I received a request to accept him at my branch, I did not have the right to refuse. I hope you understand.'

Indeed, Rochet did understand; patronage was still widely practiced.

'You mean to tell me you do not have a full record of his employment before joining the bank?'

'It is worse than that,' said Mohammed. 'I do not actually have any written record, other than his qualifications, of his activities before he came to France. All I know is that he served with the bank at home. It is not something I would like to question too closely.'

'Perhaps, then, I could talk to him,' asked Rochet.

Turkal Mohammed reached out with his left hand and, lifting the receiver, pressed with his right two buttons on the phone. He spoke briefly into the instrument in a language that Rochet did not understand and placed the receiver back in position.

'Mr Alii is on his way up.'

There was a knock at the door, and Alphonse Alii entered the room. Turkal Mohammed signalled to him to sit in the chair on the other side of the desk from Alain Rochet.

'This gentleman here, Alii, is from the police department and is investigating the death of Dr Yoreen. You will recall the sad demise of this gentleman.'

'Indeed, I do, sir,' said Alii. 'The Yoreens were new clients of ours, and I received the distressed widow only yesterday.'

'The deputy inspector', said Mohammed, 'is aware of the transaction that has taken place. He would like to ask you a few questions concerning the demeanour of the Yoreens during your initial meeting with the two of them and your subsequent meeting with Mrs Yoreen shortly before she withdrew the deposit.'

Unlike Turkal Mohammed, the impression created by Alphonse Alii was not one of open honesty. He had a certain shiftiness, but there was no apparent nervousness; nevertheless, a guarded look had come into his eyes. He seemed to have the confidence that one would not normally find in a junior manager within a small branch. Rochet did not like him.

'I understand, Mr Alii', said Rochet, 'that you joined the bank here some eighteen months ago, and before that, you had been employed in the main branch at home. Is this correct?'

'Yes, that's correct,' said Alii. 'I was trained with the bank and was lucky enough to land this posting in Nice. I enjoy it very much.'

'What I am trying to learn from you, Mr Alii, is whether there was any nervousness or any apparent discomfort being shown by the Yoreens when they deposited the money with you. Did you get the view that they were making a routine deposit of funds they had decided to entrust to a foreign bank outside England, or was this something else? Did they tell you anything that might shed some light on Dr Yoreen's subsequent death?'

Alii took his time answering the question. He went over in his mind first whether there were any advantages or disadvantages in saying the Yoreens were in a nervous state of mind or in a relaxed state of mind. In the end, he decided to tell it as it was.

'I think anyone carrying that amount of money about their person would exhibit a certain amount of nervousness. However, I would not have said that they were any more nervous or any less nervous than any other couple who would be bringing it into the bank. Admittedly, they seemed quite relieved when we took it into our custody, and we then discussed briefly how we might be able to put it to work for them. However, that was going to be the subject of a further meeting, and I then completed the necessary paperwork, and they left. They appeared to leave in a perfectly happy state of mind.'

'Are you absolutely certain that neither Dr Yoreen nor his wife mentioned anything about how they had acquired that money?' asked Rochet.

'They did not take me into their confidence, sir. I did not question them. It was not my job to do so. I really don't think I can add anything else to your enquiry, Inspector.'

Rochet knew that he had gone as far as he could at this stage of the discussion. He was still left with the feeling that this man knew more than he was imparting, and he continued to hold the view that Turkal Mohammed was nervous in his presence, more nervous than he would have been in the presence of a normal member of his bank staff. This might have been because of the relationship Alii's father had with his chief, but equally it could have been something more sinister.

'Thank you, Mr Alii, for your cooperation, I appreciate the help you have given, but if I can think of anything else that I would like to talk to you about, I will speak again with Mr Mohammed.'

There followed a brief exchange between the manager and his subordinate, and Alii left the office.

'I think that almost completes the discussion for the time being. However, there is just one final question I would like to ask you.'

'Please ask,' said Turkal Mohammed.

'On the day in question, can you give me details of the movements of your bank staff, and can you let me know of any movements that you would consider unusual? For instance, did any of them seek extra time off during the day?'

Turkal Mohammed pushed himself back into the protective comfort of the large chair and gazed hard at his left hand as if diligently inspecting it for filth.

'As a matter of fact', he said, 'on the particular day of the shooting, Mr Alii himself asked for time off to attend to a problem that he had at his apartment, but other than that, our bank staff have a very short break in the middle of the day, and all of them would have been back in their positions during the time when Dr Yoreen was shot.'

This was an interesting piece of information worthy of further investigation. Rochet made a note in his book for good orders' sake. It was not something he would forget; he determined to follow it up.

'I'd be grateful if you didn't mention this last piece of information to Mr Alii,' said Rochet. 'There may be a perfectly rational explanation as to why he had to absent himself from the bank at the very time that Dr Yoreen was shot, and, of course, there was no irregularity concerning the money or the subsequent withdrawal of that money by Dr Yoreen's wife. Nevertheless, I think it is something we would wish to examine in more detail. Perhaps you could let me have Mr Alii's home address.'

Turkal Mohammed pulled out a drawer in his desk and removed from it a small black book, and turning to the index letter A, he wrote out the first entry. It gave the address of Alphonse Alii and his telephone number. He pushed the piece of paper silently across the desk to Alan Rochet.

'You have my every cooperation, Inspector,' said Mohammed. 'If there is any further information you require from me, please call me personally.' He picked up another small piece of paper and wrote upon it his own home address and telephone number and pushed it in the same direction. Alain Rochet put it with the first piece and returned it with his notebook to his pocket.

'I am very grateful to you, Monsieur, for your cooperation. You have been very helpful. I hope it won't be necessary to talk to you again, but I cannot guarantee it.'

Rochet stood up, and Turkal Mohammed did likewise. He came round again from behind the desk and offered Rochet the small furry animal. Rochet pressed it once more and left the office. The young lady who had shown him in was there to show him out with her most glittering smile.

'I do hope we will see you again, Monsieur,' she said.

'Maybe you will,' said Rochet, but he did not mean it in the way she hoped he would.

He walked across the main floor of the bank, and Alphonse Alii looked up momentarily from his desk and then down again. Something had to be done.

Alain Rochet returned with the police driver to headquarters and went straight to Pierre Dupre's office.

'I think we have a possible lead, Chief,' he said. 'I have come up with the interesting fact that the employee who accepted the deposit at the bank from the Yoreens was actually absent from the bank at the time of George Yoreen's death. I don't necessarily think this is anything more than a coincidence, but it's one that we must follow up. I have here his home address, and I would suggest that we put him under surveillance immediately. With your permission, I will have one of my team stake out the premises and make some discreet enquiries about who else lives in the building and how much is known about him.'

Pierre Dupre granted the necessary permission, and Alain Rochet left to make the arrangements.

Back at the bank on the Promenade des Anglais, Alphonse Alii watched the clock. He dare not ask to leave early, but he needed to return to his apartment at the first opportunity. It was likely that if he did not act quickly, then his double career was going to come to a rapid and unhealthy end.

By the time the day's business was concluded and Alii was on his way home, he became aware that he was being followed. Alii needed as a matter of some urgency to talk to the hairdresser.

When he had left the bank, he took with him his few personal items. You could never be too sure what was going to happen. It was on the way to catch his number nine bus that he felt eyes on him. The bus deposited him outside his apartment at the same moment that the colourful hairdresser arrived. He took this as a sign that his luck was still running strongly. They had a brief conversation on the pavement, and Alii arranged to see her in half an hour.

He inserted the key into the top lock and, neutralising the alarm system, opened the bottom. He went into the apartment, which served as his home and arsenal.

Alii was under no illusion that the French police were eventually going to check up on him. He had, after all, been one of the people that was in contact with George Yoreen shortly before his death, and although that contact was innocent enough, he knew full well that they would question the movement of anyone known to have spoken to the Yoreens. He also knew that it would not be long before they discovered that he was not at the bank at the time of the killing. It was an unfortunate set of circumstances that had allowed George Yoreen to have chosen his bank to make the deposit. The coincidence of his employment there and the fact that the Corsican had called him to carry out the contract was uncanny. Alii had not considered the deeper implications at the time. He admitted to himself now that this was a grave error of judgement.

Alii had been motivated by the large sum of money proposed and the immediacy of the action. Being asked to execute someone on your own doorstep appeared to be the most convenient way of increasing wealth in the short term. It was only now that he realised that the facts being assembled could point to his involvement.

The first thing that he did was make a telephone call to a Middle Eastern country and requested arrangements to be made for his small house to be opened up. He next went to his desk in the corner of the small living room and took from it an envelope that contained three different passports. He selected an Algerian one, which he had purchased at considerable expense and which described him as a schoolteacher. He took the envelope and the other contents of the desk and placed them in his briefcase. He then went over to the gun cupboard and opened it. Within glistened the dark wood and silvery metal of his arsenal. It had been carefully assembled at not inconsiderable cost. He took out each of the guns and put the high-velocity collapsible rifle into a tennis bag together with the two handguns and ammunition.

Going through into the bedroom, he removed from the drawers the pieces of clothing that he felt he needed to carry with him and put them into a suit carrier along with his toiletries. All the clothes in question had been purchased in France, and anything that he left would show no direct evidence of his background. He looked at his watch; twenty-five minutes had elapsed.

In the basement of the apartment block, Alii kept a high-powered version of the Peugeot 206. He walked down the stairs with the sports bag in one hand, his suiter over his shoulder, and his briefcase in the other. At the bottom of the stairs, he opened the door into the basement area that contained the car park and descended the stairs into the car park. He stood at the entrance and allowed his eyes to become accustomed to the dim light and listened for any activity. It was as silent as the grave with the steel fire door closed behind him. It was ideal for his purpose.

He walked over to the Peugeot, and removing the keys from his pocket, he inserted one into the boot lock and turned it. The lid hissed up on its hydraulics. He placed the briefcase and the suiter at the back of the small compartment and closed and locked it. He looked around once more, but it remained quiet. He took the sports bag, and going over to the far corner of the garage where it was at its darkest, he kneeled down and raised a manhole cover that gave access to the sewerage system.

Although he had not planned it, Alii had been delighted to find, when he had rented the apartment, that this opening gave direct access to a main sewer. He always believed in examining every sensible exit point from a building in which he was living and from which, one day, he might have to make a quick exit under pressure. From the manhole cover, there descended a set of rusty steps, and he lowered himself carefully until his foot found the first rung. The smell that came up to him was not the sort of thing that Alii welcomed, but now he hardly noticed it. Working his way down the ladder, he was able to step from it onto a slightly elevated area above the main drainage channel, and taking the small Duracell torch from his pocket, he shone it onto the wall. The small beam revealed a storm entry point slightly above his head to the right.

Alii took the sports bag and wrapped it as tightly as possible around its contents and, reaching up with his left arm, found the rim of the entry, and hauling himself onto the tips of his toes, he was able with his right arm to ram the bag into the opening. It went far enough in not to be observed. It was with considerable regret that he said goodbye to his weapons, but they were replaceable. They might never be discovered, but he would never risk coming back to this town or this apartment. There was one final task.

Natalie Bosanquet did not consider herself to be a sex maniac, but she did have an interesting and varied sexual life. Being a hairdresser, she had a number of opportunities offered to her that were of an altogether non-heterosexual type. She had explored this fully and had not only gained considerable satisfaction from it but also widened as well her client base.

Her custom of changing her hair colour she had even passed on to some quite surprisingly well-known ladies.

She readily admitted to herself that her particular passion was for very fit, slim young men. It had been her experience that they were generally better stayers, and she liked to prolong the act of lovemaking and create several orgasms before she allowed her partner to indulge in his one solitary act. She had to admit that in the case of Alphonse Alii, she had not tested his prowess. He seemed to have so much nervous energy that she could not slow him down. He was exciting, though, and from the minute he entered her, she started to come.

Anticipating his visit to the apartment and remembering with satisfaction the last occasion, she quickly prepared herself for this one. A day in a hot salon is not guaranteed to present a clean and odour-free body, and therefore Natalie quickly stripped off her working clothes and took a shower. She recalled the electric effect of being without panties had had on Alphonse last time, and she considered briefly whether she should repeat it. She liked variety, though, and wanted to see how he would react to something slightly different.

Having towelled herself dry, she sprayed herself liberally with Effendi. She took the brush off her dressing table and vigorously brushed her green blonde hair. She stood in front of the full-length mirror and studied her naked body critically. Her breasts were full but had held up surprisingly well. They had dark brown centres to them, and the nipples were already partially erect. She ran her hands over her still-flat stomach and ruffled the dyed pubic hair. Leaning down, she opened one of the drawers in the dressing table and took from within a white suspender belt and clipped it round her waist. She then took out a pair of white stockings and, rolling them up her shapely brown legs, fastened them tautly to the suspenders. She pulled on the matching French knickers; it had always been a mystery to her why they were referred to as this. A short layered pleated skirt with a loose shirt tucked into the waistband, and a pair of white high-heeled mules completed the outfit. She felt dangerous.

Alphonse Alii had replaced the cover over the opening to the sewer and rapidly returned up the stairs and let himself into the flat. He was five minutes overdue at Natalie's. He quickly removed his outer garments, which he feared might have become contaminated from his subterranean activities, and pulled on a clean pair of trousers and a casual shirt. He once again let himself out of the apartment and crossed the small landing, pressing the bell on Natalie's door. She let him in.

The policeman observing Alii had reported to Alain Rochet that he had left the bank and taken the bus to his apartment. He had not recorded the fact that Natalie Bosanquet had arrived at the same time. He had remained on duty outside. It was unfortunate that he had chosen to observe the main entrance to the block. It was going to be a foolish oversight of the police that they did not allocate a second man to observe the rear exit from the apartment, which lead from the car park into the street behind.

Alphonse was taken into the small sitting room and, as before, sat down on the sofa by the coffee table. Natalie produced a glass of wine.

'What is it I can do for you, Alphonse?' she said, hoping that she already knew his answer.

There were two things that she could do for him. One was to remain permanently silent about their spasmodic relationship; he wanted no intimate details such as were available to her to be passed to the police. The second thing she could do was quite readily apparent to them both.

'I have had some rather sad news from home,' explained Alphonse. 'Unfortunately, my grandfather has died and I have to return home for the funeral.'

'I am sorry to hear that,' said Natalie, crossing one leg slowly over the other and giving him a glimpse of the upper part of her nylon-clad thigh.

'I am having to leave my apartment, and I wonder if you would be kind enough to look after it for me while I am away. There won't be anything to do, but I would just like to know someone is keeping a friendly eye on it. I will be happy to leave you my keys.'

'So long as you don't have that horribly complicated alarm system activated, I am sure I can handle that,' said Natalie. She moved her elegant legs again and noted with satisfaction the reaction that she had predicted.

'It will not be necessary for me to leave the alarm system on,' said Alphonse. 'There isn't anything I shall be leaving in the apartment that is of any particular importance. You understand, I only have it because, occasionally, I have confidential bank documents there.'

'Of course', said Natalie, 'it will be no problem. How long will you be away?'

'Oh, I would expect two weeks at the most,' lied Alphonse. 'These family funerals are sad affairs, and I don't want to stay for too long, but, unfortunately, there will be some necessary family business to transact as a result of my grandfather's death, and I won't be back before that is completed.'

'Is there anything else I can do to help you?' said Natalie. She licked her red lips, leaving a momentary high gloss. It was becoming increasingly apparent to Natalie that there was.

The need that Alphonse had immediately after one of his 'jobs' had always been satisfied by some available female. It was a new experience for him to partake of the act immediately prior to death, but this also appealed to him.

'You are a very attractive woman, madam.'

Natalie had, on a number of occasions, tried to persuade him to call her by her given name, but for some obscure reason, he persisted in calling her madam. She did not insist; it heightened for her the sexual thrill by accentuating the age difference. This young man needed an older, more experienced woman as his teacher. She knew that given the time, she could teach him a lot and that their lovemaking would be more enjoyable as a result; there was no time.

Alphonse stood up from the sofa, and she could observe more clearly now the not-inconsiderable change that had taken place. He came round to the other side of the coffee table and stood directly over her. She reached up and touched him. It was like an electric shock. She ran her fingers up the length of a very substantial erection. She stood up too, and together they went into the bedroom, where Alphonse, with indecent haste, removed his clothing. He stood facing Natalie with his legs astride, the erection pointed at her excited by the destructive act that was to follow.

'Take your clothes off.'

Slowly, Natalie removed the outer garments and kicked off her shoes.

'I said take them off,' said Alii. 'I'm not here for a striptease.' There was a new authority in his voice, and she looked mildly surprised. She thought that the titillation she was offering him would be more to his liking; she was wrong. She quickly removed the other garments and lay down on the bed with her thighs spread, her feet dangled over the edge, and Alii stood between them. It was a short journey from there, and he penetrated her instantly and deeply.

'You're hurting me, Alphonse,' she said with mounting nervousness and struggled under him. He placed his hands on the tops of her arms and held them on the bed and thrust again deeply. She cried out, but it was a mixture of passion and fear. Alii continued with the deep and penetrating thrusts, holding her totally immobile on the bed. He was nearing the peak now and suddenly transferred his hands from her upper arms to her neck and, pressing down with his thumbs on the windpipe, grasped her in the grip that was to be her death. Her eyes popped with amazement and terror. *Oh god,* she thought, *I'm coming.* She could not have been more right. He increased the pressure inexorably while continuing with his climax. She never actually reached hers, nor was she to ever again.

Alii released himself from the dead body. His upper arms were deeply scratched, and blood dripped onto the bedcover. He picked up the discarded knickers and wiped himself on them. He went into the small bathroom, and taking a towel from the rail, he ran it under the cold tap and gently dabbed the scratches. The blood flow reduced. It would mark his shirt but not come through his outer garment.

Returning to the bedroom, he quickly dressed. He picked up the discarded bloodstained knickers from the bed and put them in his right trouser pocket and, closing the door of the bedroom, left the unfortunate Natalie spread-eagled behind him. He shut and locked the door of her apartment, returned to his own briefly, looked around to see whether he had left anything, and then shut and locked his own door. He posted the keys through the letterbox in Natalie's apartment and descended the stairs to the garage. He started the car and drove cautiously out of the car park entrance. Surprisingly for him, he had not picked up the tail on the way back to the apartment, and he noticed nothing now as he left. The policeman at the front continued with his observation.

He drove carefully but swiftly through Nice and along the coast road before picking up speed and heading for the Italian border. He was heading for Milan and his exit point.

It was not until the following day, when Alii did not turn up at the bank, that they broke down the door to his flat. It became apparent that he had left. The police knocked on the door of Natalie Bosanquet's apartment but got no reply. Enquiries then revealed that she had not been to her place of work. Having interviewed the other tenants who were unable to give any real help, the police decided to enter Natalie Bosanquet's apartment, and they forced the door and discovered her body.

Chief Inspector Pierre Dupre was seething with rage. It was an inexcusable oversight not to have known there was a car park in that apartment block. Now the man who had become their prime suspect in the murder of George Yoreen had apparently disappeared without trace. Enquiries at the bank had been fruitless.

The dossier on Alphonse Alii, which was pitifully slim even accounting for the bank's full cooperation, was sent immediately to Supt Roger Schofield in London. Over the next few days, the apartment building was searched thoroughly from top to bottom, and as if for making up for their errors of allowing him to escape, the cache of weapons was found. Forensics confirmed that the Westman & Fredericks rifle was what had fired the shot that had killed George Yoreen. Made in USA, the weapon was unregistered, and all identification marks had been removed.